PRAISE FOR CHAR

"A slow-burning, beautifully writ[...]
life the Rome that tourists don't s[...]
The Times

"Immensely impressive...holds you completely enthralled throughout."
The Bookseller

"A sophisticated literary thriller."
The Guardian e

"Lambert's writing is expressive and finely tuned; he has a flair for characterisation and a sense of place which goes down very well...
Sunday Business Post

"It's a wonderful book, beautifully written."
Euro Crime

CHARLES LAMBERT

THE VIEW FROM THE TOWER

EXHIBIT A
An Angry Robot imprint
and a member of the Osprey Group

Lace Market House,
54-56 High Pavement,
Nottingham,
NG1 1HW, UK

www.exhibitabooks.com
A is for Azzurri!

An Exhibit A paperback original 2014
1
Copyright © Charles Lambert 2014

A catalogue record for this book is available from the British Library.

ISBN: 978 1 90922 366 0
Ebook ISBN: 978 1 90922 368 4

Cover design by Head Design

Set in Meridien and Franklin Gothic by Argh! Oxford

Printed and bound by CPI Group (UK) Ltd, Croydon, CR0 4YY

For Jane.

PART ONE

1

On the last morning of their marriage, Helen and Federico leave the flat together, shortly before nine. Federico has told his driver to wait on the far side of the square because the widowed sisters on the first floor complain about car fumes dirtying their scraps of washing; flannel vests, grey woollen tights, despite the early June heat. How sad, thinks Helen, glancing up at their balcony as a drop of water catches her arm. A whole life lived, a line of dripping cloth. So she and Federico have these final moments together, down the dark stairs and across the square, barely time to exchange a dozen words and say goodbye before their separate days begin.

By the time they reach the car they have both fallen silent. In any case, everything was organised before they left the flat. Helen will shop for that evening because Giacomo, their oldest friend, is coming to dinner with his new wife. As usual, Federico has planned the meal and written the list of items Helen has to buy. He's decided to keep it simple: cold cuts, veal liver and artichoke, summer fruits and cheese. On the way to the ministry, he will tell the driver to stop off in one of the narrow streets nearby, where he will pick up some Stilton from a shop that imports it directly. This evening, Helen will set the table and fill up glasses while Federico cooks and serves. He always cooks; it relaxes him after work. Helen will sit at the breakfast bar with a glass of wine and listen to his stories of the day's events at the ministry, of people who form an intimate part of Federico's world and a less intimate part of hers.

Federico takes his seat beside the driver with his briefcase lodged between his feet, the briefcase he has had since university and refuses to replace, now cracked and stained and stitched together with sailmakers' twine – a task he performs himself each summer to the amusement of Helen, who has never mended anything in her life. In the back sits one of the bodyguards assigned to Federico: two drivers, two bodyguards, what Helen calls his government issue, shifted around on a bi-weekly rota. Today's driver is Massimo, her favourite; the other one never seems to notice her. Federico is supposed to stay in the back, with the bodyguard, but prefers to sit beside the driver, whose risk is greater. He enjoys taking risks.

Massimo raises his hand in a crisp salute to Helen.

"When can we come and see your mother again?" she says.

Massimo spreads his hands as if to say she only has to name the day. "She's been bottling the new tomatoes. She hasn't forgotten you, don't worry. She's put some aside."

Federico has already picked up the pile of this morning's newspapers from his seat and is rifling through them. Helen hesitates beside the open window, then turns away as Federico grimaces at something he's read, his face disappearing behind a sheet of tinted glass. She steps back to watch the blue car cross the square, drive down towards Via Giulia and the flow of traffic on the Lungotevere, its passenger invisible behind the dark rear window.

She stands for a moment, distracted by the fluttering of rainbow peace flags from the windows opposite, then walks over to their local bar and orders a cappuccino, which she drinks while glancing at the headlines of the *Messaggero* on one of the tables. The banner is devoted to videos of the hostages in Iraq, but she ignores that and glances down to the front-page account of a minor government crisis, comparing it with what Federico told her the night before. She has that familiar feeling of being at the centre of events and yet excluded. She is tempted to tell the barman the truth of the matter, but she resists. The barman, the rest of the world, will always prefer to believe what they read. Even when events prove her right, her version will have been forgotten.

The barman's mother, wrapped in an apron, her sparse grey hair pushed up into a nylon cap, is working in the kitchen behind the bar, preparing sandwiches for later that day, cheese and ham, artichoke hearts and mozzarella, tuna and tomato. She glances through to the bar, waving the large broad knife she uses to spread mayonnaise, and shouts across to Helen that the world is going to the dogs, with a tone of immense cheerfulness, even hilarity. Helen nods and raises her empty cup in agreement.

She has three hours before work. Her shift at the news agency begins at noon, the light shift after the early morning roundup. She leaves the bar and walks across Piazza Farnese and through the market in Campo de' Fiori, remembering the way it was when she'd first come to Rome, the rickety wooden stalls, the sacks of dried beans like dusty counters, all of it smoothed away now, tamped down and neatened up. She checks to see what's on at the cinema; a Japanese film she's never heard of that won something in Venice last September. She wanders down Via dei Giubbonari, pausing to glance through the table of books outside the second-hand bookshop in the small square halfway down, where the man she thinks of as the Sad Man is sorting through old magazines by the door. He smiles at her, she smiles back; they have friends in common, well, Martin, really, but she can never remember his first name, except that it's English. Anthony? Andrew? He has red hair going grey, worn too long and held back with a rubber band, and one of those waistcoats with pockets all over it that fishermen wear. She feels she should talk to him, but doesn't want to talk to anyone this morning, she's too distracted by thoughts of the dinner this evening, and of Giacomo. She's never met his new wife, Yvonne, and doesn't particularly want to. She nods her goodbye as she walks away.

She decides to spend an hour in the American Library. She's supposed to be writing an essay on Toni Morrison, for a second degree in modern American identities she no longer sees the purpose of. It was an idea of her husband's, who worries she's stagnating, who sets her small but demanding intellectual tasks to ensure her mind remains alert. But the minute she's inside the library, she ignores the bookshelves and picks up this morning's copy of the *International Herald Tribune*.

The first two pages are devoted to the war in Iraq, but Helen is looking for stories about Italy – looking for mention of Federico. It's odd to see news of the government crisis repeated, downscaled to a squabble among minor parties, a storm in a teacup; two brief paragraphs on page three and a hint of irony entirely lacking from the domestic account. She thumbs through the rest of the newspaper, then glances round the reading room to see who else is there. A group of students, teenage boys and girls in low-slung jeans and T-shirts, two soberly dressed women, perhaps lay nuns, in the political history section. No one she knows. She's restless, waiting for something to happen. She wonders if Giacomo is already in Rome, and what he's doing if he is. She finds herself trying to imagine what Yvonne will be like, and how she'll behave with her, how polite she'll need to be. She's in no mood to study.

Leaving the library behind her, she stands in the empty courtyard, already bleached by sunlight at 9:20am. High above her head, an army helicopter crosses the bright blue square of sky, like a furious insect. The noise reminds her of her mobile. She fumbles for it in her bag, then stares at the blank display to see if she's been called, but it's still turned off from last night, her final act before she slept, with Federico reading in bed beside her from a pile of official-looking papers. Leaning against the warm stone of a column, she closes her eyes against the light. And all at once she has a vision of Federico, his tall, stooped figure, his creased blue suit, the fine hair falling across his face, as though he is standing in front of her and shaking his head, his smile both irritated and perplexed, yet still a smile addressed to her and to no one else. She almost cries out and reaches her hand towards him, her body urging her forward towards Federico, to hold him.

And just as abruptly he is gone. She looks at her watch to see what time it is. 9:27am. She thinks, I'll ask him where he was over dinner. Or maybe not. Maybe it's better not to mention it. Federico has become so superstitious these past few months, with a thousand odd ideas about fate and coincidence: the notion that it's all bound together and has sense, which reminds her of Jung and synchronicity and that business about a butterfly's wing, and strikes her as lovely and meaningless at the same time. She has always been puzzled by the need for saints and miracles, the need for connectedness; not cynically, almost with envy, as something beyond her grasp.

She holds her mobile in her hand and then, with a shiver at what she will call, for want of any better term, her vision of Federico, she turns it on. She has three missed calls and a text message, all from the same number, a foreign number she recognises from the code as French. At last, she says to herself. She opens the message.

Bored, alone in Rome. Free for half an hour? Il tuo G.

2

Giacomo hurries her into the hotel room, then takes both her hands in his and steps back to take a better look. She laughs and tries to pull away a little, unexpectedly self-conscious.

"Helen, Helen, my dear sweet Helen," he says. "How good it is to see you."

He is speaking English with her, as he always did, however much she complained; but he's acquired a French accent these past few years. He's also put on weight since she last saw him, a matter of months ago, although it seems far longer. He hugs her to him, his belly warm and firm against hers. And immediately, as though the light in the room has changed, she wishes she hadn't come. It's stupid to see him here in Rome like this, the minute he's arrived and without Federico, in a hotel room booked for him by Federico's staff. It's not just indiscreet; her being here will spoil what's supposed to be the surprise of their meeting up, the four of them, for the first time this evening. For a moment, she wonders whether it might be wiser not to tell Federico where she's been; but then she will feel like a child who has opened her birthday present the night before and has to fake her pleasure. She can be honest and spoil it for Federico, or lie and spoil it for herself. Either way, it's a risk, and the bigger risk is that he'll find out anyway. It might be Giacomo's fault – she's here with Giacomo's connivance, after all – but she knows she has made a mistake. She squirms until he lets her go, only to place his hands on her shoulders and stare down into her face with an affectionate, challenging grin until she's forced to turn her head away, laughing again, with a trace of anxiety she tries to hide. And then the mood passes as quickly as it came – how complicated life can be if you allow it, she thinks – and there is nowhere in the world she would rather be than here with Giacomo.

"So good." He pulls her across the room to a pair of armchairs near the window. "I'll phone for coffee?"

"Not unless you want some. I've had enough for one day." She glances round the room. There's an open suitcase on the bed, a magazine beside it. *The Economist.* "You're on your own. Your wife?" She listens to her voice for sarcasm, or hurt, but all she can find is casual interest.

He waves a hand in the air. "Yvonne arrives sometime this afternoon. Late. She had business to attend to in Paris."

"She's in fashion?"

"Oh yes, always." He grins again. He's misunderstood deliberately, she knows that. As if they have never been apart, and there is no new wife between them, she relaxes.

"And you didn't wait for her?"

He shrugs. "You know me. Always restless. She had some lunch to go to." He stares through the window, down towards Via Veneto and its silent flow of traffic. "Whose idea was it to put us here? In this lap of bourgeois luxury?"

"One of Federico's people. I told them you wouldn't like it."

"On the contrary, I'm delighted. These days, I only ever stay in places like this. I have a reputation to maintain."

She isn't sure if this is a joke. He pulls out a packet of cigarettes. *Gitanes Légères.* In Turin, he'd smoked *Nazionali.* Giacomo has always believed in blending in.

"You haven't stopped?"

"I haven't been quite forced to. Not yet, anyway. Which is one of many reasons for continuing to prefer Paris to other less civilised capitals." He lights up, then offers her the packet. "I assume you're still resisting."

"Yes."

He nods again, draws deeply on the cigarette. When his eyes close for a moment, she sneaks an appraising look. He's older, stockier, his good looks faded by now, but his greying hair has been cut by someone who knew what he or she was doing, and she's never seen him dressed so well, so stylishly, nor with such highly-polished, almost foppish shoes. Federico would refuse to wear a suit this perfectly tailored, on political grounds. She can already see his face when he looks at his old friend dressed like this, perplexed and disdainful; she wonders, when he does, which side she'll be on. She's glad though that she's wearing something decent.

"So tell me about Yvonne," she says.

He shrugs. "No, let's not talk about Yvonne. You'll meet her soon enough. You can make your own conclusions when you do." He stubs out the barely smoked cigarette; Federico would be shocked by the waste, as though the fact of the cigarette itself weren't wasteful enough, in a world of limited resources. But she isn't here to think about Federico.

Leaning forward, Giacomo reaches across until he can touch her knees with both his hands. She has on her favourite linen dress, buttoning at the front; it has fallen open at the hem but she doesn't want to pull it closed. He'd call her Anglo-Saxon if she did, as though nothing has changed since Jane Austen; as though he doesn't know her better than that.

"The last time we were alone was almost three years ago," he says, "in that wonderful convent you found for us."

She nods. You don't need to remind me, she thinks. Partly to avoid his eyes, she looks around the room, at the curtains with their heavy sashes and swags, the darkly reflecting surfaces of the framed reproductions of ancient Roman views.

"It wasn't quite as luxurious as this, if I remember," he says. She still can't tell if he's sneering, or enjoying the luxury. She's never been able to tell with Giacomo. "Perhaps you prefer it here."

"I'm not interested in luxury. You know that."

He is silent for a moment, as if to acknowledge her reproof. "I almost didn't come, you know. I still don't understand why Fede invited me."

How odd it is to hear him say *Fede*. Almost nobody does any longer, apart from her, and his parents; no one else is that close to him. She isn't sure she likes it in Giacomo's mouth, although it was what they both called him then, when they were a threesome, if that was the word. The three of them in Turin, setting the world to rights.

She wishes he'd straighten up. She can't talk about conferences, or convents, with the dead weight of his hands on her legs. This isn't the moment to tell him whose idea it was that he be invited. He'd be mortified if he knew how hard she'd had to work to bring Federico round.

"He thought you'd make an important contribution," she says.

Giacomo snorts with laughter. "Only you could say something that absurd without even smiling a little." He holds her knees, his thumbs working their inner sides in a leisurely, circular motion, quite independently of his voice and eyes.

"I'm not sure you should be doing that," she says, but she doesn't move her legs or push his hands away. She turns her head to avoid his gaze and sees through the window a surveillance helicopter, hovering like a soundless gnat, the sunlight picking it out. Behind it, blurred by heat and pollution, is a second, and a third. The American embassy is two hundred yards from the hotel, there must be dozens circling above their heads that she can't hear. She's about to make some comment about the hotel's double-glazing, about the price one pays for silence, when Giacomo sinks to his knees before her and buries his head between her thighs. She can feel his breath on her skin, a fluttering heat, a beating wing; she has the sensation he's trying to speak to her, to tell her something she needs to know. She wants to lift his head, not to stop him from doing what he's doing, or not entirely, but to listen. To find out what he wants to say. But instead of that, she parts her legs a little, to let him in.

Here we are again, she thinks.

3

Helen can't free her mind of Giacomo as she walks to Piazza Venezia and along the Corso. She takes her usual route, skirting the Trevi fountain and up the hill that leads to the Quirinale, where the crowds thin out as the road rises, dust-white in the heat. Federico's office is just round the corner from the room in which she and her colleagues at the English desk are gathered, five tables squeezed into a room. He has calculated the distance as three, maybe four hundred yards and she sometimes imagines the walls are glass and they can watch each other at their business, Federico slouching behind his large dark desk, cluttered with papers and bulging pastel-coloured files as though the computer hasn't been invented, Helen crouched over *her* computer in the nervous birdlike position she adopts to read from the screen, her glasses halfway down her nose. Normally, she finds it comforting, this sense that he is near, almost within reach. This morning, though, with the after-touch of Giacomo's mouth still on her, the idea of Federico being so close to her is less welcome. All he would need is to see her and he'd understand at once what she'd been doing. She'd be caught out. How wonderful, though, to find herself with Giacomo like that, his need for her so obvious, without the slightest hint of flirtatiousness. Each time it happens, even when she's planned it herself, she's taken by surprise. And how hard it is to stop her mind shifting from one to the other the way it always does, from Federico to Giacomo and back, as if they are part and parcel of the same thing.

She stops in a bar for some water, holding the empty glass against her cheek to cool it. She's five minutes late, but she isn't worried. Martin will forgive her, she's covered for him in the past, more than once. She walks through the arch, turns into the foyer and greets the receptionist, whose face changes when he sees her, as though he has seen a ghost. He stands up and walks across, placing his hand on her shoulder to guide her.

"Sit down," he says, his voice unnaturally quiet. He leads her to one of the low soft chairs arranged along the wall, where visitors wait to be met. She sits down, shaken, not curious at all, because she already knows. He picks up the phone, his back to her, and she can't hear what he is saying although she hears her own name quite distinctly, not once but twice. She doesn't know how she knows, but she does; her blood knows.

Federico is dead.

ROME, Italy (CNN) – Shortly before 9:30am today, Federico Di Stasi, a consultant at the Ministry of Employment, was assassinated in the centre of Rome. According to initial investigations, two or three men on motorcycles shot him dead in Via Rasella, less than one hundred metres from the Quirinale, the official residence of the President. The driver of the car, Massimo Monesi, 28, also died in the attack. A third man, the bodyguard, is expected to be released from hospital in a matter of days. The attack is believed to have been carried out by internal terrorists, although no organisation has claimed responsibility for the attack. There is believed to be no connection with the Republic Day celebrations tomorrow, nor with the official visit of US President George W. Bush, scheduled for Thursday.

Di Stasi was most recently responsible for controversial plans intended to dismantle the few remaining state-owned enterprises and place them on the open market. Despite government pressure, he is believed to have insisted on the need to protect those currently employed by these enterprises, most of which are concentrated in the south, by establishing a series of government-financed "buffers". These have been fiercely contested by members of the government as "hand-outs". Di Stasi has also spoken out recently against military intervention in Iraq.

"It has all the hallmarks of a warning," Attorney General Lorenzo Gaeta told reporters in Via Rasella shortly after the murder. "Even the choice of site is significant. Via Rasella was the street in which partisans killed 33 German soldiers during the last war." When asked if he saw a link between this assassination and the murder three years ago of Davide Porcu, Home Office adviser, Gaeta refused to comment.

Government spokesmen are already talking of a fresh outbreak of terrorism, accusing the so-called no-global movement, as well as unions and parties on the left, of bearing at least part of the responsibility for the murder because of the recent intensification of protests against the government's economic policies.

Federico Di Stasi was born in Rome in 1952 to the journalist Fausto Di Stasi and life senator Giulia Paternò, partisan and among the founders in 1948 of the Italian Constitution. After studying in the United States and Britain, he was briefly involved in extra-parliamentary activities during the late 1970s. He began collaborating with the Ministry in 1982 under the first centre-left administration. He leaves a wife and no children.

4

As soon as the police have finished with her, Martin Frame comes into the room and slumps into a spindly gilded chair in front of Helen. He takes her hands in his and holds them for a moment without speaking. He isn't sure what to expect, what to do; he's hopeless at moments like this. The last time he spoke to Federico they had talked about his chances of coming through the reform process alive, and Federico had said you had to live each day as if you were eternal, which is a wonderful sentiment, of course, as Martin remarked at the time, but offers little actual protection against attack. That kind of talk, thought Martin then, is one of the many ways we ward off the nastier business of reality; Federico had been involved in government long enough to know that. But none of this seems to matter now.

Martin's still shaken, shaken and appalled to have lost a friend like this, in a morning. God only knows how Helen must be feeling. She's not the type to cry, but still, how hard it must be to hold oneself together. She looks up and attempts a smile, then shakes her head, as if to say, Who would have expected this? He sighs. If it hadn't been Federico, he thinks, it would have been someone else, although he won't be saying this to Helen. Why on earth should Helen be interested in someone else?

He looks down at their hands: Helen's, lightly tanned and delicate, engulfed in his own, large nicotine-stained, like the paws of some beast, nails bitten down to the quick as they have been for the past fifty years. He's scared of how fragile she must be, as though a simple gesture might crush her. He feels he should speak, say something helpful to her, but doesn't want to seem banal, or uncaring, and can't think of anything to say that isn't one or the other, or both.

"Oh, Martin," she says finally, breaking the silence, the words little more than a sigh.

He moves and the chair creaks beneath him. For an awful moment, he imagines it breaking beneath his weight. He sees himself struggling to his feet, the chair in splinters beneath him; how unbearable that would be, how close to farce. Abruptly, he lets her go.

"One of us should be at the desk," she says, her forehead suddenly creased with worry.

"You needn't think about work, my dear. The desk is the last thing you need to worry about. I'll take care of all that." He lets her go.

"I'll be back," she says, her face set, oddly determined. "Just as soon as all this is sorted out." He wonders what she thinks she means by "this". The specific business of the police and everything that will have to be done? Or the infinite business of Federico's death?

"I know you will," he says. "I rely on you. You know that."

"I just can't believe this has happened." She stares at the ceiling; he watches her throat as she breathes. "I know it's what everyone says, Martin, but it's true. I never knew. People talk to me and I feel as though they're talking about someone else. They asked me all these questions and I kept wanting to tell them I wasn't sure, I couldn't remember, I'd have to check with Federico." Her gaze moves down towards him, as if to beseech him for an answer he doesn't have.

"You have to give yourself a chance."

"To do what?"

"To take this on board," he says. He wishes he had found something better than this tired phrase, then makes it worse by adding: "You'll need all your strength."

She looks away again, this time at the window, its weighted gauze curtains like a shroud. "They told me I'd be needed later, at the hospital." She pauses, then shudders, clutching her elbow with her hands as if to shield herself against the cold. "I suppose what they meant was the morgue."

They are in one of the rooms reserved for interviews; a long table, a score or so of brittle ornate chairs like the ones they are sitting in, over- and under-decorated at the same time. Martin is rarely obliged to attend events in here; his work is at the English desk. The walls are a pallid institutional green, the row of windows framed in swathes of heavy rust-coloured velvet, held back by gilded cord that would take the skin off a sailor's back. Outside, beyond the filtering veils of gauze, is the side wall of the President's palace. A shelf of television screens on the wall behind Helen's head flicker green and black as the stories roll in, but he doesn't read them. He can imagine what they're saying. Stories and comments on stories and the whole self-feeding business of news, to which he contributes daily as a jobbing journalist; and now the business is turning on Helen for nourishment, as she must know. She hasn't looked round to see what's being said, not while he's been here anyway, and he can't blame her for that. The longer she goes without witnessing Federico's death reported, the easier it will be for her to pretend it hasn't happened. But he can't help wondering what she's thinking; she seems so distant.

"Were they difficult?" he says.

"Who? The police?" She shakes her head. "On the contrary. They treated me with kid gloves." She shudders again. "The last time I was questioned by the police they treated me like shit."

"That must have been some time ago," he says cautiously.

"I'm sorry, Martin." She opens her bag, her manner distracted and fidgety, then snaps it shut. "No, they were fine. They just asked me a lot of questions, that's all."

"What did they want to know?" he asks, on firmer ground now.

But she doesn't seem to have heard. "You know what I've been thinking about?" she says. "Condole. The word, I mean. Is that how we say it in English? Only it sounds so strange when you say it out loud. Are you condoling me, Martin?"

"I'm trying to, my dear. Not very well, I'm afraid."

"I've been here too long," she says, and sighs. "I'm forgetting everything."

Martin has known Helen since she first came to Rome, over twenty-five years ago. A call came through from reception one morning to say that a young woman wanted to speak to someone at the English desk. Send her up, said Martin. His latest intern, a newly-arrived English graduate who drank too much and fancied himself as a revolutionary, had walked out that morning after being ticked off about a piece he'd written. Perhaps she'll be looking for a job, he thought, we could do with some fresh blood. When she came in, he was disappointed; she looked younger than he'd expected, and unconvinced, as though she didn't expect much good to come from this. It didn't take long for him to change his mind. She'd been teaching, she said, in Turin, but hated the work. She'd moved to Rome and wanted to write; she had some pieces she'd done with her and could leave them for him along with her CV. He asked her to try out the following day – he'd square it with management if she worked out, and if she didn't, they'd pretend it hadn't happened. How did that suit her? It made her smile, a smile that lit up her face; he remembered thinking, so it isn't just a cliché, it actually happens. Smiles can light up faces. By the time she'd left he was infatuated. He stayed that way for almost two months, as she learnt the job and they shared the odd coffee break, not quite in love with her, but almost, toying with the idea of it as she toyed with her spoon and packet of sugar, before leaving it unopened. Until one evening she invited him round for dinner and introduced him to a serious, blond young man who might have been her brother, but was in fact her husband, the economist Federico Di Stasi, she'd said with unashamed pride, and Martin had shaken his hand and raised an eyebrow. Yes, Federico had said before anyone else could speak. My ill fame goes before me. I don't think we say it like that, she'd said, and whisked Martin off into the small living room they had then, still filled with boxes and piles of books after what must have been months in the place. Federico will do the cooking, she said. He loves to cook.

"What was Federico doing?" Martin asks now.

"What do you mean?"

"Where it happened," says Martin, unable to say *where he was shot*.

"He was buying some cheese," she says. "For this evening."

"I thought you normally did the shopping."

"I do," she says. Is she correcting him? It's hard to tell. Perhaps she simply hasn't realised, not fully. You can know something and not know it, Martin's more than aware of that. Sometimes he thinks it's the human condition.

"Cheese?" he says, prompting her. He's on safer ground, somehow, with questions.

"Stilton. The shop he was going to imports it from a dairy near Leicester." She looks at Martin, her face contorted by pain for the first time. "That's the sort of thing Federico finds out. You know what he's like. Everything has to be authentic."

Martin reaches across and takes her hands again.

"We needed it for this evening." With a sharp, unexpected gesture, she pulls her hands away. "I can't do it," she says, panic in her voice. "I can't do dinner for people now. Not her, anyway."

"Her?"

"Giacomo's wife."

"Giacomo?"

Helen nods. "You know him," she says. "I'm sure you've met him, years ago. He's an old friend of ours from Turin. He's here for the conference."

"You don't mean Giacomo Mura?"

"Yes," she says.

"Giacomo Mura's here in Rome?"

"Yes." She sighs, an odd resigned sigh, as if she's just remembered something inconvenient that can't be changed. "He adores Stilton, you see, he always has. That was the point."

"Mura knew that Federico was getting Stilton in for this evening?"

She looks startled. "No," she says. "It was meant to be a surprise."

"So who did know?"

"The police asked me that as well," she says.

They can't have been ordinary policemen, thinks Martin, Federico was too near the centre of things for that; they must have been secret service, the branch that deals with terrorists. He saw them on their way out, two men and a young woman, attentive, polite, their jackets on, an almost embarrassing display of rectitude and concern, with the woman behaving in a hugging, sisterly fashion she must have been trained to adopt and Helen standing there, rigid in her arms like a mannequin being dressed. But for all their concern, they hadn't seemed satisfied, Martin thought as he watched them pick up their papers and leave. Of course they asked her who else knew where Federico would be that morning. He'd like to know if she answered them, because she hasn't answered him; but he doesn't want to push. He's never seen her this pale, almost grey beneath the early summer tan. He wonders now what else they must have asked her.

"Were they difficult?" he says again.

"No, I told you. They were very good with me. They just asked me about Federico, if he had any enemies. I didn't know what to say. Of course he does. He travels with an armed guard, I said. I think I may have lost my temper with them a little. Isn't that your job, I said, to know who his enemies are? And then they kept asking me about this morning, about what he normally did, what I normally did." Her voice begins to tremble. "Oh God, Martin, it was awful." She opens her bag again, closes it; he wonders what she's looking for; a handkerchief, her mobile; or if this is some way of keeping busy, of distracting herself. "It was almost as though I couldn't remember, as though everything had been wiped clean. I could see they weren't happy."

"That doesn't matter," he says, to comfort her. "What did you remember? Try and tell me. Perhaps it will help."

She tells him about a cappuccino, the American library, walking through the market. "I saw that friend of yours," she says at one point, "the bookseller. He's bound to remember me," and it sounds like a clumsy attempt to construct an alibi. She's staring into his eyes as she speaks, as if she's trying to convince him. In the end, her voice falters. "I just wandered round," she says. "Window-shopping, I suppose. Looking at people."

"Your phone was turned off?" he says.

"Yes," she says, then corrects herself. "Well, not all the time." She looks anxious. "They can check that sort of thing, can't they?"

"When did Mura arrive?"

"Giacomo?" She rubs her eyes with her fingers. "I don't know. Today, I think."

He moves in his chair, cautious, feeling it give beneath his thighs. He can't understand why she's lying. He hopes that, whatever her reasons might be, she made a better job of it with the police. He decides to try one more time. But before he can ask her anything else, her face has puckered up like a slapped child's and she's fighting back tears.

"He didn't die straight away, Martin," she says. "He was still alive when they took him to hospital. If I'd had my mobile turned on, I might have been able to get there in time. He was conscious, they said, he wanted to know where I was." Martin has found a clean handkerchief in his pocket and is holding it out to her, but she's reached across the table to a box of tissues encased in the same dark velvet as the curtains, which are not so much rust-coloured, it occurs to Martin now, as the dark and powdery hue of the dried blood gardeners use on their roses. She pulls a tissue out. She wipes her eyes, then blows her nose with surprising vigour. "I'll never forgive myself," she says.

Before he can comfort her, she glances at the clock on the wall. He follows her eyes. A quarter to three. Siesta time for some, he thinks, but the police or their assistants will be talking to the people in the bar, her neighbours, the bookseller, perhaps, the library staff; checking the times they gave against her account. A reconstruction of her morning, an ordinary morning, a *normal* morning, perfect in every detail. A morning that led her, step by step, to a place in which Federico is dead and nothing will be normal any more. That must be what she's thinking. When she closes her eyes again and leans her head back into the emptiness behind her, Martin wonders where she really was this morning and why she is lying. He would do anything he could to help, if she will only let him, because what she needs, at this moment, matters more to him that the truth. You foolish child, he thinks, anxious for her but also hurt that she should feel he can't be told.

"I didn't realise it was this late," she says.

"You must be hungry."

"Not at all." She covers her mouth with her hand. "I'd be sick if I tried to eat anything."

"Still, something to settle your stomach? A sandwich, perhaps? I could have one sent up."

She shakes her head. "Thank you, Martin. I'm fine. But you go and get something to eat. I'll be all right here for a little while."

"I'll leave you then? You want me to go?" Is this what she means? She's trying to get rid of him?

"Yes. Leave me alone for a moment."

"You're sure that's what you want? I can wait outside if you like. I don't want to leave you like this, Helen."

"No, please," she says, almost sharply. "Just for half an hour."

Martin heaves himself up, pushing his hair back from his forehead, smiling down at her in what he hopes is a reassuring way, not wanting her to see his resentment at being sent away like this.

He's standing by the door, about to turn and ask her one final time if there is anything she would like, when he's pushed to one side. A man a few inches shorter than he is, bulky, in a dark light-weight suit, is rushing across the room. Helen has half-risen from her chair, her arms reaching out. Martin can't tell if she's pleased to see the man, or shocked beyond measure, if she's stepping away from the table and holding out her arms to welcome him or to fend him off.

"So, this is where you've been hidden," the man cries, in an accent Martin can't place. "I practically had to fight my way in. I've been searching all over Rome for you!" He wraps his arms around Helen and Martin feels a stab of jealousy as she softens against the man and allows herself to be comforted, as she might have allowed herself to be comforted by him if he'd only tried. He's never been good at hugging; he's never thought of Helen as the hugging type. Martin can hear the man whispering into her ear, as one hand strokes her hair away. "I can't believe it," he's saying, "we have to be strong," and then her name, without the "H", as though she were Greek. When he lifts his face away from Helen's hair for breath, Martin sees his face clearly for the first time and recognises Giacomo Mura, older but still indisputably the man Martin remembers, from his photographs at least. Martin's gaze is returned, but Mura's expression is one of curiosity and affront, as if to say, "What do you want here? Who do you think you are?" Martin feels once again that he's being dismissed, and stands his ground, waiting for Helen to see him, acknowledge his leaving. Finally, she pulls away, her face flushed. She looks at Martin.

"I suppose I'm free to go?" she says.

5

Turin, 1977

Helen found their first place in Turin for them, while Federico
sorted himself out at the faculty. Anywhere would be better than
sleeping in a cheap hotel, she'd thought, after the second week
in a third-floor place beneath the porticoes near the station,
the corridors of which were filled with the constant whine and
shudder of washing machines. It had taken her three days to
realise that rooms in the Hotel Saturnia could be rented by the
hour, and that the women in dressing gowns she occasionally
bumped into as she headed for the stairs were prostitutes. But
she'd changed her mind about anything being better when an
agent showed her the only flat they could afford to take, a place
beneath the roof with a shared squat toilet on the landing and a
scurrying of insects as the door opened. At least the hotel sheets
had been clean; if she left the room for ten minutes a flurry of
maids would sweep in and change them.

It had taken her three weeks to find somewhere that would
do, with a deposit small enough for them to afford. A second-
floor flat in a block halfway between the station and the park:
a windowless hall, two poky bedrooms overlooking the street,
a bathroom, also windowless but with a deep white tub, a live-
in kitchen whose narrow balcony would take some pots of
herbs. The whole place smelt of something the owner called

candeggina. "*Tutti i giorni, mi raccommando,*" the woman insisted, "*usi la candeggina.*" Helen looked it up in her pocket dictionary as soon as she had paid the single month's deposit, had the keys in her hand and was standing alone in the semi-darkness of the empty flat. *Candeggina*. Bleach. She ran into the bedrooms and opened both shutters, then looked around her, wondering what Federico would think. He didn't seem to mind where they lived. "You find something," he'd said. "I trust you implicitly." The walls were beige, the woodwork chocolate brown, the floor a sort of mottled marble, like one of those fatty salamis cut into slices and squared off into tiles. Helen decided to buy paint, but all she could find that afternoon was tubs of white the size of oil drums and little squeezy bottles with colour she could stir in until she had the shade she wanted. She couldn't believe how many little bottles it took to impart the faintest tinge to the paint.

Everything seemed so primitive here; she couldn't quite cope with it. She hadn't imagined northern Italy to be so, well, post-war, she supposed, the way she remembered her childhood in the aftermath of rationing; she half expected to find bottles of sterilised orange juice in the shops beside the sparkling water and the long-life milk. And then, as if to taunt her, there was the odd glimpse of luxury, handmade chocolates in the bars along the porticoes of Via Roma and the women that bought them, their elaborate hair-dos and ankle-length fur coats, even in autumn; a luxury she couldn't have and didn't – she told herself – want.

Alone in the flat, painting the walls a paler azure than she'd have chosen while Federico went about his business, she'd stop, paintbrush in hand, and close her eyes and listen to her neighbours through the walls. A family of Neapolitans on one side, four children of school age, a father who worked on the shop floor at Fiat, a wife who shopped and cooked and hung out washing like something from a film by De Sica, her favourite director, an old woman she heard the voice of but never saw; on the other side three young men from Calabria, also Fiat workers, who argued incessantly about politics and football and were never to be found apart.

She wondered aloud to Federico about the absence of people who were actually born in Turin. It's as though they were all in hiding, she said. *Torinesi* don't live in the centre, he said, certainly not in this part of it. It's been taken over by immigrants. But they're all Italians, aren't they? she said and he kissed her and told her he adored her, which wasn't much of an answer.

She'd never planned to live and work in Turin, a city she'd barely heard of six months before. Throughout her last year at Cambridge, she'd dreamed of some sprawling chaotic southern city with palm trees and a port; Naples, Palermo. She'd looked forward to pizza and mozzarella, not steaming hunks of boiled meat and the sharp, anchovy-scented green sludge that everyone served with it. But Federico had found this short-term research post at the university and the idea of being separated was inconceivable. They hadn't lived together before: it had always been furtive somehow, sneaking in and out of each other's rooms before other people woke. In some ways, small but significant, they barely knew each other.

Their first night, in the still-unpainted flat, they ate a spit-roast chicken and potatoes out of the tinfoil container they'd come in, drank cheap red wine from a plastic bottle and went to bed too drunk and exhausted to make love. Federico was asleep the minute she turned off the light but Helen, despite her weariness, was restless and couldn't settle. There were still no curtains or blinds at the windows, nothing but the wooden shutters that let the streetlight into the room. She lay beside Federico, turned to her side and resting on one elbow, to watch him breathe, the almost imperceptible movement of his mouth, lips parted, half-pressed into the pillow, his soft fair hair curling into his neck. She lifted a curl and let it drop, then kissed the edge of his ear as gently as she could, not wanting him to wake, finally at peace with herself. This will never happen again, she thought, our first night in our first home.

Next morning, after coffee and an aspirin, they walked along the part of town they knew best, the run-down, shabbily exotic porticoes beside the station, jostled by strangers with suitcases and boxes tied with string, contraband cigarette sellers every few yards, the early shift of whores, not all of them women. Helen held onto Federico's arm. They sat outside a bar in a small square, where the road opened up. They drank cappuccinos and shared a brioche, dipping the pointed ends into the froth.

For Helen, the first few weeks in Turin were filled with novelty and with love, the habit of which was the greatest novelty of all. Sometimes she found herself smiling as she worked at her decorating and realised she'd done nothing but think about Federico for the past half hour, or longer. This is what I've always wanted, she told herself. I'm living in Italy with the man I love.

It was hard, though, to reconcile what she'd wanted from Italy with what she heard on the radio, tuned constantly to a local radical station Federico had recommended as one that *told the truth*. It was hard to believe the news that stared up at her from the papers, dense with print and grainy photographs that she'd strewn to protect the floors of the flat from paint. Murders, arrests, kneecappings, hostages, bank raids. So many new words, so few of them in her dictionary, as though the language were being remade to fit. Would she ever catch up?

In the streets below the flat, in the old-fashioned grocers and bakers where she did her little bit of shopping, nervously and using too many gestures, at the stand where she bought her copy of *La Stampa*, the local newspaper she was expected to read, everywhere she looked she saw graffiti, political, violent, often witty as far as she could tell, like the slogans people had coined in Paris nine years earlier. Helen both knew and didn't know what was happening. She was in the middle of a war, it seemed, a civil war in which lives were actually being lost, while people in England were sticking safety pins through their earlobes and calling it revolution. She read the stories and listened to the news reports with an anxious, growing diligence that left her in some uncertain place she did – and didn't – recognise; she had a sense of numbers but not of lives.

In the evenings, back from the faculty, Federico cooked and talked while Helen listened. He talked about others, his parents in Rome, whom Helen had still to meet, his research colleagues, writers and thinkers he admired; anyone but himself, the only one she cared about, or her. More than anyone, he talked of his best friend, Giacomo, who was travelling in South America. Inside his wallet he had a strip of photographs of them both, taken in a booth. Giacomo's face was Italian in a way that Federico's wasn't: large, strong features, deep-set eyes, a mass of curling black hair – a romantic face; a brigand's face. Federico's was classical, fine-featured, fair, with a northern, slightly priestly, look to him; he might have been her brother. Helen hadn't even realised he was Italian when they'd met at the Dante Society in St John's; she'd thought he was just another English graduate student looking for language practice, and anything else that might be available; glamour, romance, even love, if they were lucky. Well, she'd been right about that.

Federico and Giacomo had met in Pisa, at the *Normale*, where they'd taken their first degrees. They'd done their military service together in Civitavecchia, their doctorates in Yale. Then Federico had come back to Europe, to Cambridge, and Giacomo had gone south, on the road. You'll love him, Federico said whenever he mentioned him. I know you will. Everybody does. Helen examined the small creased strips of photographs and other photographs of him Federico showed her, always surrounded by people, and wondered if she would like him as much as Federico expected her to. She didn't like doing what everyone else did, or feeling what they felt. Besides, there was something over-masculine and swaggering about him she didn't take to. Always standing in the centre, the largest smile, the others more often looking at him than at the camera, to see what he wanted from them. She wouldn't give him what he wanted, she decided, whatever that might be.

One morning, a few weeks after she'd arrived, Helen was spoken to by a woman in a queue at the small, subterranean supermarket nearest the flat. "Isn't this so-called supermarket dreadful?" the woman said, in English, when she heard Helen's accent at the till. "We foreigners need to stick together." Helen disliked this attitude and was defensive about her pronunciation at the best of times. She would have ignored her if she hadn't felt, at the soft burr of the woman's voice, a fleeting sense of loneliness, as crippling and acute as a physical cramp in her stomach, as though it had been waiting to catch her unawares. The woman, whose name was Miriam, offered her coffee. Helen accepted.

Miriam wasn't Helen's type. If she hadn't spoken, Helen might not even have recognised her as non-Italian; she had bouffant coal-black hair and too much make-up, a salmon-pink cashmere pullover knotted round her neck and a tailored silk blouse beneath it. Her fingers were covered with rings, her wrists with charm bracelets. They left the supermarket and went to the same bar Helen had had coffee in with Federico after their first night in the flat, but she kept this to herself; she didn't want the conversation to be about men. Miriam told her to sit down, then brought the coffee over; she drank hers with extra water and pulled a face when Helen said no to sugar. "How can you drink it like that?" she said.

Miriam turned out to be an ex-au pair, who was now teaching English at the Fiat headquarters on the outskirts of the city. Before Helen could ask her how she had found the job, Miriam wanted to know if Helen had a boyfriend. This was the conversation Helen had hoped to avoid; she had no desire to talk about Federico, not yet, she wasn't sure why. She was naturally secretive, she supposed. She said no, not really. But Miriam was shocked.

"We can't have that," she said, "a lovely-looking lassie like you. We'll have to find you someone suitable."

"To be honest," said Helen, "what I really want someone to find for me is a job. I've been going round all the schools, but they don't need anyone."

"Well, why didn't you say so?" said Miriam.

The following day Helen was driven out in a two-seater sports car to meet Miriam's contact, an expensively dressed, middle-aged man in a large sunlit office with whom she was clearly having an affair. Three days after that, she was introduced to her first group of students, executive secretaries on the top floor of the main Fiat building, the heart of the empire.

She started the following Monday. She had classes at 8 o'clock every day. Each morning, while Federico shaved, she left the flat and caught the tram at the corner of her street; she sat on the hard wooden benches of the tram until it had left the centre and then walked the last part of the journey down Corso Agnelli and along the windswept dual carriageway of Corso Settembrini as it carved the Mirafiori plant into monolithic blocks, rehearsing what she would teach that day. The first few lessons, she was nervous in front of her class, her voice over-loud and tremulous; the confidence her four-week course should have given her had deserted her in the first few minutes. But she needn't have worried. Her students treated her like a child, although some of them were no more than two or three years older than she was. Perhaps it was because they were married already, and mothers. They bought her coffee from one machine and fed her crackers and chocolate biscuits from the one beside it, as though she would otherwise starve to death. When they discovered she owed her parents a letter, they pressed an office telephone into her hand. "*Sta parlando con la mamma*," they sighed to one another, entranced by the soap opera of her life, while she apologised to her startled mother for not having been in touch. They were the only Italians she came across in those early months who never talked about politics. Miriam said it was a national disease, like football in Scotland, and religion. "I just turn off," she said, "and wait for them to stop."

One morning Federico received a postcard from Giacomo, from Rio de Plata. The picture, a Technicolor-tinted image of a baroque church, had been scribbled across in red biro, digging deep into the cardboard. Federico held the card at an angle to read what was written, then laughed.

"*Vinceremos*. South America's gone to his head. He'll be full of liberation theology when he gets back, you'll see. He spent two weeks in eastern Turkey a couple of years ago and all he could talk about when he came home was the Kurdish struggle. He wanted to bring one back with him, adopt him. Any Kurd would have done. I've seen him pick kittens up from the street and find homes for them with people he doesn't even know. He persuades, you see. He won't take no for an answer."

Helen took the card from him and turned it over. The writing was small and neat, indistinguishable from the handwriting of Federico. "He sounds a bit of an enthusiast," she said, not liking her tone; she sounded disapproving. It reminded her of her mother's tone when she'd heard that Helen was moving to Italy, as though she were throwing her life away. Federico, though, didn't seem to have noticed.

"Well, yes. He can't just sit in his armchair and theorise, as he puts it. What he means is that he can't behave the way I do. He doesn't say that, of course. He always pretends to be talking about someone else when he says it. Never me." Federico smiled, with a fondness that Helen couldn't bring herself to trust, or like.

Giacomo bounded into the flat one morning in late October, unannounced, dropping his rucksack and half a dozen bags of various sizes and materials on the floor. Before anyone had a chance to speak, he ran from room to room, opening and closing doors, darting across to windows, looking down into the street, leaping back as if avoiding snipers. He turned on taps and thumped beds and stood in front of a wardrobe mirror, his face appalled. "God, I look awful!" he said, then burst into delighted laughter. "It's Giacomo," said Federico, but Helen hadn't needed to be told.

He was right, he did look awful. His clothes – a parka pulled over a khaki T-shirt and combat trousers – were faded and grubby, with ingrained dirt at the seams. The trousers hung off him; she'd never imagined him so thin. He smelt of old dried sweat and something she couldn't identify, a dusty spicy scent, oddly pleasant. When he grinned, she saw he'd lost his canine tooth on the left. Above the tangled beard, his eyes looked wild and big; hanks of hair matted into semi-dreadlocks hung over them. The lines in his forehead, the lines at each side of his mouth, were etched with grime, but he didn't, despite this, give the impression of being dirty. There was something startled and alive about him, she thought, like a large dog fresh from the sea. She wouldn't have been surprised to see him shake himself dry. He took Helen's face between his hands and kissed her on the mouth, a warm dry kiss, then leapt across and seized Federico's face and did the same to him.

"It's just so good to see you both," he said, in odd Spanish-American accented English. "So good." He hugged them both, leapt back, rubbing his hands together like a child.

"*Non devi parlare inglese per me,*" said Helen. She listened to herself, appalled. You needn't speak English for me. How prissy she sounded, how middle-aged. She heard her mother's voice again. Already he'd rubbed her up the wrong way.

Giacomo grabbed her round the waist and dragged her into a

stumbling dance around the kitchen. "*Parli un italiano perfetto*," he said, grinning with delight. But he continued in English. "You're wonderful. Fede's lucky to have found you." He held her so close his breath was in her face; it smelt of coffee and aniseed. She wanted to let him lead her, but also to push him off. Already, he'd begun to scare her. She didn't know what he'd do next.

They stayed in that evening. They ate pasta with oil and garlic, and bread and salami, and drank Barbera from plastic bottles. They listened to Giacomo, who seemed possessed, crouching forward, hands clasped together in earnestness or spread out with the palms turned up, as if he could weigh the world; swinging back until she thought the chair would collapse beneath him; laughing at odd intervals, his eyes bright with tears he didn't bother to wipe away. When they'd eaten, he emptied his bags on the kitchen floor to show them what he'd found. Music tapes, painted flutes, scraps of embroidered and woven cloth, those peg-like worry dolls, sweaters of heavy musty-scented wool with geometric designs and tassels. Helen had thought, disappointed, but this is tourist stuff. You're nothing more than a tourist. And then he dug down deeper. Beneath his screwed-up T-shirts and underpants were posters and pamphlets, cyclostyled on coarse grey paper, crumpled and ripped, books with their covers torn off and their dog-eared pages scored with question marks, exclamation marks, doodles. He pulled it all out, the fabulous mess of his last nine months, waving it in their faces until Helen was exhausted.

"They could be arrested at any time, they *live* with it, so everything they do has meaning. They live and eat and breathe politically. They *love* politically. There's a grace to them, it's extraordinary. You can't believe it unless you see it, unless you feel it. We're dead here." The tears were pouring down his face, his voice was breaking. "They aren't just empty gestures, Federico," he said. When he stood up and began to pace from one side of the kitchen to the other, Federico reached out for his arm. For a second, Giacomo seemed to want to shake him off, but let himself be held. His hand came out to Helen's shoulder and she, too, stood up and allowed herself to be drawn in by both men's arms.

He moved into the second bedroom that night. The next morning, when he came into the kitchen and found Helen and Federico drinking coffee, with Helen about to go to work, he picked up a cup and poured some coffee, then sat between them, closed his eyes and sighed. "Home," he said, his legs stretched out beneath the table. Helen glanced across at Federico, but he was reading a pamphlet and didn't look up. Ten minutes later, as she left the flat, Giacomo was fidgeting and playing with a packet of *Nazionali* he'd pulled out from his pocket.

The first few days he was in and out of the flat, looking people up, his pockets jingling with telephone tokens. He washed his clothes, one by one, in the bathroom basin, hanging them on a string above the bath. Helen tried to do them for him, but he refused.

"It's not because I'm a woman," she said, irritated. "I mean, that's not why I'm offering."

He grinned. "I didn't think it was. It's because you're good. You're a good person, Helen." She couldn't tell if he was teasing. She wasn't sure if he was right. What she'd wanted was to take possession of her flat again, against the intruder. It was unsettling to find him there when she got back from Fiat with some bread and ham for her lunch; she was never sure whether to share it with him. If she did, she felt exploited; if she didn't, she felt mean. Either way, he never seemed to notice. Often he had bags of fruit he'd throw down on the table, the oranges or pears spilling out. She'd grab them as they rolled, then take one into her bedroom to eat.

Sometimes he'd follow her in and give her newspapers to read, *Potere Operaio*, *Lotta Continua*. She cast a glance at the closely printed pages and smudged photographs, stumbled through a paragraph or two of jargon-ridden prose, then put them down, defeated. She didn't believe anyone could really care enough to read that kind of stuff until she heard, one morning as she waited for the tram that would take her out to work, two women old enough to be her mother, the day's market shopping jammed between their feet, debating the legitimacy of the use of arms. How easy it is to understand that sort of Italian, she thought – *legittimo*, *uso*, *armi* – and, at the same time, she wondered what crazy world she'd woken up in, where old women talked about something other than the weather and the price of washing powder; talked about the right to kill as though it were as normal as queuing for a bus – more normal, because no one in Turin ever queued for anything. She understood then what Giacomo had meant and wondered if what she wanted was to be part of it; if what she wanted was to be alive as they were alive, or seemed to be, and not just looking in through glass. She described the women to Federico over dinner that evening, hoping he'd be amused, but he couldn't see why she had thought them so surprising, so worthy of mention. We're not in the Home Counties now, he said, and she felt both abashed and exhilarated, as though she had opened the window wide and breathed in a lungful of cold, clean air from the not-so-distant mountains. But she still didn't know where she stood. And she was glad that Giacomo hadn't been there to hear their conversation.

6

Giacomo has taken Helen away from the agency and back to his hotel. There's no point in hanging around here, he said, and, because she didn't know what else to do, she followed him down the stairs to the waiting taxi. Now she's in his room and already she's regretting it. Yvonne, Giacomo's new French wife, is sitting on the arm of one of the chairs by the hotel room window, looking uncomfortable. She doesn't belong here either and she knows it, thinks Helen, and because she can't stop thinking, and can't control her thoughts, she imagines Yvonne in the room with them this morning, watching as Helen and her husband were making love and Helen's own husband was dying in a hospital no more than half a mile away as the crow flies. Because Helen has already done the calculations, measured the distance between where she was and where she should have been. That's what she was doing when the police were asking her questions, working out how much time she would have needed to get to him before he died.

Yvonne has barely looked at Helen since she came into the room and was introduced. She'd taken both of Helen's hands in hers in a gesture that struck Helen as ecclesiastical, as though she were performing a benediction of some kind. That's what Giacomo did this morning, Helen finds herself thinking. Perhaps it's a French thing he's picked up. Yvonne is tall and thin, not the type Giacomo normally chooses. She wonders for a moment what Federico will think of her, whether she'll appeal to him, then remembers Federico is dead and flinches as if she's been slapped across the face. She lets this knowledge seep into her once again, this sense of being here and not here, as though she is also in a place in which Federico is still alive. If only she knew where it was.

Giacomo offered to take her home, but she couldn't bear the thought of being there, not yet, not by herself. Come and meet Yvonne, he said. It will pass the time. I know, he said, I know, when she said these words back to him. It will pass the time. In the taxi, she sat in the back, her hands pressed between her knees, until Giacomo put his arm round her shoulder and pulled her in. He smelt of some male perfume he'd put on since that morning, heavy with musk, almost unpleasant. She stared ahead, not sure if she was grateful to him, nor what she wanted. At least he didn't ask her how she felt. What will she say when she's asked; because she will be. Widows are. She'd never known him so silent. And now they are back in his hotel room with its soundproof windows on the Via Veneto, and Giacomo's wife is staring at her with a mixture of pity and resentment.

Giacomo goes across to the door and lets in the waiter, with his neat white jacket and shining metal tray. Helen watches him as he places three small cups and a sugar bowl on the table and waits while Giacomo signs a chit, carefully looking at no one in the room, his eyes fixed discreetly on Giacomo's hands. He knows about Federico, it occurs to Helen, it will have been on the 1 o'clock news; maybe there was a news flash, there usually is for events like these. Everyone will know by now. She feels exposed. When he glances across at her on his way out she realises, with horror, that he might have seen her here this morning, alone in this room with Giacomo. Hotel staff know everything. She can't believe how stupid she's been, to have lied to the police. She was scared, and guilty, and had no time to think. A lie of omission, she thinks, does that count as a lie? She will have to say something to Giacomo when she has the chance.

Giacomo picks up a neatly folded newspaper from beside the television, mercifully turned off.

"Time for a cabinet reshuffle," he says. "Apparently." He opens the paper to skim the second and third pages, then throws it on the bed, his patience exhausted. "There'll be political mileage to be made out of this morning, that's for sure, though who'll be making it is anybody's guess. All of them, probably, one way or another. Squabbling over the bones like slum dogs. I don't know how you can live here, Helen. This shabby little theatre." He shuts up, as though he's only just realised how cruel this sounds. But Helen isn't hurt by Giacomo, she's known him too long for that. Besides, she's barely listening. She's watching Yvonne open her handbag and shake out two small pills from an ornate filigree box into her hand, then drop them into her coffee; that must be how she keeps so thin. Helen can't imagine what Giacomo sees in her. She certainly isn't Federico's type. Turning her head, she watches Giacomo spooning sugar into his own cup, stirring it, slugging it back. "At least the coffee's still good," he says, to no one in particular. Giacomo has always envied Federico his ability to eat what he wants without getting fat. And not only that; his seriousness, his determination. His wife. He's envied Federico, *punto e basta*. Helen knows this; she's always known it. It must have been hard for him to live with his envy, his sense of failure when measured against Federico, when everyone imagines him a success. Which is one of the reasons she still cares for him.

"I suppose they left you alone," Giacomo says.

"Left me alone?"

"The police."

Yvonne is watching the lines of cars sweep past beneath the window, her empty cup cradled in both hands. "They drive like lunatics here," she says.

"What do you mean? Left me alone about what?"

"You know, that business from the past. They didn't rake it up, I hope."

"It was thirty years ago, Giacomo. Things have changed since you left." Although maybe this isn't true. Maybe nothing has changed at all. Except that this time they are the victims. This time it was Federico's turn to be shot.

"And the fact that I'm here today?"

"Is coincidence." She glances at him, remembering the look on Martin's face when he asked her who knew about the Stilton. "Isn't it?"

Giacomo sighs. "Of course it is. You know as well as I do this conference was all Federico's idea. It's part of his grand plan to rehabilitate me in Italy."

What does this all matter to me? thinks Helen. Martin only made things worse, his silence, his sympathy when all she could feel was guilt and horror and loss. How vain Giacomo's become, though. One day she will tell him about the evening when Federico talked about his plans for the conference and she, half-joking, suggested Giacomo – he is an economist, after all, in spite of everything – and Federico shrugged, but didn't answer; she wasn't even sure he'd heard. That was what made her insist Giacomo be invited, until Federico had finally given in; that, and the fact that she and Giacomo could be in Rome together for a few days. She hadn't been told about Yvonne at that point; if she'd known she would never have suggested he be invited. Federico had said, "He won't accept, Mura won't want to dirty his hands with anything so practical." But he had. "I'll bring my brand new wife with me for your approval," he'd said, and this was the first they'd heard of her.

"You don't suppose it will go ahead?" Helen says.

Giacomo glances round the hotel room, as though he has misplaced something but can't remember what. "The conference? I don't see why not. People still have to reconstruct Iraq. Sooner or later."

"And you're still prepared to speak?"

He shrugs, and she sees at once that of course he is prepared to speak. "He wouldn't appreciate it if we didn't, after all his work," he mutters after a moment, preferring not to meet her eyes. Helen feels some shell enclosing her begin to shiver and crack, as though under pressure not from within herself, but from outside. She lifts both hands to her face and rubs her eyes, which are dry and sore from the hotel's air conditioning.

As if on cue, Yvonne stands up and announces she needs fresh air. "I suppose I am allowed to leave?" she says to Helen, as if she is being held in the room against her will. Helen pulls a face. "I'm sorry you have to be involved in all this," she says.

"Were they unpleasant?" Giacomo asks.

For a moment, she can't think what he means.

"The police, Helen." He sounds exasperated. Yvonne continues to stand beside the door; she seems afraid to leave them alone together. Helen sighs. If only she knew.

"Oh, yes, the police. They were fine." How different they were from the ones she remembers in Turin, when she'd been dragged in and held for hours and finally released after threats of expulsion from the country; their bullying, their indifference, the pall of smoke in the room. And no women in those days; all men, their jackets off, their shirts lifting out of their belts, their collars undone. Always the odour of stale male sweat and that sexual insolence men in authority had, as though they assumed you would rather be fucked by them than anything else in the world, as though they were holding something back they thought you wanted. Thank God they were gentle with her this time. It's only now she remembers that this time she's done nothing wrong. Martin asked her the same question, she thinks. Does everyone think I'm guilty?

"Did they say who might have done it?"

She shakes her head.

"What did they want to know?"

"They asked me if anything strange had taken place this morning, or last night, in the last few days. If there was anything I could remember that seemed out of the ordinary."

"And was there?"

"Of course not. You know Federico," she says. "Besides, if anything suspicious had happened when I wasn't there he wouldn't have told me. He never did. I told them that. He kept me out of that side of it. He lived with all this security fuss by pretending it wasn't important. The escort, the risk. It gets so boring after a while, Giacomo. Living with fear." She pauses. "Some of them were so sweet. We made friends with one or two. You know Federico, how he loves talking to people, finding out about them. Massimo, the driver this morning, he was our favourite. We know his family, his wife, his mother; he's got two little girls. She lives near Latina, we spent a Sunday there a couple of months ago. She sends us olives and wine and cheese. They all know how much Federico loves that sort of thing."

And now, for the first time, as if Massimo's death has broken the shell that encloses her, she starts to cry. Since she was told the news, five hours ago, she has spoken to the police, to Martin, to her parents-in-law. She phoned them from the taxi. "I'm with Giacomo Mura," she told Giulia, immediately wishing she hadn't. "Federico's old friend," she added, which only made things worse. She turned off her mobile after that because there was no one else she wanted to talk to, not now, not yet. And throughout all this she hasn't cried once. She has felt detached and wondering, an observer to what should be grief and yet somehow isn't, is puzzlement and disbelief and, more than anything, guilt and a sense of being soiled. She has waited to cry like this and now, in the end, it has come. And she doesn't know who it is for.

She cries, she is loud and messy, her saw-like gasping for breath, her face screwed up, her mouth down-turned and open like that of a tragic mask. Yvonne moves back from the door and stands behind her, one slim hand on her shoulder, the slightest possible physical contact required to indicate that she is not alone. Giacomo, slumped on the farther bed, seems incapable even of this.

Later, when she is calmer, Helen will wonder if Giacomo was constrained by the presence of Yvonne. She's jealous of the woman, although she has no right to be, and knows it. Because all Helen wants is to be held by Giacomo, as she was held in the taxi, when they were alone. To be held and comforted by someone who knows her almost as well as she knows herself, someone with whom she need hide nothing. But this doesn't happen. She cries until her throat begins to ache with the effort of it, retching sobs from deep within her that physically exhausts her. She cries until the tears run dry, and continues, tearless, her eyes staring blankly into the meaningless room of this luxury hotel Federico's secretary has booked for Giacomo and Yvonne, seeing neither of them, seeing no one. Yvonne produces a small white handkerchief from her bag and Helen looks at it, now in her own hand, as if she's been given some fabulous artefact from an alien culture, then crumples and drops it to the floor. Yvonne, with a barely audible whine of complaint, stoops to retrieve it.

"I'm so sorry," Helen says.

Giacomo walks over and lifts Helen up from the chair to clasp her to him, a clumsy rather formal embrace. Yvonne strides to the door, aggrieved, then leaves the room. Helen resists the urge to push him away before easing herself from his grasp as gradually as she can. "I'm so sorry," she says again.

"Don't be sorry. You need to cry," Giacomo says.

"Have you cried yet?" says Helen, not meaning to be cruel, although she realises as soon as she has spoken that what she is doing is measuring his loss against hers. "Did you cry when they told you?"

He shakes his head. "I can't believe he's dead. I haven't seen him for what, three years? Since Corsica that summer, when Stefania was so unhappy. That dreadful dinner, do you remember? Except in the papers, of course, unavoidably. On the news. And once or twice in corridors in Brussels. The last time was maybe six months ago, but he was with these people, I don't know, the usual hangers on, ministry people, they weren't my type. I should have spoken to him then."

"You weren't to know," says Helen. She reaches in her own bag for a tissue, hearing what she has just said, playing it back in her head. You weren't to know. I wasn't to know. We weren't to know. These are the words they're expected to use, words made for occasions like this. She wonders how many more times she'll come out with them during the next few days. After crying so much, she feels curiously light, as though she could float off at any minute; light but without enough energy to walk unaided. She'd forgotten about Corsica.

"He'd stopped to buy Stilton, you know, for this evening. For you, really, he remembered how much you liked it. I said I'd do it, but he loves running errands like that, it distracts him from his work. And I think it was a way of showing that he was happy you were coming to the house after all this time. He wanted to buy it himself. He was outside the shop when they shot him. I wonder where it is."

She looks at Giacomo, sitting on one of the hotel room's single beds. Once again, she remembers Martin asking her if Giacomo might have known what Federico was doing that morning, and shivers at what this means. He is fiddling with his mobile now, the way they all do, men and children, the girls as bad as the boys. At first she thinks he's sending a text to someone. But she can tell from the rhythm of his thumbs as they tap on the keys that he's playing a game. The snake that eats itself. The mobile beeps. She waits for him to stop.

"Where what is?"

"The Stilton." She stares down at his hands, large, strong, tufts of coarse hair between the knuckles; strong hands that have never, despite their strength, really worked. They are folded round the phone, which is small and metallic and looks like a toy. A rich man's toy, because Giacomo will be rich by now, his books, his lecture tours will have seen to that. They are all rich, more or less. Only Federico has resisted – the trappings at least. "It must be somewhere. In a box. It's probably an exhibit."

"I suppose it is." Once remembered, she can't stop thinking about it. She could so easily have gone, she had nothing else to do this morning. She could so easily have said, as he climbed into the car and picked up his papers, No, I'll get the cheese. And he might have said, yes. And he would still be alive. Now she has something new to feel guilty about.

"I'm sorry, Helen," Giacomo says in a voice so low she barely hears him.

"But why should you be sorry?" Is he talking about what he did to me this morning, she wonders.

"You know what I mean," he says. "I'm sorry, that's all. For everything. For everything that's happened. I loved him too, you know that. I know we've had problems recently, and in the past, but he was my oldest friend. My only friend, really. Apart from you."

To Giacomo the past tense comes easily, she notices, the note of nostalgia and regret. Perhaps he's had more practice; Federico isn't the first person he's lost, after all. His tone is filled with pity that strikes her as self-pity; Giacomo coming to terms with what has been lost as personal loss. Before he can say any more about friendship, about her, she changes the subject.

"Yvonne's never been to Rome before?"

"Oh yes, dozens of times. She used to model. She's planned a shopping trip. As though Paris doesn't provide her with enough opportunity for it. I told her she didn't have to come to the conference. She thought I'd gone mad." He laughs wanly. "It hadn't entered her head. I don't think she's heard of Iraq, never mind the war."

"How old is she?"

He glances up at her from his mobile. "I know how much you like Stefania," he says, "but things weren't easy." He looks sheepish and she remembers the two of them on a Corsican beach, she and Giacomo, no more than fifty yards from Stefania and Federico, lying between two beached pedalòs, fucking as though their lives depended on it.

She looks down at her watch.

"I have to go to the hospital. You will come with me?"

"Of course."

"As though there were any doubt it's Federico." She stands up. "Apparently, it's a formality. Which means it has to be done." She pauses. "Perhaps they'll have made a mistake. Perhaps it won't be Federico at all." She is torn between a nervous need to giggle at the horror of what awaits her and the return of tears, because she half believes what she has just said. That she might find a man she has never known. *I don't know whether to laugh or cry.* More words she will need. This time she holds out her arms and Giacomo comes to her, as he should have done before; but this time they are alone. He folds her to him, his stomach and hips against hers, his chin on the side of her head; he bends a little to kiss her hair, comforting kisses, and she lets herself cry into his neck in a gentler, almost resigned way. They stand together, embracing for a minute or two, more like old friends than lovers, until she becomes aware that he is no longer kissing her, that his arms are stiff and posed. She breaks away.

"We have to go. They're waiting."

"I'll need to tell Yvonne."

"You can call her from the car. She'll understand."

"Oh yes," he says. "She'll understand."

7

She hadn't expected journalists, let alone a television troupe milling outside the hotel. She recognises the nearest interviewer from a national news channel just as he recognises her. In a jaw-snapping double-take that might have amused her in any other circumstance, he also recognises Giacomo. For a long indecisive moment, with an instinct for the larger story, he seems to consider holding the microphone out not to Helen Di Stasi, the grief-stricken widow, but to Giacomo Mura, the terrorist redeemed; but he pulls himself together as she walks towards the gaping door of the waiting car. He pushes the microphone into her face; behind him, as if attracted by the scent of her, people she thought were guests or passers-by also gather and she understands that she is about to be mobbed by reporters, a scene she has witnessed so often on TV but can barely believe is happening to her. The jostling begins as tape recorders are poked towards her, followed by questions she can't quite catch. Federico always manages – *managed* – to avoid this somehow, she thinks, and she feels a wave of envy and loss so crippling she reaches out to steady herself against Giacomo. Enclosed by babble, the only question she clearly hears is asked by a woman she sat next to once at a dinner some months ago, whose high-pitched grating voice rises above the rest. She wants to know what it feels like to have lost one's husband, a question so fatuous Helen finds it difficult not to burst into appalled laughter. *I don't know whether to laugh or cry.* Before she can speak, a microphone catches her on the side of the face, cutting her lip; she feels the sting and trickle of blood, with a rush of relief. Giacomo pushes the journalist away, the others falling back as he swears and hustles Helen into the car, sitting beside her a second later and pulling the door shut behind him. The camera swoops down to film them both as the car pulls off. She slumps back into the seat with a long sigh from deep in her lungs that surprises them both. The driver is apologetic.

"That's torn it," says Giacomo. "I'm hardly ideal company for you at the moment. In the eyes of the world, I mean." He squeezes her hand and she feels herself relax. My skin remembers his, she thinks. I still have Giacomo. After a moment, gently, she pulls away.

"They were bound to find out you were here sooner or later. It's not a state secret. You used to be Federico's friend."

"Still, the two of us together like this, today of all days."

"You never used to be so discreet. You've become a politician." She turns to look at him. "Unless you're worried about Yvonne?"

"I'm worried about you." He lights a cigarette but doesn't offer her one. She never thinks about smoking these days. But she would accept a cigarette if she were offered. She turns away from Giacomo, watching Rome pass by the window of the car, people shopping, groups of tourists she might have seen but not noticed this morning, before she knew; a city about its usual business. It strikes her that the death of Federico has, in fact, changed nothing and she thinks for the first time – what a long time it has taken her! – of the people who have done this to him. Who have done this to her. She wonders who they could be, and what could have made them do it. Federico has meant nothing but good.

These thoughts are interrupted by sirens. Their driver pulls over to allow two police cars with an official blue car sandwiched between them to pass. She tries to see in, momentarily convinced against all sense that Federico is the passenger. But the windows reflect her own car. In their swiftly passing glass, she catches a glimpse of Giacomo's profile and of her own face, shadowy and pale before it's gone.

The sirens remind her of the sirens she heard that morning, no more than fifteen minutes after the shooting of Federico, and the death of Massimo. The world was already dealing with it all by then, as she made her way to Giacomo's hotel, its mechanisms of defence already in full play. She had no idea. How is it possible not to know, she thinks, after almost thirty years, that your husband has been shot less than half a mile from where you are?

"Helen, I've been wondering about something." Giacomo interrupts her thoughts. "The police must have asked you about this, obviously."

"About what?"

"About the Stilton. They must have known he'd be stopping at that shop."

"I don't know. They might have been following him and realised it was a good moment. A back street. Not many people around."

Giacomo shakes his head. "These things are planned in advance, down to the last detail. They must have known he'd stop there."

"Yes, they did ask me."

"And what did you say?"

"That *I* knew."

"And? Who else?"

"No one, as far as I know. Apart from the shop. He'd called to make sure they had some Stilton in."

"Do the police know that?"

"Yes. Although I wish they didn't."

"Why?"

"Because the shop couldn't possibly be involved, Giacomo. It's one of Federico's favourites. He's been going there for years. His mother goes there, for God's sake." As soon as these words are said she sees how ridiculous they are. "Oh, give me a cigarette. I think I'm going mad."

She smokes rapidly, holding the smoke in her lungs as long as she can, her head immediately starting to spin. She's eaten nothing since breakfast, having turned down lunch, and drunk too much coffee, more than she's used to. Her stomach feels empty and queasy at the same time. He's right, of course, but she doesn't want to think about it. To break the mood, she utters a short, forced laugh.

"I did something foolish this morning," she says.

Giacomo doesn't answer at once. After a moment, he says, "You mustn't think about that."

"I wasn't thinking about that."

"I'm sorry. I'm thinking about myself."

"I told the police a lie," she says. "About us. Or rather, not about us." She turns to him, then gives him her half-smoked cigarette, to dispose of. "When they asked me what I'd done this morning, I didn't tell them I'd seen you. I don't know why. I suppose I felt it would look bad."

Turning away from her, he stubs out the cigarette, then sighs. "Silence looks worse. I think you'd better tell them the truth, Helen." He sounds annoyed.

"What, all of it?" She is tense with him now. She wants him to tell her it doesn't matter, although she knows it does. She wants him to take at least part of the blame for what she has done. "To Yvonne as well?"

"There's so much we need to say to each other." Giacomo's voice is urgent now. "That I need to say, I mean. Helen, darling. So much I need to explain."

"About Yvonne?"

"Oh, for God's sake, Helen. Yvonne doesn't matter. About you and me. About Federico."

8

Giacomo is smoking some distance from Helen, his elbows on a windowsill, blowing the smoke out into the early evening air. He's forgotten how pleasant the first part of the summer can be in Rome, before the heat sets in. He can just hear Helen on her mobile some yards away. She sounds agitated, one hand holding her hair off her face, the other clutching the phone, her knuckles white. She is standing in a corridor in the hospital, with two young policemen beside her, their patience plainly visible on their faces and in the way their arms are clasped behind their backs, as if to render them defenceless. Giacomo glances at his watch and then at a television suspended from the wall at just above head-height, angled down towards a row of empty seats. He is waiting for the news. There have been flashes throughout the day apparently, but now the programming is back to normal, a quiz show, flashing lights, fabulous prizes. Someone will be in deep shit for this, he thinks, this insensitivity. He looks at Helen and wonders how she is coping. He wishes he could be alone with her. What a cool customer she must seem to everyone. Still elegant, more so than before to be honest, she used to look too frail, too lightweight to be really elegant. The first time he saw her, hovering behind Federico in that dreadful freezing flat they'd found in Turin, he wondered why Federico had been so proud of her. Skinny, almost anaemic, not his type at all. And now, here she is, expensively dressed, even chic. Yvonne could learn a thing or two, although he'd never say this to either of them. He has always loved women with large, generous bodies, by which he means he has loved making love to them, loved fucking them. Yet the ones that stick with him are the others, the Audrey Hepburn types, the clothes-horses. He can't regret this morning, whatever else might have happened, nor the other times, all the other times, and he doesn't think she can either, though she's trying, he's sure of that. Whatever they had, he thinks, they still have. If only he knew what that was. Perhaps Helen will know, if he has a chance to talk to her. Perhaps everything will be all right.

Helen has asked him to stay until she's seen the body, or he'd have gone back to the hotel. He's already had to cope with Yvonne on the mobile, whining that she's neglected. She wants him beside her all the time, he's discovered, within touching distance, to stroke, to kiss, to pamper. At first, he thought she saw him as a pet to fondle and distract, which amused him because nothing could be further from the truth. The truth is that, without him, she's nothing, a washed-up ex-model with tastes she can't afford to indulge. And now he knows that she also knows this. He knows because he has forced her to admit it, by withdrawing, by not meeting her demands. He has made her cry, which has reduced her value in his eyes. He recognises this, and isn't proud, but what can he do? And now, it occurs to him, he will have to contact Stefania and tell her what has happened to Federico. She'll be distraught. The way things stand between them, she'll probably find a way of blaming him as well.

Helen calls him over. "He's ready. Whatever that means. I wish to God I was." She slips her arm through his. "That was Giulia, Federico's mother," she says. "They won't leave his parents alone either." She flicks open her mobile to turn it off.

"They?"

"Oh, everyone. The papers. The RAI. *The Economist*. Federico always says they pay more attention to him abroad than here.

FT. What's that about a prophet outside his own country? Do
you know, Giulia's even had calls from politicians? Not friends,
you'd expect that. From people he's never met. They want to
rope him in, all of us in. He must have died for something,
after all. Isn't that what you said in the hotel, about political
mileage?" She grips his arm. "Oh, Giacomo," she says, her voice
faltering, "I wish I could understand what's happening."

"Don't worry about anything now," he says, to comfort
her. He's thinking about the reports of Federico's death, the
delicacy of the phrase the news agency had used to talk about
Federico, about "extra-parliamentary activities", as though all
they'd been doing was sticking up posters and spraying slogans
on walls. How *exciting* life had been then, whatever else it had
been, however shameful and destructive. How strange time is,
though, the way it folds in on itself, teases you, makes you feel
mortal and immortal all at once. He's never forgotten that first
time in Turin, when he fucked Helen in the kitchen. Talk about
teeth and claw, fingernails like a cat, that dangerous edge to
her he's always half-loved, half-feared; nor the other times, not
often enough for him, but there was all that bad feeling to get
over, that misunderstanding. It took years for Helen to forgive
him, or so she said, and then the logistics of it all – marriage,
whatever – got in the way. She could have left Federico at any
time and come to him, she'd always known that. And, as always,
he wonders what stopped her. She's never really said. He looks
at Helen now as she stands beside him, a woman in her early
fifties, which used to seem old and no longer does. They have so
much life ahead of them, he feels, almost as though Federico's
death has invigorated him; as though he has been spared.

With Giacomo close behind her, Helen allows herself to be
led down some stairs into the basement of the hospital, along
a corridor lit by humming fluorescent tubes. The walls are the
usual green and beige as they segue from the wards of the living
to the refrigerated cells of the dead. Giacomo hasn't been in a

morgue for decades and is curious to see how much they've changed, if at all. He walks a pace behind her as they enter a room and come to a halt in front of a wall of small square stainless steel doors, like the *loculi* of a cemetery except that, instead of the photograph and dates of birth and death, there is a metal pocket with a slip of paper inside it; half *loculus*, half filing cabinet. The bureaucracy of the dead.

He can't see her face, and he's glad of it, as a man in a green coat and white clogs lifts a latch and pulls out the long tray with Federico lying on it, encased in a plastic bag. The man drags back a zip and Giacomo steps forward, as if to protect Helen, although his first instinct is to see the body. For a moment, it crosses his mind that maybe the dead man is not Federico at all, but someone else, some absurd mistake, and he remembers that the same thought passed through Helen's mind in the hotel room; it feels like hours ago now. He wonders if her disappointment is as acute as his when he sees the face of Federico, drained of colour and oddly youthful, emerge from the bag. Surely *more* acute than his, he corrects himself, they've been married for over twenty-five years, they're still together after all that must have happened, her disappointments and lies, his compromises; she must be desolated by this. He looks at Federico, the hair smoothed back, less of it than when they first met over thirty years ago but still not a trace of grey, the eyes wide open with that cold, almost repellent blue as piercing as ever. He sees, as always in these situations, the total absence of the person, the total obliterating presence of death, as though the physical body really were a sort of receptacle for some living flame, some flickering quenchable soul. Perhaps we'll all get God one day, before we die. He frowns.

Helen slumps against him. He slips his arm round her waist and hugs her to him, as much for support as anything; she seems to be about to fall. She has been so brave, it can't last forever. Sooner or later, she is bound to collapse, need help, and he'll be there. When the man in the green coat starts to tug the zip further down, his gaze casts over to the wall as though ashamed or complicit in some way, and it becomes obvious that Federico is naked – but of course he'll be naked – she utters a stifled cry and turns towards Giacomo, raising her face until her eyes, as wide and blank as Federico's, are staring into his.

He cups his hand around the back of her head and guides it into his shoulder. He'd have done anything, he realises, to spare her this. Shaking his head at the man in the green coat, he leads her, almost falling, towards the policemen near the door. Surely there must be someone more senior than these two, he thinks, they look like kids. I used to be scared of men in uniform; now I feel like sending them off to find their mothers. "We've seen enough," he says.

Ten minutes later, they are sitting with the man who seems to have been assigned to them, not much hair, a thin pusillanimous face, oddly shabby for a state official. The magistrate assigned to the case. Giacomo hasn't caught his name; he's surprised she doesn't warrant something higher. He heard the Attorney General had done a PR job at the site of the shooting, but look at this character in front of them. There's a bleached, northern look to him, confirmed, as he begins to talk, by a trace of accent. Couldn't they have sent someone with a decent pair of shoes? Perhaps it isn't the magistrate at all, he thinks; this one smells more like police.

The man is asking Helen questions in a low-voiced way that might be intended to express his sympathy but is having the opposite effect. She wipes her tears from her cheeks with her hand and glances round the room, an office emptied of its normal occupants, in a fretful way. She says to Giacomo, in English, "He's treating me like an idiot. He seems to think I don't speak Italian." Immediately, the man shakes his head. "Not at all, Signora Di Stasi, please forgive me," he says, also in English, his thin voice rueful, even sad. His English sounds perfect, with an accent it takes Giacomo a moment to place: South African. "You have my deepest sympathy." To Giacomo's surprise, Helen's cheeks flush with embarrassment.

The man continues in English, beginning to ask Helen about her movements that morning, with cautious insistence. Giacomo lights a cigarette and waits, curious, to see if she will tell the truth. Why shouldn't she? She hasn't done anything wrong. Because old habits die hard? Helen has told enough lies in the past. She's lied to Federico, she's lied to me. And then he thinks, What in God's name possessed me to accept this invitation? To come back to Rome like this, so publicly? I might as well have put an announcement in the paper. Sitting duck in capital. Pot shots welcome. Because of course this terrible thought has also entered his head. Is this murder directed at me in some way? Is Federico no more than a warning? How many enemies do I still have?

"Is this necessary? I've already explained it to your colleagues this morning. Surely someone takes notes?" Helen glances across at Giacomo and makes a gesture that seems, to his astonishment, to be an invitation to kiss her, two slim fingers brushing her mouth, but is actually a request for a cigarette. He lights it for her, alert to what Helen's interrogator might do with this glimpse of intimacy. Will he have done his homework? This little man in his cheaply cut grey suit who imagines the right questions will turn up the right answers, because there are right answers, there are always right answers; it's just a matter of knowing where to look. How much will he know, Giacomo wonders, handing her the lit cigarette, how much will he know about the three of them, no, the four of them, because there was always Stefania, good solid Stefania, about the old days in Turin, when politics was passion, the real and only thing. Sexy, as well, though they didn't realise that at the time. Or maybe they did. Maybe he and Helen did. This time, though, she should know when it suits her to tell the truth. The shabby man's not to know she hasn't, of course. Giacomo's safe enough so far.

She takes a drag, then looks for somewhere to put it down, already at a loss to know what to do with a cigarette she doesn't want. She stopped before Federico, before Stefania even. Anglo-Saxon health fetishism, he'd thought at the time, yet here he is with Yvonne constantly at his throat and the sense of being hounded by clean air fascists in France of all places. Thank God they still won't let him into the States, that's one advantage. The interrogator pushes across the desk an ashtray the size of a dinner plate – Giacomo has never been in an Italian hospital that doesn't have a plentiful supply of ashtrays – and coughs discreetly, as if to say, under the skin we're the same, we're men, we understand each other. Giacomo looks at him with unexpected admiration. It's true in a way. We must be the same age, give or take a year or two, we probably have more in common than either of us dreams, we know the same things, the same flavours, the same fears, unlike those youngsters in the corridor outside who know nothing. He's right. We understand each other. Isn't that what they say? Police and thieves.

Helen stubs out the barely started cigarette, exhales a ribbon of smoke, continues: "I said goodbye to my husband at the car, where we always say goodbye. He drove off – was driven off, I mean – and I went into my local bar, the one on the corner, I don't know what it's called, I've never looked up to see, and I had a cappuccino and a, no, nothing else. A cappuccino. I spoke to the woman who owns it about something, a few words, I don't remember what…"

She is talking in a measured, almost off-hand way that would be insulting in any other situation, as though she has been pestered beyond endurance; but here, in this hospital office that is slowly filling up with smoke, it denotes something else, an exhaustion to which she, more than anyone, is entitled. "After that, I went to the American Library, it's just down the road from where we live. I wanted to work on my thesis. I'm doing another degree, in American literature, to pass the time really. It was my husband's idea."

She pauses and looks puzzled, as if she is thinking, Why am I saying all this? What business is it of theirs? Or maybe, What am I doing here? Can any of this be real? The man turns his head, in what looks like a gesture of delicacy, and stares at the wall. Giacomo is impressed again. After a moment, with a tiny shake of her shoulders, Helen goes on: "I stayed there for some time, I didn't really look at my watch, twenty minutes maybe, half an hour." She sighs. "I had the start of a headache, I thought a walk might make it better, so I left the library and decided to wander around the centre a little, look at a few shops, and wait for it to go. Walking usually helps. I didn't need to be at work until twelve, you see…"

All at once her tone has changed, become persuasive, that odd unnecessary *you see* has given her away. All at once, she needs to be believed. But why, in God's name, did she lie in the first place? He couldn't believe it when she told him in the car on the way to the morgue. I've done something foolish, she said. You won't let me down, will you? For old times' sake? The man must have noticed as well because he leans back in his chair, as obvious in his way as she has been in hers, and caps his pen. Secret service, decides Giacomo. And now I'm implicated, damn her.

"You must be tired, Signora Di Stasi," the man says before Giacomo can intervene. "I'll arrange for you to be taken home." He opens a drawer and takes out a card, which he gives to her. "I shall certainly be in touch, but if you would like to speak to me again–"

"I'll take you home," Giacomo says as Helen puts the card into her pocket. But the man shakes his head.

"I think it might be wiser, Dottor Mura, if you returned to your hotel."

Giacomo, affronted, turns to face him. "I'm sorry?"

The man shrugs. "Naturally, you are free to do as you wish. I was merely offering a word of advice."

"I'm sorry?" insists Giacomo. "I didn't catch your name."

"He's right," says Helen. "You've done quite enough already." Giacomo can't tell if he's being thanked or dismissed. He stifles his resentment.

"I'll call you later."

"No, don't do that," she says, her voice still measured, in an oddly insistent way. "You won't get through. I won't be taking calls."

"If you're sure that's what you want," he says. He opens the door for her, stands back to let her pass, but she takes his hand in hers and he can feel her trembling. "If you're sure."

"I'll call you," she says. "Later. I promise."

Then, at a volume the other man is not supposed to hear, she adds: "I have to talk to you, I just don't know where." And Giacomo nods and presses her hand before letting it go.

9

The flat is empty. Slowly, she lifts her hands to her face and holds it for a moment, skin against skin, her palms against her cheeks, as if to make sure she is really who she is, and not some other woman whose husband has been murdered. She has rushed at the stairs to be here, pursued by nothing but her growing horror of the world outside, the cars, the lights, the hustling intimacy of its demands. Outside the hospital, someone shouted as a man's hand guided her lowered head into the car, one voice above the rest, *Bravo Federico*, and she flinched but didn't turn. She sat straight-backed in the car with the police woman from that morning beside her, holding her arm the way a friend might although Helen didn't see her as a friend and wished she wasn't there. I've answered too many questions today, she thought. I shall be home soon. Part of her has been waiting to be alone for almost seven hours and now, with her back pressed to the front door, she closes her eyes and listens to her breathing as though there is nothing else to be done, as though – finally – she has what she needs.

She steps out of her shoes, the wooden floor warm and smooth against her feet. Her first thought is to take a shower, but she is suddenly so tired she can barely walk across the room to the sofa and collapse. Clutching a cushion to her side, she sits in the corner, her legs curled up beneath her, refusing to lie down, afraid she might fall asleep when there is still so much she has to do. She doesn't know where to begin, her mind is a wiped slate, so blank she has a sudden sense of panic, as though she is literally being sponged away.

When the landline rings on the other side of the room, she bites the side of her tongue in shock. The taste of blood filling her mouth, she picks up the receiver. She hears a woman's voice she doesn't recognise repeat her name, the pitch insistent, hectoring. She drops the receiver, not on the phone where it belongs but on the pad, beside a number and a date, written in Federico's hand, a doodle. The voice continues, the furious buzz of an insect trapped in a jar. Her name and a plea to be answered, a plea that is also, it seems to Helen, a threat. It is 7 o'clock. The news will be starting. Now everyone will know. Friends and others. Some people, it occurs to her, will be pleased. She pulls the pad free of the receiver and stares at the doodle, a flower in a vase; Federico must have made it the day before. What was she doing while he drew this? Who was he talking to? Someone she knew? She doesn't recognise the number. The date is for next week. Next Tuesday. A week today. The doodle blurs. Eventually, her hand shaking a little, she puts it down.

And now what shall I do? she asks herself. She starts to cry again, slow effortless tears. Not even her home is safe; she has the sense of being hounded by savage beasts, as though beyond the door there is no longer the familiar hall, the worn-down stairs, the furled umbrellas waiting to be used; as though she has become detached from that. The world seems hostile and unknown. She should feel safe here, in her own sitting room, surrounded by all the objects they have chosen, yet how empty the flat is without him, how silent and indifferent; although he was never home by this time. He never gets back before nine, he works too hard. Normally, *that dreadful word*. She turns on the television and makes herself a snack, some olives that Massimo's mother has sent them, a handful of cashew nuts; she pours herself a glass of wine or beer, and sits on the sofa to watch the news. She waits for Federico. *Normally*. But this evening, she isn't hungry and doesn't want to pour herself a drink. She is afraid that once she starts she won't be able to stop, because *normally* it is the thought of Federico finding her drunk that stops her after the first two glasses. And she can't believe that might not happen.

Sitting in the car on the way here, she planned to call Giacomo as soon as she arrived, ask him to come over. But she realises now, alone in the home she's made with Federico that what she wants to do, more than anything in the world, is to talk not to Giacomo but to Federico, and she won't be able to. As if for the first time that day, she understands that she'll never be able to talk to Federico again. But this time it is worse. Before this, some part of her has told her that he'll be back, that he's away on business, but he'll be back; he always comes back. And now this part has fallen silent and she feels a flush of pain and rage, so strong it takes her breath away. Who has done this to me? To us? She stares at the phone, which has started to make a curious noise, then replaces the receiver on the handset. Immediately the ringing begins. She lifts it to her ear. It is Giulia, Federico's mother.

"I've been trying to get hold of you for hours, Helen," she snaps. "Your mobile's turned off."

"I couldn't stand it any longer, Giulia." Talking again, Helen tastes the blood in her mouth. "I was being pestered by journalists."

"You've only just arrived home?"

"Ten minutes ago. The police brought me back in the end. I've been at the hospital all afternoon. I had to identify him, Giulia."

"How dreadful for you. You aren't still with that Mura man, I hope?"

"Giacomo left me at the hospital. He was a great comfort."

"They could have asked me." Giulia pauses. "Oh, by the way, the president's called. He has to talk to you."

"What about?" For a moment, Helen wonders who she means. The president of what?

"Fede was such an important figure, especially at the moment." Giulia's voice fills with pride. And now Helen understands that this is what will happen, for Giulia at least. Federico will become a hero and then a martyr. Perhaps it is happening already. What she stops herself saying, just in time, are the words: *He isn't dead yet*. Without putting down the phone, she stretches out to the remote control and turns on the television to see what is left of the news, the volume off. Giulia's voice, with that undertow of offence, continues to talk of Federico and his achievements, but what Helen sees is herself and Giacomo as they climb into a car, and a smile on her face she doesn't remember, followed by a glance of complicity between them, accusing them both. And there are more pictures of Giacomo, on a demonstration in France, standing with his arm round the shoulder of the man who bombed the McDonald's branch, the one with the moustache, and then a photograph she hasn't seen for years, from his first driving licence, the one all the newspapers used when he was on the run. Appalled, she tries to tell Giulia that she has a headache, she can't talk any longer but Giulia insists that Fausto has something important to say to her first. Helen expects her father-in-law to cry and feels her own lip tremble. He hasn't been able to speak to her until this moment. Before she can answer, or protest, Fausto is on the line. "Turn on the news," he says, his voice breaking.

"I know. I'm watching it."

"But what on earth were you thinking of?" She's right: he's close to tears. "What did you imagine people's reaction would be? Today. On the very day..." He pauses. "Giacomo Mura, of all people. All that terrible business had been forgotten and now, now that Fede's—"

The news moves on, Giacomo's bleached-out bearded face is replaced by footballers training, the wedding of a couple she recognises from the gossip magazines.

"I just don't understand." She interrupts him, her own voice breaking. "Why is everyone so angry with me?"

"I'll speak to you tomorrow," Fausto says.

"Yes," she says. "That's the best thing. We'll talk tomorrow." She can hear Giulia's voice in the background, and Fausto saying yes.

As soon as she has put down the phone, with the receiver deliberately off the hook, she raises her eyes to the ceiling. "Oh my God, Federico," she says, out loud, her voice unexpectedly strong, as though she is calling him from the next room. "Help me get through this without you."

She goes to the kitchen and opens a bottle of wine from the fridge and sits in front of the television, with the sound turned off, to drink it.

PART TWO

1

Rome, Wednesday, 2 June 2004

Helen wakes up at six, her head throbbing. After hours of fitful half-sleep, the top sheet pushed away in a sweat and then pulled back, she has had a dream in which she and Federico are seated together on a train as it passes through the countryside around Turin, low hills and houses, the mountains behind, the neat green woods. She lies there, her eyes still closed, her temple pressed against the pillow, and struggles to remember what she has seen, as she always does, in that state between sleep and wakefulness. For a moment, absorbed by her efforts to recall the dream, she is calm, even happy, despite the dull but insistent pain in her head; she will tell Federico what she has seen, as she always does, when he comes back from the bathroom, toothbrush in hand. And then, with a wave of emptiness, as though she is being filled with it, stifled, she knows where he is. She opens her eyes, the dream wiped out, and hears herself moan. Her hand reaches out to his pillow, to stroke it, but also to check, because it can't be true. What she knows to be true cannot be true. She lies there, alone on her side of their bed, and thinks, I shall never get up again. How can I?

Three hours later, Helen sighs at the voice of Fausto, muffled and urgent, over the entry phone. She still isn't dressed. After waking and remembering, she somehow went back to sleep, and woke again, and remembered again. When the doorbell rang, she was on the point of calling Giacomo, sitting with the mobile in her hand and his name staring up at her, afraid of what she might say.

She stands by the open door in Federico's old towelling robe, hearing her father-in-law's feet slow down as he climbs to their floor, until, at the corner of the final landing, he makes an effort and almost runs up the final few steps to embrace her. He is carrying a case. He begins to cry and then so does she, and she is filled with such gratitude, because this is what she needs, someone whose grief is as simple and uncompromised as hers should be. She hugs him to her, her hand on the back of his head, her mouth pressed into his coarse grey hair. They stand on the threshold, the case squashed between them, until Fausto eases her gently away from him and guides her back into the flat. He closes the door behind them, then puts down the case with a little sigh as he bends over.

"There are people in the street outside. Journalists. Not too many yet. They will take it in turns to pester us for the next few days, I imagine. All of them with their little tape recorders as though pen and paper have never been invented. Television people too. No sign of the police. You'd have thought they could provide some kind of guard. Perhaps they're all needed at the parade."

"Parade?"

"You don't remember? Of course you don't. It's the military parade this morning, for the Republic. All these helicopters, you haven't heard them? Federico will have received an invitation. Perhaps he forgot to mention it. He's been so busy these past few weeks."

"Federico never goes to that sort of thing."

"I should have been there," Fausto says. "Giulia wanted us all to be there, you two as well. She says we should show ourselves a united front. Against what, I don't know. I only wish I did.

Sometimes the company you are forced to keep is less palatable than that of the enemy. Giulia doesn't see things that way, of course." He shakes his head. "She's there now." He runs his hands through his hair. "I wanted her to come with me, to be here with me. I don't understand her sometimes. I didn't want her to go, but she insisted. She said that someone had to show their face." He sighs again. "It's all so clear for her, even today, so clear where her duty lies." His face puckers and she thinks he's about to cry again.

"Please don't," she says, resting her hand on his arm for a moment. "I'll make us some coffee." She turns towards the kitchen, expecting him to follow. But Fausto touches his heart.

"Not for me, my dear."

"Tea? There's some green tea somewhere. That's good for the heart."

"No. Nothing." He sounds distracted, but not by grief. He's staring at the floor beside his feet.

"That's Federico's case, isn't it?" Helen says, the two halves of the coffee pot damp in her hands. He doesn't seem to hear. He has walked across the room and is sitting in the office chair they use when they work at the computer. She asks him again.

"Yes," he says after a moment. "It's his laptop. He forgot it yesterday." He rubs his forehead. "Not yesterday. The day before."

"I didn't know you'd seen each other. I thought he'd been at work all day. At the ministry, I mean. He didn't say he'd seen you."

"Didn't he?" says Fausto.

"Federico didn't tell me everything," she says. She's hurt but doesn't want to show how much.

"We were working on the conference. He disliked working on it at the ministry. The conference was his idea, it had nothing to with the department. He must have told me a hundred times these last few weeks it was the only thing that kept him sane."

"Sane?"

"You know that it hasn't been easy recently, at the ministry, I mean. He had too much on his shoulders." Fausto sounds reproachful. Helen wants to say *Of course I know*, but the truth is that she doesn't. She hasn't known anything about her husband's threatened sanity until a moment ago and now she can't understand why no one has spoken to her about it, Federico above all; even more, that he has chosen to speak to his father. "He wanted to talk to us about a document he'd been working on. Something to do with the opening."

"Us?"

"His mother, Helen. Me." As if to say, who else? He pushes the chair away from the desk with impatience, using both hands. His feet barely touch the floor as he comes to a halt. With a moan of pain, stretching the muscles in his back, he crosses the room and takes the two halves of the coffee pot from her hands. She is startled, she's forgotten she's still holding them. She watches him rinse the pot under the tap again. "I'll do that," she says, but he waves her away. Neither of them speak, as though the business of making coffee is all they need to distract them. It is bubbling up before he turns to look at her.

"I didn't want to tell you this, but Giulia will if I don't and I think it's better coming from me. The PM has been trying to persuade Bush to extend his visit by a day, so that he can be present at the funeral."

"I'm not having Bush at the funeral," says Helen. "Fede despised him. It's out of the question. What funeral anyway? I haven't even had a chance to think about the funeral yet. Why haven't I been asked about this?"

"There'll be pressure though. For a state funeral." He hesitates. "Giulia wouldn't mind one either. She's taking it with great courage. I'm not surprised, of course, knowing Giulia. I don't know how she can bear to have gone to that thing this morning, standing there with everyone looking at her to see how she's coping."

"It's the last thing Federico would want." Helen shudders. "I don't know what Giulia's thinking of." She can see her mother-in-law now, her tight drawn face and exquisite tailored suit, her hair in the chignon retired ballerinas adopt to show off their necks, stiff as a ramrod, as the troops file past her, too proud to show emotion, her one child dead. She'll be planning the funeral in her head, thinks Helen with a kind of fury. Federico, sane?

When the coffee bubbles up and over the ring, she pushes past Fausto to turn off the heat. She picks up a cloth, then stands with it in her hand, her anger suddenly turning on him, who lets himself be led, who has brought her this news about Federico. She wants to tell him to leave the flat, but doesn't know how.

He takes the cloth from her and squeezes her hand, more firmly than she likes, a hard bony grasp, but she doesn't pull away. Just as suddenly, and against all sense, she is filled with love for this anxious old man who has lost his son and is standing in this room with her, with this bond and this barrier between them. You must know more than you've told me, she wants to say, Federico always spoke to you before he spoke to me, about these things at least. She allows him to hold her until his grip loosens finally, then eases her hand from his as slowly and gently as she can and embraces him a second time.

"You can cry with me," she says, "I need someone to cry with." She presses his head against her neck, feeling his hair on her lips. He hasn't been able to do this with Giulia, she thinks, for all her celebrated courage. And they call it a marriage. She feels a moment's triumph. She wonders for a moment what the word marriage means.

By eleven, Helen is showered and dressed, and alone. She looks in the fridge for something to eat, because she feels she ought to eat. But all she can find is a crust of parmesan and a brown paper bag containing three vine tomatoes. It was her job to do the shopping yesterday, her job to buy the cold cuts and salad and

artichokes they would have eaten, and the fruit and the fresh
crisp pizza bread to go with the Stilton, wherever that is now, in
some forensic freezer made of stainless steel, or forgotten and
starting to stink in a plastic bag in some office. Or maybe it is still
inside the shop, because she still doesn't know at what point he
was shot, on his way in or leaving. She still doesn't know what
happened, not entirely. She still doesn't know how he died,
how long it took the ambulance to get there, how many times
he must have asked for her and wondered where she was. No
one has told her about his last few moments, in the hospital,
whether he was aware or not, aware that he'd been left to die
alone. She tries to imagine what it must be like to know you
are about to die, your hand pressed hard where the bullet went
in, to staunch the blood, your cheek against the sawdust on the
shop floor and beneath that the smoothness of the tiles. Your
last sensation the coldness of the marble, the smell of cheese,
shouting that slowly fades away until you're being lifted up and
jolted back to life as they carry you into an ambulance and you
hear the sirens, which move with you, which are there for you.
She isn't sure why she is imagining this; to do as much harm to
herself as she can, perhaps. "I'd do anything for it not to have
happened," she says out loud, her voice sounding strange to her
in the silent room, then pauses, as if waiting for an answer, as
if her claim might be challenged. As if Federico might ask her
about Giacomo and she won't know what to say.

Eventually, she closes the fridge door and discovers in a
cupboard half a packet of biscuits, slightly stale. She makes
herself some weak Italian tea, without milk or lemon, to dip
them into. When the biscuits are eaten, she sits with her elbows
on the worktop, holding the cup in both hands, and lets her
eyes drift round the room, the piano, the paintings she has
bought and hung, the new books piled on a painted wooden
chest; moving closer, into the space of the kitchen, a woven
plait of garlic, the blackboard with the row of keys hanging off

it and Federico's last written word, OLIVES, scribbled in English only moments before they left the flat; she'd have forgotten them, she thinks now, and he would have been annoyed with her, and sent her out to find some. They settle in the end on Federico's small bone-handled knife, his favourite. How many times she's envied the deft way he uses it to slice courgettes, slice open packets, crush garlic; he's had it as long as she has known him, since their time in Cambridge. She picks it up and holds it with the edge of the blade against her palm and then higher, at the level of her wrist. She thinks, as she often thinks with knives, a little pressure, that's all it would need, although she has never seriously wanted to take her own life; she has merely wondered what it might be like to want to, and then to do it. She has never been as close to it as she is now, it occurs to her. Suicide must be a kind of numbness. A friend of hers, years ago, who believed in séances and divination, told her that a palm with a single line across it, in which the head and the heart line are one, had been enough to convict a man of murder in the middle ages. The hand doesn't lie, she said, and Helen often looks at palms in search of this single line, but has found it only once, on the hand of a man who'd asked her for money in the street. She stepped back, startled, as though she'd seen a ghost. As if that were all it took, she thinks, to identify a murderer. A show of hands to see who the guilty one is. The way they used to make us all hold our hands out after school assembly to make sure they were washed. Rows of girls with their arms outstretched, palms up, sleeves pulled back to the elbows, waiting for one of us to be dragged off by the wrists into the bathrooms, wondering who it would be.

When the doorbell rings, she starts with shock and nicks her wrist on the knife blade. She crosses to the entry phone, lifting the cut to her mouth to lick the blood away. The last word he wrote in his life was OLIVES. We never run out of olives, she thinks, I must buy olives, then brushes the thought away as too painful. Perhaps this time it will be someone she wants to see and not a journalist, and she will let them up. She picks up the phone. There, by her feet, as if to taunt her, is Federico's laptop in its neat black case.

2

Giacomo is woken at 7am by the noise of traffic, the overhead droning of helicopters. He lifts his head from the pillow and sees that Yvonne has opened the bedroom window and is staring down into Via Veneto. She is wearing a pale, translucent robe he has never seen before that barely covers her bottom, and he is excited until he remembers, with a sensation akin to panic, that Federico, his oldest friend, has been shot and is lying dead in a hospital no more than a mile from their hotel. And because he can't bear to think of Federico before him on a metal shelf, beneath a plastic sheet, he lies back and lets images from the news the previous evening return to him. He didn't get to bed until past 2am, what with specials and news flashes of one sort or another, although there was nothing new to report. Comment is news of a kind, it's what stands in for news and then all at once the event has ceased to happen, there is only its reverberation. That's a nice idea, he thinks, abruptly cheered, and is about to jot it down in his notebook when Yvonne turns into the room towards him and he sees her small breasts through the floating fabric and whispers to her to come over, his voice early-morning rough. She shakes her head.

"Who are you?" she says, her bottom lip in a pout that might be serious or merely playful; he doesn't know her well enough to be sure.

"I'm sorry?" He'd tried to make her watch the TV with him, so that she'd know what they are talking about. Not just Federico now, but then. And not just Federico, but all of them. Layers of truth and lies so artfully blended no one knew which was which. "Look," he'd said, thinking she *must* learn Italian sooner or later, *must* make the effort, for him if for no other reason, he couldn't spend all his life interpreting for her. But she'd turned her back to him; asleep or faking, it came to the same thing.

"What were they saying about you on TV last night?" she says now. "Those photographs of you and your name all the time. Giacomo Mura this, Giacomo Mura that. I heard them say your name a hundred times, as though you were the one who has been murdered and not your friend. If that's what he was."

"I've already explained it to you." He wants her to come to bed, badly. He sits up, pushing the sheet away from him to free his hips, and reaches to clutch at her robe. But she moves away with a whimper of distaste.

"I don't think I want to make love to you," she says, and it occurs to him how incapable he is of reading her tone. Is this flirtation? Distaste? "Now that I know what a wicked man you've been. A violent, naughty man." It never worried Helen, he thinks, the secret names, the subterfuge. Even the boring parts exhilarated her, like the *longueurs* of the films they used to watch with such passion, skyscrapers and sleeping men and the slow mute churning of washing machines, the riveting boredom of endlessly repeated acts. She followed him once, from one side of Turin to the other, imagining she hadn't been seen, darting from door to door like an actress in some two-bit film noir. He led her a merry dance, but she deserved it. He wonders if she remembers now, or whether she has chosen to forget, the violence and the excitement of those days, as though the world would actually be changed by what they did. That was when she told him something she'd heard at Cambridge: a crank is a small thing that starts a revolution. He hadn't understood at first, not until Helen explained the double sense of crank, and then he'd loved it, quoted it endlessly, convinced of its truth, convinced that madness, his own or the collective madness of them all, would change the world. A hand on a crank, a hundred, a hundred thousand hands. Maybe he still thinks that; it's just that his notion of madness has changed. Now, when he thinks of power, he sees a strutting demagogue in a double-breasted suit surrounded by goons, and wonders what drives him, and others like him, scattered across the palaces of the world. Is all this madness too? And if it isn't, might madness be any better? Ten minutes later, sitting on the lavatory while Yvonne, humming, makes up her face in the bedroom next door, Giacomo is reading an article about himself in that day's copy of *Il Foglio* with a mixture of disgust and satisfaction. The journalist is a man he remembers not by his real name, Adriano Testa, but as Little White Mouse, *Topino Bianco*, a codename provided unwittingly by his then girlfriend. She'd used the term one morning to describe his dick, though naturally he hadn't been told. And what was *her* name? Anna Something. Utterly mortified when she found out, he remembers now, amused. You can't call him that, she said. He'll realise. Now, there's naïveté, he thought. It wouldn't hurt to tell him now, though. Pompous piece of shit.

The article isn't bad, he'll admit that. Most of the facts correspond more or less to the truth as Giacomo recalls it. The six months spent without trial in San Vittore after Moro's death, followed by his release for lack of evidence. High-profile campaigning against the special anti-terrorist laws, using his own case as an example. Enemies made, etc. A list of the great and good. His subsequent arrest as the brain behind a series of ideologically motivated bank jobs, security van heists, break-ins. No actual blood on his hands, no careless gun fire. No deaths. No one has ever accused him directly of that, although what was the money stolen for if not for arms? What was the purpose of the arms if not to kill? Court appearances, declamations, manifestos, silence. Sentenced to eight years, increased on appeal. Elected to the House of Deputies as a radical, released to take his seat. Little White Mouse makes it all sound like snakes and ladders, but wilful too, and as though something infinitely nasty was lurking beneath it all. Immunity revoked, but by that time he'd left his seat and moved to France, making a name for himself as a man with an intellectual mission. The then president persuaded by popular pressure (that is, by a handful of journalists that included Federico's father) to issue an official pardon. Now ageing *enfant terrible* in Paris. Settling his buttocks more comfortably, Giacomo skims through the piece again. Nothing overtly stated, everything implied. The photographs part of the overall effect. Next to the classic image of Aldo Moro, the kidnapped elder statesman, newspaper in hand with the five-pointed Red Brigades star on the wall behind him, there is Giacomo standing beneath a banner with the same crude star on it, his Che Guevara beret impeccably tilted to the left, his right hand raised in a fist. Cheap, but effective. And that isn't all of it. Giacomo, grinning behind the bars of the cage in the court room, like some chained beast. Giacomo entering Parliament to take his seat with the same fuck-you grin, in a suit he'd borrowed from someone – Federico? He doesn't remember – that didn't quite fit, too tight across the chest; already putting on weight, the easy life just about to start. An older, altogether tidier and more affluent Giacomo with Mitterrand, a particularly spiteful choice this one, the two of them looking as though they've just had sex, by some physiological fluke smiling dreamily at each other, with no one else in sight. Has everyone else been whited out? Photoshopped out? But by whom? The Stalinist training showing through. Altogether, a more than competent hatchet job, thinks Giacomo, nothing quite libellous, nothing worth getting the lawyers in for. Little White Mouse has been itching to do this for years, lousy in bed and bitter with it. Decades of hating Giacomo, hardly surprising given his own rather less spectacular career trajectory. From pseudo-Maoist in 1976 to jobbing hack for the self-appointed king of dumbed-down television, dumbed-down politics, dumbed-down Italy. He isn't exactly going to love me, thinks Giacomo as he raises himself from the lavatory to see what he's produced, then puts down the paper, satisfied, to wipe his arse. Could have killed two birds with one stone, it strikes him a moment later, as he straightens up to flush. Could have wiped my arse on the article. How much his having read it has made him feel that he is back in Italy, at home. This use of a good man's death to settle an old score.

A quick splash at the bidet and he is on his feet, but his legs have gone numb after crouching too long. He staggers to the bed, stumbling across it as Yvonne turns round from the mirror to examine him, splayed out. That sonnet by Shelley, about Ozymandias, comes into his head. "Look on my works, ye Mighty, and despair," he declaims, but Yvonne sniffs and goes back to her own work, mascara wand in hand, shoulders hunched in concentration, her bra straps lifting off the skin above her breasts. Good thing she doesn't pick up the reference, he thinks, she could use it against me. Never mind, she'll have ample opportunity for that before all this is over. Nothing beside remains. Round the decay of that colossal wreck. As the blood flows back into his legs, he feels strangely invigorated by his morning's reading. There's nothing like a decent evacuation and an article dedicated entirely to one's own sweet self to put one in the mood for breakfast. That and the first faint stirring of an erection. God, though, she's thin. Half the size of Stefania. But wasn't that the point?

"I don't suppose you'd like to smudge your lipstick?" he says.

She doesn't hear, or pretends not to. Giacomo lies sprawled across the bed, playing with himself in a desultory way, tempted to simply wank in front of her and have done with it. Helen would take him up on the offer, he thinks, and feels himself stiffen, though part of his brain knows full well that Helen was never as available as he would have liked, as though she's always known that some small part of the fun – because it *has* been fun, even yesterday had been *fun* – has nothing to do with her and what she offers, but draws its sustenance from Giacomo's cuckolding of his best friend and rival, now slotted into a grey steel cabinet for the dead a couple of miles from this hotel room. He looks around the walls, hand motionless, shell-like, on his groin. Decent room, *tutti i confort*, as they still say, provincial as ever. Funny place to pick though, Via Veneto, as if Rome hasn't moved on since Tyrone Power punched paparazzi in the face. Now it's nothing but lard-arsed tourists and glove shops and a particularly shabby Hard Rock Cafe.

These last few weeks he's been getting messages of various kinds from Federico, emails, faxes, the occasional text on his mobile. He isn't sure he'll say this to Helen, nor anyone else, he hasn't quite admitted it to himself, but the impression these messages have given him is of a man on the slipway to some state of, not madness exactly, exaltation. The tone of a man anointed by the Lord, or of one who thinks he is. Not like Federico at all. Messages filled with references Giacomo hasn't bothered to look up, to tree huggers of various kinds, Taoists, heaven knows who else. Flat earth fundamentalists, intellectual-stroke-spiritual-stroke-stark raving bonkers Taliban. With trepidation and not entirely without that pleasure one derives from a friend's misfortune he's been looking forward to whatever Federico's contribution to the conference might be and now that there will be no contribution, unless from beyond the grave, he feels both thwarted and relieved.

His erection has faded, so it is particularly galling that Yvonne should choose this moment to come and sit beside him on the unmade bed in her bra and panties and place one fine-boned, moisturised hand on his thigh. Flexing her fingers, drawing her varnished nails across the hair and flesh, still firm, still muscled enough, she glances at his penis, now retracted deep into the foreskin, looking like one of those twirls of sand you find on the beach. What makes them? he wonders. Worms? Lugworms? She purses her pale pink glistening lips, then stands up to dress, humming the same tuneless melody as before as she lifts down a skirt from the wardrobe and steps into it.

"Darling?"

"Yes?"

"Why can't we go back to Paris today?" she says. Her back, naked but for the bra straps, is turned to him, her tone without urgency, as if making conversation. Giacomo, though, knows that she has been preparing this question all morning, perhaps all night. Yvonne is single-minded in the purest sense, he thinks, her mind possessing no more than one whole thought at a time, one thought that must be dealt with, concluded in some satisfactory way, for her to move on, to see what new thought might appear.

"Paris?" he says. Her head disappears, re-emerges from a pale silk top. Her tone becomes plaintive, kittenish. "We don't have to stay here any longer, do we?" Her back is still turned, he imagines the set of her mouth and jaw, murderous; no wonder she doesn't want to be seen.

"But I thought you had shopping to do?"

"Oh no, darling. I can do that so much better in Paris. To tell you the truth, I'm always *disappointed* by Rome. It's lovely and historical and all that, I know, but there's something rather provincial about it." She pauses, her face turned away. "Something a teeny bit vulgar." She slides her feet into her shoes, white strappy things, no tights, he likes that, that sense of her skin being within reach. "I don't know how poor Helen can bear it."

"Helen?" This surprises him. Yvonne enlisting Helen to achieve her own ends. He saw she was jealous yesterday, she even made a scene over dinner in the restaurant. Apparently he'd kissed her too long, too hard. And now it is *poor* Helen and he is expected to agree.

"What will she do now, do you think?"

"Do? I've got no idea."

Yvonne darts over to him, across the thick beige carpet that could be anywhere, and stands beside the bed, looking down, her bottom lip pushed out in a pout. Swinging his legs off the bed, he sits up, wishing he was dressed as well. His stomach obscures the view of his penis. This is what eunuchs must be like: dickless, obese. You're going to seed, he thinks. You're gone.

"Please, let's go back to Paris."

He uses his most mollifying tone. "But Yvonne darling, we can't. We have to stay for the conference. Besides, the police may need to speak to me again. They asked us not to leave. Don't you remember? In any case, I can't just abandon Helen. I promised we'd go round to see her this morning."

"This is like some ridiculous film," she says, indignant. "We are held here against our will." She spins away from him, into the bathroom. "There won't be any conference now, Giacomo. Your friend is dead." He listens to the rustle of cloth against cloth, the hiss of cloth against skin, as she hikes up her skirt and slides her panties down, followed by the rustle of paper when she picks up the newspaper he's been reading. He listens to her pee as she flips through the pages.

"I see now why you don't want to leave Rome," she shouts through when she's finished, with a note of triumph. "All this excitement, this attention. Two whole pages devoted entirely to you. Photographs. Mitterrand! Giacomo Mura is *such* an important man."

"A prodigal son." But he can tell from her voice that she's impressed. And so she should be.

"Is that what it says here? That you are a prodigal son?"

"Not exactly. It says I'm a bit of a shit, to be honest. If not worse. You know how bitter journalists can be."

"And where are the photographs of your poor Helen?" She drags out *Helen*, a ridiculous lengthening of the vowels. But you can't blame her for feeling jealous. Walking into the bathroom, he squats on the bidet beside her and takes her nearest hand, prising it off *Il Foglio* and lifting it to his face, covering the soft hot palm and fingers, which smell slightly of her urine, with a series of butterfly kisses. She drops the paper and strokes his head with her free hand, guiding it down towards her crotch. He reaches awkwardly behind to flush and feels the faintest sprinkle of water on his face. She sighs. "Poor Helen," she says again, as the hotel phone begins to ring.

"That will be her," she says, standing up and brushing him off so roughly he falls back onto his arse, banging his hip against the corner of the tub. He struggles to his feet to answer the call, wishing once again that he was dressed, aware of the ridiculous figure he cuts as he stands beside the bed, holding the receiver in his hand, stark naked.

He doesn't recognise the voice at first, nor the man's name. Not until the man reminds him who he is.

"I'm investigating the murder of Federico Di Stasi. You were with his widow yesterday when I spoke to her. At the hospital."

"That's right," says Giacomo. "I was." He looks around the room to see what Yvonne is doing and there he is, pasty and overweight in one of the mirrors the place is littered with, as though all people wanted to do in hotel rooms was admire themselves. "I'm sorry," he says, "I didn't catch your name."

"Cotugno," the man says. "Piero Cotugno."

"Yes, of course," says Giacomo, sucking his stomach in to see what difference it might make, letting it out with a grimace of disappointment.

"I wonder if you could come round to my office. I think you may be able to help me. There are one or two things I think you may be able to help me clarify."

"Certainly," says Giacomo, curious now, indifferent to his reflection. Yvonne is standing by the door, tapping her fingers against the plastic key in its slot. "Just tell me when."

"A car will pick you up in fifteen minutes. I hope that gives you sufficient time."

Giacomo looks at his watch, the only thing he's wearing and the most expensive thing he owns, apart from cars and houses. Unless you count Yvonne. It's just before 8 o'clock. "Yes," he says. "That will be fine."

Cotugno is dressed more smartly this morning, in a white shirt, grey tie and a pale blue suit, the jacket buttoned at the waist, that fits him a little too loosely; he must have lost weight recently. He doesn't look well. He shakes Giacomo's hand and calls for coffee, then gestures that he sit down.

"I'm sorry to have to bring you in so early," he says. He glances up. "Pressure from above," he says, and there's an assumption that he's talking to an equal that throws Giacomo off for a moment.

He crosses his legs and grasps his calf. He's wearing shoes without socks, something he would never do in France; his ankle looks pale and unwholesome against the soft black leather of the moccasin.

"Do you mind if I smoke?" he says. Cotugno shakes his head and reaches to move an ashtray towards him. It's a wide desk, cluttered with files. You can see the importance of the man from his surroundings, though; yesterday, in the hospital, he was harder to place. Giacomo offers Cotugno a cigarette, then lights his own. Cotugno is silent, observant. Caught off guard, Giacomo's about to ask how he can help when the coffee arrives.

"You must miss this, living in Paris," Cotugno says, handing him a cup.

3

Martin walks out of the agency and grabs a roll and glass of wine at the nearest bar because he has no time to go back to the flat for lunch. The last thing he did before leaving his desk was make a phone call to a friend of his, or, more precisely, to someone he has known so long, and had dealings with so often, not always pleasant, that familiarity has bred a sort of reluctant affection. The friend's name is Corti. He has a first name, but Martin can never remember what it is. He learnt at school that first names were special, implied a difficult intimacy, and one of the reasons he has stayed in Italy so long, he tells himself, is that Italians agree with this. They also use surnames to mark out territory, just as they use handshakes to establish contact. He's been here so long he's uncomfortable in England, where people he's barely met call him Martin and either refuse to touch him or cover him with kisses. It's a funny old world, he says to himself, as he leaves the bar and heads off down the hill.

He's about to do Helen a favour, although she doesn't know it. At least, he hopes that it will be a favour. He's still ill at ease about the way she seemed yesterday, stunned with grief, certainly, he'd have expected no less, but evasive as well. He's convinced she has something to hide, and is irritated, and hurt, that she doesn't trust him enough to share it with him. Hasn't he proved he can be trusted in the past, both to her and to Federico?

And then there's Giacomo Mura, turning up on the day his oldest friend is murdered, with all the bad blood that must have flowed between them, however often they've patched things up. He's seen and even spoken to the man several times in the past, once in Rome at a reception organised, as far as he can remember, by Federico, once at a book presentation in Milan, when he was visiting friends there. And in Paris as well, but that was soon after he'd been released, when he was still fresh meat on the dinner circuit and someone had thought it would be fun to introduce Martin to the latest *enfant maudit*. There's still affection in certain Parisian circles for terrorists who haven't quite reneged and know how to behave in company. But Martin can't forget the way he and Helen held each other, and the whispering that went on between them; and the sense, most galling of all, that he wasn't needed any longer. When he read the piece about Mura in this morning's *Foglio* he wondered how long it had been festering in some drawer, because surely not even a man with a grudge could turn out something that rich with vitriol so quickly. He knows the man who wrote it, not well, but well enough to give him a ring, share a drink for old time's sake. Martin's not much fonder of Mura than Adriano Testa is. He'll have things to say that might be worth hearing. It set his teeth on edge to see Helen in that man's arms.

It's a warm day and Martin is sweating by the time he reaches Piazza della Rotonda. He takes off his panama and rolls it between his hands, then puts it back on again and crosses the square. If Corti isn't here yet, he promises himself, he'll nip into the Pantheon and refresh his spirit in the temple to all the gods, the only temple he could ever worship in. He'll stand and look up at that hole, the mystery of it the product of human engineering and nothing more. But the usual table is occupied. He raises his hat and waves it. Corti struggles to his feet, moving his chair back into the tiny space left for it, awkwardly turning to offer his hand to Martin. He's a short man, with too much sun-streaked hair and a pearl grey linen suit. His feet are set at ten to two.

"*Buon giorno*," he says.

"*Buon giorno*," says Martin, releasing Corti's hand and sitting down. They conduct their conversation in Italian, using the polite third person form throughout. It's a pleasure to do business like this, thinks Martin, as he places his hat on the table and calls a waiter across.

"Can I get you something?"

"A coffee," says Corti. "Decaffeinated, alas." He lifts a hand to his breast pocket, pats it. "Heart."

"Sorry to hear it," says Martin.

Corti shrugs. "How can I help you, Frame?"

Oh good, thinks Martin, straight to the point.

"Di Stasi."

Corti smiles. "I imagined that would be the case," he says. "You work with his wife, I believe?"

"I'm impressed," says Martin. "You're well-informed, as ever. It's hardly an affair of state."

"That's for the state to judge," says Corti, with the same conceited smile.

"I suppose you still have access to cell phone records?" says Martin, impatient suddenly.

Corti nods. "Of course."

"Di Stasi's wife," he says. "I think she may be hiding something. Nothing incriminating, of course," he adds smoothly. "I just want to help her if I can."

"Ever the knight in shining armour," says Corti.

The coffee arrives. Corti stirs three packets of sugar into it, then downs it in a gulp.

"Are you in a hurry for this information?"

"I'm always in a hurry for information," Martin says.

"It won't be easy," Corti says.

Martin calls the waiter over and pays the bill. "How is your wife, by the way?" he says as Corti fastens the middle button of his jacket. His shirt is white, his tie a slightly darker grey than his suit. As ever, Martin feels shabby and defensive about his own clothes, thrown on this morning, crumpled from the wash. Corti glances at Martin with distaste.

"Thank you for asking," he says. "She's well." He tugs at his cuffs, plays with the cufflinks for a moment. They're large and shiny, gold with some sort of crimson stone in the middle. "I'll tell her you asked after her."

"There's no need to do that," says Martin. He stands up, shaping the brim of his hat before holding his hand out. "As soon as you can manage it, then? And Di Stasi's too, if you get the chance. No need to put yourself out, of course. Tomorrow will do."

Corti nods, then touches Martin's hand with the tips of his fingers. "We understand each other, Frame. We have always done, I think?"

"Oh yes," says Martin. He has a sudden picture of Corti's wife being bundled into a taxi, her coat half off, crying her eyes out. That was more than thirty years ago now. Still, a favour remains a favour. Martin is still owed something.

They're leaving the table when Corti turns. "It's a funny set up altogether," he says. "This murder."

"Is that what they're saying at the ministry?"

"And not only at the ministry." Corti shakes his head.

"Any theories?"

"None that I know of. Certainly none that I'm prepared to talk about. But I think you may be barking up the wrong tree with the widow. I hope so, for her sake. The last thing she needs is to be bothered by this sort of thing. Infidelity is such a squalid business."

Martin's climbing the stairs to his flat when he remembers a call he received this morning, from someone called Martha Weinberg. He knows the woman, though not well. She's an

American, New Yorker, been here for years. She used to be an
actress, as far as Martin recalls, came over with the first tour of
Hair, or claims she did. Bit of an ex-hippy, dabbled in avant-
garde film, fringe activist, ban the bomb, women's stuff. These
days she'd say she was a journalist, but Martin would dispute
that, despite the magazine she claims to own. She chatted for
a while about the situation in Iraq, the anti-war demonstration
organized for Saturday, the state of the world; pleasantries that
paved the way to the real purpose of her call: Helen. Weinberg
has been trying to call her, she told him, ever since she heard
about the shooting, but her phone is always turned off. Now
why would you want to speak to Helen? Martin asked her. I
didn't know you knew each other. Weinberg hedged a little
here, said Helen had agreed to help out with the Saturday
demonstration, essential that people stand up and be counted,
another Vietnam, and so on. Martin let her speak herself out,
then waited until the silence was too much for her. And I need
to talk to her about her husband, she said eventually. Her
husband? Is there anyone in Rome you don't know? he teased
her. She laughed, a throaty laugh that almost endeared her to
him. Just tell her to get in touch with me, she said. Tell her I
need to tell her stuff she needs to know.

He lets himself into the flat and makes a pot of coffee, then
drinks it from his unwashed morning cup, standing beside
the sink, his free hand cradling the dull ache in his stomach.
The last time he lived with someone else, his second wife, she
trained him to sit at a table to eat and drink, but even then it
struck him as time wasted. After she'd left him he'd returned to
his old ways, relieved, his use of plates and cutlery reduced to a
minimum once again. Sometimes he can get through the whole
day on a rinsed cup and a fork.

He'd call Helen now to see how she is, but knows she'll be
unavailable. He's tried a dozen times already today, only to find
her mobile turned off and the land line permanently engaged.

He can't blame her, but he wishes she'd call him, give him the chance to help a little. Yesterday afternoon at the agency, she seemed stunned with grief, incapacitated by it. He could have done more then, he knows that, the image of Helen in Giacomo Mura's arms continuing to rankle. Still, there is more than one way to lend a hand. He thinks of Corti, thinks of the evening he'd rescued the man's wife from the flat of her lover, hanging by his neck from the light flex in the bathroom. He'd helped Corti by clearing up the mess, speaking to people he knew at the British embassy, where the man had worked, smoothing things over until there was no more risk of embarrassment, or damage to Corti's career, which hadn't, after all, been quite as triumphant as he'd hoped. And now he will help Helen.

He walks through his shabby, unlit flat to the room he calls his office and searches through a drawer full of business cards until he finds what he's looking for.

4

Helen watches Giacomo and Yvonne climb the stairs. Yvonne is two steps behind her husband, dragging her feet, while Giacomo bounds ahead, panting with the effort. This morning, he's dressed in a light wool suit and freshly pressed linen shirt, open at the collar, expensive, tailor made. She thinks of the first time she saw him: his T-shirt and combat trousers, filthy, worn to shreds, and of how he simply moved in with them. He has always treated my home as though it were his. He has always treated me as though I belong to him in some way. And I've never discouraged him. She wishes he had come alone.

"Can't move for journalists out there," Giacomo says.

Helen nods. She holds him by the jacket cuffs as though afraid to take his hands in hers, then lets him go.

"They want to know if you're ready to come out to speak to them." Yvonne offers her cheeks to Helen to be kissed, her lips caught in a little *moue*.

"I'll never be ready to speak to them. They've been buzzing to be let in all morning. I wish to God they'd all go home and leave me out of all this." Her words are angry, but what she most feels is weariness. She'd like to sleep, but can't. Whenever she closes her eyes, she sees Federico. She must have fallen asleep at one point, because she actually did see him, standing in front of her and asking her what she was waiting for, and she woke herself by crying out that she didn't know what she was supposed to do.

Giacomo spots the trace of blood on her wrist and winces with concern, but Helen shakes her head. "It's nothing." She grimaces. "I've been playing with knives."

"Giacomo is exaggerating as usual. They are two very young people in jeans and pullovers." Yvonne is amused. "Like identical twins. Perfectly innocent, sitting together on the doorstep, reading different novels by John Grisham, I think, in Italian. They wanted to know who I was and I told them. I had to spell my name for them, letter by letter, but I still don't think they understood. Is that possible? That they are journalists and don't know the English alphabet? It was really quite sweet. They must be… what do you call them? That funny word the Americans use? Yes, cub reporters. Like little baby animals."

Ignoring Yvonne, Giacomo takes Helen's hand and turns it to examine the cut, then lets it go. "You should be more careful."

"I'm at my wit's end," Helen says, pulling away, also ignoring Yvonne. She picks up the laptop case and unzips it, her hands shaking. "Federico left this with his parents on Monday. Fausto brought it round earlier. He'd been round there talking to them about the conference. I thought he'd been at work all day." She flips open the computer and turns it on. "I can't believe he lied to me."

"Where did he say he was?"

Helen doesn't answer at once. "He didn't," she says eventually. "I suppose I didn't ask." She holds the laptop out to him with a sort of resignation. I'm using anger to protect myself, she thinks, but that isn't true. She's never felt so hurt.

"So, how do you feel this morning?" purrs Yvonne, slipping out of a pale blue linen coat, beneath it an artfully simple dress made from the same material, the lining of the coat a shimmering dark grey, almost black. She lets the coat fall to the sofa, touches Helen briefly on one arm as Helen waits for Giacomo to take the laptop from her, then moves away. "Would you like me to make you some coffee?" she asks, hands stroking the bracelets around her wrists, as if she has offered to roll up her sleeves and scrub a floor for the first time in her life.

"No. You can make some for yourself if you like," says Helen, then realises how ungracious this sounds. She has no reason to be unpleasant to Yvonne, a woman she barely knows, she tells herself, although she knows how absurd this is; she has every reason. She would give anything for Yvonne not to be here, standing between Helen and Giacomo like an unwitting chaperone. "I'm sorry," she says. "I didn't mean to be rude."

Giacomo takes the laptop from her as Yvonne drifts off towards the kitchen. He looks at her, quizzically.

"*Non parla italiano*," he says, gesturing towards Yvonne with her head. "*Non capisce niente. Possiamo parlare con tranquillità.*"

Helen is shocked. "We can't do that," she says. "How awful."

He shrugs. "So, what do you want me to do with this?" he says, holding the laptop in one hand and brandishing it up and down, like some unwanted creature that has attached itself to him and won't let go.

Irritated, she takes the laptop back and sits down at the table. "I wanted you to open it for me. I wanted you to see what Federico has been doing. I've been sitting here looking at it all morning. I just can't do it alone. I saw a doodle he'd made when I got back last night and I couldn't bear it. I felt as if he were still alive for a moment. I kept waking up all night and remembering." She looks at Giacomo, who has sat down opposite her, his hands on the table, an unlit cigarette between them. "I don't know if I could face him if he was alive. If he walked in now and saw you here, and Yvonne in the kitchen, I don't know what I'd say."

"I'm not such a terrible shock, surely?" says Yvonne. She's made a pot of coffee and found a tray to put it on, with cups Helen never uses.

"You've made coffee," Helen says, unnecessarily. "Thank you."

Giacomo has spun the laptop round to face him and opened it. "What do you expect to find here?" he says as they wait for it to boot up.

"I've no idea," she says, and means it. What most frightens her is that she has no idea what Federico has been working on these past few weeks. How little she's spoken to Federico these past few months, if not longer, years perhaps. They've lived in a silence she thought was companionable, but wonders now how true that is. He's talked, she's talked, but to what end? It's not just the conference; she's never been the wife he'd have liked in that sense, she knows that. She's never regarded his work, or anyone's work, as fundamental. This is another way in which she's disappointed Giulia.

"Well, let's see." He clicks on Documents. The most recent is a Word file called Juggernaut. He clicks on that and finds a blank screen. "That's odd," he says. "Juggernaut mean anything to you?"

"Juggernaut? As in truck?"

"I don't know. I can't see Federico writing about trucks. Doesn't it mean something else as well? Isn't it that Indian thing that crushes everything in its way?" Pleased to have something to do, Giacomo takes off his jacket, closes the file, then opens it a second time. The same blank screen. "Juggernaut." He whistles. "So, where is it?"

"There's nothing there?"

"No," he says. "Odd though, isn't it? To delete the contents and leave the document. Why not delete the whole thing? I imagine it wouldn't take much to retrieve what was in it either." He clicks on *paste*, just in case, to see what might happen. Nothing. "As though they want us to find something." He taps on the touchpad. "Of course, it might be someone who doesn't know how to use a computer." He glances at Yvonne. "It's the kind of thing you might do," he says.

Helen stands up, her arms crossed tightly across her chest. Her breathing is tight, she thinks she might faint.

Giacomo, with a snort, walks across to the door, beside which he has left a pile of the day's newspapers. "I don't suppose you've seen any of these?" he says to Helen, who shakes her head. "Responsibility's been claimed by something that calls itself *Nucleo Comunisti Armati*, apparently. Never heard of them."

He throws the newspapers onto the table in front of the sofa, just as Federico did when he came in from work, for Helen to flick through while he cooked and talked. These gestures, which hurt so much, which repeat themselves, thinks Helen, of their own accord; they have no meaning after all. It is all repetition. She sits down, suddenly unsteady.

"Apparently they were involved in the Porcu killing," Giacomo is saying. "They claim to be the heirs of the Red Brigades, exactly what you'd expect them to say. I tried to read their statement in the car, the same old jargon-ridden nonsense that's always churned out on these occasions. God knows what good anyone ever thought it would do, though, let's face it, it used to convince us, didn't it? Do you remember?"

Helen doesn't answer; she's barely listening. She wishes Yvonne would leave so that she could talk to Giacomo about something that matters. Oblivious, Giacomo sighs. "Class struggle. Hegemonic rule of global capitalism. Economic imperialism. It's not that they've got it wrong, God knows. It's just that it's all so stale. The funny thing is they've used that typeface the old Olivettis used. What's it called? Courier? For that touch of credibility, I imagine. If it *looks* like the kind of thing we banged out in Turin in the old days then it must *be* the kind of thing we banged out. I wouldn't be surprised if it had been written by the secret services, to throw people off." He pauses and looks around the room, as if for support. "Oh well," he says. "Life goes on."

"I think you are shocking and cruel," says Yvonne, "to talk like this. We have come here to comfort Helen, not to talk about these wicked people who have..." She pauses, turns her head to

Helen. "I don't know how you can bear to listen to him," she says. "It is all politics."

"So, no one knows who they are," murmurs Helen, not answering Yvonne, not knowing what else to say. Until she can bring herself to believe in it, with her heart as well as her brain, Federico's death has still not happened. So how can anyone be responsible? How can there be a murderer with no murder, no victim?

"In France we had '68 and then, *pouf*, everything was back to normal," says Yvonne.

"Don't make yourself sound any sillier than you are," Giacomo says, so quietly Helen wonders if she is the only one supposed to hear. Certainly, Yvonne gives no sign of having noticed, drifting around the room with her back arched and one hand stroking the nape of her neck, the image of petulant boredom. Helen watches Giacomo walk across and silently replace the receiver on the telephone, and she thinks, with a surge of infantile rebellion, *Well, if it rings now, you can bloody well answer it yourself.* It strikes her for a second that he's been told to do this, and she wonders by whom for a moment – Is there no one she can trust? – before the idea is forgotten. Yvonne collapses with a weary sigh on the sofa and picks up a newspaper, the top one on the pile, and glances at the photograph on the front page.

"You look so sad," she says, pursing her lips in what might be sympathy, holding the paper out for Helen to see. But Helen doesn't need to take the paper from Yvonne to see the photograph, which occupies the top third of the page. Against her will, she glances at this brutal, stolen image of herself. Of course I look sad, she thinks. My husband has just been murdered. But now, as she takes in the image with greater attention, she sees that Yvonne is wrong; the Helen in the picture doesn't look sad so much as puzzled, as though she has been asked a question she can't answer, or understand. She is standing beside a powerful blue car, one hand at her throat, her head turned from the camera, the image very slightly blurred. A man she doesn't recognise is opening the door for her and as she steps over finally and takes the newspaper from Yvonne's hand to examine the scene more closely, because her curiosity has got the better of her, she has a sense of estrangement from what she sees, as though the woman in the photograph is an actor who wears her clothes and has learnt her mannerisms, who moves as she does because she has been told to do so; she imagines for a moment that this is not her in the picture, but someone standing in. She drops the paper to the floor and picks up another and sees the same woman there, and what she feels is no longer shock, or violation, but a sort of envy she can't understand, as though this woman, who looks so like her, despite her bewilderment, possesses some certainty she doesn't. No, not certainty; its opposite perhaps – some leeway, some possibility that things could still be set right. The photograph was taken before she had seen Federico's body, she's sure of that, when there was still some chance, however faint, that a mistake had been made. What she would like to do now is to sit with these papers and these photographs and make some attempt to understand what has happened and what, even more, is expected of her, but she needs to be alone to do this. The nausea she has kept at bay all morning begins to rise. How odd that grief should affect the stomach, she hasn't expected this. But she hasn't expected grief.

"Aren't you going to tell Helen that you met with the magistrate this morning?" says Yvonne.

Giacomo glances furiously at Yvonne, who gives him a little serves-you-right smirk before straightening her skirt, then at Helen, who is staring at him, open-mouthed, in what looks like a state of shock. Before anyone can speak, the landline rings. Helen shrinks back, then raises her hands as if in self-defence. Giacomo puts his hand on the receiver, avoiding her eyes. "No," she cries, her voice breaking, but he has already picked it up. He turns his back on both Helen and Yvonne to answer, relieved to have something that might distract them, or distract Helen, and is told to wait, something he hates. Normally he would put the phone down, but today he does what he's been told to do.

A moment later an instantly recognisable voice says "Signora Di Stasi."

Impressed despite himself, he pulls a face, then covers the mouthpiece with his hand and turns back to look at Helen.

"It's your beloved PM," he says, holding the receiver out to her, unable to suppress a grin. "He seems to think I'm you."

"Oh no," says Helen, shaking her head. "I can't."

"I'm afraid she isn't available," Giacomo says, adding, with a sense of his own naughtiness: "Perhaps I can take a message. Who is that?"

The line falls dead for a moment. The first voice, a man, returns to ask when Signora Di Stasi can be found. He passes this question on to Helen, who gestures helplessly.

"I don't know. Never," she says.

"Can't be done," says Giacomo. "Sooner or later you'll have to talk to him." Helen stares at him wretchedly. Then, with a shudder, she walks across.

"Give it to me." She grabs the receiver from him and swings away, visibly furious. Immediately, Giacomo regrets what he's done.

"*Pronto.*"

Giacomo moves off. Helen is silent, her body clenched. She says *sì* and *no* and *grazie*; she could be talking to anyone at first, her tone polite but cautious. For a moment, Giacomo wonders if he's misheard, if the man on the other end of the line isn't the prime minister at all but a journalist, or someone playing some dark idea of a joke. But he'd know that voice from a thousand. Then Helen begins to shake her head.

"*Mi dispiace, è fuori discussione.*"

"She says it's out of the question," he whispers to Yvonne, who doesn't seem to have understood what's going on, and is still enjoying the discomfort she created a few minutes ago. "It's the prime minister," he says a second time. This time she nods, but looks bemused. She's a child, he thinks, she's lucky to know so little. What in God's name am I going to do with her?

Helen is holding the receiver slightly away from her head.

"*Mi dispiace, ma lei non può decidere ciò che sarebbe piaciuto o non a mio marito*," she says, her voice overloud, slightly tremulous.

"She's saying he can't decide what Federico would have wanted," Giacomo tells Yvonne, who has shown no sign of wanting to know what Helen is saying. She's got guts to talk to him like that, thinks Giacomo. He isn't used to people saying "no". I'd love to see his face.

Helen pivots on her heels and holds the receiver out to him, making an odd sound, almost a whimper. He steps forward to take it, listening to silence, followed by a click. As soon as he has put the receiver down, the phone rings again. After a moment's hesitation, he picks it up. This time, a woman asks for Helen in a sharp, impatient voice that expects to be obeyed. Before Giacomo can answer, the woman says, *Le dica che sono Giulia.*

"It's Giulia," he says to Helen, who is standing beside him, beaten down by the brutality of what is happening.

"You don't have to speak to her," he says, and he's about to make some sort of excuse. But Helen takes the receiver from him with startling brusqueness and begins to speak.

"You told him to call me, didn't you?" she says. "You told him I was at home. You told him to call me here." After a moment, during which she looks at Giacomo with an expression of horrified disbelief, she continues. "I don't believe it. Federico doesn't *belong* to anyone, Giulia. Hasn't he done enough for this fucking country already?" Another silence. Helen's knuckles are white. Then, "I don't think you know what you're saying,

Giulia. How can you talk about his death like that?" She is shouting now. "Giulia! He didn't *want* to die!" So, that's it, thinks Giacomo, the old woman wants her son to be seen as a martyr, like one of those Roman matrons who'd give their own flesh and blood a dose of hemlock for the sake of the republic, who'd slit their own wrists in the bath. And then Helen sinks into the desk chair, grabbing the edge of the desk as the wheels skid under her weight. "He can do what he likes," she cries. "I won't listen to any more of this." But she does listen, gripping the phone, tears streaming down her face. She'll listen until the woman has said whatever it is she has to say, imagines Giacomo. He knows the type. She's like the PM, she won't take no for an answer. She'll ring back and if the phone's off the hook she'll be round ten minutes later and banging on the door until it's opened.

"I need to go now," says Yvonne behind him.

"She's always hated me," says Helen, covering the mouthpiece with her hand.

"Not now," he snaps.

"But I need to go now," insists Yvonne.

"And I've hated her," announces Helen.

Giacomo jerks his head towards the corridor. "There's a bathroom down there."

"I don't mean that," Yvonne says. "I mean leave this apartment."

"We're not going anywhere," Giacomo says. "Not yet."

Helen puts the phone down. Giacomo can just hear the voice of her mother-in-law trapped within it.

"No," she says, "I do want you to go. Please. I'll be all right. Don't worry about me."

Giacomo shakes his head. He doesn't try to stop Yvonne. When he hears the flat door slam behind his back, he's relieved, and not only because he can't leave Helen alone like this. They have been through so much together, whatever she might have said to Federico. And now here he is, in Federico's flat, in Federico's city, at Federico's bidding, with Federico dead. Giacomo could so easily have refused to come to this conference; the last thing he needs is what Helen, typically insensitive to political nuance, has called an act of rehabilitation. On the contrary, it's likely to do him more harm than good in some quarters. But he wasn't thinking about his reputation when he agreed to come. Helen had been the main attraction, he'll admit that. But there was also Federico, and their friendship, which was rivalry, of course, but not just that, which predated Helen and might have outlived her, if the chance had been given them. And now he finds himself here in the midst of this pointless anachronistic murder that reminds him of nothing so much as of one of those endless sequels, *Rocky VII*, *Superman III*, in which nothing is left of the original but an infinitesimal homeopathic dose.

"I'm glad you're here," says Helen. She's crying again. When she reaches out for him, he takes her in his arms and holds her the way he might hold someone injured, some car crash victim, perhaps, the extent of whose wounds are still unclear, whispering words of comfort while waiting for more certain help to arrive.

5

Early in January, when the snow was still on the mountains that seemed to surround the city like a barricade, Helen was called to the office of Miriam's lover, up on the executive floor. He offered her coffee, asked her how she was settling in; his English had taken on Miriam's Scottish burr. She said she was happy, which was true; she'd begun to enjoy teaching, enjoy the company of her students, not only the secretaries she'd started out with, but all the others, from upper management to the shop floor. She said it had given her an insight into the real Italy. He was glad she felt that way, he said, she was much appreciated. He'd heard nothing but good of her. She blushed, she told him she was pleased to hear it. When she said this, his tone immediately changed. He became brisk, business-like, his almost flirtatious amiability shelved. He told her he had a favour he needed doing, and she was just the person. No one else would do, he said. She stared into her empty cup, too anxious to answer or look up; she didn't trust the word "favour". He asked if she'd be prepared to give individual lessons to a man that Fiat was moving to its South Africa branch. She'd be paid extra, naturally, at a higher rate than usual. Relieved, curious, needing the money, she said she would.

The following day, after her classes were finished, she was taken to a room in a part of the building she didn't know, near enough to the factory itself for the muffled sound of machinery to be heard. It was empty of furniture, apart from a small wooden table, two chairs and a stool. The student was sitting on one of the chairs, his leg stretched out before him on the stool, the knee bandaged. Helen recognised him as someone she'd taught until a few weeks before Christmas, one of her best students, a trade union steward called Eduardo. She'd spoken to Federico about him with such enthusiasm that he'd seemed, unexpectedly, jealous, and then over-curious, as though he'd wanted to know what he might be up against. Helen was amused. He's the kind of man you can't help but admire, that's all I mean, she'd protested when Federico asked her, half-teasing, how her favourite pupil was behaving. She'd tried to imply that admiration wasn't love, although surely, it had occurred to her afterwards, it should be part of it at least. Could she have loved a man she couldn't admire, she asked herself. Federico had let it drop in the end, when Eduardo left the group and she stopped mentioning him. She thought he'd been transferred; she hadn't been told why – no one seemed to know. But now, with Eduardo before her, struggling to stand despite his bandaged leg, she could see what had happened; he'd been kneecapped. She was shocked, she said she was sorry. The man who had brought Helen backed out of the room, closing the door behind him. When they were alone, Eduardo raised his eyebrows and nodded, then tried to smile.

"I know you are sorry, Helen. It must be strange to you, this violence, this armed struggle." The last two words were said with irony. His English had improved since the attack.

"It ought to be strange to everyone," she said. There was an embarrassed silence. Helen wasn't used to individual lessons, and she was too fond of Eduardo, and too unsettled by what had happened to him, to know how to start. It didn't seem right to begin with the usual routine about what they'd both been doing since they'd last seen each other. She'd lived her normal life, while Eduardo had been shot, had been taken to hospital, had convalesced, had lived in fear of what might happen next. There were no words for this.

Finally, because nothing else came to her, she asked him what he thought he would need to know in South Africa. He said he would need to learn to brake his tongue. In English, she told him, the expression is "hold your tongue". He sighed, shaking his head. "How can I live in South Africa? I despise apartheid," he said.

"Do you have to go?" Helen said. "Why don't you change your job? You could go to another city, surely?" He looked at her, with pity, or worse, contempt, as though she had chosen to be foolish.

"I have a family," he said. "A wife, two sons at university, one of them your age. Here in Italy I'm a marked man. In any case, in my business, Turin is the only city. No one else makes cars in Italy."

"But you represent the union. I thought you were fighting to defend the workers," she blurted out. "I can't understand why they should want to hurt you."

"They?" he said. "Who do you think *they* are?"

"What do you mean?"

"You make it seem simple, Helen, when you say 'they'. You make it seem that the lines are made clean with a knife between one person and the other, one idea and the other. It isn't simple. I might move over these lines and be shot, or shoot. I have been shot, this time. But I don't know who 'they' are. Who do you think they are?"

"I don't know," she said. "I don't know what they're fighting for." She looked at him. "You would know, wouldn't you? If you shot someone?"

He shrugged, then winced, pressing his hand to his knee.

"I have a family," he said. "I would shoot for them. I would shoot to kill. And now I must live as a white man in a racist state for them. I think I would prefer to shoot, but that is not possible." He grinned, his face lit up; he looked like a boy. He was old enough to be her father. Opening his hands, he held them out in an unexpected gesture, less of resignation than acceptance. I love you, she thought, although that wasn't what she meant. It was just that, at that moment, she would have given her life to spend it beside this small neat man, with his large hands and bristly cropped grey-black hair. He seemed to be the only man she knew.

"And now you must teach me the words I will need to explain to the people I will work beside, all these white people, why I am not a racist and cannot share their view." That evening she listened to Giacomo argue with Federico, when they had finished dinner and both men assumed she would clear the table, as she generally did. She listened to their talk of hegemony and autonomy, workers' control and the ethics of auto-reduction, by which they seemed to mean evading tram fares and stealing food from supermarkets. All at once they stopped arguing and began to laugh about a professor they both despised at the department, where Giacomo was also working, although not, as far as Helen could tell, being paid.

She was the only wage-earner in the flat; Federico's research grant was still tied up in some bureaucratic way she didn't understand. They were living on pasta and beans, vegetables and round bread rolls with a crusty little nipple at the top that Helen always broke off and nibbled first. And local red Barbera, bought by the litre from a local *vineria*. Giacomo was putting on weight. He had barely trimmed his hair and beard. That was the evening she said he looked like one of the Red Brigades leaders, who'd been arrested the year before and was still in jail, awaiting trial. She found herself comparing Giacomo and Federico with Eduardo. Beside that small heroic man, his wounded leg propped on the stool, they seemed like untested boys to her; she wondered how she'd translate the word "callow" into Italian while they mopped up the last dregs of sauce with their bread.

The following morning Giacomo's beard was gone. That afternoon he went to the barber's and had his hair cut short. That evening he came home for dinner in plain grey trousers and a v-necked sweater over a nylon shirt. They barely recognised him.

"You look as though you're in disguise," she said, not sure whether to laugh or be disturbed. "You've cast off all your bourgeois intellectual trappings," teased Federico. "You'll have to be careful though. They might not let you into the department looking like that." Helen thought the new Giacomo was like some character from Turgenev, a pale inconspicuous anarchist biding his time in an office until the moment came. He looked more dangerous, not less. She couldn't take her eyes off him. She wondered what Miriam would make of him.

She still saw Miriam once or twice a week. They'd eat a roll together for lunch in one of the bars in the centre, or meet up in one of the English pubs for a drink. Miriam had guessed that Helen had a man, but didn't press for information. "We girls have to make do with what's available," she'd said. Miriam introduced her to all the other girls from her Highland village, au pairs to some of the richest families in Turin. It was odd to see them together, over-dressed, drunk and raucous, their make-up smeared by tears of laughter and sweat, and imagine them the following morning in the Liberty villas of their employers, preparing their charges for their private schools, while drivers waited below in expensive cars, armed against kidnappers. They had their days free, and seemed to spend them in beauty salons. Helen had sometimes wondered what happened in such places, but turned down their offers to take her with a nervous smile. One of them, usually Miriam, would drive her home, then watch her until she was safely in the building. They worried she had no money and needed new clothes. Everyone wants to mother me, she thought, except Federico. She wasn't sure how much she liked it.

She didn't tell Giacomo about Eduardo; Federico did. She'd heard enough of Giacomo's views by then to know what he would think, and she was right. He said it was sentimental of her to suppose that Eduardo's disgust and acceptance and anger were more important than anyone else's, to which she said that of course no single person was worth more than any other single person, she knew that, although she wasn't sure she believed it. She told him that it was *through* Eduardo that she understood the others. That's what she said, but she heard herself speaking and wondered what she meant. Was she afraid to say what she really thought, that none of this violence made sense to her? She'd heard Giacomo use the word "injury" to describe kneecapping. It seemed so bland, so anaemic, as though being shot in the leg were a sort of accident, like falling off a kerb. It might have been no more than a blip in his otherwise perfect English to use the word in this way, but she didn't think so. She thought it reflected his state of mind.

She couldn't be sure how Federico felt. When she told him about the extra lessons, and the reason for them, he listened with what looked like sympathy. He didn't seem to be jealous any longer, which puzzled and upset her, though she couldn't have explained why. He asked her questions she couldn't answer about Eduardo's union work, about how it was seen within management. Was he seen as a collaborator? he wanted to know. What effect had his kneecapping had on morale? he asked her, as though that mattered. He wanted the best for everyone, she said, he's a good man, although she couldn't know this; it was just what she felt. Federico listened and nodded, silent. The idea that she was missing something, some larger sense, stayed with her and made her uncomfortable.

6

At the top end of Via del Tritone, with helicopters circling above his head, Martin strides out. He's had a brief siesta and now he's sweating slightly in the late-afternoon heat, marvelling at the tawdry bazaar-like feel of the tourist shops, their amateurish window fronts, the dark unwelcoming bars, handwritten signs in broken English and Japanese, the *démodé* displays of ties and bags and gloves. It's odd the way this side of Rome has survived, he thinks, as though people still came to the city for its leatherwork and silk, expecting bargains. He pauses just before reaching the *Messaggero* building, wondering if snipers have their rifles trained on him, because there are always snipers on days like this, days of parades and state festivities, dotted like urns above the gutters of the buildings, visible to one another and the hovering pilots. A helicopter's shadow skims above him like a cloud. He glances up, tempted to wave, catching his hat as it slides off. When the impulse passes and he looks ahead, he sees Adriano Testa standing beside the newspaper kiosk in a pale blue polo shirt and linen trousers, and is pleased to find him both balder and more out of shape than Martin is. With a bound of contentment, his hand outstretched, he walks across.

"No joy with this damn thing," Adriano says, waving his mobile in the air. "It's these fucking helicopters everywhere."

A gun-grey copter obligingly appears above their heads. Martin sighs and nods. "It's the price we pay for our security," he says.

Adriano looks at him warily, unsure of Martin's tone. Martin opens his hands and holds them out in the classic gesture of someone with nothing to conceal. "Joke," he says.

Adriano shrugs. "I've got a place round the corner," he says. "We'll go there."

Martin follows him as he slouches off ahead, into shadow. Five minutes later they are sitting opposite each other at a small square wooden table, the kind used in *trattorie*, in a barely furnished flat. "Bolt hole," says Adriano. "Can't be expected to get home every night." He grins. "Things pop up."

"I'm sure they do," says Martin.

"Come on then," says Adriano. "Spill the beans. I haven't heard from you for years and now you'd 'like a chat'. What's up?"

"I don't have any beans to spill," says Martin. "I was hoping you did."

"About what?"

"I read your piece this morning."

Adriano gives a shifty grin.

"And?"

"You must have had it waiting for some time."

"Everything comes to he who waits."

"I imagine so."

"So, you're interested in Mura?"

Martin shakes his head. "No, not Mura. He's just a poseur in the end. The one I'm interested in is Di Stasi."

"The man of the moment." Adriano makes a low whistle. To Martin's surprise a cat appears from somewhere in the flat and presses itself against his leg.

"Not mine," says Adriano. "Comes in through the window. Lives on the roof. It's a mystery who feeds it."

"You knew him too." Martin says this slowly, as if to caution Adriano that pretending otherwise will serve no purpose. He did his homework before leaving his flat. He knows that Adriano went to school with Federico, before being separated by military service and university. And then the tidal wave of the struggle, the *lotta armata*, had swept Federico up but left Adriano behind, apparently, although Martin isn't convinced of this. Adriano has subsequently re-emerged as an expert on the secret services, often quoted, rarely contradicted. He's teased Martin a couple of times in the past about episodes Martin would rather forget, as though he knows more than he lets on.

"Did I?" says Adriano, then nods his head. "I suppose I did. Though he didn't exactly seek me out these past few years. I suppose he had bigger fish to fry."

"Is that why he's dead?"

"Don't ask me. Big fish, big pond," says Adriano. He stands up and crosses the kitchen to the fridge, coming back with two cans of beer. Martin opens his can, then reaches down to stroke the cat. It leaps onto the table, brushing against the hand that holds the beer.

Adriano drinks from his can, looking round as if for something misplaced, then opens the top three buttons of his shirt.

"I suppose you're wondering who killed him," he says.

Martin nods. "That had crossed my mind."

"You're not the only one."

"Really?"

Adriano scratches his chest. "These damned mosquitoes. They're eating me to death. Don't they bite you?"

Martin shakes his head. "My blood doesn't seem to appeal to them. It must be too refined."

Adriano ignores this. "There's something wrong about it. Seriously wrong." He finishes the beer, his head tilted back, his gullet working, then fetches another can while Martin strokes the cat, now settled on his lap. "Remember the Porcu business, what was it? Three years ago. Shot on his way to the office. Didn't have an escort, of course. That all came later. They still don't know *exactly* who did it, the hand on the gun, I mean, but that's not the point. There was never any doubt about where the bullet came from, if you follow me. Everyone knew damn well it was one of the last half-dozen Trots left in Europe." He drinks and pulls a face, surprised, as though the beer has suddenly gone off, or he's lost his taste for it. "This time, though, there's something extremely bad-smelling about the whole thing. It doesn't tie up with anything. Nobody's taken responsibility for it."

"I thought–?"

Adriano snorts. "Come on, Frame. You weren't born yesterday. A splinter group no one's ever heard of? That communiqué? It stinks to high heaven. Killing someone with an escort? That hasn't been done since Moro. It's just not worth the trouble. Killing the escort as well. Leaving one of them alive to tell the tale. The whole scenario's wrong. I'd say it was an inside job if it made any sense, but Di Stasi wasn't that important. Now, if there'd been an election coming up in the next week or two–"

"So?"

"So." Adriano slaps his forearm. "Shit. Missed the fucker."

Martin senses that something remains to be said. That all he has to do is wait. "Does it have a name?" he says.

"What?"

"The cat."

Adriano ignores this too. "You work with Di Stasi's wife. Well, widow now, I suppose."

"Yes."

"That's Rome for you. Everyone knows everyone. That's what makes it so fucking sticky," says Adriano. "Everyone's fucking face in everyone else's fucking mess."

The cat jumps down from his lap and runs to the door. A moment later, they hear a key turn in the lock. A woman comes in with a bag of shopping. She looks at Martin and then, with surprise and a trace of annoyance, at Adriano, while the cat twists round her feet.

"You don't know Alina," Adriano says.

Alina puts the bag down on the table between them.

"I thought you were supposed to be calling me today," she says, ignoring Martin, who moves his otherwise untouched can of beer away from the bag as it slumps and empties its contents onto the table. A smell of fresh bread fills the room, and meat. Mortadella, maybe, *prosciutto crudo*. Unexpectedly hungry, he wonders if they will ask him to stay for dinner and what he will say if they do; he has no other plans. He looks at the woman, sizing her up. She's young enough to be Adriano's daughter. Perhaps she is, although he doubts it. She is pale and thin, with breasts too large for her frame. Her T-shirt, mauve and sequinned, has sweat stains under the arms. She reminds him a little of Helen, of Helen reduced and compromised. He breathes in unobtrusively to see if he can pick up the scent of her on the air. What did Adriano say? Things pop up.

"No signal. Honestly. I've got a witness," says Adriano, and it's hard to tell if the explanation is required or merely demonstrative. He takes his mobile from his pocket and points it at Martin, who ducks his head slightly in an affirmative bow and hazards a wry smile to distance himself from Adriano.

"Yes, right," she says. She gathers her blonde hair behind her neck with one hand, reaches in the pocket of her skirt with the other for what turns out to be an elastic band, which she uses to tie the hair back.

"Martin's just going," says Adriano. Leaning in her direction, still not standing up, he pulls her in towards him until her hip is against the hollow of his shoulder. She isn't relaxed, Martin can see that. He's noticed an accent that isn't Italian. Polish? East European? She is looking at him in an odd way, as though she expects something from him but hasn't decided what. She's like Helen in that as well, he thinks, you never know where you stand with her. He realises that he is staring at her, and turns away

"I'd better be off then," he says. "You know where to find me if you think of anything that might be of any use." He's sounding like a TV detective. He fumbles in his pocket and puts a business card on the table, for Alina's benefit. He'll ask himself what possessed him later, when he has forgotten the presence of her, and the effect it had on him. "Just in case," he says, holding out his hand to her. "Alina. It's been a pleasure."

She looks down at the card and then at his face, as if estimating the likelihood of his playing a trick on her, springing some trap, the way she might look at a client she doesn't trust, because Martin is convinced by now that she is on the game, and both wants her and wants it not to be true, for him at least.

She takes it and gives him a cautious, knowing smile. "The pleasure's mine," she says.

Back at home some hours later, with most of a bottle of wine already drunk and nothing left on his plate but a crust of cheese and some olive stones, Martin is thinking about Federico and the last time they spent an evening together. Helen had gone to bed early, and he and Federico had stayed at the table, finishing the wine and opening another bottle, and finishing that. Martin had drunk most of it, but Federico had had far more than usual and was turned towards Martin, both elbows on the table, his voice slightly slurred, loquacious in an untypically confidential way. Normally they would speak about Federico's work, in the wider sense, issues rather than personalities, inner-circle gossip of a sort but with a sense of probity that rescued it from vulgarity, Martin thought, with occasional passing regret; a peck of insider dirt never goes amiss. He'd enjoyed it though, this sense of being Federico's interlocutor, an elder, more experienced operator in the world of policy and political expediency; he'd enjoyed living up to this role that Federico had assigned him, adopting a laconic, avuncular manner, offering advice when it was called for as a representative of the press, an intimate outsider, a foreigner in the know. More in the know than Federico ever guessed.

But that last evening, leaning towards Martin, his shirt cuff brushing the trace of sauce left on his plate, Federico had

lowered his voice and asked Martin if Helen seemed strange
to him, if there was anything odd he'd noticed about her.
Martin said, No, why? thinking, Dear God, don't let her be ill
with anything. Don't let her die. I think she's having an affair,
Federico said, his voice resigned, even relieved, because he
had said the words, Martin decided later. But at the time it had
seemed that it wasn't the words being said but the idea of it that
had given Federico relief. Embarrassed, also relieved, Martin
said, A what? An affair? What on earth makes you think that? I
can't imagine it somehow. Not Helen. Federico wiped the sauce
from his cuff with a napkin, shrugged in that characteristic
Italian way, elbows pressed into his sides. She's different. It's
as though she has some sort of, I don't know, outside interest.
She's doing this degree, Martin said. Federico shook his head,
apparently amused. She's behaving like someone in love, he
said. She's in love with you, said Martin. She always has been.
I know that, Federico said, impatient, as if what Martin had
said were so obvious as to be insulting. I'm not suggesting she
doesn't love me, Martin. But she's distracted. I don't know. Her
head's in the clouds. He lowered his voice again, leant forward,
this time avoiding the plate. She's better in bed, he said, more
energetic, as though she's been charged up somewhere else
and needs to wind down with me. Aren't they the signs of
an affair? Martin didn't speak; he hadn't known what to say.
Embarrassed, head low, he glanced towards the shelf in the
kitchen where the wine was kept and was on the point of
fetching a bottle across, but Federico grabbed his arm and held
him down and began to talk again. I don't suppose it's more
than an infatuation, what's that word you use? A throw? A
fling, said Martin with a smile. Whatever it is, Federico said,
his fingers gripping Martin's bare flesh. I've seen no change,
said Martin, already asking himself if this was true. Was Helen
really the same as usual? The notion that she might be having
an affair struck Martin as brutally unreasonable, though less

to Federico than to himself, who had often tested the ground with her, with infinite delicacy and tact, perhaps too much. Perhaps she had never even noticed his attempts to woo her – *woo* was precisely the word, he recognised this, his discretion like something from the previous century. But I *am* from the previous century, thought Martin, that's where I was made and grew old. I might have died before the start of this one, this brave new millennium, the odds were in favour of death after all, my heart, my drinking history, cigarettes, the paraphernalia of the hard-boiled, hard-nosed journalist; it's a miracle I'm still alive. But I'm thinking about myself again, I'm letting myself get in the way as usual. I'm supposed to be thinking about Helen. Is Helen the same or different? he had asked himself. And he'd wondered, with a shiver of unexpected, inappropriate pleasure, if Federico had thought for even one moment that he, Martin, might once have been the secret life, the fling, and was asking him these questions merely to see what his reaction might be. Federico's last words had been *I wouldn't mind, you see. I wouldn't mind if she was. It's just that I'd like to know.* Was that some kind of absolution addressed to Martin?

And now, as though it were the most logical step in the world, he finds himself thinking about the woman he has met this afternoon, in Adriano's flat. Alina, who has his card. If he had some way of making contact with her at this very moment, he'd use it.

7

Giacomo watches Helen fill a pan with water and place it on the stove, then stare at the small bone-handled knife in her hand as if on the point of speaking, before thinking better of it, taking a clove of garlic from the head, to peel and chop, taking another, her head bowed as if she is trying to avoid his eyes.

"You're doing pasta," he says, to remind her that he is here.

"With what there is, which isn't an awful lot, I'm afraid. I was supposed to have shopped." She pauses. "Thank you for staying," she says, slitting open a chilli pepper to empty out its seeds. "I can't bear the thought of being alone here."

Giacomo grates cheese into a small deep bowl, green with a thin white slip of glaze applied to it that, held to the light, appears to shimmer. He sees her bite her lip as she pours olive oil from an unlabelled bottle into a small copper pan and he says, "Do you know, I've never seen you cook before? In all these years," the words slipping out before it occurs to him how cruel this is, to remind her so brusquely of Federico. She nods, looks at him properly for the first time since he phoned Yvonne to tell her she would have to eat alone. "It's odd," she says, "but that's just what I was thinking," her voice unnaturally calm as she scrapes the garlic and chilli from the chopping board into the pan. "Do you remember this knife? He had it in Turin."

And then, to his surprise, Helen puts down what she is doing and walks across to hug him in a clumsy ungainly way, bending over him as he half rises from the chair, half tries to turn towards her in order to embrace her back. But she has trapped both his arms in hers, he would have to wriggle or break her grip to escape and that would be unforgivable, he thinks, as she begins to take deep breaths against his scalp, harsh retching gulps of air, and so he lets himself be held and waits for her to cry as one waits for rain.

But Helen doesn't want to cry. Eventually, her breathing calms.

"I can't forgive him," she says, her soft mouth warm against Giacomo's ear. "I've been trying all day, but I can't. It was so *selfish* of him to put himself at risk like that." Her lips have never been this close to him, he feels, although she has kissed him a thousand times, kisses of circumstance and passion, kisses that have had nothing to do with this intimacy, this inclusion at the cost of others. "I've been telling myself that it wasn't his fault, it was just the job he was doing." And now she pulls away. "But he *chose* the job, Giacomo. He knew how dangerous it was, how easily something like this might happen, and he just went straight ahead. He didn't think about me at all, about what I'd do if he died." She stares at Giacomo, her eyes damp, but she's too angry to cry. "I thought I'd be safe with him, you know that, don't you? I thought he was the sensible one." She thumps Giacomo on the chest, lightly at first and then with more force. "I thought you'd be the one to end up dead, not him." He grabs her wrists, holds her off before she hurts him. "I got it all wrong. All wrong, right from the start. He's lying dead in the morgue," she says, pulling away from him, her face accusing. "And you're alive. You're safe, in Paris, everything rolls off you." She stares at him, as if waiting for him to answer, defend himself, before speaking again, in a voice he barely recognises it's so laden with anger and accusation. "Why couldn't he have been like you?"

"I'm sorry," he says, and means it. At this moment, in his heart, he would rather it had been him. He's never felt so worthless. "What can I do?"

"Do? I don't know. What can you do?"

"To help you, I mean."

"I'm just so furious with him," she says, and now her tone is softer, almost pensive, as though she is thinking aloud and Giacomo isn't even here. "I can't stop remembering all the times I've felt left out, neglected. As though I'd just been tagged on to his valuable life. You don't know how often I've thought of leaving him." She glances at Giacomo. "Not just for you, though I've thought of that too." Before he can respond to this, she continues. "But I've always changed my mind, it's never lasted long. I've wished him dead sometimes, God help me, so that I wouldn't have to decide. Not wished his death, Giacomo – wished his absence." She looks around the room. "It's odd, isn't it? Normally, when I'm with you, it's as though Fede doesn't exist – that's a terrible thing to say, isn't it? But it's true, you block him out somehow. And now he doesn't exist any longer, now he's dead, I can't get away from him. I've never been so aware of his presence. Never. He's everywhere I look, his books, his pans, his little knife. His best friend. He's here between us, and I can't see round him." She holds out a hand for Giacomo to take. After a moment's hesitation, he does so, leads her to the table. They sit together. "And now it's just the two of us," she says, "and I can't bear it."

An acrid smell, of burning, comes from the stove. Giacomo stands up and hurries across, whipping the pan of chilli and garlic from the heat. The pan with the water must have been boiling for some time, but he hasn't noticed. He doesn't know what to do. He's never loved Helen as unreservedly as he does now, at this moment.

"I'm hungry," she says. She walks across to where he's standing and puts her arms around his waist, from behind. He feels her rest her head against his shoulder. "I've barely eaten since Monday evening." She slides some pasta into what's left of the boiling water and takes two bowls from a shelf. She shakes the garlic, burnt to a crisp, and chilli in the pan, then tips them into the sink. "It's time to start again," she says, then smiles to herself.

"I'll open some wine," says Giacomo.

"Everything goes on, doesn't it?" she says, taking the knife once again and chopping more garlic and chilli, pouring some oil into the same small pan. His pan, thinks Giacomo, his knife. "As if nothing has happened. But I've already said that, haven't I? I can't remember what I've said and what I haven't. Giulia says I've got the brain of a pea-hen."

"She has a way with words." He pours red wine into glasses.

Helen sighs. "She thinks I'm completely incapable, she always has. She's never forgiven Federico for choosing me, when he could have had one of her cronies' daughters. One of the daughters of the revolution. Her revolution, that is. She's responsible for all this," she says, with surprising venom. She shakes the pan. "Mustn't let this burn as well." When Giacomo offers her the glass, she takes it, then looks at him.

"What was that Yvonne said about you having to see the magistrate?"

He hoped she'd forgotten. He sips his wine. "He wanted to know what I knew about Federico," he says, "which, these days, is almost nothing. As I said. He asked me about the old days, in Turin. I think he may have had a personal interest."

"Really?"

"Yes. He grew up there. You didn't notice yesterday because he was speaking English. His accent in Italian is pure *torinese*."

"Did he ask about me?"

"No," he says. "Surprisingly, he didn't."

She lifts a thread of pasta from the pan. "*Al dente* all right?" she says.

When they have eaten their pasta and the bottle is finished, Helen asks him what he intends to do.

He laughs. "What with?" he says. "My life?"

"I was thinking about this evening," she says. "Yvonne must be wondering where you are."

He shrugs. "I'll sort Yvonne out later," he says. He plays with his empty glass for a moment. "I know what I want to do."

"Yes." She glances at his hand and then, more intently, into his eyes. She looks tired, a little scared, younger than she has seemed for years, despite her exhaustion, as though some patina has been rubbed off and left her exposed. She looks the way she used to look in Turin, he thinks, wary, bare, without resources or subterfuge, needy in a covert, antagonistic way. No wonder he loves her.

"If you'll let me."

8

Half an hour later Helen is naked in bed, the sheet pulled up around her. Normally she'd read a novel from the stack beside her, knowing that Federico won't be coming to bed until he's finished whatever work he's brought home. But this evening she lies and listens to Giacomo in the bathroom, brushing and spitting, peeing and flushing, as Federico did, as all men do. She lies there, thinking that she has never felt so alone, so distant from herself, when the dream she had that morning comes back to her and she remembers where it came from, as vividly as if the scene were being played before her eyes. It was one Sunday morning almost thirty years ago, when she and Federico had gone to the station in Turin and taken the first train out. The train passed through an area with shallow hills and lines of trees as windbreaks, poplars maybe, and there were low square farmhouses with arches and porticoes along one side, some built from brick and others plastered over with ochre, rose pink, lemon. The sun had come out and they were hot enough to take off their jackets, although it was still early spring. Federico's shirt-collar was sticking up at one side, which made Helen want to reach across and tuck it in; some fluff from his jacket collar had snagged on the stubble of his neck. They were alone in the compartment, and the sunlight was pouring in as they headed towards some town whose name she has

forgotten, and then there was a tunnel, quite unexpected
in that landscape, as though someone had placed a hill in
that precise spot, purposefully, to create a theatrical effect,
perhaps of detachment. They came out of the tunnel, the
train moving slowly as if approaching a station, and there
was the finest house they had seen up to then, with tall
symmetrical windows and a squat tower at the centre and a
wide arch that ran right through the structure so that they
could see the fields beyond. They were sitting opposite each
other, staring out through the window like children, when
Federico turned to Helen, his face radiant with sunlight, and
said: "We could buy that house and live there, just the two
of us," and Helen nodded, too moved by happiness to speak,
not even daring to look at Federico any longer, deliberately
looking away, just staring out as the house went slowly by.
When people have said they thought their heart was going
to burst with happiness, Helen has thought of that house,
disappearing behind a line of poplars, and the figure of
a woman she saw at a window, reaching out to close the
shutters against that unexpected late-winter sunlight, her
white blouse and her naked arms suddenly closed away,
enveloped by the darkness of the room behind.

That was her dream, she thinks, that day, that journey,
that house, that happiness. But she can't see Federico in the
dream. She can't remember who she was with, however hard
she tries.

During the night, she wakes to find Giacomo beside her in
the bed, in Federico's place. For a moment, feeling the heat
of another body, she thinks it *is* Federico, and rolls into him,
forgetting that he's dead. Then, with a shudder of revulsion
and fear, she cries out, pushing herself away with all her
force. But Giacomo catches her shoulder and moves against
her, his naked chest against her arm, his stomach brushing
hers. "You're all right," he whispers. "It's all right. It's me.

I'm with you now. It's going to be all right." And she falls back onto her pillow, unresisting. "What time is it?" she says. His fingers touch her lips. "Hush now," he says. "Help me," she says, not knowing what she means. How on earth can Giacomo help her?

It takes her an age to get back to sleep.

PART THREE

1

Fighting an almost manageable hangover, Martin struggles to conclude the English desk's daily round-up of the national press. Federico's assassination is yesterday's news by now, replaced on most front pages by images from the latest video of the Italian hostages in Iraq, the statement by their families that they won't be taking part in Saturday's anti-war demonstration, despite the kidnappers' demands that they show themselves as a gesture of solidarity with the people of Iraq. Well, yes. Quite. This hardly bears reporting, thinks Martin, but taps a brief sentence out to round off the piece. Nobody cares about other countries' hostages in any case. Japanese dying by the cartload, Filipinos too, and barely a peep in the western press. Yesterday's military parade went off smoothly, as expected. There are photographs in some papers of Federico's mother standing beside the defence minister, comments that range from the admiring to the affronted. No mention of Helen, thank God. Fifteen teenage girls arrested for climbing over a barrier. Balloons banned from Rome air space. Worth a mention? Hot air against imposing show of military force? No, better not tempt fate. Government talk of pulling the troops out of Nassiriya, immediately contradicted by government talk of a strong Italian presence in the province, the having-it-both-ways strategy that satisfies no one, but is always more newsworthy than silence. What else? Research shows fewer cases of clinical depression in Italy than elsewhere in Europe. Research shows Italians have fallen in love with hole-in-the-wall cash machines. Some connection worth making perhaps? Martin writes, deletes, writes. And so the muck mounts up. Agency statements by MPs no one has heard of to pay off private debts to lobbyists. Disagreement among leaders and would-be leaders of the centre-left. Martin sighs, reads on. A talking head on one of the PM's channels, now Euro-candidate for the boss's party, comes out as "homo-affective", whatever that means. Claims to have Alexander the Great syndrome. Too "local"? Church slant? Why not? Go for it, boyo. All at once, Martin feels better. After a burst of anticlerical energy he calls down to the bar for coffee. Double espresso. Writes his concluding paragraph, his Italy in a nutshell, worms and all. Bangs *Enter* and off it all goes, as it does every morning, onto a thousand, a hundred thousand blinking screens. The truth. The news.

Finally, Martin picks up the phone. Time to call in another favour. For Helen.

Alina hasn't called.

2

Giacomo is woken by what sounds like a bell. He lies on his back, holding his breath, waiting for Helen to move. But Helen is fast asleep, her mouth pushed open by the position of her head on the pillow, which makes her look vulnerable and slightly infantile, the puckered cherry-like mouth of a china doll, so unlike her mouth awake. Her hair is damp with sweat and broken into strands on her cheek and forehead. Giacomo raises himself on one elbow and is about to lift the hair away from Helen's face with the tip of a finger when he hears a noise from somewhere in the flat.

A woman's voice calls out, in Italian. "Helen. Helen. Are you here?" Then, more quietly, but still loud enough for him to hear: "Where on earth can she be? That stupid girl."

Beside him, Helen stirs, mumbles. Giacomo shakes her shoulder gently. "There's someone in the flat," he says, his voice as low as he can make it. Helen's eyes start open in a look of absolute terror; he wonders for a second if she's forgotten he's here. "Don't panic. It's a woman," he says, adding, to reassure her: "She knows you. She thinks you're stupid." When the bedroom door swings open, they are both sitting up, Helen with the sheet clutched across her breasts like a Victorian heroine, Giacomo bare from the waist up, his hands in his lap. An old woman, slim, with dark grey hair twisted up into a tight ballerina's chignon, wearing pearls and a neat black dress, walks into the room, her heels click-clicking on the wood. I know you, Giacomo thinks.

"Good morning, Giulia," says Helen, in Italian.

"I expected something, I must admit, but not this," the woman replies. "Not this degradation."

"I don't know what you mean." Helen's voice is icy. Giacomo fights back the impulse to laugh. He slips a hand beneath the sheet and grips Helen's thigh.

"You were never fit to be Federico's wife. I knew that of course." Giulia is stiff with contempt. "You never made any real effort to be his wife. And now this. This filth."

"How dare you," Helen says, pushing Giacomo's hand away, letting the sheet fall down from her body. It sticks for a moment to the damp skin of her breasts, then slides into her lap, where she lets it lie. With a shiver of disgust, Giulia turns to leave the room.

"Wait a minute," says Helen. "Where are you going? Who gave you permission to walk in here like this? This isn't your house. Who do you think you are?"

Giulia has changed her mind. She stalks across to the chest of drawers and picks up Giacomo's lighter, plays with it, weighs it in her hand, an expression of grim satisfaction on her face. For a moment, Giacomo thinks she's going to burn them all alive. "You don't imagine you can get away with this, do you?"

"Did Federico give you a key? He never said anything to me."

Giulia puts down the lighter with a brisk slap and turns once again to leave the room. "We'll discuss this when you're decent." As if to emphasise the unsuitability of the word, she repeats it: "Decent." When she can no longer be seen from the bed, she adds, in a louder voice: "I won't leave, you know. Not until I'm ready. You might be free of my son, but you won't be free of me that easily."

"You'd better deal with her," Giacomo says. "What do you want me to do? Shall I leave?"

"For God's sake, no. Did you hear what she said? Don't leave me alone with her, whatever you do. Make us some coffee while I talk to her." She scrambles out of bed, pulling the top sheet away with her, her back and arse exposed as she crosses the room towards a chair. Giacomo lies naked on the mattress, his penis half-erect. He'd pull her back if he could. "You'd better put something on," she says. "You've shocked her enough as it is." She slips on a short cotton skirt and singlet, taking a towelling robe from a hanger and throwing it across to him. "Put this on," she says. "I'll go and sort her out."

Giulia is waiting at the table, the house key beside her hand. Helen sits down opposite the older woman, resisting the urge to reach across for the key and slip it into her pocket. The ridge of varnished wood at the front edge of the seat is hard and cool against her thighs. She has decided that she will see what Giulia wants to say before speaking; she doesn't want to pre-empt or misdirect her. Perversely, she feels a sort of gratitude. After years of evasion and patrician indifference on the part of the older woman, after all those words not said or not quite said, the haughty silences and callous asides, Giulia will finally tell her what she really thinks of her. And then she will do the same to Giulia.

"The telephone's off the hook. Your mobile's turned off. You don't even answer the doorbell. I hardly like having to enter the house like this, like some common thief, but you do realise that you can't just disappear, Helen," Giulia says. Her tone is unexpectedly conciliatory. "There's so much to be done. I don't know where to start."

Helen stretches her arm out for the key, but Giulia is too fast for her.

"This doesn't belong to you," she says, slipping the key into the pocket of her dress.

"Well, it certainly doesn't belong to you."

"I won't pretend to like you," says Giulia after a thoughtful pause, as though she has just been asked to do this by someone else and has needed a moment or two to consider. Well, Federico must have asked her, thinks Helen, and Federico is there before her, the abrupt and dreadful absence of him, for the first time this morning. Federico must have given his mother the key. She feels that she has been woken by a slap across her face.

"You never have."

Giulia shrugs, impatient. "Everything I have done for you I have done for Federico. You know that. As though we haven't suffered enough."

Helen can't bear her mother-in-law's appropriating *we*. "You aren't here to help *me*, I know that," she says. "If you'd wanted to help me, you'd have come with Fausto yesterday, instead of going off to that ludicrous march. I don't know why you're here today. I don't know what you want. I know I don't want you." She has said it, she thinks. Finally, she has said it. Now, perhaps, the woman will go away.

But Giulia leans forward with an urgency, a violence that startles the younger woman.

"You know why I'm here," she says. "We can't let Federico's sacrifice pass unnoticed."

"You make him sound like some sort of animal. Federico wasn't sacrificed," says Helen. "He was murdered."

Giulia snorts her derision. "You've no idea how strange he's been these past few weeks, have you? He thought you were having an affair, you know that, don't you? You thought you were being so clever. And he was right all the time, though even he hadn't imagined you were betraying him with someone he thought was a friend."

"He spoke to you about me?"

Giulia smiles grimly. "He spoke to his father, of course. He spoke to Fausto. Fausto spoke to me. Married couples do that, you know. They speak to each other about the things that matter. Surely I don't need to tell you that?"

Don't you tell me what married couples do, thinks Helen. I've seen the way Fausto looks away when you're on some hobbyhorse about something. You bore him. Why do you think he's always got the TV on, flipping from one channel to another? But before she can say this, a more important thought comes to her.

"You've been sent, haven't you?"

Giulia ignores this, standing up and crossing the room. Before Helen realises what her mother-in-law is doing, Giulia has replaced the receiver on the phone, lifting it to assure herself of the dialling tone. She puts it down once more, with a sigh, then glances round the room.

"Your mobile?" she says. "Where is it?"

"What?"

"Where have you put it? You have to turn it on, Helen. You can't carry on pretending not to be here. There's been more than enough nonsense already. You seem to have forgotten your responsibilities. Federico wasn't just anyone, you realise that? His chief secretary has been calling you all morning. It's already gone ten."

"Calling me?"

Giulia tut-tuts, as though Helen were behaving like a stubborn child. "You can't bury your head in the sand. Decisions have to be made. And you have to make them, though you're clearly incapable."

"Why don't you leave her alone?" says Giacomo, who has finally come into the room, barely covered by Federico's dressing gown, which is too small for him. No, thinks Helen, please don't. You'll make it worse. But Giulia pays no attention to him. She walks over to Helen in her usual brisk way, placing a hard cool hand on her shoulder. Helen fights the urge to push her off.

"He's worked so hard," Giulia said. "He's given his life to his work. Surely you can see that. I know you've never really cared. You were the worst sort of person for him, I've always known that. What Federico needed was someone who would support him, someone who cared about Italy." Not some foreign woman with her own life, Helen thinks, hoping her silence will egg Giulia on. It's doing Helen good to be treated like this, knowing that she could hurt the woman so much, if she wanted to. But she's changed her mind about that, for today at least. Federico never spoke about her. He always made such an effort to do what she wanted, the holidays, the lunches, the friends of the family that had to be entertained, yet he never once said to Helen that he loved her. He never once said, I love my mother. Federico understood duty, he learnt that from Giulia. But duty wasn't love. What a weight the woman's hand is, as though she is actually bearing down on her, pinning her down by brute force. Helen wriggles to shake her off but the fingers tighten.

"Someone who would give him a child," says Giulia.

When the phone rings, Giacomo moves to answer it, but finds himself blocked by Giulia, who darts across the room with unexpected speed. She, in her turn, is stopped by Helen. How farcical we must look, she thinks as she picks up the receiver.

It's Fausto. "Can I speak to Giulia?"

"So you knew she'd be here."

"How are you?"

"All right," she says. "And you?"

"I didn't sleep," he says. "I couldn't." After a moment's silence: "Can you pass her over to me?"

"You're in this together."

"I don't know what you mean," he says. "I'm sorry." He sounds both hopeless and determined. This isn't Fausto, she thinks. Fausto has always been on my side. Giulia is standing beside her, as close as she can get, her foot tapping briskly on the parquet floor. Helen can feel the heat coming off her and smell a sourness that must be the woman's sweat. She wants to tell Giacomo to drag her off, but thinks better of it. She turns her shoulder to block the older woman, grips the receiver. "Tell her to leave me alone," she cries down the phone as Giulia tugs at her arm with her bony hands. "For Federico's sake."

"Give him to me," says Giulia.

"What does she want from me, Fausto?" Helen is close to tears as Giulia's hard old fingers prise hers away, first one, then two together. Helen threshes out, catching her mother-in-law in the face, and Giulia staggers back, then snatches the phone from Helen's hand. Rigid with shock, Helen sees a trickle of blood on Giulia's cheek, where her engagement ring must have gashed the skin. She starts to shake. Giulia snaps into the phone, "I'll call you back," but doesn't put the receiver down. Fausto must have said something to make her listen. Giacomo has walked over and is holding Helen; she can feel his hand on her hair, stroking it over and over again. She gasps for breath, her snot on his robe, her eyes tight shut. "I'm sorry," she says. "I'm sorry." She lets Giacomo lead her to the bathroom, closing the door behind them. "I can't take any more of it," she says. She stands by the basin like a child while her face is splashed with cold water and wiped dry.

"It isn't just what *you* want, Helen," Giulia says from the other side of the door.

"Just fuck off and leave me alone," Helen shouts out, in English, then listens, hand over her mouth, as Giulia walks away.

"I can't go out," she says to Giacomo, who tries to embrace her. But almost immediately, as if she is dreaming, she has pushed him off and is standing in front of Giulia, seated once more at the table as if waiting to be served.

"You really are beyond me, Helen," says Giulia, apparently unaware of the blood on her cheek. "You've done everything wrong so far, you realise that. You've ignored the press when all you needed to say was a word, *a single word would have done*, you've locked yourself up in this house as though you had something to hide. You've refused to cooperate with the government or the president or anyone else. You've behaved like a spoilt child and it isn't acceptable." She glares at Helen, her contempt unconcealed. "And look at you," she continues, with spite. "Already in bed with someone else, on the *second* night. And with *that* man. That loathsome man." She stops short, as though something has only just occurred to her. And, of course, it has. Helen watches the colour drain from her face. Giacomo is smirking behind her, but she has no time for that.

"You were with *him*, weren't you? You were with *him* when Federico died. Those lies you told the police were designed to protect *him*."

How odd, thinks Helen, that this simple fact, this irrelevant coincidence, should finally make the woman feel something. Because Giulia has no right to talk about grief. What does she know about the way Helen feels? What does she know about lies to the police?

"What makes you think I lied?"

"Don't brazen it out with me."

"You have your spies, I suppose," says Helen. "Old habits die hard."

Giulia stands up. "I belong to this country, as Federico did. As you never will."

"I'm glad I don't belong." Helen is incensed. "I don't care two figs about your fucking country."

Giulia gives a scornful laugh. "Do you really think you're fit to make decisions about my son? A woman who can't wait forty-eight hours after her husband's murder before being caught in bed with a convicted terrorist." For the first time, her hand rises to touch the scratch on her cheek. She strokes it thoughtfully. Perhaps she has only just noticed the pain. "Of course," she says, after a moment, "if you were prepared to listen to reason."

"Reason?"

"Fausto says they're prepared to send a car round for you."

"A car?"

"You have to speak to the PM," Giulia is saying. "He won't take no for an answer, you know that perfectly well. I despise him quite as much as you do, we all do, but that isn't the point. He's not entirely unreasonable. Listen and let him tell you what he wants."

Without realising what she is doing, because she hasn't really understood – her mind is on Giacomo, who is still in the bathroom – Helen moves her head in what might be a nod. Giulia leans over to pat her daughter-in-law's hand. "Leave it to me," she says, as though she has won her point and can afford to be generous. She hurries to the phone, punches in a number she obviously knows by heart, glancing back to see how Helen is taking it.

But all Helen wants to do is walk. She wants to leave the flat for the first time, it occurs to her now, since the day Federico was shot, which seems a lifetime ago. How strange time is, entirely emotional, whatever the clocks and calendars might say. She wants to leave the flat and walk, without purpose, across Via Giulia and take the steps down to the river, along the bank as it narrows and widens, past the hospital on the Isola Tiberina and the synagogue up to her left and on towards Testaccio. She wants to leave the old city and see the gasometer and later, much later, when the sun is in the right position, the light that reflects on the gold of the mosaic of St Paul's Outside the Walls. She wants to walk in her own sweet time past the gypsy camp and the old dog track and leave the river behind her as she clambers up the dried long grass that covers the bank into what starts to feel like open country, although there are buildings everywhere, ugly and low, in all directions, most of them newish, houses and workshops of one kind or another, small factories, allotment sheds, warehouses. She and Federico would cycle round there in their early days in Rome, Federico stopping to talk to people with that earnest curiosity he always has, or had, because curiosity is a feature of the living, perhaps the most important. Federico would listen and later, when there were just the two of them, jot down notes of what he'd heard. This is where it all starts, he liked to say, tapping his notebook, these words in here. He'd done this in Turin as well, with Giacomo laughing behind his back. Always the three of them, and then Stefania, and then, at a distance, the others. She wants to walk until there is no one and nothing left but the dark coarse sand of the coast and the empty sky, and then, after all this, she will breathe. She tries it now, in the poisonous air of the flat, a deep breath in, a forced breath out, her mother-in-law whispering into the phone only feet away, lowering her voice each time she utters Helen's name.

"What's that about a car coming for me?"

"Later," says Giulia. "We'll talk about that later." She picks up her bag. She seems to be on the point of leaving when something, some thought, stops her. She stares at Helen with a pained expression on her face.

"We mustn't argue, you know. There mustn't be bad feeling between the two of us, not now. We have Federico's legacy to think of." She glances towards the bathroom door. Moving closer to Helen, she adds, in a confidential, intimate way: "He isn't important. You know that, don't you?" She taps Helen's wrist with a finger. For Giulia, this must be a gesture of affection, Helen thinks. "And you needn't worry about your phone. I've made sure no one can pester you."

Giulia has been gone for five minutes before Helen sees that she's forgotten the keys after all. She walks across to the kitchen blackboard to hang them on one of the hooks and sees the word OLIVES in Federico's writing, then goes to the bathroom and pushes open the door. Did Federico really give his mother the key to the flat? And not say a word? Sometimes she wonders if they were married at all. Maybe Giulia is right.

She stands there, her hands stretched over her head to hold the frame. She pushes until she feels the strain in her shoulders. Giacomo is slumped on the loo, his head thrown back against the wall, Federico's towelling robe drawn round him, tight across his stomach. His eyes are closed, but he opens them immediately.

"You'll send any car away, won't you? she says.

"Of course."

"Hadn't you better call Yvonne?"

"That won't be necessary," he says.

He's been thinking about how it all might be managed. Yvonne won't be a problem. She's almost as bored with him as he is with her. She might already have packed her bags and left, as she threatened to do last night. And what would I feel about that? he asks himself. It doesn't take long to find the answer. Relief. He won't deny it. Why should he? He's always been ready to admit his mistakes and move on. It's been obvious for some time that she'll leave him, sooner or later. Sooner would be a generous miracle. She will sue him for cruelty or indifference and he will have to provide her with money, he imagines, more than she is worth, more than he can comfortably afford. He will have to get back on the lecture circuit and postpone his book, see if the States are prepared to have him yet. He's been told he has a cult following on certain campuses. He has it in mind to do something on Federico. No theory; a sketch, some memories, observations both wise and paradoxical. Nothing too tame. A little thing to move the waters. He'll talk to Helen when the time is right, see what she thinks. They'll have time for that, and for everything else. He's never understood before how right she is for him. It was wonderful to see her stand up to that dreadful old woman. He'll have to bring Giulia into it, the influence of the mother, the role of women in Federico's life. Maybe Stefania will have some thoughts worth sharing.

Which reminds him; he must tell Helen that Stefania called yesterday morning. She'd just got back from one of her field trips in Africa and only just heard of the murder. She was crying dreadfully, she couldn't stop. He waited until she'd cried herself out. She wanted to come to the funeral. What funeral? he said. No plans have been made yet. It's up to Helen. Helen, she said, and started to cry all over again. I'll call her, she said, you must give me her number. The shock will be like this for a while, he thought then, like waves moving over the surface. Just as one person gets used to the loss of Federico, another will begin the process of understanding it. How long will that process take, he wonders, looking inside himself as Helen sighs and sits beside him on the edge of the bath, holding his hand in both of hers, her head bowed. He thinks she's about to cry. He's ready for that. He welcomes the chance to comfort her.

And after Stefania, whose turn will it be?

3

It's years since Martin last played this kind of cloak and dagger nonsense. He can't quite believe he is sitting in his car, the windows up, outside the abandoned acres of the old Mercati Generali, waiting for someone he doesn't know from Adam. When the metallic blue Fiat Brava draws up beside him, he glances across and sees a young man, overweight or over-muscled, it's hard to tell, his head shaven smooth like everyone else's these days, the loveliest people in Europe transformed into a race of skinhead thugs. He is wearing a high-collared white shirt, tight round the biceps, and those wraparound sunglasses that look like the eyes of a fly, with mirrored orange glass. In any normal world, thinks Martin, he'd stick out like a sore thumb.

The man nods and pulls away, along Via Ostiense in the direction of St Paul's. Martin follows. He expects to be taken out towards Ostia and, sure enough, the car in front turns right onto Viale Marconi and right again onto Via del Mare. Martin has always avoided this road on the odd occasions he's had to go to Ostia these past few years. He's hardly a sun-worshipper, his skin comes out in livid blotches at the least exposure. Via del Mare is said to be the most dangerous road in Italy, hard though it is to believe, this sun-dappled avenue of maritime pines, straight as a die, the ruins of Ostia Antica appearing on the right as they leave the city behind them, pass under the ring road, clogged as usual with traffic.

The man in front is maintaining a healthy speed, at the upper limit of what's allowed, and Martin is amused to see how often they're both overtaken. There's a line from a Dylan song he's always liked, that you have to be honest to live outside the law. How true that is, he thinks, his eye on the speedometer, the needle just kissing seventy. Invisibility is the best revenge. He is leaving enough space for one car to squeeze between them, but no more. It isn't the first time he's followed, or been followed for that matter, and, as usual, he's enjoying himself. He's always enjoyed what he thinks of as the game and it strikes him as strange that in the last fifteen years he hasn't missed it more.

The car turns off to the left before they reach Ostia, and into the pine woods that run parallel to the coast from where they are now, all the way down to the president's estate between Ostia and Torvaianica. Martin continues to follow it down a dirt track, increasingly amused by this subterfuge, a simple phone call, a simple request for information, has to lead to this. It's the way we're wired, he thinks, he recognises it in himself. Why make it simple when you can play the game?

The car is twenty yards in front of him when it drives into a picnic area, a dozen wooden tables with benches attached, and almost stops. This is the signal. Martin pulls over and watches the Escort drive off and it is only now that he notices the appropriateness of the model chosen.

He winces as he climbs from the car, arthritis in the hips and knees, he doesn't need to be told he's overweight, but what other pleasures are left to him? His sex life, such as it is, has dwindled to nothing since his doctor put him on medication for high blood pressure. Now, there's an irony, he thinks. High pressure everywhere but where it counts. He thinks of Alina. Perhaps she has special techniques for men like him, he thinks, then feels ashamed.

He pulls his linen trousers away from the crotch and tucks his shirt back in, letting his stomach rest for a moment on his hand. The June sun is directly above his head and he realises that he shouldn't have worried so much about looking conspicuous and brought his panama – the real McCoy, an old man's whim – to protect his scalp. It will itch tonight, that low-level constant itch that stops him sleeping without sufficient alcohol, and even then he wakes up in the early hours of the morning and has to swab it with some pink lotion the dermatologist has given him that sometimes works and sometimes doesn't. But these days hats draw attention to themselves so much.

Wiping his forehead on a handkerchief, he walks across to the nearest bench and sits down, his back to the table. He doesn't look at his watch. He expected to have to wait, and here he is, alone in a derelict picnic area in the heart of the Ostia pine woods, waiting for someone he hasn't seen for over a decade. A man, it occurs to him, he has never seen in places other than parks, and stations, and woods. Always in the open air, even in winter, always in places where no one is watching them or listening, although they can never be certain, they both know that.

What in God's name am I playing at? he thinks abruptly and has to remind himself that he is here for Helen; here to help Helen understand why her husband is dead. "We can't talk like this, on the phone," Picotti had said when Martin asked him for help, intriguing Martin although he'd known it might have meant nothing at all, nothing more than the reflex of a stiff neglected muscle. And so the arrangements were made.

Picotti doesn't arrive in a car. Or if he does, he's left it some distance away so that Martin is startled when a pine cone bounces near his feet and a second one catches him on the shoulder. He jumps up, turns round sharply and there the man is, the same as ever, irritatingly bright and thin, his naturally bald head gleaming in the sun. Martin sucks in his stomach, sadly aware that it makes no significant difference, except that the pressure of the belt buckle on the flesh is momentarily reduced.

Picotti darts across the picnic area, his hand outstretched, his grin as curved and luminous as the new moon. He is dressed for holiday, those odd half-mast trousers with superfluous pockets round the knees and rubber toggles dangling off them, a style called *pinocchietto*, according to one of the younger men on the French desk, who's actually worn a khaki pair to work. Little Pinocchio, Martin thought at the time, suppressing a grimace, whatever next? As though we have to dress for the outward bound course our lives have become. Picotti's T-shirt says something in English, but he is still too far away for Martin to read it without his glasses. He thought the fashion this season was Spanish obscenities, but maybe he's wrong. He generally is these days. His understanding of fashion, he's discovered, was infinitely fallible. He'll have to ask Jean-Paul.

He holds out his hand. Picotti takes it, squeezing harder than Martin likes, then slaps Martin's stomach with the back of his own hand, a hard, almost vicious slap.

"Hey, Martino," he says, "we let ourselves go a little these past years."

"Your fault," says Martin, forcing a smile.

"My fault?" Picotti feigns shock, falls back a step, hands rising to his chest. His grin flips down at the corners into clown-like tragedy.

"Plural, old chap. *Colpa vostra. La dolce vita.*" He wouldn't choose to conduct their conversation in English, but he knows this isn't up to him. It's Picotti's favour, Martin can't set the rules of play. Even "Martino" has to be swallowed without flinching. It has always been Picotti's way to reduce him to a state of impotent irritation before coughing up what is called for. Not that there is any guarantee of that, there never was. The cards played closest to the chest are all too often the ones that have nothing on them.

"Long time, no see," Picotti says, waving a hand towards the bench. "We're getting old and the world is more full of horse shit every day. It's not our world any more, Martino, we're two old men." He shrugs, sits down, hitching his *pinocchietto* up almost to knee level, waiting for Martin to sit beside him. When Martin does, he puts a hard dark hand on his knee. Martin ignores the hand, observing Picotti's face with as pleasant an expression on his own face as he can muster. He is close enough to see that the T-shirt bears two green feline eyes on a black background. "All Cats Are Leopards in the Dark" it says and, below that, *"Ethiopian proverb"*.

"The bambini are in charge, Martino. What's that beautiful idiom you English say? The lunatics run the asylum." Picotti starts to laugh, then coughs, squeezing the flesh above Martin's knee with startling force until Martin, still forcing a smile, itches to brush him off. "English humour. Very nice. We don't have your sense of humour here, you know that? We have to make do with being the best lovers in Europe, maybe in the world. It's hard. But we make ourselves content." Martin nods, relieved as the hand on his leg relaxes. "I've missed you, Martino," Picotti says. Despite himself, Martin is touched by the sincerity of his tone.

"I've missed you too," he says, but doesn't quite mean it, not as much as Picotti seemed to. He's forgotten the way the presence of Picotti fills him with a sense of unfocused shame. This is the second time he's felt ashamed today.

Picotti leans back, his elbows on the table. "And now this stupid bloody war, I ask you, who needs it?" he says. He taps out a cigarette from its soft pack, offering it to Martin, who refuses. Picotti raises an eyebrow, then takes it himself. Still smoking MS, Martin notices. *Morte Sicura*.

He can see now that Picotti has aged at least as much as he has. His face is lined, the skin beneath the tan looks crêpey and tired. When he smiles, as he invariably does, his teeth seem larger, more widely spaced than ever, the menacing smile the sort a horse might make. Horses also lack a sense of humour, thinks Martin.

"Your friend Di Stasi agreed with me, right?"

Martin didn't mention Federico when he phoned, and is both startled and alarmed. "Di Stasi?" he says, his tone deliberately bemused.

"Di Stasi, right. He didn't want this fucking war. Who does?" Picotti watches his cigarette burn, then flicks the ash into his hand and blows it away, the way a woman might blow a kiss from her palm. "Oil and money. Money and oil. Good men are dying there." He rubs the ash into the dirt with his sandal, a gleaming complicated affair of straps and buckles. His feet are brown, the toenails a little too long, the toes curved in after decades of over-tight shoes. "Like that," he says. He looks at Martin. "Men like us."

"People have always died in wars," says Martin.

"What do you want to know?" says Picotti, suddenly impatient.

"Di Stasi," says Martin slowly. "My friend. He was killed. Shot dead in the street for no apparent reason. I wondered if you might know who would want to do a thing like that. And why."

Picotti throws back his head and laughs. "Martino," he says. "You ask me a question like that, what can I do? What do you think I can do now?" He slits his throat with a finger. "You want blood?"

"I want help," says Martin.

Picotti, serious now, looks up at the sky, where a helicopter is heading towards the coast. They watch it turn left, towards Castel Porziano and the presidential estate.

"It's a busy time. Too many important people to look after. Too many lunatics. All the asylums are one now, you know? One big Yankee asylum. One big boss. I don't have the stomach for it, that's how you say, right? The stomach." He smiles. "Not like you, Martino, not like you."

He stands up, pushing the legs of his *pinocchietto* down to below his knees.

"I have a new young wife. You didn't know that, did you? They keep you young, no?" He smiles more broadly. "Young clothes, I mean. Like this. She says it makes me look good, it makes me look sexy, but I'm not so sure. An old man, it's too easy to take the piss. Don't worry, Martino. I don't ask you what you think."

When Martin is standing beside him, wriggling his own trousers loose at the crotch, Picotti throws his arms around the larger man and pulls him close in a clumsy embrace that startles Martin, who stiffens, but immediately relaxes. If his own arms were free and not pinned to his sides, he thinks, he would hug Picotti back. He wants to ask him about his first wife, whom he has never met, but fears the answer, whatever it might be. He already knows it won't be good news. Divorce or death. Acrimony, illness. He knows that whatever it is would be hard to stomach. Yes, that's how we say it, Picotti. To have the stomach for it.

Picotti pulls away.

"That was my son, my *bambino*. The one who took you here. Big boy, eh? Tattoos, the lot."

Martin nods. "You're keeping it in the family. Wise man."

"Hey, Martino. If you can't trust family," Picotti says. He slips his arm through Martin's and steers him gently but firmly towards the car.

Martin has already opened the door and is about to slump down into the stifling heat inside, disappointed but not surprised that Picotti has offered no help, when Picotti gives him a slip of paper with a phone number scribbled on it.

"Leave it with me, Martin. I do what I can."

4

Helen carries the pot over to the table and pours them both coffee, watching its glutinous trickle puddle and fill the cups.

"I can't believe Giulia treated me like that," she says.

"You were wonderful with her," says Giacomo.

"I wasn't. I was horrified. I think she's gone mad. She wants to see her son carried home on his shield, that's all she can see. She'll do anything to get it. Her beloved republic. I just can't bear the thought of Federico being used to bolster up something he hated."

"But worked for?"

Helen shakes her head. "He didn't, Giacomo. He worked against it. From within."

"I'm not sure that can be done."

"I'm not sure either. But Federico thought it could."

Giacomo lays his hand on Helen's. Helen looks down at their hands, then raises her head to smile. "I'm glad you're here."

"I'm glad I'm here as well."

They are both silent. They haven't eaten but Helen isn't hungry and, in any case, there is nothing in the house. This can't go on, she thinks. I'll die in here if I let myself. Giacomo's hand is warm and heavy on hers. For a second, she wants to pull it away. She can feel his eyes on her: cautious, anxious, almost oppressive. Is she glad he's here, or not? She can't tell. This is the first time in her life she's been with Giacomo without betraying anyone. She imagines them leaving the building together, arm in arm, and walking towards the river. Is this what she wants? To lose one man and take on another? She eases her hand away. She's restless, stifled.

"I suppose I'd better turn on my mobile," she says. "Giulia's right. I can't just hide away like this."

"They'll expect you to answer it if you do."

"I know that." Helen stands up, turns on her mobile, stares blankly at the screen as she tries to recall her PIN, inserts it, sighs. "I don't care. I'll go and talk to him if I have to. Why shouldn't I? I'm not afraid of him. It doesn't mean I have to do what he says."

Immediately, the mobile starts to ring. She answers without even looking to see who it is.

The first call is from a reporter, a woman she worked with once on a cultural insert for *L'Unità*. She's freelance now, she says, her tone more desperate than she'd like. Of course, she knows how awful it must be for Helen, how inappropriate it is of her to call, but–. Well yes, interrupts Helen, it is. I do understand, the woman says. Thank you so much, murmurs Helen, I really can't talk, not yet. Yes, yes, I do understand but, the woman says again as Helen hangs up. At once, the mobile makes the guttural sound that indicates the arrival of a text message or missed call. She sees that Martin has called once, but left no message. Another colleague, Martha Weinberg, has called, for the third or fourth time in the past few days. The mobile continues to cough in her hand. The other missed calls – all seven – are from numbers she doesn't recognise. One of them has an England code, which intrigues her briefly, but not enough to call it back. There is nothing from Giulia but, of course, there won't be. She'll use the landline, now being vetted for Helen's protection, thanks to Giulia. She's surprised her mother-in-law still has the clout to engineer it, and shocked that someone should be intercepting calls on her private line.

Federico has been saying for ages that their line is under surveillance. He said it went with the job. "But my calls don't go with your job," she told him, meaning: I don't go with your job. "I know, I know," he answered wearily, "I don't like it any more than you do." She'd felt guilty about insisting.

The second call is from Martin.

"I've only just turned it on," says Helen, apologetic. "You called earlier."

"Don't worry, my dear. I just wanted to tell you that I'm working on your behalf."

"On my behalf?"

"Asking questions."

"Oh yes, of course," she says. "I'm sorry, Martin, I'm only half here."

"How are you coping?"

"Come round," she says. "That'd be better. I hate the phone."

"Are you alone?"

"No," she says. "Giacomo's here. But I'd love to see you."

"Oh, that reminds me. I had a call from Martha Weinberg."

"What did she want? She's been calling me as well."

"Yes, she said she had. She wants to talk to you about Federico."

"She doesn't know Federico."

"Maybe you should give her a ring, see what she has to say."

"I will," she says. And does.

"Hello, Martha, it's Helen."

"Oh, my dear, how are you?"

"I'm fine," says Helen, pulling a face, as if to say, How else can such a question be answered? "You've been trying to get in touch. I'm sorry. I've had my mobile off."

"I'm not surprised. You must have had so many people pestering you after what's happened. I wouldn't have bothered you, but I felt I had to talk to you. It's about your husband."

"Yes, Martin told me," says Helen. "That's why I'm calling."

"He didn't tell you? That he'd been in touch with me?"

"No," says Helen. "He's been very busy these past few weeks." Why am I making excuses for him? she thinks. "What did he want?"

"Well, he wanted information."

"Information?" Helen is startled.

"Yes, he hummed and ha-ed a bit, then I got short with him and he said he wanted a contact address for this piece we'd done on the church and anti-globalisation."

"And what did you say?"

Martha laughs, a hoarse, smoker's laugh, then thinks better of it. "I said he should try using one of his own researchers, I mean, they came with the job, didn't they? He thought that was funny. I told him to look at our website."

"Was that it?"

"Well, no, it wasn't. About two weeks later, so we're talking about, what? less than a month ago, he called again. He wanted to meet me. I told him I didn't have time."

"He wanted to meet you?"

"Right. I didn't believe it either. This man is redesigning the Italian labour market and he wants to meet me? I started to wonder if it was someone else, some sort of weird hoax. But I saw him on television a couple of days later and it was his voice sure enough."

"A piece on the church, you said?"

"Yes." Martha pauses, before saying, in a cautious voice: "Look, I don't know if you're ready for this."

"For what?"

"He offered us money," says Martha. "From his own pocket or somewhere else, he didn't want to say, I don't think. I didn't ask."

"Federico?" Helen is incredulous. "He offered you money, personally?"

"Huh-huh. Well, for the magazine, obviously. He wouldn't give in."

"What do you mean?"

"He'd keep calling. Three, four times a day. I asked him what he expected to get in return. I thought maybe he was trying to buy our silence, I don't know. Nothing, he said."

"And what did you say?"

"I said he could take out a subscription. We don't do bribes."

"And did he?"

"He sent me a cheque that day."

"For how much?"

"Well, let's just say he bought quite a few subscriptions."

Helen is silent.

"Look," says Martha, "I'm really sorry to have to tell you all this, but you know, I figured it might be important. I didn't want you not to know now, and then find out."

"No," says Helen. "Thank you." She's about to hang up when Martha says something else that she doesn't catch.

"What?"

"Saturday?" says Martha.

"What about Saturday?"

"The demonstration against the war? Iraq? I mean, I know this isn't the right time to mention it but, well, I just thought. If you want to be on it, for Federico's sake as well, we'd love if you could be with us. We'll be gathering our forces at the office. You know where we are. Out by the gasometer. You don't need to let me know. Just turn up. We'd be so proud."

"I'll think about it," promises Helen, barely aware of what she is saying, and ends the call. Giacomo is sitting on a low chair in the corner of the room, tinkering with Federico's laptop. He looks up, curious. The mobile rings again. A private number Helen doesn't recognise. She lets it ring, then, when it's too late, picks it up.

"Patience is a virtue," she says. "You don't say that in Italian, do you? Not like we do, I mean. As though we meant it."

"Perhaps because we don't think patience *is* a virtue."

"What are you doing?"

He beckons her over. "Come and look at this," he says. As she walks across to where he's sitting she's struck by how anomalous this is, this sense of normality, as though she and Giacomo had always been here, and of strangeness, the absence of Federico like a scent in the air. Why were you giving money to that woman? she wonders. She feels that there must be some way she can talk to him, and knows how insane that is, to still feel he's available to her. Giacomo is sitting where Federico used to sit to tie his shoelaces, and check his briefcase before leaving the flat. With a stab of anguish, she thinks, his briefcase, where is it? I must ask that magistrate, he'll know. He'll help. He seemed to be someone she could trust. I can't bear to think of it lying in some office. Oh Federico, she wants to say. Why did you lie to me? Who were you? It's as if, within the great loss, there is a smaller, more focused, loss.

Giacomo is pointing at a window on the screen. "I thought I'd take a look at this Juggernaut file," he says. "There's still nothing there, of course, but look here." He points, and she sees the words *Last printed* and a date and time beside them. Monday 1 June 2004 14.43.00.

"That's impossible," Helen says. "Fede was already dead."

"It isn't impossible. It just means Federico didn't do it. You say that he left the laptop at his parents?"

"Yes."

"Well, there must have been something to print. And look here." He points again. "The last time it was modified was fifteen minutes later. That must have been when the contents were deleted."

"All that stuff Giulia said about Fede being strange," says Helen.

"Yes?"

"Martha Weinberg just told me something odd."

"Who's Martha Weinberg?"

"She edits a magazine called *Futuri Prossimi*. She's American, she's been here for years. She used to live down the road from here, on the other side of Piazza Farnese, but she was thrown out because she had too many cats. I don't know her very well. Federico hated her magazine. He couldn't stand these fringe people. He said they ruined everything, like spoilt children at parties trying to get all the adults' attention." She can hear herself speak. She thinks, I'm rambling. Concentrate, Helen.

"So what did she say?"

Helen tells him.

"Well, it makes sense in a way. I wasn't going to mention it to you, not yet anyway, but he's been sending me strange messages these past few weeks." He hesitates; she can tell he's wishing he hadn't started. "New age sort of stuff. Not like Federico at all."

"So, is that what Juggernaut's all about, do you think?" she says, nodding towards the laptop.

"You should ask Giulia," Giacomo says.

Helen laughs, without humour. "I suppose I should." She pushes her hands through her hair. "I'm going to lie down for a while," she says but doesn't move.

"Do you want me to come with you?" he says, his tone hesitant, hopeful. She's never seen him like this, unsure of himself with her. She doesn't know how to deal with it.

"No," she says. "You can answer the phone for me, though. Say I'm sleeping." She pauses. "I think you should call Yvonne as well. I feel very bad about her."

"I followed you once, you know," says Helen an hour or so later, after she has slept more deeply than she'd expected or could have hoped. "When we were all living in Turin."

"Really?"

"Yes. One afternoon. I was looking at shoes in a shop and I saw you come out of a bar a few yards away from me and walk off towards the station. I was going to call out to you when something stopped me, some impulse – I don't know what it was, embarrassment? shame? curiosity, probably – and I thought, I'll see where he's going. It was quite exciting, actually. I remember thinking this must be one of the reasons people do it, the thrill of it. It seemed to justify itself. Then you met up with two other men. I followed you all into a part of Turin I didn't really know, out towards the cemetery. There was no one else around but us. I was sure you'd turn round and see me and I wouldn't know what to do. Then you went in through a gate. I waited to see if you came out, but you didn't. After about twenty minutes I walked over to the gate and looked in. And that was it really. You'd disappeared. I didn't wait any longer. By the time I got back to the flat I felt as though the whole thing hadn't really happened."

"Did you tell Federico?"

Helen shakes her head. "God, no. I've never told anyone. It was such a foolish thing to do really, but it didn't seem to be then. It seemed almost normal. You were doing it, weren't you? Following people around, suspecting people. It was that talk about patience that made me think of it, I suppose."

She closes her eyes. "You don't remember, do you? Federico wasn't home when I got back, but you were in the kitchen. I must have shown how startled I felt, how caught out, because you took me by both hands and kissed me. It was the way you did it, the way you looked into my eyes. You saw me, I thought. You know exactly what I've done. 'You look as though you've seen a ghost,' you said."

Helen doesn't say what happened next. She doesn't say that she was taking off her coat when Giacomo came up behind her to help, lifting it off her shoulders. She doesn't say that she let herself flop back into him, be lifted until she felt his beard against her neck, and then his lips. That she turned round slowly, her coat sliding off to the floor, and kissed him, then pulled back while he raised an eyebrow and gave her a rueful smile, as if to say, Are you sure? and she nodded, also smiling, and kissed him

163

again, pulling his head towards hers. His hands easing round to the zip of her jeans and pulling it down as she moved her hips away a little to give him room, not breaking the kiss, pushing her mouth against his, her arms around his neck, her hands behind him, groping the air like someone about to drown. He knew what he was doing, he'd done it before. She doesn't remind Giacomo of the way she breathed in sharply, then bit the inside of his lower lip, not hard, as his fingers slipped down inside her panties and he pushed her against the wall and she fell away from him, her head thrown back as he slipped to his knees and started to tongue her, slow and hard. She doesn't say that she clenched her fists in his hair and moved his head with them the way she liked it, the way she moved his head only two days ago, in the hotel room, with Federico dead. She doesn't say that what she feels most strongly as this scene returns to her, other than a flush of sexual excitement she can hardly bear, is shame.

"I didn't tell anyone, you know," she says. She can't tell what he remembers. It's better that way, she thinks.

"No," says Giacomo. "I don't expect you did. Neither did I."

They are silent for a moment. Then Giacomo stands up and paces round the room, pushing his hair away from his forehead with both hands. When a mobile rings out, they both jump.

"It's mine," said Giacomo. "Relax." He takes the phone into the hall, where he can't be heard. It's Yvonne, thinks Helen, wondering where the hell he is. But Helen is wrong. When he comes back a few minutes later, he is smiling and shaking his head.

"I don't believe it. That was your father-in-law. He says he needs to talk to me. I can't imagine why, unless he wants to tell me off about being here with you."

"He's coming to the flat?"

"No. We're meeting at the hotel in half an hour. You can come if you like. That'll give him a surprise."

Helen pulls a face. "No," she says. "There are things I need to do."

"I'll call you later then?"

"Yes. Do that." When he glances at her, quizzically, she frowns. "I mean it," she says. "Don't let me down."

As soon as Giacomo has left, Helen goes into the bathroom and turns on the shower, adjusting the temperature of the water until it is almost cold. She takes off her clothes and steps into the cabinet with a sharp intake of breath as the jets hit her skin, then stands and lets her head take the force of it, enjoying the respite from the water's chill as the hair flattens slowly out and seals to her neck and shoulders like a cap. Lifting it from her face, she takes the sponge and soaks it beneath the jets, then squirts shower gel onto it and wipes herself down, her arms and shoulders and breasts, until her skin feels smooth. She lets the water carry away the scented foam, her eyes closed, her head tilted backwards so that the water is beating against her face, thinking, for the first time that day, of nothing. It is only when she steps from the shower and reaches for a towel that the image of Federico returns to her, as though she has stepped back into the world. She thinks of his rapid nervous fingers as he unbuttoned and buttoned her blouse, impatient, almost clumsy, the way he sometimes had of looking into Helen's eyes at the oddest moments, as if for reassurance.

Her body still damp, she puts on the robe that is hanging behind the door and walks across the wooden floor into the kitchen. She opens the fridge door and takes out a bottle of white wine, opening it and reaching for a glass. She carries them through to the living room. Putting them down on a small table beside the sofa, she crosses to the window, cautiously moving the light curtain that covers it until she can see down into the square. There seems to be no one there, other than a handful of tourists, people going about their business. The bar is open, as always, two small tables on the pavement outside. No TV vans, no cars of journalists, as far as she can tell. No one seems interested in her. She opens the window a little, to let in some air. She can hear the insect-like drone from above of a helicopter, another one or the same as the one she's been hearing for days, as though it were following her every move.

Stepping away from the window, Helen calls Giacomo, suddenly needing to hear him, but his phone is turned to voicemail. She hesitates before speaking, says "It's me," then ends the call. How she hates these things. Of course he will have turned it off, he'll be with Fausto. In a fit of irritation with herself for having called, she throws the phone onto the sofa, where it bounces on a cushion before falling to the floor. Oh God, she thinks, it's broken now. She picks it up, calls Giulia's landline without quite knowing what she'll say, relieved as it rings out to see that the phone still works, even more relieved when Giulia fails to answer. The woman will be about her business, as ever. She stares at her own house phone, silent, its calls being filtered for her protection. Giacomo closed the shutters and windows before leaving, against the heat. In the half-darkness, the flat has never seemed so empty. She sits down on the sofa, then snuggles into a corner, her arms around her knees, like someone waiting, and afraid.

Half an hour later, she wakes up with a start, her head full of confused images she can't quite grasp, Giulia and Federico, and Martha in a driver's uniform, her mad grey hair spilling out of her cap. She dresses, then goes through the drawer in which Federico kept his odds and ends, boarding cards, foreign coins, out-of-date passports. This is where he'll have put the key to his parents' flat. Two can play at this game, she thinks. She finds three bunches, a spare set for the car, a set she recognises as belonging to their weekend place down the coast and the third, on a simple ring, composed of a large key for an outer door, a security key and a Yale.

She is slipping them into her jacket pocket when her fingers touch the visiting card the magistrate gave her. She sits down with the telephone beside her, and dials the number on it.

Let's see what Giulia will make of this, she thinks, imagining a bored man in a room somewhere perking up and turning on his recording equipment.

"This is Helen Di Stasi," she says, when the call is answered. "I have an apology to make."

5

Turin, 1978

Giacomo left the flat at the beginning of February. He had a new girlfriend, a dark-haired, rather sombre woman from Florence called Stefania, who also worked in some undefined way at the faculty. Stefania had asked him to move in with her, and he'd bundled his books and clothes into his rucksack and disappeared from their lives as swiftly as he'd arrived, like a bird that had entered by one window and left by another. Helen missed him, and resented his absence. She was eager for news of the faculty, and of Giacomo, eager to learn more about Stefania, whom she'd met for no more than half an hour and wasn't sure she liked. But Federico had no gift, or inclination, for gossip. He was out most of the day; after dinner, which he prepared, they'd read together or go down below the flat for an ice cream. She was lonely, it struck her. After her lessons were over and she'd eaten some lunch in the flat, or a sandwich in a nearby bar, she took to walking around the centre in the afternoon, window-shopping, imagining different lives for herself, hanging around the shelves of the English bookshop in the hope that someone might strike up a conversation, startled and hostile if anyone did. That was when she'd spotted Giacomo in the street and followed him, and then he'd followed her, back to the flat and made love to her, only to disappear a second time, leaving his mark on her, she felt, the way a tomcat might have done. He left her feeling excited, and soiled. She'd never betrayed anyone before. She was glad he hardly ever came round to the flat any more. Sometimes she wondered what it must be like for Giacomo to work with Federico every day, in the same small room, and know what he'd done. It occurred to her once that he might have told Federico. Isn't that what men did together? Share their trophies? The awful thing was that she could imagine Giacomo telling him, perhaps as an act of bravado, as though she didn't matter, but not Federico's reaction. She had no idea what he might do. She told Miriam one evening in the pub; she'd drunk too much. Miriam laughed. "You don't need to worry about that," she said. "Better to have two irons in the fire than one." She giggled. "Especially if they're pokers." Helen wished she hadn't told her.

Later that week, Helen was half-asleep at the kitchen table with her teaching books strewn about her when Federico brought both Giacomo and Stefania home. He had a spit-roast chicken and potatoes from the *tavola calda* at the corner, like their first night together in the flat, when she and Federico had been alone. Giacomo had wine; Stefania a *tiramisu* she'd made herself; it looked as though the evening had been planned. Helen pushed her books to one side, uncomfortable, letting herself be kissed by all three of them as she struggled to wake up properly. By the end of the evening, when they were all quite drunk and talking, as always, about what she called, in letters home, "the Italian situation", she'd managed to relax enough to take a liking to Stefania, and even feel a little sorry for her. It couldn't be easy to be in love with Giacomo, she thought. She wondered how many other women he'd fucked in kitchens when their boyfriends were out. She had a twinge of jealousy, not of Stefania, but of these other women he might have had. Helen was shopping for food one afternoon soon after that, when a crackling voice came over the supermarket loudspeaker system. She never listened to these voices; she could rarely understand them through the interference and, when she did, they were calling people who worked there to the telephone. She stood in the queue to pay for her bread and wine and onions, working out what they would cost and counting out the money, as the voice droned on. The message was longer than usual. Before it was over, the woman at the till stood up and slammed the cash drawer shut with a bitter laugh, and an "I-told-you-so" toss of the head. Helen mumbled something, her basket in her hand, as the woman scooped up her handbag from beneath the till. She looked at Helen with a disbelieving air.

"*Non hai capito niente?*" she said. "*Hanno rapito Moro.*"

"*Cosa?*" What hadn't she understood? What or who was Moro? Raped? Did *rapito* mean raped?

The woman gave an exasperated sigh and began to unbutton her overall. Her purple top beneath was shot with silver threads, the kind of top Helen might have expected to see in a disco. She was old enough to be Helen's mother.

"*Sciopero,*" she said. "*Capisci sciopero?*"

Of course Helen understood *sciopero*. She heard the word every day at Fiat; she saw it in banner headlines at newsstands and taped onto tram stops to general exasperation; the personnel manager who'd prepared her contract had said that people on *sciopero* should be shot. *Sciopero* was strike.

Looking around, she saw the other customers abandon their baskets and trolleys and walk towards the doors. The scene reminded her of a Fifties sci-fi film, one of those alien take-overs in Middle America; an invasion of colonising implants triggered by a recorded voice, their host bodies snatched and carted away. Only her foreignness or ignorance of the language had saved her. Still, she hurried to join the others, to blend in among them, invisible, as they wound among the shelves and filled the aisles and streamed towards the exits.

Half an hour later, the entire city seemed to have come to a halt. Helen went home and waited for Federico. In the meantime she looked up *rapito* in her dictionary and found that it did mean rape, but in the old sense, as in rape of the Sabine women: kidnapped. But who or what was Moro? Her dictionary said "Moor", but also "dark".

When Federico burst in, she'd been back at the flat for over an hour, unable to concentrate on anything, wishing they had a television, listening to the radio without understanding more than a few words at a time, as though she'd just arrived. So many names that meant nothing to her, so many acronyms, so much anger. Federico had a newspaper, literally hot off the press; his hands had blurred the headline. He threw it on the table. "It's started," he said. "Get your coat."

"What's started? Who is this Moro man?"

"Aldo Moro. He's one of the top men in the Christian Democrats," Federico said. He whistled, then picked up the paper and slapped it against the table. "It says here it was the Red Brigades."

"Oh my God," said Helen, shocked. "They murdered his bodyguards." She was looking at a black-bordered row of photographs, mug shots of young men, with their ranks and ages beside the names, the kind of faces she saw outside the Fiat gates every day.

They spent the rest of the day with colleagues of Federico who had a television, watching interviews with Moro's associates, members of the opposition, figures from the church and the three major unions, which had declared a general strike. Helen stared at Moro's face for the first time; she'd never noticed him before. She still wasn't sure who he was, nor why he mattered. What she saw was the face of a weary, cynical patrician, ascetic and long-suffering, clearly no fool; the face of a man who'd seen too much human weakness to be surprised; he looked more like a cardinal than a politician. The journalist announced that he was being held in a people's prison. A prison run by the people, she thought. That's new, outside China. By the people, for the people. Which people? Who decides? She couldn't understand the mood of those around her: exalted by what was happening, at moments almost jubilant; when there was anger or contempt, it seemed to be directed less at the kidnappers and murderers, as she saw them, than at the government. She didn't have the confidence to question this; she questioned herself instead – perhaps she had missed something. Giacomo and Stefania weren't there; she imagined them sitting in front of a different television, in another room, in the same inexplicable city.

When she and Federico were in bed that night, unable to sleep, she asked him where he'd been that morning. He raised both hands in the air, letting his book fall to the sheet, and grinned. "It wasn't me," he said.

Helen arrived at Fiat the next day to be told there was a letter waiting for her from the security office. It said she should no longer accept lifts from Fiat employees, who were regarded as particularly at risk in the current climate of political unrest. Fiat would not be held responsible for her should anything happen. The language was formal, opaque. She read it out to her students to make sure she'd understood. They laughed nervously and told her it was just a precaution. There was nothing to worry about, they said. When she showed it to Eduardo later that day, he sighed.

"Why have they kidnapped Aldo Moro?" she asked him.

He was on the point of answering, but stopped himself, then shrugged.

"This is not your struggle," he said. "You should go."

A few days later, Helen heard from Miriam about a Scottish woman she'd made friends with, a teacher from one of the language schools she'd dropped into when she'd first arrived, in search of work. The woman's flatmate had been arrested, and was awaiting trial, for terrorism. The woman, whose name was Katy, had let herself into his bedroom and burnt the books and leaflets that might have incriminated him, badges with Che Guevara on them, Little Red Books, absurd things really, the trinkets of revolt. Then Katy was arrested too, for having lent her car to someone who had raided a bank. Federico and Helen tried to get into the police station to see her, but it was hopeless. Federico lost his temper, called the police fascists and dogs. He was dragged away, but released that afternoon. Stefania gave them the name of a feminist lawyer who said she'd do what she could. Federico promised her money, all the money that might be needed, and the lawyer had looked at him as if to say, Well yes, you surely don't expect her to be released without money, while Helen wondered what he meant. They had no money. Katy, in the meantime, had denied all knowledge of the bank raid, as she would, whatever the truth might have been. Released without being charged, her hair cut short, she claimed to have been raped by the police. All the fun had been knocked out of her, all the desire; she flinched when anyone touched or tried to comfort her. She spoke about leaving, about going back to England, until things cooled down. Two days later, Stefania drove her to the station, then came back to Helen's flat, unable to calm down. The Moro business scared her, she said. It was all too much, too soon. The kidnap was factional, divisive. There was no support for it among the masses. The masses didn't care. Helen wondered how Stefania knew all this and what it meant to say *too soon*. Was that what it was, a question of timing? Stefania sat in Helen's kitchen, hunched over the radio as if for warmth, listening to bulletins with scorn on her face.

Helen couldn't believe that Katy had been involved, but the man who told her what had happened, a colleague from the school she'd bumped into while shopping at the same supermarket as before, said she shouldn't be so sure. Someone else she'd heard about, but not met, an older man from another language school, had simply disappeared, the colleague told her.

No one's immune, he said, as though the spores of violence were in the air and could settle on anyone. She felt as though what she'd seen at first as simple numbers was breaking up and taking physical form in some way she couldn't understand, becoming faces, names, affections. By now there were people she knew on both sides of the barriers, wherever they were drawn. A woman in the grocer's said the government was holding Moro prisoner in a cellar near where she lived, and nobody seemed surprised, as though any absurdity were permissible.

She woke one morning with the face of Moro in her dream, his drawn sad face, weary with suffering and disbelief. She wanted to say this can't be right, but wasn't sure who would listen. She didn't mention the dream to Federico. That was the day the papers had photographs of the man in his shirt-sleeves, brutalised, the Red Brigades symbol at his back, as proof that he was still alive. There was the face she had dreamed, on every front page in Italy.

A week after that, she found herself on a demonstration against police brutality, shouting out slogans with the best of them.

When Giacomo and Stefania dropped in one evening, she told him she thought the whole business was shameful. Federico and Stefania had left the kitchen to talk about work; they were sitting in the room that Giacomo had used, now Federico's study. Helen and Giacomo had opened the final bottle of wine. "I don't see why the government can't just buy them off," she said, pouring it into their tumblers. "To save his life. They could always deny it later."

"All right, Helen. Let me tell you something you don't know. Nobody in Italy wants Aldo Moro alive, except his wife and children. The people who've kidnapped him probably care more about his state of health than the people in his own party. Nothing would suit them better than to have him dead. He's a liability, Helen."

"You don't know that," she said, but she knew he'd won. It wasn't just knowing more, though that was part of it. It was the fact that he knew what he knew, no more no less. She thought his sort of clarity was despicable if what he knew was wrong, but she wasn't sure it was. Nothing she thought made her feel better, or less confused. "He wouldn't have been running the party if they hadn't thought he was the right man."

"Don't be naïve, Helen."

"Why is any opinion that isn't yours naïve?" She was angry, but also elated. Arguing with Giacomo wasn't like arguing with Federico, who listened to her and then corrected some small error, so that by the end of it she'd forget what her point had been. Giacomo was broad strokes, theatre.

"Well, obviously," he said, with a taunting grin. "Because it isn't mine."

"And what is your opinion?"

"About what?"

"I don't know," she said. "About Aldo Moro?"

"You want to know my opinion?" He made the word sound opportunistic. "All right, I'll tell you. My opinion is that Aldo Moro isn't a man at all, not in any meaningful way. He isn't anything. Come on, you've read Barthes. He's an empty signifier, a box you can change the label on to suit whatever you put into it, or whatever you want the buyer to think might be in it. He's a martyr, so stick on the martyr label, he's the man who invented the historic compromise, so call him a statesman. He's a builder of bridges, a saint, a sinner, a strategist, a bargaining counter, a corpse. He's whatever you want. That's what makes this kidnapping so fascinating in its way, and so ambivalent."

"And Moro the man? The husband? The father?"

"Is insignificant. Like you. Like me. You don't really think we matter, do you?" He paused to light a cigarette. "Life goes on, Helen." For a moment, as he held the smoke deep in his lungs, his face looked tragic, another expression that suited it. "They'll have to kill him, of course."

6

After she has made her phone call, Helen leaves the flat. Her car, a yellow Smart, is parked on the Lungotevere. The last time she drove, it strikes her as she pulls out into the traffic, Federico was at work. He'd asked her to bring him some files he'd left on his desk at home, just over a week ago now. She'd been angry; she couldn't understand why he hadn't sent someone over to pick them up. He couldn't do that, he'd explained, the files weren't strictly connected with the ministry. It would have been an abuse of his position to occupy the time of someone employed by the state on a personal matter. She'd have liked to say she was busy, her life was too full, but she'd been watching a DVD Martin had lent her, of Buster Keaton shorts; she'd been curled up on the sofa with a bottle of iced tea and some imported ginger nuts. She hates driving through the centre of Rome, she'd resented every minute of it. She wonders now, with something like rage, why she didn't open the files and look inside. The thought never arose, as though nothing they might have contained could provide her with fuel to melt the iciness that Federico's distance, Federico's mission, had created within her. As though she had no right to know, or care; her role was to fetch and carry, and open the wine for the world as it passed through his life, to which she was a mere accessory. Or maybe Giulia was right, she's never really cared about Federico's work. She's let herself be sidelined so easily these past few years. All it took was a word from Federico that something wouldn't interest her and she'd nod and turn elsewhere for her entertainment; over-priced packets of biscuits she had to hide in her desk drawers, *CSI*, silent comedy. Giacomo. When, all the time, she might have had the answer to her questions in four green A4 files, flung on the seat beside her. If she had cared to look.

She lets her speed be dictated by the cars around her, shoulders hunched forward as though she were carrying a secret parcel on her lap. Her eyes are fixed on the car in front of her, a pale green Panda, as she goes with the flow along the Lungotevere towards Ponte Milvio. The car is moving faster now, the set-back arches of Ponte Milvio to her left, lights glinting from the hill beyond, Fleming no more than fifteen minutes away if the traffic doesn't get any worse. She'll soon be there. For a moment, she asks herself what she expects to find, assuming the flat is empty. If it isn't, she'll have to face Giulia. She'd turn back if she could and drive home, but by the time she's almost reached the bridge and that's possible she's changed her mind again. She feels the nagging onset of a headache. The Panda has been replaced by a group of teenagers on scooters, hilarious and unpredictable, helmet straps swinging as they swerve together and then apart. She'd better concentrate. The scooters pull off as she slows down and swings round to the right. Moments later she's crossing the Tiber, then turning right and heading up into Fleming.

She hates this part of Rome, its Sixties apartment blocks squatting like toads on the sides of the hill and narrow, winding roads lined with expensive cars. Federico used to say he'd rather die than live here, surrounded by its smug monocultural values, though not when his parents were within earshot. And so she's reminded again.

Five minutes later, she finds a place to park and pulls up fifty yards from their building. From the car, she calls her in-laws' landline once again, her nails tapping out their impatient tune on the steering wheel as the call tone rings out, unanswered. Fausto, she supposes, is still with Giacomo; the risk is Giulia. Shifting her jacket, she takes the bunch of keys from the pocket, slipping them onto her finger by the ring and clasping them to her palm as though they need to be hidden, or protected. She doesn't want to have to stand in the street and draw attention to herself by searching for them.

The foyer is empty. She waits for the lift, staring as she always does at the printed mural, an eighteenth century scene of the Tiber, bucolic, blown up to fit the wall. A row of large-leaved plants, overwatered and yellowing, stands by her side in a cast-iron trough.

The flat is dark, the shutters wound down against the summer heat. Helen goes straight to Giulia's room, at the end of the corridor. The top of the desk is empty apart from a laptop, which Helen turns on, and a fax. She waits for the laptop to boot up, her hands on the polished green leather surface, looking at the door and then around the walls, at the bookcases and photographs, framed in black, of Giulia and famous people she's known or met. Khrushchev. Picasso. Jimmy Carter and his wife. Popes. Wojtyla. Luciani. How odd, she thinks, that Italians always call Popes by their surnames, as though they were butchers. Others she doesn't recognise. Giulia is in all of them, never smiling, except on one with Federico, when he was made a *Cavaliere del Lavoro*. This is the only photograph of Federico. She was thrilled to bits, you could see that. Helen was there as well, behind him and his parents, slightly turned away from the lens, as though she'd been on her way to somewhere else.

Giulia's laptop is running Windows 95. Giulia is famously dismissive of technology, but she's clearly become attached to this small laptop, some years old now and surprisingly heavy as Helen adjusts it a little to suit her position. She opens Word. The documents have names that mean nothing to her, dates she doesn't know. Some of the files are so small she wonders what they might contain. She clicks on one, at random, and finds herself staring at a blank page. She tries another file, with the same result. Juggernaut, she thinks. The empty file of Juggernaut. Of course. What did Giacomo say about someone cancelling what the file contained out of ignorance? Giulia doesn't know how to delete files. She imagines the stiff old woman, sitting there with her finger on the delete button, patiently watching her son's words being eaten away.

She pulls open the central drawer. Scissors, a stapler, a bottle of correction fluid, some drawing pins in a small glass jar. A stack of cards with Giulia's name and *Senato della Repubblica* written underneath. She opens one of the side drawers. This is full of files: green A4 files like the ones Helen ferried across Rome. She lifts out the top one to find that it contains clippings from newspapers, as does the one below. Beneath this file is a stack of paper sheets attached by a paper clip. She catches her breath when she sees Federico's characteristic use of Courier. She picks the stack up and begins to read.

```
The first mention of the Juggernaut was in the
journal of Odoric. "At every yearly feast of the
idol, the king and queen, and the multitude of the
people, and all the pilgrims assemble themselves,
and placing the idol in a most stately and rich
chariot, they carry him out of their temple with
songs, and with all kind of musical harmony,
and a great company of virgins go procession-
wise singing before him. Many pilgrims also put
themselves under the chariot wheels: and all
they over whom the chariot runneth are crushed
in pieces, and divided asunder in the midst, and
slain right out. Yea, and in doing this, they
think themselves to die most holily and securely,
in the service of their god."
```

Juggernaut is any literal or metaphorical force regarded as unstoppable; any force that will crush all in its path. If you Google the word, you'll find it's associated with something incapable, in the final resort, of listening to what lies beneath it. But the word itself comes from the Sanskrit term Jagannatha, "Lord of the universe", one of the names of Krishna.

There's a class of words known as antagonyms, words that mean both themselves and their opposites. Overlook is one of these words, as is anabasis, or cleave. Juggernaut is also a kind of antagonym, not only destructive, but also a force for the good; not only the image of Krishna, beneath whose wheels his acolytes crush themselves, but also the name of Krishna, lord protector of the world. Juggernaut is both power and sacrifice.

Maybe nothing exists without self-contradiction. Peace-keeping missions. Friendly fire. Sacrifice itself is a word that unsettles. It's a word that asks us questions we aren't prepared to answer. Still, it's not to be denigrated, the afterlife of the martyr.

Helen's hands are shaking as she reads. Can this really be what he was writing for the conference? It isn't Federico's style at all. She turns over a couple of pages and reads again.

not all to feel guilty about. I used to think I'd confess to Giacomo that he was jailed in my place, that one word from me, one gesture, and he'd have been released. But I didn't have the courage. And then, when I did have the courage, I saw that it would deprive him of what he most valued, his

notoriety. It would turn him into a victim, even
worse, my victim. I never told Helen for the
same reason; she always needed an excuse to
respect Giacomo. My father knew; he'd never
have fought for Giacomo's pardon otherwise.
That's when my father stopped worshipping me.
He thinks it was before, when I was on the
other side, but it wasn't. He respected me
then.

And now I've told my mother what I intend
to do, in a moment's weakness, because I was
scared, and I know she assumes, because what
other explanation can there be, that I'm
delirious, insane. She thinks it's the illness
talking, not her son. Perhaps it is.

How many secrets are there, she wonders, appalled. Is it
true that I need an excuse to respect Giacomo? What did
he mean by that? Often she's felt more respect for Giacomo
than for Federico. She's respected his flair and energy, the
largesse of him, seen them as implicit criticism of Federico's
cautious, scrupulous approach to life. She's seen him as
bountiful and Federico as penny-pinching. She's continued
to desire him after her desire for Federico dwindled to
almost nothing.

And this talk of illness. What illness?

She turns to another page.

days, I look at Helen as she talks to me
and I see her lips moving and she might be
laughing or anxious or angry about something.
And I want to tell her what I feel but I
have no words for it that she'll understand.
Because I don't trust her anymore, or she

doesn't trust me. I can't tell which came
first. We no longer have the words. We babble
to each other.

When you say you trust someone what you're
saying is that you share a language, you have a
language in common and can use it, not always
or even necessarily to tell the truth, because
even within trust there are secrets, but to
be with that person, as much to commune as to
communicate. Conversely, the loss of trust is the
loss of that language you share. You watch the
other person speak, you watch the movement of
their lips, with love perhaps, with bemusement,
with anger or irritation. But who or what that
person is or believes or needs is beyond you,
mysterious, and finally less than mysterious;
without interest. It's like an aphasia of the
soul. After a while you cease to listen to the
noise the person makes. But I can't believe that
this should be the case with Helen.

And if it is, how far am I responsible? How
far is my silence responsible? Speaking to Martin
the other night I almost told him, but something
stopped me. Respect for Helen? Perhaps. I'm filled
with doubt. Besides, Martin

This is the worst, Helen thinks, this is the worst since he died.
It can't get any worse than now. But to have him speak to her
like this and to have no way of saying that she is sorry, and that
she doesn't understand, and that whatever he might have told
her she would have heard if she'd known. If she'd only known.
This is the worst.

7

Giacomo and Fausto are sitting in the bar of the hotel, while Yvonne sulks in their air-conditioned room on the fifth floor, "Please Do Not Disturb" in five languages, including Arabic and Japanese, dangling from the door. Giacomo hadn't expected to find her there and suggested she go back to Paris alone, not only because he doesn't want to leave Rome, or Helen, but to see if she will actually go without being taken. She's a hopeless traveller, or pretends to be, constantly losing small articles of clothing and needing them to be retrieved, always without the right amount of change in the appropriate currency; although the Euro, bless its otherwise unlovely heart, has put paid to that, at least between Paris and Rome. But she shrugged and pouted and said he only wanted to get rid of her.

He was surprised to get the call from Fausto, but not for long. He's always respected Fausto and the fact that he knows the respect isn't mutual has given his own respect for the older man an unselfish, ethical aura, reflecting well on him and giving him a sort of advantage. And he's grateful for the way Fausto assisted in his defence from the pulpit of more than one newspaper, not to speak of strings he must have pulled behind the scenes. It's good to see the old man again, Giacomo acknowledges to himself, magnanimous in victory, curious to see what role he might still have. There's nothing sadder than someone whose power to influence events has been wrested from him, thinks Giacomo, who can only imagine this appalling fate. Of course, there are ways and ways, he knows that. He's been quoted as saying that, in politics, there are buccaneers and there are bookkeepers. Giacomo, despite his ever more sensible and pondered manner, his handmade shoes and tailored suits, his wasted hours in airport lounges and at meetings, is convinced that he's still a buccaneer. Fausto, in his own way, has also played a reckless, even dangerous game: partisan, prison, internal exile. And now, sitting opposite Giacomo in the bar of this luxury hotel, he is talking about the moral question, an expression Giacomo has almost forgotten, and Giacomo is trying to concentrate.

"Federico knew he was running risks, of course," says Fausto, shaking his head. "But we never imagined this, this moral desert."

"Risks," repeats Giacomo, lost for a moment.

"It wasn't a political appointment. But he was expected to do something that mattered, not only by the minister, but by the people who knew him, who knew what he really wanted to do."

"And the minister pulled one way and Federico pulled the other? That was inevitable, surely? Did you see the point of what he was doing?"

"I mean," says Fausto stiffly, "that everything he tried to do was in vain. The practice of government in this country is nothing but shameless self-interest."

Well, yes, thinks Giacomo, but how surprising is that? How new? Your lot managed to stay in opposition for forty years and, as soon as they had the chance to govern, you and a bunch of others got on your ideological high horses and rode off. You pulled out in time. Now you complain about other people's low moral standards. You never had the chance to be corrupted. You never had anything to sell. And that's what the practice of government is. And that's why I've always stood outside, deliberately. But he doesn't say any of this, partly out of pity, but primarily because it's all been said before. He has the feeling that Fausto, too, is talking for the sake of it, talking until something that actually matters can be slipped in as secondary. Fausto pauses, resting his squat liver-spotted hands on the low table between them, the hands of a worker; although Fausto, to Giacomo's knowledge, has wielded nothing heavier than a pen since the war. Strong, small hands, like paws, on the gleaming wood.

"I think he was going mad," says Fausto, almost in a whisper. "These last few months."

"Yes," says Giacomo, relieved that the purpose of their conversation has finally been broached. "I think so too."

"What did he say to you?" says Fausto.

"All kinds of things. We didn't actually talk, but he sent me emails, text messages. He said we were governed by forces that have nothing to do with politics, that would never be understood. It was madness to think we had control over them in any rational sense."

Fausto nods, apparently reassured, eager to confide in Giacomo now that his doubts about Federico have been confirmed. "Yes, yes, that's exactly the sort of thing he said to me. Forces. Dark forces. He called them dark forces. I didn't know what he meant at first. I thought it was some sort of metaphor for, I don't know, globalisation, the free market. I never for a moment imagined he thought the forces were real. He looked so ill. These last few months, he'd lost weight. I don't think he was eating, though Helen didn't seem to notice. He talked about the need for sacrifice, you know; I don't know what he meant, some final sacrifice. Isn't public service sacrifice enough? He couldn't even move without bodyguards." Fausto shakes his head, helpless. "I went into his office one day and he was sitting there with a bowl of crystals. He had his hands in it, playing with them. I couldn't believe my eyes. He looked across at me and said he was absorbing their auras. I was absolutely dumbfounded. 'Are you sure you're all right?' I said, and he started laughing. 'Don't worry, Dad,' he said. 'I'm not completely mad.' He pushed the bowl to one side and started talking about something else, something serious. I didn't know what to make of it. I still don't." He crouches forward, stares intensely into Giacomo's face. "Did he talk about crystals to you?"

"No," says Giacomo. He picks up his empty coffee cup and uses his spoon to scrape out the dark brown crust of sugar at the bottom. "Didn't Nero play with crystals?" he says. "Crystals, precious stones? He said it relaxed him. They are believed to have curative powers, aren't they? Perhaps that's why Federico was doing it: to relax."

"Did he mention the conference in these messages he sent?"

"Not really, no."

"He told me he was working on something that would make everyone sit up. He said it would end the war."

"You don't know what?"

Fausto shakes his head in a hopeless, exhausted way. This odd, earnest, loveable little man, thinks Giacomo, who has wasted his whole life on a futile quest for utopia, who still, in his bones, believes in Marx and the Marxist dream though he's learnt not to say so and prefers to talk of social democracy like everyone else. This decent little man – with his paw-like worker's hands and his squared-off pugnacious bullock-like build continues to worship the notion of social perfectibility, in spite of Auschwitz and Buchenwald and the gulags and Hungary and Gaza and 9/11 and Madrid, in spite of the fact that the bigger the dream the greater the toll of the dead – continues to worship rationality and safety nets for redundant workers and the movement to stop the war, while the country he's fought for, and been imprisoned by, and been prepared to die for, goes down the plughole.

And now, as Giacomo watches him run his fingers through his stiff white hair in a sudden intensely upsetting gesture of desperation, so that Giacomo wants to comfort him in some way, Fausto cries out, his voice trembling: "Why did they kill him? Why did they have to kill Federico? Do you know why? It makes no sense." He looks at Giacomo, eyes wet with tears. "You don't know, do you? You'd tell me?"

Giacomo shakes his head.

"All I know is that there's something fishy about this whole business." With Fausto in front of him, about to weep, he can't bring himself to say the word *murder*. "It's the kind of thing that used to go on in the Seventies, in my day, not now. The world's moved on. And yet someone's done this here and now, this stupid brutal thing, and it's in no one's interests at all: it's pointless, anachronistic. It doesn't solve anything." Giacomo lifts his empty hands, exasperated. "It isn't even terrorism. Who's terrorised? Who's threatened, apart from a handful of civil servants and academics? They've simply destroyed a life for some trivial political vendetta. Terrorism's moved on. It hits the innocent. That's how things work now. Hasn't anybody told them?" He pauses. "Don't ask me who did it. I wish I knew."

Fausto is too emotional to speak.

"I'm sorry," says Giacomo, taking pity. He should have kept his mouth shut. "There's no justification for what's been done."

They are both about to stand up when Giacomo reaches across and touches Fausto's arm.

"Can I ask you a question?" he says. "It's something that's been bothering me for years."

Fausto sits back in the chair.

"Everything you did to get me released from jail, my pardon. I've always known you didn't like me. There was no reason why you should. I know you thought I was a bad influence on Federico. But I didn't know then how many strings you'd pulled for me. I only found out later, after the pardon came through, when I was in France. I'm grateful, of course," he says as the old man's face sets into a look of irritation, almost anger. "But I don't know why you went to so much trouble."

"I don't believe anybody should be jailed for crimes of opinion," says Fausto stiffly, the stress falling, unflatteringly, on anybody.

Giacomo smiles. "Well, that's noble. But that isn't why I was jailed." He leans forward, abruptly serious, his hand once again on Fausto's arm. "Don't you remember? I was charged with conspiracy to murder. Possession of firearms. I was charged with having taken part in a bank raid during which two people died. They said I'd stolen a car that was used in a kneecapping episode. The irony is that none of it was true in material terms. What I mean to say is that I may have done these things, or similar things, on other occasions. But not on those occasions. I don't know who it was who did it. But it wasn't me."

"You didn't say this at the trial."

"I didn't say anything at the trial. I was a political prisoner, remember? None of us did. We were pledged to silence. How annoying we must have been."

"You were treated unjustly," insists Fausto, red in the face, inexplicably furious.

Giacomo nods. You aren't going to tell me, he thinks. He watches the old man leave the hotel, then sits down again and thinks of Helen. He wants to call her, hear her voice, but something tells him to wait. She'll call him when she needs him. Yvonne finds Giacomo in the hotel lounge, his feet on the low table in front of him, his shoes kicked off beside them. He is watching television. He has been alone for almost two hours, although she doesn't know this and would be furious if she were told. He smiles at her and lifts a hand, as if he expects it to be kissed. What he actually intends to do is guide her down into the seat beside him, a gesture so cavalierly inappropriate, given her evident rage, that he lets the hand fall immediately.

Taking his feet off the table, he slips on his shoes, then pats a plump little cushion beside his leg. He parodies the face of a child caught out in some mischief, pretending to be contrite, but Yvonne isn't amused. She stands beside the overstuffed divan, her neat foot tapping the marble, until he speaks.

"Calm down," he says.

"I'm perfectly calm. I'm leaving."

"Leaving what?" he says. He can't help it, he loves a risk.

"Don't tempt me, Jacques." She uses the French version of his name, which he hates, playing with the clasp on her bag, clicking it open, clicking it shut. "I've told the man at the desk to send someone to pick up my luggage and arrange for it to be taken to the airport. Now I expect you, or someone else, I don't really care who does it, to change my flight."

"You can't go now," says Giacomo, grinning. "You'll miss the reception. You know how much you want to press the flesh of Mr Bush. Besides, things are just beginning to get exciting." He points towards the television screen. With obvious reluctance, Yvonne turns her head. What she sees is a woman dressed in black, in late middle age, screaming and waving her fist at the camera as it backs away. She wrinkles her nose with distaste.

"You know who this is, don't you?"

"Some dreadful peasant," sniffs Yvonne.

"On the contrary, she's the mother of Federico's driver, the one that was shot. She's accusing the government of his death. She says it was all a plot. Her son had already warned her something like this might happen. There'd been talk at the ministry. Voices in corridors, and car parks presumably."

"Only in Italy," says Yvonne.

"Well, naturally, a government as blameless as the one you have in France wouldn't dirty its hands with anything as sordid and demeaning as murder." He shudders.

"France is *civilised*," says Yvonne, incensed. "That may not seem much to you, Jacques, as an *Italian*, but those who are born and bred in France know how to appreciate it. It's in the air we breathe."

"I don't believe it." Giacomo rubs his hands together in a parody of glee. "We seem to be about to have a political argument. Of a sort."

"You amuse yourself," says Yvonne, with hauteur. "No one else."

The screaming woman has been replaced on the screen by a man with the melancholy face of a clown.

"He's one of the PM's right-hand men," says Giacomo. "Ex-communist, apparently. Priceless, isn't it?"

When Yvonne comes down with her case twenty minutes later, Giacomo is fast asleep on the same sofa. Someone has turned the sound off but the news is still on and she sees the face of her husband's dead friend, his hair too long, at some meeting or other. She wonders what he saw in Helen. The taxi arrives before she has a chance to wake Giacomo and tell him what she thinks of him, which is probably just as well.

8

Helen has left her car in Via Giulia and is walking without any clear sense or purpose, walking in a way that is as close to running as she can manage without drawing attention to herself. She walks beneath her building, but doesn't go in. No one in the street below is waiting, no journalists, no cameras, and this surprises her, but also leaves her with a sense of loss she can't explain to herself without feeling uncomfortable, as though she needs the attention of the world to still have Federico belong to her. Without it, she's on her own.

She sees a group of teenagers tapping in text messages a dozen yards ahead of her as she strides across the square and down to the Lungotevere, sweating a little because the air is still warm this late in the evening and she is moving more quickly than she normally does alone; alone, she likes to dawdle, observe, eavesdrop. Sometimes she finds herself adjusting her step to that of a couple talking half a yard in front of her, to hear what they might be saying, almost unaware of what she is doing. She has heard extraordinary things like this, intimate things, and told them to Federico that same evening, amused to see his shock. "People don't talk like that," he'd said once when she'd told him about a conversation she'd overheard between lovers, about what they'd do to his wife, to her husband, if they had the chance, appalling forms of torture that sent the couple into fits of laughter until they became aware of Helen, staring into a shop window, her shoulder almost touching the shoulder of the man; aware that she too was laughing. "You've got no idea what people say," she said. "You spend too much time at your desk." Will she ever have that kind of conversation with Giacomo, she wonders. Whenever he enters her head, he comes in company; he comes with a sense of guilt she can't shake off.

She stands at the top of the steps that lead down to the river, hesitating. This is the walk she has taken with Federico a hundred times, heading west towards the sea as the river does, not only on summer evenings like this one, but whenever they needed to get out, when his work was going badly or she needed comfort for some disappointment: a friend's disloyalty, a contract falling through. It was always empty at night, which was what he loved, the silence apart from the low rush of the water, the patches of darkness, the feel of the stone and short uncared-for grass underfoot. They would walk without talking until things fell back into place.

Now though, alone, she has no desire to be alone. The papers are in her bag, but she can't bear to look at them again, not yet; perhaps she never will be able to. She walks a hundred yards or so, then turns back towards the centre, down Via Arenula towards Largo Argentina. She is trying not to think, but can't; trying only makes it worse. She can't not think about what she has read, and what Federico meant. Because she is no longer sure of anything. When a police car goes past, its siren blazing, followed by a dark blue van and a second car, she finds herself on the brink of tears.

At Largo Argentina, she waits for the traffic to let her through then stops beside the wall. She stares down into the brightly illuminated ruins to watch the cats preen and sleep, as close to the heat of the spotlights as they can get.

"Hello."

Startled, defensive, ready to snub whoever has interrupted her thoughts, she turns and sees Martin beside her, in his old cream suit and panama, for all the world like someone out of a film. He is with that friend of his, the bookseller. The one she calls the Sad Man.

"Hello," she says back, relieved. She leans forward to be kissed by Martin, then gives the other man her hand. He takes it, gives it a brief shake, looking uncomfortable. "I'm so sorry about your husband," he says, then looks at Martin. "I'd better be off." Before either of them has a chance to speak, he has gone.

"He's probably the last person I spoke to while Federico was still alive," she says, watching him as he hurries away. She can't get over the sense of fracture, the before and after of it all.

"Should you be out like this?"

"I'd go mad in the house."

"You haven't been by yourself?"

"Giacomo stayed," she says. She will tell him what she has found, she decides, but not yet. First, she would like a drink. "You didn't come round, did you? I thought you might."

Martin shakes his head.

"Giulia found us in bed this morning," she says. To her surprise, her voice comes out over-loud and on the edge of breaking. She doesn't know whether she wants to giggle or cry. I'm hysterical, she notes. I can't go on like this.

"In bed?"

"Together. We hadn't done anything, honestly, but she doesn't know that. Now she thinks I'm a whore, on top of everything else."

Martin takes her elbow. "You need a drink, my dear," he says. His voice is slightly slurred, she wonders how long he's been drinking. She realises she has just told Martin that she and Giacomo have slept together, and feels relief. Martin is her oldest friend in Rome, which makes him her oldest friend in the world apart from Giacomo, and friend's not the word for what Giacomo is, though she can't think of any other, whatever word Giulia might choose. She lets him lead her back towards the river, turning left into the road that will take her to her own house. More police – *carabinieri*, this time – are standing in a small group at the corner. She wants to point them out to Martin, to see if he's also noticed how many armed men are out this evening. But almost at once he is guiding her into the back room of a bar she's never used, where Martin is clearly known. They sit down at a table in the corner, Martin taking off his hat and placing it on the chair beside him, Helen wondering if he'll be driving home to his place near Latina that night or staying in Rome. He's in no condition to drive, she thinks, as he orders a bottle of prosecco for them both. Perhaps she should offer him a bed. Then Giulia can find her with another man.

"How are you feeling?" he says, patting her hand.

Before, she's bridled at this question, but with Martin it's different. She thinks for a moment before she speaks. "I wish I knew. It's so hard to know what to say. I don't want to sound too brave, or too pathetic. Half the time I feel numb, which makes it worse when I think about him and the pain comes back." She pulls a face and watches him fill their glasses. "I'll survive."

"It won't be easy. But you don't need me to tell you that."

"What's worse is that I feel I'm losing him all over again."

"How's that?"

"That last evening," Helen says, "when you came round for dinner and I went to bed early, do you remember? You stayed for ages after I'd gone. I lay there. I could hear your voices, but not what you were saying. I asked Federico what you'd been talking about the next morning, but he wouldn't say. It was so unlike him. Sometimes he wakes me up, you know, to tell me what's been said. He was strange, I don't know, cagey." Her voice is urgent.

"Surely not," says Martin. But she doesn't believe him. He's lying too.

"What do you know about this conference?" she says. "Is that what it is, Martin? Is that what he was hiding? He was up to something, wasn't he?" She pauses. "I've found this thing he was writing, called Juggernaut."

Martin looks relieved – she wonders why – and shakes his head. "I've no idea, Helen. He didn't mention the conference to me that evening. I don't know what he had in mind. I imagine it was just a conference." After an awkward pause, he adds: "Juggernaut, did you say? That doesn't sound like Federico."

"It doesn't, does it?" she says. "Fausto says he was planning some surprise. I suppose he may have been. He didn't say anything to me." She hears the hurt in her voice and stops, then empties her glass. After a moment, she starts talking again, as Martin fills both glasses up. "Do you think he ever slept with anyone else?" she asks Martin. "Apart from me?"

Martin waves the bottle towards the bar in a plaintive fashion. "I don't know," he says slowly. "I don't have any reason to think he did."

"I know men talk about these things," she says, although she can't see Martin and Federico sharing that kind of intimacy, if that is what it is. She can't imagine intimacy between men somehow. Was Federico ever intimate with Giacomo? Did they talk about me? What on earth would they have said?

"Because I have," she says. She is close to tears, with relief and shame. She looks away when the barman brings over the bottle and opens it with an ironic flourish. Martin waves him off before he can fill their glasses. "I've been an awful wife," she says. Martin reaches over to stroke her arm, embarrassed, knocking over her glass. He is sweeping the prosecco off the table with the flat of his hand when she says, "I feel I've let everyone down. I've always wanted to do the right thing and I've never really had any idea what that was. Not really. I've just flopped round from one thing to another. I've never really been convinced by anything I've done, whether it was the right thing or not. Is that normal? Not to be convinced? I've let people tell me what to do and then when I've done it they've always been disappointed in me. It's never been enough. I've never been enough."

She pauses. She wants Martin to speak, rebuff her in some way, but he carries on mopping up the spilt drink with paper napkins from the metal dispenser on the next table. After a moment, she continues. She feels as if she is speaking to herself, which gives her strength.

"Federico always made me feel I hadn't understood. Years ago, just after we were married, we'd had dinner in this couple's flat and the woman was sitting at her husband's feet while he pontificated – I can't remember what about – and she interrupted him to say she didn't agree, he was wrong, with this little thread of a voice. It was obvious she'd been steeling herself to contradict him. I think she only did it because I was there, she felt ashamed of him in front of me. He was so boring, so full of himself. A dreadful man. And do you know what he did? He *patted* her on the head, I couldn't believe it. He said that she didn't really *know* enough to disagree, he'd explain it to her later. She just dissolved, it was awful, this tight little smile, but all she wanted to do was cry. He really thought he was being helpful, you see, and she knew that, *really* knew it, and there was no way out of it. She was stuck. And I despised her because Federico had never treated me like that; I wouldn't have let him. I was absolutely convinced."

She passes her ring finger through the trace of prosecco still left on the surface of the table, licks it dry, then clutches Martin's damp hot hand in hers. "And now I wonder if I'm any better than she was." She stares into Martin's eyes, willing him not to look away. "Did he know, do you think? About me?"

Martin flinches. "I'm sure he didn't."

"I see," says Helen. "I couldn't bear it if he knew. Not now. Because I can't explain it to him now."

"He'd understand."

"What? That I'd fucked his best friend to give myself a sense of purpose?"

"That's not the whole truth," says Martin.

"I've slept with Giacomo on and off for years. It started ages ago. But I was already with Federico when I did it. Not slept, exactly. Fucked. We fucked whenever we could, in the kitchen, in the back of cars. I don't know why, or I didn't then. I think I do now. I was with him just after Federico was shot, you know. I haven't told anyone." Apart from the magistrate, she thinks, with relief, who already seemed to know. And then there's Giulia, who's guessed.

She lets go of his hand, leans back.

"I'm seeing the PM tomorrow."

"I thought you'd decided not to."

She fights back tears. "It can't be avoided. I have to face up to things. I spoke to the magistrate this afternoon, you know, the one who's investigating Fede's death. I told him the truth. He wants to talk to me again, he says, on Saturday. He was nicer than I'd expected. Compared to Giulia, who isn't?"

"Well, she's had a rough time. Exiled during the war, jailed," says Martin. "Tortured, by all accounts."

"Giulia the martyr," says Helen.

"I didn't mean that." Martin takes his hand away from Helen's. "Is that how she sees herself, as a martyr?"

"No. She sees herself as a servant of the constitution, as though the thing has been written in blood. Her blood. Which I suppose it has, in a way; I suppose she does have blood."

"And a martyred son."

Helen nods. "Yes, Federico's the martyr now." Her eye is attracted by someone entering the room, a thickset man with a shaven head, who glances at them both. For a second she thinks he might be a journalist and she wants to leave, she reaches for her bag on the floor with a brief involuntary shudder. Martin turns round to see who's there but already the man has gone. She shakes her head. It was nothing.

"I've been doing a bit of nosing round," he says.

She wonders how much more she wants to know.

"A friend of mine had a look at Federico's cell phone records." He pauses, lifts his shoulders, his bottom lip jutting out. He's not looking well, she thinks. His flesh is soft and pasty, like dough that children have played with, that has picked up the dirt from their hands. He needs to comb his hair and change his shirt. Out of the agency, away from his desk, he is beginning to look like a lost old man. It breaks her heart to see him reduced to this, his fingers fiddling with the cigarette pack in the pocket of his jacket like a rosary. And she wonders what he's done to get this information, not only today but in the past.

"What did they show?" she says.

"His secretary, his assistants. His father two or three times a day. His mother rather less often. You, obviously. A priest."

"A priest?"

Martin wondered how she'd react to this.

"Yes, not your usual PP though."

"PP?"

"Sorry, my dear. I forget you've never belonged to the mother church. Parish priest."

"I don't think Federico had a parish priest."

"Not your parish. Someone in Umbria. Bit of an odd fish by all accounts. His name is Don Giusini. He's one of these anti-global types. Quite an activist. He got himself into trouble during G8, when they sent the police in to kick shit out of those kids." He glances across. "I'm surprised you weren't there."

"I should have been. I wish I had been."

"Masochism, my dear."

"You don't understand, Martin. I was having a dirty weekend with Giacomo," she says. "In a convent, of all places." She sighs.

"Time well spent, I imagine," he says, giving her a cautious smile.

"It was embarrassing for him," she says. "When all the trouble blew up he was asked to write a piece about it, his impressions and so on. Except that he didn't really have any. He could hardly write about what he'd really been doing."

When her mobile rings, she reaches down for her bag, beneath her chair, pushing aside the printout to retrieve it. She looks at the screen.

"Talk of the devil," she says.

"Are you alone?" says Giacomo.

"No," she says, "I'm with Martin Frame. Are you?"

"Yes," he says. "I've been abandoned."

"Oh dear."

"I thought perhaps I could come to your place?"

"Yes," she says. "That would be nice."

She stands up. "I have to go," she says to Martin. She looks for her wallet, but he stops her.

"Are you sure you're all right?" he said.

"No," she says. "No, I'm not." She smiles. "You can walk me home if you like." She touches his cheek. "The air will clear your head."

PART FOUR

1

Rome, Friday, 4 June 2004

Giulia and Helen are sitting together in the back seat of the
official car that Giulia appears to have acquired the right to use,
a car identical in every way to the one Federico died against,
apart from its colour, which is black. Both women are as close
to their respective smoked windows as the width of the car seat
will allow, silently staring out at streets deserted of everyone but
groups of tourists in shorts and sun hats, at the shuttered and
barricaded shops of the Corso, at parched yellow grass as the
driver takes them slowly round past the Villa Borghese horse
track. Sitting beside the driver in the seat that would have been
Federico's, Fausto throws the occasional glance behind him, but
Giulia either doesn't notice this or chooses not to acknowledge
him, leaving Helen to smile at him with a gratitude he can't
quite see.

They are going to look at Federico's body, laid out in what
Fausto has translated as the ardent room, a minor reception
room inside the ministry. Helen and Giulia, in agreement for
once despite Fausto's doubts, have refused to consider a space
with religious connotations. *La camera ardente*. The ardent room.
"I don't know what it's called in English, I'm afraid. I've never
been to one before," Helen said in an apologetic way, touched
despite herself that Fausto should be using English with her, as

though she were a child and needed to be made to feel at home among adults. "I expect it'll be something to do with *morte*. Mortuary. Morgue. Something like that."

"Mortuary chapel," Giulia announced, reprovingly. "I remember being privileged to attend Churchill's lying in state, to pay my final respects, my country's final respects, to a national hero." She'd looked through Helen's wardrobe for something suitable, finally settling on a black dress Helen hasn't worn since singing in a concert more than ten years before, a linen dress that now hangs loosely on her, giving her an unattractively shrunken, gaunt look that seems, nonetheless, to gratify Giulia, who is also, although more stylishly, dressed in black. She must have an extensive collection of appropriate mourning outfits by now, thinks Helen, neatly cut suits like this one; her colleagues and friends, the old republican guard, have been dropping like flies these past few years. One ardent room after the next. How odd that it should be *ardent*, though; surely there is nothing icier and more indifferent than this trooping past the body of someone dead. Because what she feels most strongly as she sits in the back of the car with her mother-in-law is indifference, not to Federico, not *essentially*, but to this display, this performance, that she has allowed herself to be talked into by Giulia.

Now, as the car cruises past ranks of mourners and comes to a halt inside the ministry courtyard, Helen's instinct is to tell the driver to drop the others off and take her home. But it isn't her car, or driver; she doesn't have the courage, or the right.

The door is opened for her by a middle-aged man whose anxious, troubled face she recognises, who offers her his arm as she leaves the car and says, in a low voice, as if to remind her: "Remondini." She nods. Of course she knows him, he worked with Federico. She's seen him at their flat a dozen times, over dinner, staying on behind when she went to bed and lay there in the dark, not sleeping, wondering when Federico would come to bed and whether it was worth staying awake, knowing that he would wake her in any case, whether she cared or not, to tell her what had been said.

She rests her fingers on his forearm and is about to thank him when her mobile rings. She turned it on in the car, to call Giacomo, who left her flat early that morning, but lacked the courage. "Switch that thing off," hisses Giulia behind her, but Helen, aware that she is being childish, opens her bag, pulls out the mobile and sees that it is Giacomo calling her. With a protective gesture, Remondini steps briskly between her and the group of people at the door to the room where Federico must be waiting. But, of course, Federico isn't waiting. Dead men don't wait.

"I can't talk now," she says, giving Giacomo just enough time to say that he loves her before she turns off the phone and replaces it in her bag. She looks behind for Fausto, who walks up sharply beside her and takes her hand in his. He leads her past the waiting people, hardly a crowd, no more than a dozen, who murmur and shuffle away from her, their eyes avoiding hers, as Fausto also moves to one side, to allow her to enter first.

They have put him at the centre of the room, on a table draped with some heavy crimson material. He is out of his plastic bag and lying fully dressed in a coffin and she wonders where the suit has come from as she walks across, Fausto one step behind, Giulia talking briefly to a man she doesn't know beside the door. It is newer than anything he owns, and more expensive. She looks at this man in his satin-lined box who is no more Federico than the table is, or any piece of wood or marble or made-up flesh, the flesh of some slaughtered animal. She looks at their efforts to make him seem alive and human, the black suit Federico would never have dreamed of wearing, that someone must have bought for him, the tie, the polished shoes more pointed at the toe than he would choose, as though he himself were the mourner and not the mourned, his normally wild blond hair brushed back from his forehead and gelled into place, his lips and cheeks just touched with colour but still clown-like. Oh no, she thinks, this final indignity, this absence, at least he isn't here to see it, because it is clear to her at this moment that there is no Federico left, no trace of him, even less than yesterday, she realises now, or was it the day before? Two days ago in the morgue, with Giacomo beside her and Federico on a metal tray, like half-wrapped meat. She still hasn't seen his wound. Perhaps that would make it real for her, some visible damage to the flesh and bone of him. She's read of grief-torn women throwing themselves into coffins to lie beside the corpses of their husbands and wonders what possessed them. There was a moment in the car when she'd imagined herself seeing him move and crying out, "He's still alive!" Or she'd kiss him and feel his mouth move against her mouth, respond to it. It wasn't a thought, nor even a hope, so much as a kind of absence of thought or hope, a wiping out of what had happened, like children when they ask for the same story twice because there are no guarantees that, the second time, it won't have changed.

Only his hands look real, unscathed, *his*. Expecting to be stopped by someone, some other hand – Giulia's – reaching out to slap her, she reaches in to stroke one and it is cold, so cold she starts back, a cry caught on her lips. Nothing has changed. Fausto is close enough to whisper that they should go, they've stayed long enough, and she is once more aware of the others.

"Where's Massimo?" she says, looking round.

"Massimo?" says Fausto, glancing behind him. A queue has begun to form at a slight distance from the family party, to see Federico.

"Federico's driver," she says, her voice rising. "Why isn't he here with Federico?"

"Take her out of here," says Giulia, with a tone of contempt.

"They killed him too, didn't they?" says Helen. She sounds

hysterical, the last thing she wants. She has promised herself she will stay calm.

"You're all right, my dear," says Fausto.

She wants to pull away and say *I'm not all right*, but something prevents her, a sense of dignity if that weren't Giulia's preserve. Perhaps of shame. I would make a scene, she thinks, if I were strong enough.

They are leaving the building, Helen one step in front of her parents-in-law, when a man she doesn't know comes up to her. Younger than Helen, in his thirties at the most, he places himself squarely in her path before anyone has a chance to stop him. He is wearing a black suit and dove-grey shirt. At his neck, she sees a white dog collar. Through the corner of her eye, she is half aware of Giulia urgently summoning help.

"You don't know me," he says. But I do, she thinks, although she doesn't know his name and has never seen him before in her life. What had Martin said?

"Don–?"

"–Giusini." He sounds relieved. Two large men in double-breasted suits appear from nowhere and grasp his elbows, but Helen shoos them away, excited by her power as they fall back into the crowd. By now the courtyard is teeming with people.

"Federico spoke of me?"

Helen tosses her head back, a brief and not quite affirmative gesture, but otherwise doesn't answer.

"I would like to be able to talk to you when I can," he says. "About your husband. About Federico." He is the same height as Helen, delicately made, with large brown eyes and a day's growth of beard, like a model's. His hair is thick, roughly parted and pushed behind his ears. There is an urgency about him that reminds her of Giacomo, not Giacomo now but the Giacomo who came back from South America, enraged and ecstatic, almost three decades ago. The priest glances round with impatience, as if to say *Who are these people? What do they have to do with us?* then, apologetically it seems, smiles at Helen, his eyes on hers so that nothing will be missed. A smile of complicity.

"I don't have time," she says. "Not now." Giulia is tugging at her sleeve like an impatient child, while Helen does all she can to ignore her. Outside the entrance to the ministry courtyard, held back by a dozen uniformed porters, camera crews wait for them to leave. She sounded colder than she intended, and hurries to make amends. "This afternoon, after lunch. Come to my house. You know where I live?" Before he has a chance to do more than nod, Giulia pulls her away with startling force.

"If you dare do that again, I'll slap your face," says Helen. "That won't look very good on the news this evening, will it?" She nods towards the cameras, the journalists ready with their microphones. "Haven't you seen them, gathering?" Giulia's fingers relax enough for Helen to pull her arm from their grasp. She wants to push the old woman away from her with both hands, push her hard in her chest, hurt her in some deep way. Humiliation will do, even better than pain; she's learnt to tolerate pain, she's fed on it; she's fed on grief.

"Don't you dare touch me again," says Helen, as Giulia, her face flushed, calls for the car. Don Giusini has fallen back a few paces, arms crossed, watching the scene. Because it is a scene, thinks Helen. I'm finally making a scene.

"This afternoon," she calls out to him. "All right? You know where I live?"

Once more, he nods, his eyes fixed on her. She walks away from them all, from her parents-in-law, from the suited men gathering round her, stifling her, and hurries across to the priest, who takes both her hands in his as she holds them out. The cameras edge towards her, but she doesn't care about them.

"What do you want to tell me?"

The man glances down, to the marble floor of the courtyard, and then up, directly into Helen's eyes.

"Federico was dying," he says.

2

Giacomo heads up from Piazza Barberini, but has gone no more than fifty yards when he finds his path blocked. The area outside the American embassy – indeed, the entire width of Via Veneto – has been cordoned off by the military. He will have to find an alternative route to the hotel. Frustrated, he tests the weight of the cordon, lifting the roped post fractionally from the pavement. Two soldiers approach and wave him away with the tips of their machine guns, their eyes invisible beneath the shadow of their helmets. They're American, he notices, and his first instinct is to ask them what right they have to block a road in the capital of a sovereign state, but he resists.

He looks at the soldiers, fresh-faced, one with acne, the other Hispanic. They're the age that he and Federico must have been the last time he stood outside the embassy, with thousands of others, in parkas and those stiff Peruvian sweaters that stank of yak, holding hand-written posters and candles and guitars. They'd gathered to protest about US involvement in the first 9/11, when Allende was assassinated, and Victor Jara. How did that last song by Jara go? The one he'd written with his hands already smashed? Giacomo can't remember a note of it now, although he knew it once by heart.

What he remembers best about the event is being pulled from the crowd and taken to a police van, his arms twisted up behind his back, terrified, thrilled, finally aware *on his own skin* of what it meant to be the victim of fascist brutality. How simple things were then, the words always ready when they were needed. That was the first time Giacomo had been arrested, though not charged, held for a night with others, roughed up and documented, released. Years later, a girlfriend of his, with access to the appropriate offices, had found the immigration file on Mura, Giacomo (born Rome, Italy, October 1953), a bulging folder containing the mug shot the *carabinieri* had taken that morning, his left eye dark and almost closed where he'd been hit. Visa refused. How proud he'd been.

He is still beside the cordon when fifteen motorcycles in a V formation sweep out of the embassy grounds, followed by five Cadillac limousines, each bearing on its hood the American flag, and a further group of motorcycles. And somewhere in the middle of all this screaming horsepower, all this protection and visible immensely vulgar show of power, is the man himself, the ruler of the world.

Giacomo recalls, as he invariably does in these situations, the first time he saw Mitterrand, dwarfed by the ring of men around him, the crème de la crème of exquisitely dressed bodyguards, the President's feet invisible so that he seemed to be floating on a cushion of air, a portly and trivial presence at the heart of brute force exemplified. All emperors are the same, he thinks, new clothes or not. Thank God he's never been tempted. How difficult it must have been to be Federico these past few years, tailoring to the court, when he could have been like Giacomo, an irritating presence on the fringe of it all, enjoying the crumbs as they fell from the master's table, nipping at their ankles and darting off.

He is glad that Fausto called this morning to tell him the conference was cancelled, as he'd expected. But this doesn't mean he's ready to leave Rome, leave Helen.

Federico is already cold news, he discovered over coffee in a bar. Today's front pages are full of the hostages, the Italian embassy in Baghdad attacked by mortar fire, political infighting, the US emperor's visit. Not much space given to the claims of the old woman, the mother of the murdered driver, but that's only natural. It's in no one's interests, finally, to give her credence. He wants, he realises, to call the woman *widowed*. There's no word for a woman who's lost her child, it occurs to him, perhaps because it should never happen, it goes against the natural order. But it happens all the time. The emperors make it happen, and their advisors. Perhaps there was a word for it in Latin, in ancient Rome, he thinks, when it must have been needed all the time.

Federico has been shuffled back to the third or fourth pages or even further. Interestingly, the papers owned by the PM and his family have relegated the story to national news, as though his murder has the status of a mafia killing or kidnapped child. As though it isn't political at all. These are distinctions most people don't make by now, thinks Giacomo, unless the murderer is Muslim. Muslims are the only real terrorists these days, driven by ideology, because it is easier to see the threat as external; it makes us feel better about ourselves now that we've put history and ideology behind us. It was different in our days: they couldn't tell the terrorists from their own children. We were their children. And now Helen's standing beside her husband's coffin in a room in a ministry, at the heart of the country's power, and he's wishing they were both in bed again.

She was strange last night. You'd expect her to be distant, but he'd hoped she'd share it with him: her grief, her need for comfort. He's never been so attentive to a woman's demands in his life, he thinks – this wonderful, fragile creature – as though his ear is pressed to the shell of her. This is the first time since they met that they've both been single, free. He hasn't said this to her, it's too soon for that; but he wonders if she's thought it too. She must have done. This morning, when she said she was going to the *camera ardente* and then onto wherever else they took her, she'd decided to play the game, he'd looked at her and seen her as she was; alone, without Federico. This is how it's meant to be, he thought. Everything he might have said, about how unwise it was to let herself be led, he bit back. He wanted her to make her own decisions for once. The whole Helen, finally, for him.

He turns round and heads back to Via del Tritone; the hotel can wait. Walking down the hill, he squints into a place selling postcards and sees a woman in a T-shirt with a line of sweat on her upper lip, and feels attracted to her, always a relief, that automatic response. Like waking up in the morning and checking his pulse, to be sure it isn't a dream. Still potent, still alive. Five minutes away to his right are Via della Vite, Via Condotti, Via Borgognona, Yvonne's world, with its stage-lit museum-like windows and bone-thin shop assistants, though presumably this isn't what they're called any longer. Consultant *somethings*? He wouldn't be surprised. Yvonne would know, but he isn't likely to ask her. She'll be back with her rake-thin friends in Paris by now, dissecting salad leaves in some overpriced cellar, still bottled water in their glasses, dishing dirt. His step is light. He thinks about calling Helen again, but decides against it. She'll call him back when she's ready.

3

She expected to be accompanied by Giulia and Fausto, but a middle-aged man in a pale grey suit takes Helen by the elbow and, with the gentlest pressure, removes her from their company. She experiences a sense of panic – even Giulia would be better than nothing – as he steers her to a waiting lift, letting her go as soon as they are both inside and the doors have smoothly, swiftly closed on the faces of her distant in-laws, left far behind her in the hall. The lift is carpeted, mirrored, an ornate gilded cornice concealing the light. Looking into the mirror to her left, she can see where the man's hair has been combed across his bald patch and has to suppress a smile. He turns to her, the mechanism of the lift almost soundless so that she has the sense of being suspended in time as much as space, and offers his condolences in an unctuous whisper, his accent southern, his eyes sliding over her and off, as though she is dressed inappropriately. Perhaps she is. But what had the priest meant? *Federico was dying.*

She follows the man along a corridor into a room that must be directly above where Giulia and Fausto are waiting; more carpets, flimsy-looking gilded chairs along the wall, a row of long, elaborately draped windows overlooking the street. A group of men is gathered at one end of the room, around a desk at which someone is sitting, concealed from her. She recognises his voice at once, the Milanese accent, the self-satisfaction. He is telling what sounds like a joke.

"–and the Pope are walking along the banks of a river when the Pope drops his Bible in the water. Immediately, I walk on the water and pick the Bible up. Next morning," – professional pause for effect – "*l'Unità* has the front page headline: 'Prime Minister can't swim!'."

The man who has brought her is waving towards the group in a frantic way, but no one notices him until the joke has been finished and appreciated. It is only when they part and the PM sees her that the laughter dies away. One of the group whispers hurriedly in his ear. He stands up and walks across to her at once, his features flushed with displeasure. It isn't the first time they've met; Helen has been introduced to him on two or three earlier occasions, but he clearly doesn't remember this, and hasn't been reminded. He takes her hand in both of his, soft and warm, and squeezes it. He is shorter than she is, though not by much.

"*Le mie condoglianze più sentite,*" he says. She lowers her eyes and nods, thankful that he hasn't tried to speak to her in his cruise-ship English, as he has done in the past. This close, she can see the matt beige powder on the forehead and cheeks, the sides of the nose toned down. She wants him to let her go, but doesn't like to pull her hand away.

"I greatly admired your husband," he continues, in Italian, the corners of his mouth twisted down as though trying not to smirk, to suppress his instinct to flirt. "His work has been of inestimable value." She knows he's lying. Federico has told her a hundred times how close he's come to being removed from his post by the PM's boys at the ministry. But his lies don't surprise or shock her; she hasn't expected the truth. No one has told her the truth, she thinks, not yet. Except, maybe, Don Giusini. But how can that be true? *Federico was dying*. The PM is talking about everything Federico has done for his country, for *our* country, he says, squeezing her hand. And now it is their turn to do what can be done for him, he is saying, to show him that his death has not been in vain. To demonstrate to their enemies that they stand united against those – cowardly, illiberal, terrorist, intolerant of freedom – who would intimidate them.

She's heard of his charm, even his enemies acknowledge it, albeit in a qualified way, the charm of a salesman, a card-sharp, and for a moment she succumbs to it, like someone who finally allows herself to drown after hours in the water, who welcomes the water into her lungs because it is useless to resist any longer. And then it occurs to her that she has heard this speech before, or speeches to this effect. It is part of his repertoire.

He must have seen some change in her because his smile flickers back, the lips sealed together, the effect vaguely comic despite its intention, which is surely not to amuse but to express, in the midst of grief, an understanding, a solidarity. He is suddenly what Helen's mother used to call, with contempt, a "ladies' man". Ladies' men also have their repertoires, she thinks. She tugs her hand free and the smile disappears, as if some mechanism has been brought into play. When he shifts his head to one side, to summon one of the other men in the room, one of his band of assistants, she sees the faintest line along the jaw where the make-up comes to an end. "I trust you to do what you can," he says to her in a stern, admonitory tone, his hard eyes fixed on hers, "your husband's wishes must be respected. For the good of our beloved Italy. Its international standing. The eyes of the world upon us." And then, as briskly as he approached her, he turns on his heels and struts away.

A few moments later, in another formal room, she is asked to sit down and is left alone. She has a sudden impulse to laugh, as much with relief as anything. She hasn't given in. Beloved Italy, indeed. Opening her bag, she takes out her mobile and switches it on. There is no coverage, so she can't call someone who might share the absurdity of this. Martin would be ideal. But what did Don Giusini mean? As the PM's face returns to her, so close she can see the powder in the pores, she remembers Federico one evening, preparing their meal, the noise of the television in the background. The best way to destroy the PM and people like him isn't assassination, he said, his knife in his hand, but humiliation, constant humiliation. One day, I'll tweak his nose in front of the cameras. Laughing would do it, if enough of us were prepared to laugh. Laughing out loud each time he opens his mouth and utters his platitudes and lies. That's what he's most afraid of, to appear ridiculous. But he already does, she said. I don't understand why everybody can't see that. I might just do it one day, he'd said, when I've nothing to lose. I wish you would, she remembers saying. That's what *I* should do, she reflects now, with the useless cell phone in her hand, in front of everyone. Tweak his nose, laugh at him to his face. She looks up, drawn by some noise, and sees a closed circuit camera pan round the room. A moment later, a man walks in.

She's seen him on television, one of the shouting matches that pass for political forums, but can't remember his name. He is younger than she is, short-haired, almost shorn to the scalp, rat-faced, the kind of man who might just as easily run a market stall as a ministry these days. He doesn't introduce himself; he seems to assume he's known to her, with the arrogance these people have.

"You know the Prime Minister depends absolutely on your agreement," he says, without preamble, in an accent that takes her back to Turin, in a tone that takes everything for granted, her obedience above all. She raises an eyebrow but doesn't answer. Let them sweat, she thinks. He begins to describe the work Federico has done, his contribution to the state, his dedication, none of it false and yet all of it unreal to her, as it would have been to him, she is sure of that. And it strikes her that what the man is doing is not describing Federico at all, but the dead man in the ardent room, in a suit he'd never worn, the man with make-up on his face, who isn't Federico either. I might as well let them do what they want, she thinks, with relief, as though she has been holding her breath without realising it, and has now let it go. They can have their hero and I can have my husband.

And now he plays what Helen recognises immediately as his trump card, when he says the President of the United States has intimated he would be prepared to postpone his flight to France to take part in the funeral. She should be honoured by such a presence, he says, his tone increasingly unctuous. The fight against international terrorism. The Axis of Evil. It's vital that everyone play their part. How stupid you are, she thinks. You almost had me. If you hadn't brought up Bush.

She is about to ask to be taken back to the car when Giulia and Fausto appear at the door, Giulia holding her handbag, Fausto a handkerchief, both looking oddly lost, like supplicants from the provinces and not, as they are and know they are, cogs in the governing wheel. The young man waves them in, welcoming them as moral back-up, although Helen wonders if that's true. Giulia, yes. But Fausto? He was so against the idea of a state funeral. Now, though, she isn't sure. Normally, he'll stand up to Giulia, in the end. That's why they are still together, Federico used to say. Because he answers back when he has no other choice. He's the grist to her mill. Am I the grist to yours? she'd thought.

The man is turned away from her but she can see his face through a mirror in this palace of mirrors, just as she saw the bald patch of the other man in the lift and wanted to smile. She can see his look of irritation and pleading, addressed to Giulia, the way a teacher looks at the mother of an intractable child. Can't you do anything with her? his face is saying. She's being naughty. She won't play along.

Giulia stalks across to her.

"Well?" she says.

"Well, what?" says Helen.

4

Giacomo can't wait any longer and tries to call Helen, but his mobile is dead. Everyone's mobile is dead. He stops at the side of the road, the Quirinale a hundred yards away, and wonders where she is. The body of Federico is no more than five minutes' walk from where he's standing, and it occurs to him to go and see what the mood is there. Perhaps someone will know where Helen has gone; she can't be that far away. He feels trapped beneath some kind of bell jar, a sensation exacerbated by the cowl of heat on the city. He hesitates outside an empty bar for a moment, then turns up the hill towards the ministry.

He's expected a line of people, but the room is almost empty by the time he arrives and no more than a minute or two passes before he is standing beside the coffin. It has always struck him as barbaric, this practice of displaying the dead, but now, with Federico in front of him, he is struck by the blandness of it, as though death weren't involved. Removed from the antiseptic surroundings of the morgue, Federico looks the way he's looked so often, distant, slightly aloof, his mind on other things. He was shot in the stomach and the heart, of course, which helps. He won't tell Helen he's been, he decides, because nothing he is likely to say – if he is honest – will comfort her. A woman behind him coughs and Giacomo steps aside to watch her bob at the knee and cross herself and touch the wood and kiss her fingers. It's the rituals that invest the business with sense, he supposes, and wishes he'd been trained in them, or believed in what they stood for. Still standing by the coffin, he observes the woman, middle-aged, grey trousers and a blouse, walk off towards the door, alone, her duty done. Is she a friend of Federico's, he wonders, or a colleague or simply a citizen paying her respects to a servant of the state? Whatever, she has at least as much right to be here as he does. He might have stood here longer if a man hadn't crossed the room and asked him if he felt all right. I'm fine, he says, but the man stays beside him until he walks away and leaves the room, feeling like someone who's behaved suspiciously in a jeweller's. For a moment he experiences a trace of guilt. Not because of Helen; that's also Helen's choice. Because there have been times he's wished Federico dead, and now he is. He has had his wish. Is that why I'm here? he wonders. To gloat? Is that why I slept with Helen last night and the night before last, not to comfort her at all, but to take possession, as though I were exercising my *droit de seigneur*? The middle-aged woman is standing outside the *camera ardente*. She turns to look at him as he leaves. It's terrible, she says flatly. He was a good man. Giacomo nods. They walk together towards the street, without speaking.

Giacomo is deciding what to do next when a black car pulls up. The door nearest to him, the back door on the right, is flung open. What appears to be a scuffle takes place inside the car, raised voices, the sound of something like a slap. He starts to move away, unnerved, when Helen stumbles from the car, tripping against the kerb. Giacomo is close enough to catch her, almost before he has seen who it is, a woman falling from a car into his arms. Helen pulls herself onto her feet and hugs him, gasping *I can't believe it, I can't believe it's you*, as another woman – Giacomo recognises Giulia – wriggles across the back seat of the car towards the open door. Giacomo sees a man's hand reach round from between the two front seats to restrain the older woman, whose head emerges from the darkness of the car like a caricature of rage and begins to keen, a dreadful noise. Giacomo breaks free from Helen and slams the door on Giulia, not caring if the woman is hurt, not caring if her black-gloved hand is trapped by the frame of the door, hoping deep down that it is. He slaps his own hand against the body of the car, as one slaps a horse to make it move and, after a moment, it pulls away and is gone. Behind him, Helen begins to laugh and cry at the same time, gasping for breath.

"Let's get out of here," she says.

And then, as the car drives off and Giacomo turns to face her, she says, her face excited, her voice hoarse: "Fuck them, Giacomo, fuck the lot of them. I need your help. Can you get hold of a car at the hotel? Mine's back at the flat. For God's sake, Giacomo, come on!"

5

Martin swings his panama between his knees. He's finished his second coffee and is thinking of ordering another one, or maybe a draught beer, a small one, if the waiter comes across, but so far he's been left on his own, with his thoughts. He had a call from Alina this morning; she said she wanted to see him. Of course, he said. This afternoon.

He is sitting in the second row of tables, protected by the awning. The first row, the farthest from the bar, is dedicated to tourists who need to tan, the third to knots of older men who might, or might not, have ordered something in the last hour. He's where he likes to be, neither here nor there. His first wife called him ambiguous, but didn't explain what she meant, and he hadn't insisted. He hadn't wanted to clarify his ambiguity. What was it Socrates said? That the unexamined life is not worth living? He's always preferred George Eliot's line about a window providing more enlightenment than a mirror. He is alone in his row, which is a source of satisfaction to him. He wonders what Alina wants from him, and what he wants from her.

There is something missing, he knows that, something essential, something the size of St Peter's. But he can't put his finger on what it is. He'd ask Picotti if Picotti, he's started to sense, weren't somehow part of the problem. He's spent some time this morning reading up on Don Giusini and the man seems genuine, decent, slightly off the wall as these anti-global Franciscan types tends to be, a pain in the arse to the church but allowed to do pretty much as he wants, for now at least. There is nothing that doesn't ring true. Part of the problem? Part of the solution? Martin is waiting for Corti, his cell phone contact, who might have been able to lay his hands on some of the transcripts of conversations the priest has had with Federico, but he doesn't hold out much hope. Corti sounded unforthcoming, even furtive, on the phone this morning. "I'll see what I can do. A coffee later, maybe? After lunch?"

Martin said, "Yes, why not? The usual place."

"I'll see what I can do," Corti said again. Like most attempts at reassurance, this failed to reassure.

Martin is about to leave when Corti waves from the other side of the square.

"Sorry, Frame. Held up by all this security," he calls out, twenty feet from the table, as though he and Martin were alone in the square. "They wouldn't let me through," he says, stressing *me* in an affronted way. He isn't used to having his movements impeded. He sits down moving the ashtray in a finicky way, then uses a paper napkin to wipe the sweat from the sides of his nose, the corners of his mouth, dropping it on the floor after a rapid offended glance at the smear of grease he's gathered.

"Don't worry," says Martin. "Drink?"

"I'd rather not," Corti says. "Stomach." He glances across to the door of the bar. "A glass of water if he comes."

After they have both been silent for some minutes, not looking at each other, as though gathering their thoughts, Corti turns towards Martin and spreads his hands in a gesture of surrender. "No luck, I'm afraid. I did my best."

"You mean the conversations weren't recorded?"

"I didn't say that."

"But there aren't any transcripts?"

Corti purses his lips. He has some kind of gel on his skin, Martin notices. Either that or he's been waxed. He's certainly been promoted, he has a slick of power about him that wasn't there in the past, when Martin helped him salvage his career.

"Not now. There were. That is, there might have been."

"They've been removed?"

Corti pushes his thick grey hair from his face with both tanned hands, momentarily reminding Martin of Sandra Dee. Martin knows that he is lying.

"Can't say." Teasing.

"Won't say?" Teasing back. Martin hates this.

"What's the difference?" He pauses. "There is something else that's rather odd." Corti's tone is confidential. "I thought I'd have a look at one or two other mobiles, to see what they've been up to."

"Which other mobiles?"

"Well, his wife's to start off with. You never know. The bosom that harbours the asp and so on. But no surprises there. Then I had a quick look at his father's. Nothing of any consequence. Calling his son, constantly, which is rather sad as things have turned out. You wonder what he'll do with himself." He glances at the empty tables around them, lowers his voice.

"His mother's, though, that's another business entirely. She has two numbers, did you know that? Well, why should you? You know who she is, of course. Giulia Paternò? Battleaxe of the Republic? She must be in her eighties by now, ninety maybe. Not the kind of woman you'd expect to be so wired up. One of them is used for family and friends, but the other one isn't. Not by a long chalk. She's got two or three interesting friends for an octogenarian, even if she is a senator."

"One of them called Picotti by any chance?" Martin says, on a hunch.

Corti sucks in his breath. "I didn't say that."

"Of course you didn't."

"If you already know..." Corti sounds annoyed.

"I hadn't realised I did," says Martin.

"If you take my advice," says Corti, in a tone that recognises the unlikelihood of this, "you'll drop the whole thing right now."

"Drop what?"

"The whole thing. Di Stasi." Corti leans back in his chair. "Look at it this way, Frame. He's dead. He'd have been dead in any case. Maybe not today. Next week. Next month. You knew that, surely?" His voice is cold. "Drop it."

"I'm sorry?" says Martin. "Dead in any case?" What the hell does he mean? So he has read the transcripts after all.

"Ask his confessor."

Corti stands up, smoothing the wrinkles from his trousers, tugging discreetly at his crotch.

"Look after yourself, Frame."

"You too, Corti."

Martin goes into the bar to settle the bill. He is about to leave when his attention is caught by a small television in the corner. It is the midday news. Martin watches as Helen walks away from the cameras, having refused to speak to the waiting journalists, surrounded by dark-suited people he doesn't know, wearing a black dress that doesn't suit her. He sees Giulia hop beside her like a rickety diminutive crow, her hair bound tightly into a dancer's poll, black mourning gloves in one hand, the other constantly touching the shoulders, the back, the arm of her widowed daughter-in-law as she follows her towards the official car. He notices Helen glance out of the car towards the cameras with an odd look of interest, as though she has only just seen them and is wondering what they want. He sees the black car pull away towards the Quirinale and disappear, replaced by a panning shot of the crowd outside the ministry, a ragged line of mourners, and the voice of a journalist talking about the people these people represent, the loss to the nation, the mooted arrival of Bush, as yet unconfirmed, committed to the war on terrorism in all its forms, on all its fronts.

He looks at the clock on the wall. He needs to get home. He wants to shower and change before Alina turns up.

6

Half an hour later, Giacomo and Helen leave Rome along the Via Pontina in a car Giacomo hired at the hotel. Helen has taken some sunglasses from her bag and put them on. This dress she's wearing does her no favours, thinks Giacomo. With the glasses on, big wraparound things with D&G on the side in glittering paste, she looks like a typical Italian widow. As, of course, she is.

"Did I tell you I had a premonition?" she says. "Not really a premonition, because it wasn't pre anything. More of a vision, I suppose. I saw Federico the morning he was shot. He was standing in front of me, smiling in this odd puzzled way as though he'd been told a joke he didn't understand, you know, when you smile without knowing why. I looked at my watch, I remember thinking: I'll have to ask him exactly what he was up to at 9:27. He was shot at 9:27. It makes no sense."

"I didn't know you believed in that kind of thing."

"I don't." She sounds upset. They are driving along an avenue flanked by maritime pines and oleander that makes Giacomo think of travelling into the warmth of the south. Perhaps we can have a holiday later this summer, he thinks, when it's all blown over. Somewhere in Sicily. He still has relatives there.

"But I think Federico did," says Helen. "I know it sounds stupid, but I think he may have had the strength somehow to make me see him, I don't know how." Giacomo, who hates this sort of thing, is about to tell her not to be so foolish, but before he has a chance he hears a stifled gulp and a sob. He reaches across and touches Helen's knee, his hand on the bare skin where the dress has ridden up.

"I don't know what I'm going to do about you," she says, not moving his hand, or her leg, perhaps waiting for him to do so.

"Do about me?" He laughs, but removes his hand. "There'll be more than enough time to think about that."

"Oh," she says. He can't tell if this has satisfied her or not. She's tired, shaken by the events of the morning. Either way, he thinks, it is true. There will be time for everything, for them, if not for Federico.

"Are you sure you want to go and see this woman?" he says, swerving to overtake an *Ape*. "We can just go home if you'd prefer."

Helen shakes her head. "No, no. I need to speak to her. It won't take long."

Half an hour later, she tells Giacomo to turn off to the left. The new road winds uphill, zigzagging as it goes, with the sea some distance beneath them, first to the right and then to the left. The higher they go, the wider the green-blue line of it becomes. Finally, Helen says: "Here we are. It's down this road."

They pull up outside two houses, the first one fine old stone and semi-abandoned, the second constructed out of concrete blocks plastered over and painted mud brown, with bronze-coloured aluminium frames at the windows. They hear a dog bark and a door being opened and closed as they walk across to the second house. Three other cars are parked on the unpaved area outside the houses.

When they are still some yards away, the front door is opened by a young man.

"He's Massimo's brother," Helen whispers. "He must be. He looks just like him." Holding out her hand, she says, in a slow, slightly formal Italian, as though she has been practising the phrase in the car: "My condolences for Massimo. I'm deeply sorry." She pauses. "I'm the widow of Federico, Federico Di Stasi. Helen. I wanted to speak to your mother." Giacomo is startled to hear her say *widow*.

The young man takes her hand, then lets it go. He doesn't appear to have noticed Giacomo. His eyes are red from crying. "My mother isn't here," he says. "What do you want?" His tone is surly. He looks back into the room and shouts at a dog to be quiet, at someone else to take the dog away.

"Where is she?" asks Helen, clearly hurt.

"They took her away somewhere safe, where she won't be bothered," the man says, his face set, staring with inexplicable hostility at Helen. He isn't going to ask us in, thinks Giacomo. He is wearing black trousers, part of a suit, black shoes, a V-necked T-shirt, as though he has just come back from a funeral and taken off his jacket and shirt to relax. Perhaps he has. Giacomo wonders if Massimo has been buried that morning. Would they have known? Would Helen have been told?

"They?"

"The *senatrice*," the man says.

"*Senatrice*?" says Helen, her voice low and shocked.

"Your husband's mother," he says in a tone that mixes scorn and respect, as though there is only one *senatrice* in the world and Helen has no right not to know. "She said that she'd help us and she did. She sent a car."

Helen covers her face with both hands, then rubs her eyes.

"When?"

"After the funeral. This morning. My mother didn't want any visitors. There have been too many people here from the television, journalists, they wanted photographs of Massimo when he was a boy, photographs of his bedroom, they wanted to…" The young man's eyes fill with tears. "They're jackals."

"Where have they taken her?"

He shrugs.

"You have a number for her? A mobile number?"

"No."

Giacomo takes Helen's arm to lead her back to the car, but Helen pulls herself free. "Your mother said something about a plot. Do you know what she meant?"

"She didn't mean anything. She was overwrought."

"She said that Massimo had told her something might happen. That they were in danger. She must know something."

He flushes with anger. "My mother's an old woman, she's confused, she's just lost her first-born son. It's natural she'd blame someone."

"Is that what Giulia said? That she was confused?"

"The *senatrice*? I don't know what you mean. At least she said she'd look after us."

"The funeral?" says Helen. "I didn't know. Why wasn't I told?"

"They said you knew. We thought you'd be there. My mother asked after you." The young man is silent for a minute or two, considering. "There was no one, no one from your family. Massimo used to talk about you all the time. He worshipped the ground you walked on, you and your husband. My mother couldn't believe it. It broke her heart a second time."

"But I love Massimo. I love your mother. I wasn't told, you must believe me. Nobody told me." To Giacomo's astonishment, Helen flings her arms around the young man, hugging him to her. He resists for no more than a second, then lets himself be held, returns the embrace. He is at least a head taller than Helen. Giacomo sees them together: the man's brown arms against Helen's dress, her fine pale hair pressed up against his chest, and is unexpectedly jealous, when the young man's eyes meet his. He looks away, with a sense of shame he doesn't understand. He isn't to blame. But someone must always be to blame, he thinks, isn't that what the young man just said? It's natural to blame someone.

They are about to leave when a teenage girl runs from the house and presses a jar of olives into Helen's hands.

"She'd want you to have these," she says.

7

Once she's checked no one is waiting outside the house, Helen asks Giacomo to drop her at the edge of the square. "I'll call you later this evening," she says. "There's something I have to sort out." Giacomo seems happy with this. It makes such a change to have someone doing what I want, she thinks. She's always imagined Giacomo would be the last person to be manoeuvred into doing things he didn't want for someone else. Does he love her? she wonders. Does she love him?

She lets herself into the flat, kicking her shoes off, unzipping her dress as she closes the door behind her. Her first thought is to take it off, to free herself of the shroud-like dress, to let her skin breathe. She drops the dress to the floor, pushing it into the corner with her bare foot. She stands there in her bra and knickers, forcing her elbows far enough back for her to feel the strain, then lifting her hair away from her neck and letting it fall.

Silence. How odd though to find the empty flat so full, so airless. She's spent so much time in it alone these past few years, with Federico increasingly absorbed by his work. She's resented it, she's felt betrayed by Federico; her rival has been a cabinet of files, a schedule of meetings that left him no time for anything else, a sense of duty that made her feel shallow and inconsequential. She's been alone so much here it ought to feel no different. But now, as she walks from hall to kitchen to living room to bathroom, aching in every limb, it's worse than it's ever been. As though room after room of silence were itself a sort of presence so dense she can hardly push her way through it.

Don Giusini sits down at the table without being asked. Helen has pulled on a skirt and T-shirt and is barefoot behind the kitchen counter, making tea for them both. He is waiting for her to finish, not speaking. She can sense him looking round the room, at the pictures and the books, at the blackboard with OLIVES written on it in Federico's hand, looking at her, in the same slow way, as though it is only by looking carefully at everything that he can reach an understanding of it. He held her hand at the door with both his hands, and she let him, wondering if it would help, if he possessed some healing power. I'm so fragile, she thinks, resenting him a little, so needy; I'll take my help from any source that's offered. But she hasn't done him justice, she sees that now. What he does, as she has learnt to say from American TV, is *calm*. Don Giusini does calm. The sheaf of papers from Giulia's desk is now slipped into the drawer of her desk, some of it still unread. She isn't ready yet, but she will be soon. She carries the teapot across to the table.

"Milk or lemon?" she says, then corrects herself. "No, I'm sorry, it'll have to be lemon. I don't have any milk."

He smiles. His front teeth are chipped and slightly crooked, she notices; his parents couldn't have had the money to have them fixed.

"In that case, lemon. And sugar. Sugar. I have a sweet tooth."

She pours the tea out, fetches a lemon from the fridge, and sugar. The knife she uses to slice the lemon is Federico's.

"I didn't know you existed three days ago," she says, discomfited by the silence. "And now here we are together in my kitchen. Drinking tea."

He smiles more broadly. For a moment she wonders if he is making fun of her.

"Together in your kitchen," he says, looking round. "To talk about Federico."

She doesn't know what to say. What she wants to do is listen.

"I spoke too soon this morning," he says. "I was cruel, my words were cruel, but I wanted to be heard. You didn't know me; you might have sent me away. I didn't want that."

"I understand," she says, waiting.

"Federico met me at a conference some months ago. It was a small thing, a handful of people against the war. I suppose you could say that Federico was the star." Don Giusini looks at her to see if this makes sense. When she nods, he carries on. "I was a little in awe of him and also, to be honest, a little distrustful, but that soon passed. He helped us see what needed to be done because he understood his world. As we did ours. But Federico's world was also their world, the war makers' world. He helped us see what might be effective and what not." He pauses. "And then we met again, the two of us alone, sometimes in Rome but more often in my home. It was easier for him to travel than for me. My parish is in the Abruzzi, near Teramo, and one weekend he came without warning to my house. He was tired, I thought he wanted a place to rest, no more than that. A refuge. But I was wrong. He wanted to confess."

"I didn't know," she says.

"He told me straight away that he had played a part in the death of a man in Turin. Almost thirty years ago now. It happened when he was stealing money from a bank for what they called the struggle. Someone else was arrested. They knew it was Federico, but no one said. He let the other man go to jail for him." He looks at her, puzzled. "You were there – not at the bank raid, I know that, but in Italy at that time – this will make sense to you in a way it can't to me." He spreads his hands out in despair. "I wasn't born when it happened. It isn't my place to judge, but I'm a human being, I can't not judge. I listen and try to understand. I try not to judge. I do my best, Signora Di Stasi.

Helen. May I call you Helen? What Federico told me shocked me, because I couldn't understand. He tried to explain how it was, but I had the sense that he didn't understand either. Not any longer. But that didn't stop him judging himself. He couldn't forgive. He didn't seem to want my forgiveness, in a way. I wasn't sure what he wanted. He wanted to talk. He'd done other things at that time, he said, and told no one."

"He could have talked to me," says Helen.

"He couldn't do that, I don't think. Not after so long." Don Giusini stirs sugar into his tea. "He could have talked to you then, perhaps, after it had happened, but he didn't. I think he was scared at first, that you might not love him, or talk to someone else. And then he was too ashamed to talk to you. He'd lied to you for so long. I think perhaps he was most ashamed that he'd lied."

"He never said a word about it. Or anything else. He didn't tell me everything, I didn't expect that."

"Silence is also lying."

"I know it is," she says. She sips at her tea. "This morning. You said he was dying."

"Yes. He told me some time ago. He said he had spoken to no one else. He'd only found out a few days earlier, although he'd suspected something for some time. He had a tumour in his brain, in his frontal lobe. He'd been suffering from headaches. You'll have noticed?"

With tears in her eyes, Helen nods once more. "I thought he was working too hard. I didn't realise."

"He found out three months ago. He was told he had four, maybe five months to live. The tumour was fast-growing, inoperable. It was beginning to affect his behaviour; it would continue to do so, unpredictably. To remove it they would have had to remove a part of his brain. He would have been a vegetable."

"It's a mercy he died the way he did, then," says Helen. She is fighting back her anger with Federico, his reticence. His deceit.

So this was the illness. He spoke to his parents, to Giulia and Fausto. Why not to her? Because there was that wall of – what was that word he'd used? Babble.

"And so he knew that in any case he was going to die," says Don Giusini in a soft, cautious voice that alarms Helen. "And that gave him freedom–"

"What do you mean?" she says, startled.

"He had a plan."

"What kind of plan?"

"He wrote it all down, he told me. He had started to make notes for his speech for the conference before he had the news about his tumour. He'd wanted to shake them up, in a gentle way at first, to make them think. The conference wasn't really about reconstruction after the war, he told me, whatever people thought. At first he'd wanted to talk about what peace might mean. He'd wanted to surprise them, lead them somewhere new. And then he learnt that he would outlive the conference by what? A matter of weeks? Two months at best. And so he changed his mind."

"Is what he wrote called Juggernaut?"

"You know about it?"

"Yes. I think I've read some. The first part, before he knew." She is silent for a moment. "And then other bits. A later part, I think it must be. After he'd been told."

"He never showed me what he had done," says Don Giusini. "Not all of it, anyway. He would read sections to me, but he said it was a work in progress, it would never be finished except with his death."

"He was right. He told his parents about it as well, you know. His mother, anyway."

"Yes, he told me that he'd spoken to them. He would have spoken to you as well, before the end. He promised me that."

"The end?"

"I said that he came to confess to a crime," Don Giusini says.

"I should be, I know," says Helen, still thinking about Turin, "but I'm not surprised he let someone down like that. They thought they had a right to do anything. I should say 'we'. I was there, after all. We thought we could take the world into our own hands. We had no respect for anyone who got in our way."

"You don't understand. That wasn't the crime he confessed to."

"I'm sorry?"

She watches Don Giusini stand up and walk around the room, staring at the floor as though he has lost something. After a moment, during which she finds herself wanting to reach out and grab him to make him stop, he sits down beside her. He is very young, his face is smooth. There are traces of acne around his mouth, beneath the fine beard.

"He wanted my approval, my absolution I suppose, for something he still hadn't done."

8

One day, just after lunch, Giacomo met Helen off the tram. She'd finished her morning's teaching at Fiat and was on her way home. It was a fine day, one of those spring days that felt like summer, although there was still snow high on the mountains outside the city and out of the sun the air was cold, even bitter. He took her arm and frog-marched her off, ignoring her protests. He wouldn't say where he was taking her. Helen had a scarf on but her coat was open; Giacomo was wearing the parka he'd been wearing when he came back from South America, and a T-shirt ragged at the neck, and jeans; he looked the way he had done then, his hair had grown a little, he hadn't shaved for a day or two. After a few paces, he stopped and they both laughed. There was something about his manner that intrigued her; he was the way he'd been at first: playful, charming. He pulled a bar of chocolate out of his pocket and broke some off for her; it was the kind she liked; milk with hazelnuts. He knew that, things like that; Giacomo was always observant, attentive to detail. He seemed to know more about her than Federico did, she thought, her foibles, her preferences. In the cinema he would let her sit beside the aisle, something Federico never did until she reminded him that otherwise she'd panic. Federico still had to ask her if she wanted sugar in her coffee, or added long-life milk – the only kind they could find – which was worse. I'm sorry, he'd say, as she poured it away. I always forget you don't like it; and she would think, how can you always forget? Giacomo never does.

She should have found this attractive. Perhaps, deep down, she did. But, however much she told herself they were party tricks, like remembering which court card someone had chosen from a pack, Giacomo's awareness of what she wanted or didn't want, his awareness of her, upset her and left her on edge. It made her wary, as though there would be a price she would have to pay one day for this attention.

They walked for a few moments, not speaking. Then Giacomo said, in a teasing way: "I've got something to show you."

She stopped. "What do you mean?"

"It's nothing forbidden," he said. "Don't worry."

"I'm not worried, Giacomo. I'm just in no mood for games."

He took the ends of her scarf and tied them together, pulling her in towards him until their faces almost touched, she could smell the chocolate on his breath. If he'd pulled any tighter, she might have choked. She thought he was going to kiss her, and she'd have let him; but he moved away.

"It isn't a game," he said, in a quieter voice. "It's important. Well, maybe not important. But, well, significant. I think you'll like it." He was pleading, almost pathetic. She wanted to laugh. Is there any difference between important and significant? As if the first were my word and the second his? Perhaps they would never have the same language.

"All right, all right," she said. "But let me go. I won't run away."

They stopped at the corner of a street she didn't recognise, in the university quarter, not far from the department where he worked with Federico. "Close your eyes now," he said. She did. She let him lead her twenty, thirty yards; her heart was beating absurdly, she felt like a child in thrall to an older, more dangerous child. "Keep them closed," he whispered. "Trust me." They were in the shade of the buildings; the air was colder, she began to shiver. She heard him turn a key and open a door. "Come on," he said, coaxing. He guided her up steps, and then more steps, closing the door behind them. The temperature dropped once again. His hand was strong and warm around hers. "You can open them now. Just for a minute."

She was in an enormous room, bare, decorated in a formal way, some sort of entrance hall. There was scaffolding on the far side. Giacomo took her across the marble floor to a lift. "Close them again," he said. She held her breath as the lift went up. It took far longer than she'd expected. He led her out of the lift and into a biting, unexpected wind. "Open them," he said, and she did.

She could see the city of Turin laid out beneath her, the roofs of the old centre, the station with the mesh and tangle of rails out to the rest of Italy and Europe, the tramline to the factories, the dull grey ribbon of the river, the parks; the city's layers, one on the other, nothing quite concealed however concerted the effort, nothing quite whole; and beyond it all the broken bowl of mountain, its summits frilled white with snow, where the cold air started. Giacomo pointed the sights out to her, one by one, Superga, Mirafiori, Palazzo Reale, the Duomo, the Chapel of the Holy Shroud. He didn't need to; she knew where she was. She was equal to him, she thought, pulling her coat around her. I live here too. He pointed down to the streets filled with traffic, the headlights on by now, to the people, tiny, mysterious, banal, about their business.

"Tempted?" he said, with a grin, sweeping his arm towards the horizon. "It's all yours. If you want it enough."

"Don't be stupid. How did you do it?" she said.

"Do what?"

"Get us into this place. Get the key. It's always been closed, ever since I got here."

He put his arm round her shoulders.

"Friends."

"That's a very Italian answer. I thought you hated all that. Favours. I thought you said no favour came free."

"Don't complain. You know how much you wanted to come up here and now you have. Be grateful, Helen. Learn to be grateful." Leaning out, he waved his other arm towards the street below. "Just look at the people. This is the point at which we're supposed to say they resemble ants, right?"

She laughed. That was the problem with Giacomo, that he had the power to amuse her. "Well, they do, a little. Less organised perhaps."

"Look, you see that woman there," he said, pointing. "The fat one with the shopping trolley and the fur coat."

"Not really."

"Use your imagination, Helen! Say yes."

She laughed. "Yes."

"What would you say if I told you it was all her fault?"

"If all what was her fault?"

"Oh everything. War, death, torture, everything. All the injustice, all the cruelty." He squeezed her tighter. "All the bloodshed."

"I'd think you were mad."

"But suppose it was true," he said, the pleading tone back in his voice. "All the world's evil concentrated into that one small figure there. And you had a gun. What would you do?"

"I'd miss," she said. "Obviously. I can't aim for toffee."

"So, you'd shoot?"

"Don't be silly. Of course I wouldn't."

"But how could you justify not shooting?"

"Because you can't just shoot people. That's how."

Giacomo moved away from her. "There's a story I read," he said, "I don't remember who wrote it. About a perfect world, without injustice or suffering, it's fairly vague about the economic details of course, it would have to be, but there's a sense of harmony and balance, it's just what anyone would want. A bit too mediaeval for my taste, but a perfect world in practically every aspect. There's only one snag." He paused, one eyebrow raised. She did what he expected. She asked:

"Which is?"

"In the heart of the capital there's a house with a cellar and inside the cellar there's a child, naked and starving, covered in sores, bleeding, in constant pain. And the child is forced to work at some menial task, day in day out, without interruption except for the briefest sleep, deprived of all but water and the most basic food, without attention, without love, provided with just enough heat and air to keep it alive. Gradually going blind as it works, although never enough to stop."

"And why doesn't somebody do something?" she said, playing her part.

"Because everyone's wellbeing depends on the suffering of the child. Without the child their perfect world would collapse like a house of cards. As long as the child is ill they can be well, as long as the child works they have leisure, as long as the child is denied love they can love. Their clothes and food are ensured by the nakedness and hunger of the child."

"And if they let the child go? What would happen then?"

Giacomo shrugged. "Well, obviously, everything would go wrong. They'd have to get their hands dirty. One person's suffering, on the other hand, and everyone else is safe, and happy, and well. The equation's the same. One death, a hundred million lives."

"So, what would you do?"

He held his right hand up in the air, index and middle finger pressed together, the other two gripped by the thumb, his strong hard hand in the shape of a pistol as a boy would understand it, then brought it down to point towards the street. The woman with the shopping trolley and the fur coat, if she had ever been there, had disappeared, but that didn't matter. Giacomo aimed his pistol, the weapon of a child, into the distant crowd of shoppers and people hurrying to their homes from offices and factories and shops, exhausted, hungry, startlingly cold as the warmth of the spring sun drained from the air and the streetlights came on and the park was swallowed up by the darkness. His whole heart was in it, this make-believe that wasn't. He said:

"I'd kill the child." He shook his head. "I can't bear suffering."

"You don't mean that," she said. "You couldn't kill a child. Besides, there's no comparison. Your stories aren't analogous at all."

He pulled her to him with his free arm. He gave her his hand, the gun.

"Go on," he said. "Fire."

After they'd left the building and were walking towards the flat, Giacomo said: "Do you miss me?"

"What do you mean?"

He stopped, so that she was obliged to stop. "You know. What we did? Do you miss that?"

Of course she knew. "Yes, I do." Whatever he said, or did, she missed him physically. She wondered how often he made love to Stefania, if they were fulfilled. She wondered, for a moment, if she was.

"We must be very different," he said. "Federico and I. In that way, I mean."

"Yes," she said, thinking, How coy he is, he can't say the words. He can't say *fuck*. He can't even say *make love*. "You are. You're very different."

"Some people, women especially, used to think we were lovers at Yale, did you know that? Because we were always together there, we did everything together. And we're more physical than you Anglo-Saxons, we'd touch each other and so on, and people assumed there was, well, more to it." He smiled.

"I'd have been more than willing, to tell you the truth, out of curiosity as much as anything. I'd have slept with Federico. I still would, given the chance. You know what Voltaire was supposed to have said: Once a philosopher. I'd have allowed myself that, with Federico. You think you know a person, but how can you? What can you know when that whole sphere is excluded?" He stared into her eyes, until she felt abashed and wanted to turn away. "I know you better than I'll ever know Federico. And you'll know me better than he ever will. And that's a pity, I think. He's missing out on something."

"Sex isn't that important," Helen said, because she had to say something and she couldn't say what she thought. What she thought was that maybe Giacomo had explained to her why both men loved her and allowed her to love them back.

Years later, when she thought about this episode, she wondered if Giacomo had ever taken Federico to the top of the tower, as he'd taken her, and tempted him, as she'd been tempted. And she wondered if it was true that Federico and Giacomo had never slept together, or fucked, or made love, because they had had the chance so often. Sometimes she'd come home from work and find them together in the kitchen, or Federico would be sitting at his desk with Giacomo sprawled on the bed, *their* bed, beside him, and there was an air in the room, a density, of something that wouldn't be said, an air she'd chosen not to question. And then there was that flat they took together, that Federico didn't tell her about. Later, when everything went wrong and Giacomo was arrested, she'd seen Federico so beaten down by it all, so lost. That was when she'd almost convinced herself that they really had been lovers, maybe not often but, still, there was that complicity between them. Once a philosopher, she'd thought.

9

Martin calls Helen on her landline and then on her mobile, but she isn't there, or isn't answering. He hasn't planned to leave a message but finds himself telling her voicemail that he'd like to talk to her later that afternoon if she has a moment. He's supposed to be going to the reception at the American embassy, one of the perks of the trade, and of his seniority, not to speak of favours done in earlier, less simple days. Against his better judgement he's decided to go, although there is nothing he enjoys less than formal events and the kind of outfit he is obliged to wear for them. He's had the full kit cleaned and pressed. It's hanging, cadaver-like, from the back of the bedroom door in one of those flat nylon suitcases that open out into a long black sack. The case was a parting present, so not entirely well meant, from a woman who thought that all he really lacked to be smart, to have some respect for himself, as she insisted on saying, were the accoutrements of elegance. How wrong she was. What little respect he is capable of feeling would be wasted on himself. He glances down at his hands, then reaches into a drawer for some nail clippers, the size made for feet, and sets to work.

When he's finished and is satisfied with the result, he tries Picotti's number again, for the fourth time this afternoon. Martin knows he's being foolish, more than foolish, foolhardy, but he doesn't care. On the way back from meeting Corti, he bought a half-bottle of brandy at the Trevi supermarket and a couple of flabby sandwiches in cling film, one of which, half-eaten, is lying beside his phone on the table, the mayonnaise separating in the heat. The brandy is mostly drunk and he has the familiar dull throbbing in his left temple which tells him he has had too much. He has lost today's battle. A scrap of Shakespeare comes to him. How does it go? *Tomorrow in the battle think of me.* Is that it? Well, he'll do his best.

He's using Picotti's special number, the one he was given as they said goodbye. Perhaps it was part of the plan to throw me off, he thinks. He wanted to make me feel so privileged I'd keep my mouth shut. There is anger now as Martin presses the redial button and waits. This time his wait is rewarded.

"Martino." Picotti's voice is filled with reproach.

"What the hell's going on?"

"What do you want from me, Martino?"

"The truth."

Picotti begins to laugh, a sad exhausted laugh that ends in a fit of coughing. Martin waits for him to stop.

"I smoke too much," says Picotti.

"We haven't always been honest with each other," says Martin. "I know that. It wasn't possible. But I always thought we were on the same side."

"The side of the good and true."

"Not necessarily. Our side's made mistakes."

"Mistakes? Is that what you think, Martino *mio*? That we were two brave soldier boys fighting together, shoulder to shoulder, in defence of liberty and civilisation? And sometimes we made mistakes?"

"Di Stasi? Was he a mistake?"

"He's dead, Martin." People keep telling me this, thinks Martin, almost amused, as though they imagine the fact might have slipped my mind.

"And Di Stasi's mother?" Martin says. "You know her, of course. You must do, surely? Wasn't she on one of those commissions that looked into your goings-on once? Quite the busybody, wasn't she? Until things went quiet. Still, I expect she's past it by now. How old is she? Eighty? Eighty-five?"

Picotti doesn't answer at once. When he does, his voice is cold and far away, as though he is calling across an empty space, calling some words of warning that Martin can't quite catch, although the tone is clear enough. "You don't need to do this," he says. Another pause and the edge of disappointment, of regret that absolves Picotti of all responsibility, returns. "Oh Martino, *vecchio amico mio*. Why did you have to get involved in all this foolishness?"

Martin's about to pour himself a final drink when the entry phone rings. At last, he thinks, I'd given up on you.

"Hello."

He doesn't recognise the voice so much as the trace of accent.

"Second floor," he says.

Alina's dressed for the occasion. A short white skirt, some sort of green satin top, bare legs, stilettos. She's got one of those foolish little bags just large enough for lipstick and a packet of condoms, the money stuffed into the bottom, a mobile. She smiles, not coming in at once, not wanting to appear too brazen, and he steps back to invite her to enter. She sits on the sofa and slips off her shoes.

"They hurt." She rubs her toes with her left hand. "Shoes like this aren't made for human feet." Her legs are thin and strong; her calves stand out as she flexes her feet, looking down at them the way a ballerina might, as tools of her trade. "I don't know what they're made for."

"To make you suffer," says Martin.

"You must be very sad," she says, "about your friend." She sounds concerned. Oh dear, thinks Martin, she'll want to help me absorb the blow. And why not? He could do with some counselling.

"Not incurably," he says. He walks across and sits on the sofa beside her. Now she's here he doesn't know what to do, nor what's expected of him. He's drunk, he knows that; she's part of the reason. He tries a jocular approach. "Are you here to help me get over the shock?"

Alina nods, but doesn't otherwise move. Martin strokes her hair back from her face, hooking it behind her ear. She has small ears, redder than the skin around them, as though chapped. His other hand rests a moment on her leg. She is staring straight ahead. Following her eyes, he sees what she sees, the two of them framed in the mirror on the opposite wall, his torso twisted, ungainly, his stomach showing white and flecked with hair beneath his untucked shirt, the woman's pale face and neck and indifferent, slightly peeved expression, her heavy breasts loose behind the satin top, her narrow impoverished shoulders. There is no grace in this, he thinks. We both deserve more than this. She turns from their reflected faces to look into his eyes.

"Is everything all right?" he says, confused.

She laughs, a humourless impatient laugh, then parts her thighs with a brisk muscular jerk. His hand falls away.

"I didn't come here for this," she says.

"You didn't come here for this?" He's flushed with humiliation.

"I didn't come here to have sex with you and be paid for it. That didn't come into your head? That I might have had another reason?" She moves along the sofa until there is no contact between them. "You are all the same. Adriano thinks I stay with him because I have nowhere else to go."

"Why do you?" Why else would anyone stay with Adriano, thinks Martin.

"Why do you suppose? Because I love his cat." She laughs again. "I love all small defenceless creatures."

Martin stands up.

"Is that what I am to you? A small defenceless creature?" This sounds flirtatious, but isn't meant to. He asks because he wants to know what she thinks, how she sees him. He wants to know if anything can be redeemed.

"Oh yes," she says, her tone engaging for the first time. "I think you are waiting to be rescued, to be given a home."

These words strike Martin with the force of truth.

"I would like to be rescued very much," he says, with a smile, "although I don't know from what, other than my own clumsiness and stupidity."

"I came because I wanted to tell you something." Her voice is warmer now. "I wanted to warn you." She opens her bag and takes out a piece of paper. "After you'd gone, Adriano called someone. He spoke about you."

"And what did he say?"

"I wasn't supposed to be listening, and so I didn't, to begin with anyway," she says. "But it was the way he spoke, I didn't like it. Adriano's nothing special, I know that, but he can be, I don't know, angry? He can be cruel. Sometimes he forgets I'm there. Sometimes he doesn't. My life isn't easy."

"Why are you telling me this?"

She smiles wryly. "Because I think you are a gentleman. Despite everything."

Martin considers this for a moment, then asks her a second time, in a gentler voice: "What did he say?"

To his surprise, she blushes. "That you were breaking someone's balls, I didn't hear whose. That you needed to be taught a lesson."

"I've behaved badly, Alina," says Martin. "I'm so sorry. I misunderstood. If there's anything I can do to make amends?" His first instinct is to offer her money, but he's not stupid.

Alina stands up, adjusts her skirt, then walks over, still bare-footed, and takes his face in her hands. She rocks his head a little from side to side, her mouth reproving, motherly. "Treat people with respect, Mr Frame. Even if you think they don't deserve it. Even if you think they can be bought. Do that for me. To make amends."

"All right," he says, filled with emotion. This wonderful woman, he thinks, her hands on my face like this. He wants to cry. He nods, and her hands nod with him.

"I will," he says. "I promise."

She is leaving the room when, on an impulse, he calls her back.

"Alina?"

"Yes?"

"Do you speak English?"

"Enough," she says dryly. "Why?"

"Are you busy this evening? With Adriano?"

"No."

"Can I ask an indiscreet question?"

She laughs. She has an attractive laugh, open and infectious, her head thrown back a little. "Haven't you been indiscreet enough, Mr Frame?" she says in English.

He hangs his head. "I've been more than indiscreet," he says. "I've behaved unforgivably."

"So what is your question?"

"Are your papers in order?"

She's surprised. "I didn't expect you to ask me that," she says; she sounds offended. "But, yes, Adriano has served for something. I have a permit to stay. I'm his chambermaid, I believe you say."

Martin smiles. "Yes, we do say that."

"Why should you want to know about my legal status here?" she says. "Do you plan to report me to the authorities?"

"Because I have an invitation for two people and, well, as you can see, I'm alone here. I'd be flattered if you would accompany me."

"An invitation to what?" she says and he can see that she is both flattered and suspicious. "To do what?"

"To the American embassy. To meet the President of the United States."

10

Helen is putting food on the table. Pizza bread, the cheese and meat still in their wrappers. She's washed some rocket and sliced a handful of tomatoes. It all has the atmosphere of a picnic, improvised and yet with a sense of occasion, a treat. She'd opened a bottle of wine before Giacomo arrived.

"These are the ones from Massimo's mother," she says, moving the bread to one side to make room for a small bowl of dull green olives. "They don't look much but they're wonderful."

Giacomo takes one. "I'm glad to be here," he says.

"I had a visitor today," says Helen, seeming – or pretending – not to have heard, absorbed by other thoughts. She sits down, fills both their glasses. "A priest called Don Giusini. Federico's priest."

Giacomo takes a second olive.

"He knew more about Federico than I did in the end," Helen says. "Unnerving, isn't it? All that time I thought Federico disliked the church as much as I did, and there he was, seeing a priest, doing all the confession business. I wonder where he got it from."

"These are very good olives," says Giacomo.

Helen picks one out of the bowl but doesn't eat it. She rolls it between her fingers and thumb until the skin there is moist and greenish in the reflected light. She stares at the olive as if it were a jewel she has found, some precious mysterious stone, and then looks up, but not at Giacomo, at the blackboard. Giacomo follows her gaze and sees the word OLIVES. "I'll have to rub that off," she says, but doesn't move. He thinks: She already knows she'll not be able to rub it off. And then: I could have written that. We write the same, Federico and I, we have the same neat hand. "He told me Federico was going to die. He had a brain tumour."

So he would have died anyway, thinks Giacomo, but a shock goes through him, as though someone has told him of his own death. "Do you believe him?"

"I have no reason not to. Federico might have lied to him, I suppose, there's always that chance. But I don't think he was lying to me."

"Wasn't there anything he could have done?"

"Apparently not. But that isn't what he went to Don Giusini about. It wasn't the tumour he wanted to talk about." Helen puts down the olive with what looks like a grimace of distaste, as though she's already tasted it and found it bad. "He'd decided to take advantage of the fact that he didn't have more than a few weeks to live."

"Take advantage?" So little time, thinks Giacomo.

"Yes. He wanted to do something dreadful. He said he was going to die anyway so his life had no value. He was set free to do something that might save thousands of other lives. I still can't believe it." She pauses for a moment. "Giacomo," she says, and her voice is harsh and incredulous, as if she is repeating a vicious lie she had heard about herself. "He asked his secretary to arrange a meeting with the PM, with Bush if he could, with anyone she could rustle up, a meeting at the conference. And then when they were all together, all these important people, Federico was going to blow himself up and take them with him."

"Blow himself up?"

"The tumour was affecting his brain, the way he thought, the way he behaved. He was afraid he wouldn't be capable of anything if he waited too long. I think that's what he was thinking about from the minute he started work on the conference. They'd all been invited. It was a photo opportunity, that's what Federico's secretary said. I spoke to her this afternoon, while I was waiting for you. Nobody misses a photo opportunity, she said. She sounded disappointed."

Giacomo is imagining a tumour, its steady growth inside the brain, under the bone; the pressure of it, cancelling thought as it pushes for space, cancelling sense, identity, cancelling life itself. This is the proof that he was mad, thinks Giacomo, the notion that such a thing might be possible. No one of any weight would have come to his conference. He'd have been lucky to get a couple of under-secretaries. And then it occurs to him that Federico had wanted Giacomo to be there. At the kill.

"It wouldn't have been the first time he'd been involved in murdering someone," says Helen. "That was another surprise. He was part of that bank raid in Turin as well, when someone was killed, the one you were arrested for. Well, you'd know that, of course, wouldn't you? You were there too. He never told me about it. He never told anyone, not until recently anyway. His father maybe, I don't know. Maybe he told his father. And that's not all. He thought that he should have gone to jail instead of you." She looks at him, hard. "You knew, of course. You've always known."

Giacomo is silent for a moment. "The priest told you this?"

"Fausto found out later, when Federico wanted his help to get your pardon. He always spoke to his father, you see. He trusted him in a way he's never trusted me. I could never understand why it mattered so much to Fausto that you be released. But I do now." Helen wipes her nose on her bare arm, then empties her glass. "I feel as though I've lost him all over again," she says. "Actually, that's not true. I feel as though I've never had him, as though it was all a lie, all these years. I feel betrayed, Giacomo. Isn't that awful?" Her face is drawn, her eyes almost frighteningly wide. "When ten minutes after he'd been murdered I was with you."

Helen leaves the room without saying anything more, coming back after a minute or two with a sheaf of papers. "He left me this, except that he didn't really, not to me anyway. I don't think I was supposed to see it." She thumbs through the sheets until she has found what she wants.

"Read this," she says.

I have never forgiven myself for what we did, killing a man in cold blood. At the time I thought he was nobody special. A bank guard. I found out later he was involved in the struggle himself, in his own way as much of an activist as I was, but that isn't important. It doesn't make him more deserving of life. I thought then that what I was doing was right, I thought I had learnt to swim, as Kafka said. I'd never told anyone before I told Don Giusini. I thought it might help but it hasn't. It stays with you. What did Kafka say? I have a better memory than the others. I have not forgotten the former inability to swim... But since I have not forgotten it, being able to swim is of no help to me; and so, after all, I cannot swim.

Yet now, despite this, I am on the brink of killing again, because I think these deaths will solve something, will save the lives of others. This is why my repentance is worth nothing. Because I haven't changed. I don't expect anyone to understand but

"I didn't know Federico thought like this," says Giacomo. He remembers the bank raid, a cold day, drizzle, a wide road in the

252

outskirts of Turin, three of them and the driver, as if it were yesterday, the excitement, the panic, the horror; but he's never felt that Federico deserved to be arrested any more than he did. It was the luck of the draw. How strange that it should have worried him all these years, that he should have expected his father to pull strings for Giacomo. No wonder Fausto hated him and yet turned to him. If Giacomo hadn't been arrested and needed help, Fausto would never have known what his son had done. What a curious notion of fairness in the end, when a man was dead.

"Neither did I," says Helen.

"Where did you get this from?"

"His mother had it."

"This is the file, isn't it? The one on the computer?"

"Yes. Juggernaut. Ploughing roughshod over the lot of us."

"How did you get it?"

"I broke into their flat yesterday. Well, not exactly broke into. I let myself in with a key, just as she did here. Federico had thought of everything, you see. She was the one who deleted the file as well, at least I think it was her. You were right. She doesn't know how to do it properly, she just sort of empties it out like an old sack." Helen shrugs. "There are other possibilities, of course. Federico might have given it to her, or to Fausto. It's quite likely he'd mentioned the file to her, or to Fausto, and she'd wanted to take a look at it." Her tone is bitter. "They were very close."

Giacomo thumbs through the sheets of paper, reading the odd phrase. So much of it makes sense, but a skewed sense, seen through some crumbling prism of guilt and fervour. The man was genuinely, clinically mad, he thinks. Like mother, like son.

"You never told me you were innocent," Helen says.

"I didn't think I needed to," he says. "I thought you understood. In any case, I wasn't. None of us were innocent."

"I always thought Federico was," she says. "I haven't understood anything, have I? The two of us, for example. All that time Federico was alive and we were seeing each other when we could, I never once felt that it was wrong. And now he's dead, and we're all each other has, I do. I think it's wrong and I don't know what to do about it."

"Do you want me to go?"

"I don't know." She looks up at him. "Yes," she says. "I think I do."

There is another sheet of paper from Federico's file she could have shown Giacomo, if only to prove his state of mind beyond all doubt, but she chose not to. It was too horrible, and too private. As soon as she is alone again, she goes into her bedroom to find it. She sits on the side of the bed, holding it in her hands, trembling as she reads.

```
a dream last night, which woke me. A black
child, no more than five years old, the kind you
see on charity ads during famines: big staring
eyes, enormous round head on a stalk of a neck,
his stomach distended. A man was using an office
stapler to pin the child's arms to the top of
a wooden table, the arms so thin the staples
contained them, three staples to each arm. My
eyes in the dream moved down across the raised
veins of the belly to where the man was moving
the child's legs out of the way, legs like hanks
of chewed gristle, and pushing his penis into the
child, who didn't move, who lay there weeping in
a puddle of his own blood and his own mucus.
    What do I do with a dream like this? I know
it's the war that's doing this to me, it must
be, that's pressing on my head like this and
distorting it, but is that all? Am I that man?
```

Do I deserve it in some way? Where do I begin
to understand my complicity? I almost woke
Helen, but didn't. I felt ashamed. I lay there
and looked at where her face must have been in
the dark and wondered if she would blame me for
having dreamed such an awful thing. And I didn't
know the answer.

So he did go to the top of the tower with Giacomo, she thinks.
And she wonders who took whom.

11

Alina, in a dress Martin has bought for her, new shoes in the same colour, her hair freshly done – he's still shocked at the sums of money he's spent; he had no idea how much these things cost – is playing the part of the diplomatic wife with exemplary skill, shaking hands, smiling. He's been shaken by her, he has to admit, shaken by what he can only call her self-respect. How do we manage that? he wonders. How do we manage to respect ourselves? Martin can't remember the last time he's had occasion to respect himself, nor to expect respect. Yet here she is, this woman, no more than twenty-five, who's been taken from her home and bought and sold as a chattel as far as he can tell. They've been talking for hours, but in a way that old friends have, as though certain areas of trust and silence can be assumed. Her English, it turns out, is better than her Italian, which is already good. She has a natural charm that shines through her shyness. He's keeping an eye on her, not because he's worried she might let him down, but because she's wonderful to watch. He feels like Pygmalion. Here she is, holding her glass with the elegance you'd expect from someone bred to these things, these dreadful false events that carry so much weight. The only time she seemed uncomfortable was when they were frisked before entering by the embassy's men. They asked to see a document and he wondered, for an acutely embarrassing moment, if she'd been lying, before she produced an Italian identity card, glancing across at him with a smile as she handed it over to be checked. Afterwards, she took his arm and squeezed it. "Get me a drink," she said. "I hate those moments too." Once inside, she looked around her at the size of the ill-proportioned room, the over-bright lights, and smiled, a little pleased with him, intensely pleased at her own implausible presence in such a place. He's glad he brought her. She's a credit to him. He can't remember the last time he enjoyed an evening like this. Even his hangover seems to have been smoothed away by the sparkling wine he's been drinking since he arrived.

And now Alina has met George Bush, rather in the way that Martin once met Margaret Thatcher – a briefly stroked hand, not even pressed, in a line of hands, that piercing glassy stare she was known for, although clearly she'd no idea who he was, nor had she cared to know. But Alina, touchingly, blushed and even bobbed her head, and Georgie boy gave her a second glance, as though making a mental note. How odd these powerful people are, thinks Martin, taking a glass from a passing tray. How much they need us and despise us. They think we're their slaves when, really, it's quite the opposite. They're ours. And now he really is drinking too much, he'd better slow down or eat something. The canapés are decent, the home culture winning out over that of its illustrious guest. He listens to Alina explain in her elegant English to a short man in an over-tight dinner jacket that the end of the USSR has changed so much in her country, so many things for the better, so many for the worse, and he wonders if she even remembers the Wall coming down. She'd have just started school, if that. He's about to do the maths when he notices someone from the agency, one of his superiors.

"I'll be back in a second," he says and Alina, her face slightly flushed with wine, he supposes, and the glory of the occasion, smiles briefly and nods her permission.

After a few moments of awkward conversation with a woman whose name he can't remember, who clearly wants to ask him who his partner is but doesn't dare, Martin comes back to see Alina being led to the dance floor by a man he has never seen before, his plump hand in the small of Alina's back. He has a twinge of jealousy, which he struggles to overcome. Perhaps I've changed her life, he thinks, perhaps she'll find a man who deserves her. How sentimental I am. To think she came to tell me that I was in danger. And I'm doing *Pretty Woman* on her. He wonders if there might be something in it, he won't deny Picotti has unnerved him, though it's hard to imagine him counting for much. But neither does Adriano Testa count for much. And there is always danger, according to the statistics. Fear death by frying pan. He takes a glass from a passing tray and watches her dance. How beautiful she is. When she chose the dress, it looked nothing, he couldn't believe how much a scrap of fabric like that could cost, but look at it now. A vision. He has an urgent need to piss. As he moves off to the bathroom, he sees her eyes seek him out. He makes a foolish little wave with his hand, mouths "I'll be back," and is gratified to see her nod her head and smile. The man she's dancing with turns to stare at him as he wanders off.

Sometime later, Martin waits by the main door into the room for Alina to come back from the bathroom. He's more than ready to leave but when she gets back she begs to be allowed to stay a little longer and he can't deny her this one-off pleasure, watching the fag end of a diplomatic reception, the musicians leaving the rostrum, the speeches made, the waiters surreptitiously starting to clear away as the last dozen people wonder how much longer they'll be served.

"I think it's time we went," he says when a waiter catches his eye.

Alina stands up, tucking her new bag under her arm, smoothing the creases from her brand new dress. "I've had a wonderful time," she says. She kisses his cheek. "Thank you."

Together, their arms linked, they walk towards Piazza Barberini. No decision has been made about where they will go, but Martin's plan is to find a bar and talk about taxis; he doesn't intend to make the same mistake twice. There's no one about, the area directly around the embassy has been closed to traffic. Martin's weaving slightly from side to side, surprised by the warmth of the air after the air-conditioned salons of the embassy.

They're entering the square when a motorbike carrying two men in unlabelled leathers and full-face helmets swings in from the side street to the left and turns with a squeal of brakes in Martin's direction. When the bike is almost beside him, the driver swerves up onto the pavement, the back wheel skidding as it judders and mounts the kerb, the driver revving and braking to keep control. Martin's reactions are slow. Turning, stumbling slightly as the motorbike hits him, he's caught at the hip and lifted, flung up by the handlebars, flopping like a doll across the crouched figure of the driver, landing with a thud. Alina starts to scream as the pillion rider, without leaving the bike, lifts what looks like a baseball bat and hits Martin twice with it, once on his legs and once on his head, the crack of bone quite audible each time.

"I'm here," she says, reaching beneath him to open Martin's collar, her hands smeared with his blood, bright black on the white of her skin, on the pale silk of her beautiful new dress, as she pulls her arms cautiously from underneath his chest to feel his legs and see what damage has been done. "I'm a nurse," she whispers, then corrects herself. "I was a nurse. Before."

PART FIVE
1

Rome, Saturday, 5 June 2004

Helen is roused by the alarm on her mobile ringing in the kitchen, where she left it beside her glass last night. She starts into wakefulness, not sure where she is at first, then half-staggers, half-rolls from the sofa, banging her knee on the corner of the coffee table. She has barely slept. She stayed up drinking after Giacomo left, reading and re-reading Federico's papers, the legacy she was never meant to have. It made her feel dirty, in the end, as though she'd read his diary, some private part of him she'd not been meant to see. And then she was angry again, because marriage wasn't supposed to be a place for secrets. And then she was ashamed, because she'd lied to him so often. And then, because there was no end to this, she turned her shame on him, and blamed him for not loving her enough, for placing his work before his marriage, for talking to his parents instead of her, for writing all these words she had never been meant to read, which hurt so much, and then allowing her to find them.

She slept on the sofa because she couldn't bear the thought of sleeping in the bed, imagining the dried sweat and powdery dust of Giacomo and herself, of Federico, of all the skin the three of them had sloughed in it. Her final act before lying down and pulling a throw across her had been to set the alarm for 8am. She had an appointment with the magistrate at half past nine. She didn't want to be late.

And now it is 8am, and she is standing in her bra and panties, rubbing her knee, and turning off the alarm. Her neck is stiff from the position she's been in. The last thing she remembers is seeing daylight seep into the room through the slats in the outer shutters; she'd left the inner shutters open by mistake. Normally, Federico would close them before he came to bed. Normally, she thinks. This is the fourth morning without Federico. She wonders when she will lose count; if she will ever lose count. She fills the coffee pot and goes for a shower.

At half past nine, she is shown into the magistrate's office. He is dressed more smartly this morning, as though he's made an effort for her. He holds her chair, slides it in beneath her as she sits down.

"Thank you for coming," he says. His South African accent seems more pronounced today, although she was probably in no fit state to notice the last time she'd seen him, in that awful room in the hospital. Not that this is much better, piles of books and files everywhere, a trolley suitcase by the door that he must use to move his papers from one place to another. This reminds her, with a jolt, of Federico's briefcase.

"I'm so sorry," she says. "About lying to you, I mean. I don't know what I thought I would achieve. I've only made your work more difficult."

"I understand," he says, sitting down opposite her, his voice reassuring. "I would have done the same, in your position."

"I suppose Giacomo told you, in any case? When you spoke to him on Wednesday?"

"Is that what he said? That he'd told me?" When she shakes her head, he continues. "There was no need. By that time, I must admit, we already knew where you'd been. I took the opportunity to speak to Mura for another reason."

She's surprised, but doesn't speak. He opens a drawer and pulls out an envelope.

"I'd like to show you something," he says. "I hope you don't mind."

She doesn't know how to react. She watches him open the envelope and take out a photograph. He looks at it for a moment, without expression, before handing it across to her.

She hasn't seen this photograph for almost thirty years. She is sitting in the college room she had in her final year, laughing at something. It's a sunny day and the light coming in through the window has created a sort of aureole around her. She looks illuminated, far prettier than she ever was, she'd thought then, although now she wonders if perhaps she had been that pretty all the time and had never really known. She's wearing a T-shirt and jeans, her hair is longer than she normally wore it; despite this, she has a boyish look, but not androgynous; *gamine* is the word that comes to her now. She can't remember who else was in the room with her, but she remembers the moment; she remembers, if that's possible, her laughter. She's never liked photographs of herself, she's thrown them away when she's had the chance; but this is one she loved. She flips it over and sees, in her handwriting, a dedication and a date: *To my favourite student, May 1978.*

"Where did you get this?"

"My father had it."

"Your father was Eduardo?"

"Yes, Eduardo Cotugno." The magistrate smiles. "You were his teacher in Turin."

"I know that. I gave him this photograph just before he left. He asked me for one and this was my favourite. It was the only copy I had."

"He didn't know that, I don't think. He'd have been more deeply touched than ever."

"He didn't?"

"Yes, he died two years ago."

"Oh," she says, shocked. "I'm so sorry."

"He often spoke about you. He said you were the only person he trusted during his last few months in Italy. You gave him the strength to continue. My mother made it hard for him. He felt alone. You helped him cope."

"I don't know how," she says. She is shaken, shaken and moved, to find herself thinking once more about Eduardo. She looks at the man opposite her, as if for the first time. "I remember him telling me he had two sons."

"Yes, my brother stayed in South Africa. My father lived with his family for the last few years of his life, in Durban. He's a doctor."

"And you came back to Italy."

"Yes, eventually." He smiles. "My father thought I was mad."

"He didn't want to go away at all," says Helen.

"Oh, he loved it there. He got himself into trouble almost immediately. You know what my father was like." He laughs. "But when things changed, when apartheid came to an end, he was vindicated. He could never have come back to Italy after that."

"Why not?"

"Because he was living in a place he'd fought for. And because the people who'd driven him out of Italy were running the country." He looks at Helen. "I'm sorry, I didn't mean to imply–"

"No," she says, "don't apologise, you're quite right," as memories of Eduardo rush back. Sitting there with his leg on a chair as they ran through the paradigms of irregular verbs before he persuaded her that what he needed was conversation, to talk about the world. Running his hands through his hair, which was like his son's hair, she sees as she looks at the man before her. She remembers Eduardo as an older man, but he must have been ten years younger than she is now, in his early forties at the most. He'd thought his life was destroyed, but he'd been wrong. Lives can be remade, she thinks, with a little courage.

"Was he happy?" Before he can answer, she says, "I'm sorry, I can't remember your first name."

"Piero," he says. "Oh yes, he was happy, most of the time. He was challenged, but he inspired great respect, great affection. It suited him; he'd have been stifled here. He spent his last years in the country, until my mother died – they had a farm – and then my brother took him in, as I said."

Helen puts the photograph on the desk, face-down. "Did you bring me here to show me this?"

"Yes," he says, with a sheepish grin. "I've brought you here under false pretences, but I thought you would want to know that you made a difference to someone's life. He would have wanted you to know that. So often people don't. It's all we *can* do in the end, isn't it? With any luck, for the better."

They sit together for a moment, in silence. Eventually, when she can stand her thoughts no longer, Helen speaks.

"Do you know who killed my husband, Piero?"

"No," he says. "Do you?"

"Knowing won't bring him back," she says.

She's leaving his room when the site of the trolley case reminds her.

"Federico's briefcase. He had it with him when he was shot. I don't suppose I could have it, could I?"

"I don't see why not," he says. "I'll see what I can do." He's picking up his phone when Helen's mobile rings in her bag. It's Martin.

She's about to tell him she'll call him back when she hears, not Martin, but a woman speaking. "Is that Helen? Am I speaking to Helen?"

"Yes. Who's that?"

"I'm a friend of Martin's. I'm calling from the hospital. I have some bad news for you."

2

Helen keeps saying *It's my fault* as she drives to the hospital across a city whose traffic, always chaotic, has been slowed down to a virtual halt, in preparation, she supposes, for the demonstration later in the day. It takes her forty minutes to reach the hospital gates. She is stopped by the sentry, who glances into the car in a bored, desultory way before waving her on. Frantic, already playing with the clasp of her safety belt, she drives into the grounds.

A thin blonde woman in evening dress, with a dark stain in the lap, is sitting in the corridor. She jumps up when Helen arrives.

"Where is he?" Helen says. "I want to see him."

"He's through there," she says, pointing to a door. The woman steps across to open the door for Helen. Her eyes are dog-tired, ringed with black, she couldn't be more than twenty-five. Helen walks past her, confused. "Why didn't you call me sooner?" she says. What she wants to ask is who the woman is, but this isn't the moment.

"I didn't know who to call. I waited until Martin could tell me."

"But if he'd died," Helen says, her hand to her mouth. "I couldn't have lived with that, I couldn't have coped."

"There's no danger of that," the woman says. She has switched to English, but Helen only realises this later, when she replays the scene in her head. "Not now. The doctors say he'll pull through. He'll feel the worse for wear for the next few weeks, that's all."

"He's conscious?" says Helen, still standing at the door, abruptly afraid to go in. Who is this woman? she thinks.

"Yes. But they've told me to say that he can't have visitors for long."

They go into the ward. There is only one bed, near the window. Martin is lying down, the left side of his head shaved clean and criss-crossed by stitches along a jagged gash. His face is swollen and bruised, with ragged wounds on the cheek and forehead and the tip of his nose beginning to scab. A tube is attached to his nostrils by a flesh-coloured clip. Helen wouldn't have recognised him. Other tubes dangle from the sheet, draped across some sort of tent to protect his legs, ending up in a bottle attached to the bed frame or rising in an arc to a flat plastic bag full of drip, dangling from a stand. Next to the bed, on a metal trolley, is a box with dials and flashing lights to which Martin has been wired up. Helen stands by the bed, while the young woman in her blood-stained dress smoothes the sheet on the far side with a calming, professional air. Helen sits down in a chair beside the bed, watching Martin's eyes move round the room, to see who is there. He smiles when they rest on her. "Hello, my dear," he says. His voice is surprisingly strong, but distorted, as though he is holding something soft, a marshmallow, a ball of cotton wool, in his mouth. "The more the merrier," he says. He winces when Helen kisses him. Pulling back, she sees that his lip has been cut and stitched. When he opens his mouth to speak again, she notices he's lost two teeth.

"You've met Alina," he says, raising a hand to indicate the other woman in the room. "She saved my life. She's my guardian angel now." He smiles. "I hope for some time to come."

"Did you see who it was? Who did this?" says Helen, turning to Alina, who shakes her head.

"They were wearing helmets." She spreads her hands in a gesture of helplessness. "They were men, two men, on a motorbike. In Piazza Barberini."

"The number plate?" Helen says, insistent. "Did you get their number?"

"I looked, of course, but the number plate was covered. Maybe there wasn't a number plate."

Martin waves his hand impatiently.

"Not important," he says. "I know who did it. I'll come to that. Right now, I want to talk to both of you. I want you to know what I think. If we all know, we'll be safe. I'll be safe."

"All right, Martin, all right," says Helen, reaching for his hand and holding it. He tries to raise his head from the pillow, but the effort is too much for him and he lets it fall back with a sigh. "Bloody drugs," he says, then smiles. "A good shot of whisky might do the trick. No chance of that, I suppose?"

"I'll see what I can do," says Alina, smiling, but Martin has started to speak in an urgent, breathless way.

"I know who did it, or I think I do. Not this," he says, waving his hand impatiently towards his legs, "Federico. Who killed Federico. I spoke to one or two of my old friends, Helen; you knew that's what I'd do, I didn't need to tell you who. But they weren't my friends at all. Or not only mine, at least. They were Giulia's friends as well." He looks at Helen, as if for confirmation. "That's her name, isn't it? Federico's mother? Giulia?" She nods, and he stares at the ceiling, satisfied. "They were Giulia's friends." He stops to breathe, while Alina bathes his lips with a strip of dampened gauze. "She's been phoning someone I used to know. That's bloody odd, I thought, something fishy about that." He laughs, as if to himself, then grimaces at the pain from his mouth. "She's been calling him. She's got a special SIM card for her phone. It's all in the records. Check it, you'll know someone who can check it. If you all know, you'll be safe. We'll all be safe. They can't kill all of us."

"He's spoken enough," says Alina. "We must leave him to sleep." She stands up, ushering Helen out, but shows no signs of leaving herself.

Helen stands in the corridor, breathing deeply, in and out. Martin is delirious, she thinks, and she can't understand why nothing he has said, his impossible accusation, has shocked, or even surprised, her. She waits until her heart has calmed, then takes her mobile from her bag and calls Giacomo. Please let him still be here in Rome, she says to herself as his phone rings out. He might have left for Paris already, after the way she dismissed him last night. Please God let him still be here. When he answers, she can barely talk for the relief.

"I have so much to tell you," she says.

3

"But of course it's possible," said Helen. She is back at the flat, with Giacomo. "She's capable of anything." She's been calling her in-laws' flat for the past half hour, at first on her mobile from the car and now with the landline, but it's constantly engaged. The more often she tries, the more frustrated and enraged she becomes. Right now, she's half a mind to go round there and make a scene. But when she announces that this is what she plans to do, Giacomo dissuades her.

"No, not yet. We need to talk about this," he says. "We mustn't jump to conclusions. Because what you're saying is insane, you do see that, don't you? You're saying she had her own son murdered."

"She'd have done it herself," says Helen. "With her own two hands if necessary. I know Giulia. I've known her for thirty years. I know what she's capable of."

"But why?" he says, although she's explained half a dozen times.

"To stop him embarrassing her," she says. "He was a loose cannon. He might have done anything. He might have killed someone." She remembers what Federico wrote about the Juggernaut, riding roughshod over all in its path to save the world. That's how he saw himself, she thinks. She imagines him standing there on the stage, with the cameras clicking beneath him, surrounded by the great and the less great, holding the briefcase that he's had as long as she's known him, each stitch along its seams his own work, the weight of the bomb. He'd have used his briefcase, she's sure of that. No one would have questioned him. And Giacomo would have been beside him, ally to the last.

"Embarrassing her? I don't believe it." Giacomo is scornful. "In any case, Federico's no murderer."

"It wouldn't have been so hard to believe thirty years ago." Frustrated, infuriated by his tone, which seems to diminish her as Federico's had so often in the past, Helen directs her anger at him. "You wouldn't have had any problems with it. Neither of you. Not then. What about Moro? What about all the others? Don't you see? The minute Federico knew he was going to die, it made perfect sense."

"Things were different then," he says.

"Things were the *same*, Giacomo, don't you see? You were no different from Giulia. Giulia's obsessed by the state. She talks about the constitution as though it were her child. *Her* constitution. We bled for it, that's what she says. We gave our blood. She's never talked like that about Federico. She must have thought, I don't know, can you imagine what people would say about Italy if Federico really did do something stupid? Blow himself up and take half the world's leaders with him? He wasn't just anyone, was he?" She feels like striking Giacomo, slapping him across the face to make him listen. To make him see. "He wasn't just a consultant at the ministry, although that's bad enough. That's scandal enough. He was her son. The only son of Giulia Paternò, the founding mother of modern Italy." Her voice is ripe with sarcasm. "It would have destroyed her."

Giacomo nods, but doesn't speak. He looks uncomfortable. Helen doesn't care. She wants him to look uncomfortable.

"Besides," she says, feeling fully alive for the first time since Federico's death, as though she's been shaken into wakefulness, as though what she's needed to do is *think*, "whatever he did would have played straight into the PM's hands. She'd have known that. He'd have used it to declare a state of emergency, martial law, God knows what else." Eduardo, her wonderful kneecapped student, comes into her head. He was right, she's known that all this time, violence begets violence.

"But Federico would have thought of that, Helen." Giacomo sounds defensive now, as if she were also accusing him.

"Federico was sick. Whatever he'd done thirty years ago, he'd never have contemplated killing anyone now if he hadn't been, I don't know..." – she searches for the words she needs – "...well, off his head."

"And Giulia?"

"Giulia's got what she wanted all the time. Her son is a martyr. She's won."

"Well, it's a theory," says Giacomo, perplexed. "Martin's theory. Isn't that what you're saying? That this is what Martin thinks, after having been hit on the head by a motorbike?"

Exasperated and a little taken aback, because Giacomo doesn't *want* to understand and she's never seen him as obtuse, whatever else he might be, Helen changes the subject.

"Have you heard from Yvonne?"

Giacomo laughs briefly and waves his hand in the air.

"She's back in Paris, I imagine."

"She didn't say?"

"Her sudden departure and subsequent silence are eloquent enough, I'd have thought." He sips his coffee, grimaces, reaches for the sugar, pausing between the first and second spoonful. "I heard from Stefania. She wants to speak to you."

"Stefania," says Helen. "She must be so shocked."

"She's been waiting for something like this to happen to one of us. She thinks we got away with it all scot free. It isn't fair. She forgets that some of us did time. And now she feels guilty, as though she's brought this punishment down on Federico's head herself."

"Stefania has nothing to feel guilty about," says Helen.

"She wants to know when the funeral will be," he says.

"Yes." Helen nods. "She should be here for that." She's restless. "I need to get out," she says. "I've had enough of this place."

She reaches for her bag, but something interrupts her, some thought of Federico leaning back in a chair, his legs stretched out, his hands behind his head, so young he's no more than a lanky boy. He is laughing about something. And then, with a flash of recognition, she sees in her mind's eye the photograph she was shown earlier this morning by Eduardo's son, Piero Cotugno, magistrate, in which she is also laughing. She remembers that Federico had been there with her in that room in college, her final year, already in love with her, she was confident of that although they hadn't made love at that point; they'd hardly been alone together before that day. It all comes back to her: the light, the warmth in the room, which was usually cold and damp like most of those old college rooms, the shirt he was wearing, which had worked out of the waistband and showed his navel when he stretched. She'd wanted to put her finger in it, she remembers, her tongue. He'd made some mistake in his English and she'd started to laugh, despite herself, because there is nothing worse than to have someone laugh at your mistakes, and he'd had a camera beside his chair. They'd spent the morning playing tourists. And he'd caught her laughing, he'd leaned forward in his chair with the camera in his hand and said, "I have made your photo. You will be mine forever." Had he thought of what he'd said, this first declaration of love for her, when she gave the picture away to Eduardo? Had she hurt him? She'll never know.

All at once, for the first time in almost three decades, Helen and Giacomo find they have nothing to say to each other. Helen looks at her watch. It's almost noon. She sips her coffee while Giacomo turns on the TV for the 12 o'clock news. The screen fills with scenes of Rome, cordoned off for the demonstration.

"The march," she says, shaking her head. "I'd forgotten all about it. I was supposed to be helping out."

"You're going on the march?" says Giacomo.

"You think I shouldn't? Giulia went on the military parade, didn't she?" says Helen. "Of course I'm going. And you're coming too. For Federico's sake."

"Is this what Federico planned? To take part?"

"I think so, yes." She stands up. "Unless he'd already done something stupid." She rubs her face with both hands, exhausted, then pushes her hair off her face. "If only he'd spoken to someone. To me." She looks at Giacomo. "To you."

He takes hold of Helen, not in a possessive way, his fingers lightly circling her arms above the elbows, and stares into her eyes. "He never forgave me, did he? Not really."

Helen doesn't pull away, although she'd like to.

"For taking the blame? Or for taking me?" As gently as she can, she frees herself from him. "There was nothing he needed to forgive," she says.

4

Turin, 1978

Stefania wasn't happy. Helen found her waiting outside the building one day, when she came home from work, a wrapped tray of cakes hanging by its ribbon from her finger. While Helen filled a saucepan with water for tea, Stefania undid the ribbon and unwrapped the tray. She started to eat, icing sugar drifting onto her bosom as she licked the cream from the top. She was getting fat, Helen noticed, and wondered for a moment if Giacomo preferred his women fat or thin. Stefania complained that she was having problems at the faculty; she wasn't being taken seriously in the way the men were. She'd imagined the academic world would be different from everywhere else, that was how stupid she'd been. She finished one cake and started another. They were small and beautifully made, like toys. How good they are at this sort of thing, thought Helen, the little pleasures: cherries drenched in liqueur and wrapped in chocolate, packaged in individual twists of layered paper and foil, like tiny bombs. Then Stefania began to talk about Giacomo, and Helen began to concentrate.

"I thought he had another woman to start with," she said. She looked hard at Helen. "He doesn't, does he?"

"Not as far as I know," Helen said, finally taking a cake. It would take so little to tell her what she and Giacomo had done, but for what? To clear the way for more? Besides, she enjoyed her secret. "Why would he want anyone else? I'm sure you're enough for him." But Stefania wasn't listening.

"He's hardly ever at home. At work he's distant, then, when he does show up, he's always reading or listening to the radio or banging away on his typewriter, stuff he won't even let me see, although he won't come out and say so, he just hides it away. He's been talking about buying a TV, he says I'm elitist for not wanting one, but it's not that. I just think he'll end up watching it all the time and ignoring me. What's Federico like with you? Is he the same? Always thinking about something else?"

"No, not really," said Helen, although this wasn't true; the picture Stefania had painted was distressingly familiar. Only her reluctance to play the wounded co-conspirator stopped her admitting it. She loathed the way some women seemed to relish in the sisterhood of suffering, as though the truth of a relationship lay in its failures being picked over with friends. She'd barely seen Miriam since her affair with the manager at Fiat had come to an end.

"And I'd like to know why he needs that other place," said Stefania, increasingly aggrieved.

"What other place?"

Stefania licked a blob of cream from her thumb. "The one he's sharing with Federico, near the faculty." She glanced across. "You do know about it, don't you?"

Helen's resolve faded. "No," she said. "I don't."

"Oh God, I'm sorry," said Stefania, raising her hand to her mouth. "I thought he'd have spoken to you. It's only for work, I'm sure. You know what it's like at the faculty, everyone's on top of everyone else. I shouldn't have said anything. They haven't had it for long, I don't think. I'm sure they wouldn't use it for anything else." Stefania took another cake, licked off the cream; she couldn't conceal her gratification at having told Helen something she didn't know. Helen wondered how much she suspected, and how this other flat was being paid for.

"He has a study here," she said. "What's this other place like?"

Stefania shrugged. "I haven't seen it. I know where it is, though. I can tell you, if you like."

Helen rang the doorbell first, to make sure no one was there, then let herself into the flat with the key she'd found in Federico's briefcase. The light switch wasn't where she'd expected it to be, to the left. Hearing the noise of someone on the stairs, she hurriedly closed the door behind her and fumbled, like an idiot, like a thief, in the dark, thinking of Federico as he entered this flat, as much his as the one he shared with her on the other side of Turin, his hand reaching out for the light without even thinking. He has two homes, she thought, and she wondered if that was all and where he imagined he really lived: in this place or the place they shared or maybe in his own home, the home of his parents, who continued to pass him money, because how else could he possibly afford to pay this extra rent, as he clearly did? She wondered who he was, and why he'd never told her. Giacomo would never lie to her like this, she thought. Although, of course, he hadn't mentioned it either.

She found the switch and turned it on, then walked down the hall. Kitchen and bathroom on the left. On the right a living room, bare of furniture apart from an armchair, books piled on the floor beside it. At the far end of the hall a bedroom, a single bed with a dark green blanket tucked in so that she could see the metal frame beneath the mattress. Federico told her he'd been a model soldier, and she could see that from the way his possessions were folded and piled like goods in a shop on shelves along one side of the room, his shoes placed side by side and lined up under the window, their toes facing in. She knew how neat he was, how ordered; but here the neatness seemed as much of a mask as the clothes he wore. Maybe that was too harsh; a sort of self-discipline, an imposition. There was a table against one wall, with a straight-backed chair beside it. She walked across and picked up the first thing that caught her eye, a pad of lined paper, the kind of pad reporters use in films, the spiral along the top. Flicking it open, she found sketches of faces, poorly drawn, diagrams that made no sense at all; there were street maps of places she didn't recognise; towards the back of the pad a list of names and dates in pencil. Some of the names had crosses beside them, others question marks or symbols that must have meant something to Federico, but not to her. Turning the page, her eye skimmed down until it came to a name she recognised. Eduardo Cotugno. Her kneecapped student. The question mark beside his name had been rubbed out and replaced by a tick. She put the pad down and opened a drawer, her heart beating against her ribs. She wasn't looking for anything in particular, she wanted to distract herself from what she had seen. The drawer contained papers, department business, bills; she saw what looked like a permit to stay and pulled it out from under the other things. It was made out in the name of a man, a German, the space for the photograph was empty. She pushed it back into the drawer.

She only saw the other door as she was leaving. She tried the handle, opened it and found herself in another bedroom, identical to the first. I'm dreaming, she thought, as she looked at the single bed, the desk, the order, and felt her heart pumping as though she'd been running. She walked across to the desk and would have opened the drawer if she hadn't heard a noise from somewhere nearby, she couldn't tell exactly where, whether it was inside or outside the flat. She seemed to have lost all sense of space. She turned tail and hurried down the corridor. Outside the flat, with the empty lift where she'd left it, she leant against the wall and breathed deeply until her pulse had returned to its normal rate.

Two days later, the police discovered Aldo Moro's body stuffed brutally into the boot of a Renault Four in the centre of Rome. When Helen asked her students who they thought had done it, they shook their heads. Some of them shrugged. Nobody seemed upset. They agreed the placing of the car, halfway between the headquarters of the Christian Democrats and the Communists, was a message. But what did the message mean? she asked. At once they divided into feuding camps. Everything meant something else, it seemed. Then someone came in and told them the lesson had been cancelled because a national strike had been declared. A few nights later, in the English pub, Miriam said, What was the point of that? It wouldn't bring anyone back to life. Any excuse would do for a national strike, it was a wonder anything ever got done in this crazy country. All they were interested in was death and sex.

She didn't tell Federico she'd been to the other flat. She felt ashamed, as though she'd done something wrong herself, as though the lies she would always tell, to protect herself from the truth, were worse than his.

Three weeks later, Giacomo was arrested. He was in jail, awaiting trial, when she and Federico married.

5

Helen spots Martha at once, although they've rarely met. All their collaboration has been conducted by phone and email. She's seen her occasionally at press conferences and parties, they've chatted a couple of times with glasses in their hands and their eyes not quite on the other, roaming the venue for more congenial company. She's nothing against the woman, merely a sense that what she offers, beyond an outlet for certain articles no one else would publish, isn't in Helen's line. There's a fussiness about her, an untidiness, the scouring pad of unkempt steel grey hair, over-large hippie-style earrings, a way of positioning herself, face thrust towards the other person, large, nicotine-stained teeth, her lips drawn back, that strikes Helen as aggressive. When Helen steps back, Martha steps forward; she's the kind of woman who forces other women into corners. Helen has never seen how she behaves with men.

"I'm so glad, and so touched, really, that you're here," Martha says. She touches her own heart before patting Helen's arm with an expression of concern. "I guess what you're going through must be really hard right now."

"Yes," says Helen. "It is." She turns her face away from the slightly stale odour of Martha's breath. They are in the office of *Futuri Prossimi* and it is just as Helen imagined it, identical to similar offices all over the world, post-its curling on the walls and monitors, tangles of wires, anti-war posters, too many ashtrays.

She has spent time in rooms like this in Cambridge and London and Turin, even, briefly, in Rome, when she first arrived, before she joined the agency and became a real journalist. Today the office has the air of a party that is due to begin before too long. Twenty, twenty-five people, most of them middle-aged, dressed in jeans and shorts and T-shirts against one thing or the other, some of them witty, some not, more than a few home-made. Helen is wearing a well-cut cotton dress, sleeveless, in an olive green that suits her, and moccasins made from tobacco brown leather so soft it might have been used to make gloves. When did she stop dressing like a student? she wonders. When did she and Federico decide not to wear their beliefs on their chests? Martha's armpits, she notices, are dark with stubble, which is surely the worst of all options.

Giacomo is talking to some young woman Helen doesn't know by the door. Martha has taken her elbow and is steering her towards a small wicker sofa piled with books. "We can hide ourselves away here," she says, shifting some to the floor, pushing others to one side, while Helen tries to catch his eye, attract him across the room to rescue her. She is beginning to wonder what made her come. Martha seems determined to talk about Federico.

"You say he didn't so much as mention me?" she is saying as Helen moves a book from beneath her leg.

"No," says Helen. *We babble to each other*. She must be thinking we had secrets. Well, she's right. The secrets we shared and the secrets we didn't.

"He sent me an article," Martha says. "It arrived the day after he died. I've been so busy I didn't even realise until this morning. I only just had a chance to read it before this whole crowd started turning up. Not properly, I just took a look at it." She pulls a face. "It's pretty weird. I mean, it's not the kind of thing you'd expect from someone who's, well, in a position of power," she says, investing the last words with a disdain that strikes Helen as cruel, given the circumstances, although she isn't hurt, merely startled. Martha can't hurt her.

"What does he say?"

"I haven't read it properly, so don't get me wrong, but it's – oh, I don't know – it's like he's defending the kamikaze." At this Martha grimaces, as if to say, Haven't we moved on from martyrdom? It's so last century. "It's full of quotations. It shifts, like, from Plato to George Galloway, for Christ's sake. Voltaire. Angela frigging Davis. It's like he's using them all up before he dies." She covers her mouth. "Oh my God, I am *so* sorry."

"Are you going to run it?" says Helen. "In the magazine." Should I be asked? she wonders. All this – his legacy – will be up to me.

"Use it? You mean publish it?" Martha is astonished. "Are you kidding?"

"Because it advocates violence?"

Martha shakes her head slowly, hair rigid as a wig. "That would be reason enough," she says. "I mean, we are a voice for pacifism. But it's just so weird. Some bits of it don't make sense. It's like he's being dictated to by someone he can't quite hear, if you get me." She lowers her voice. "Was he, you know, all right?"

"All right? What do you mean?"

"Let me tell you something. Parts of it read like he's, I don't know how to say this. Deranged?"

"I don't suppose you could let me see this article?"

"I'd have to find it," says Martha, looking away. She hasn't got it, it occurs to Helen. She's given it to someone else to read. But surely she must have realised I'd ask to see it? And who would she have given it to? But now she's confusing incompetence with conspiracy. She's been with these people too long. She takes a deep breath, then glances round the room.

"I'd very much like to read it," she says, briefly enjoying Martha's embarrassment. "Which desk is yours?" She starts to get up from the sofa, but Martha catches at her arm to prevent her.

"By the way, I heard about Martin Frame," she says. "I'm stunned."

Helen sits back, her moment of naughtiness over. She ought to be with Martin, she thinks, not sitting in this sad confusion of a room. Who was that woman with him, what was her name? Alina? Is that a Russian name? Where did she appear from? She seemed to know Martin so well. She saw Martin watching her with what looked like love. Well, Martin deserves a little love, she thinks. He seemed so battered and bruised in that hospital bed. She could never be grateful enough, she thinks, glancing towards the door to see Giacomo, still talking to the same girl, gesticulating as the girl laughs.

"Yes," she says. "So am I."

"You think it was a mugging?"

"What do you think it was?"

"I've never really understood him," says Martha. "He's a strange guy. Not bad, heavens, I don't mean that." She touches Helen's knee. "I know you're not just colleagues." She waves a hand to silence Helen. "It's just that he's so private. Did I say private? If he were a woman he'd be frigid." She smiles in a confidential way. "I guess he's just English," she says, as though this explains everything. Then, to Helen's surprise, before Helen can say *I'm English too*, Martha leans in towards her, lowers her voice. "Do you think he's gay?"

"Martin? Gay? No, I don't think Martin's gay," Helen says, annoyed by the cosiness in the woman's tone, as though they have something in common. "Do you?"

Martha shrugs. "I guess not." After a moment, as if that subject has been exhausted, she adds: "It certainly doesn't look like a mugging to me. Is that what they're saying, that he's been mugged?"

To Helen's relief, Giacomo walks across and crouches beside her, resting his hand on Helen's knee. "How are you feeling?"

"I'm fine," says Helen. "Martha's just been telling me something else I didn't know about Federico."

Giacomo's eyebrows rise. He glances at Martha, who says, hurriedly: "He sent me a piece he'd written. I only read it this morning."

"A piece he'd written?" The heat is rising. Helen can feel a trickle of sweat running down her back, oddly cold on her skin. "How much longer do we need to wait?" she says, hearing a note of panic in her voice. The girl Giacomo was talking to has wandered across and is standing half behind and half beside him in a wary, proprietorial fashion. Helen is on the brink of tears. Federico was utterly mad and I didn't know. What was the word this dreadful invasive woman used? Deranged. My husband was deranged and I didn't notice. Where was I? Where have I been hiding? Helen and Federico. Stefania and Giacomo. And now Federico's dead and Giacomo's dumped Stefania for a woman who seems to have dumped him. And I have dumped Giacomo too, she thinks, while his hand squeezes her knee with an air that might express possession or the desire to comfort her, because she has no idea what he thinks of her, or wants from her any longer, now that she has closed him off. Maybe he loves her as much as anyone has ever done, including Federico, although she doesn't think so. She can see the girl watching his hand. I don't miss anything, she thinks, I'm always so observant. So why didn't I notice Federico was deranged? Because I was being loved by someone else? Because I wouldn't have accepted it if I had known? Because I didn't care?

I'm sorry, she thinks and almost says, her dry lips moving to accommodate the words. I'm sorry, Federico. But there is no excuse; she has left it too late. Giacomo's hand is unbearably heavy, but to move it off her knee would lend it more weight than it already has. They were neither of them enough for her, she realises, and now there is only one of them left it is like

having no one at all. She thinks of the flat the two men shared
in Turin, of what she'd seen there, the list of names, the tick
beside Eduardo Cotugno's name, the passport. What did they
do together in that flat, what plots did they contrive, the two
of them? Their two, identical rooms like the closed language of
twins, so that she has never known which was which. Because
it only occurred to her months later, when Giacomo was in jail
and she was already married and she'd come across the postcard
Giacomo had sent them from South America, that the desk
might have belonged to either of them, they had both learnt to
be tidy during their national service as soldiers. All she had had
to go on was the handwriting on the list. And she had never
been able to tell their handwriting apart. But by that time, it
was too late. She'd made her choice.

Before they left the flat, Helen had checked her email. But she'd
also opened Federico's. As she'd expected, there were over a
hundred new messages. Amazon. Harvard. Alitalia. Government
stuff. She scrolled down to four days earlier, and saw that
among the first unopened messages was one that had been sent
by Federico to himself. The subject was 'final thoughts'. She
called Giacomo over. The timeline said: 31/05/2004 19.47. She
clicked to open it.

It wasn't that long. She read the first paragraph.

    What I don't understand is how can you be what
    you are and yet still be the opposite of what you
    are. There's a poem by Robespierre I read years
    ago, at university, and didn't appreciate at the
    time, where he says that the worst thing that can
    happen to a just man is to realise, the moment
    before he dies, how much he's hated by those for
    whom he has given his life. Is this what will
    happen to me, to realise this?

6

Giacomo can't remember the last demonstration he took part in as a civilian, although perhaps civilian isn't the word he wants. As no one. Normally, he'd be linking arms with other stars and starlets of the radical protest industry, fringe politicians, philosophers, actresses, performance artists, writers. He'd join in for half an hour, his assistants would have told the press, the television cameras, because there is still this lingering respect for intellectuals, in France at least, as *personalities* at least. What was the expression Topino Bianco had used in that fucking article? *Ageing enfant terrible*. There'd be an interview of some sort and then the usual round of goodbyes and kisses until the next time. Each would give, in his or her own way, what he or she had to give.

Today, though, he finds himself under the banner of a magazine so poorly edited, so insignificant, it has to be paid for through the proceeds of some illicit slush fund, a tax loss, some anxious benefactor buoying it up with conscience money. Because it surely can't pay for itself. How anachronistic to see these people gathered beneath the handmade placards and swash of cotton sagging with the weight of its own painted slogan, touching in its naïveté: NO MORE IFS AND NO MORE BUTS. As though there could be a world without ifs and buts. As though the world weren't being re-invented daily through, at best, prevarication and doubt, at worst, mendacity. They might as well all have joined hands to sing "Imagine". And yet, despite or perhaps because of all this, he is happy to be here. He is happy to be anonymous, at least for now, and to have his arms linked on one side with Helen, who's been ignoring him for the past hour, and on the other with some girl he's just met, no more than twenty, a girl who had never heard of him before this morning and now adores him. He is happy to be introduced to Don Giusini, who recognised him, and shook his hand in a rather solemn judgemental way that amused Giacomo, because they were all in the same business in the end, the business of making up stories that made up the world, and there is no moral higher ground. He is happy to find himself caught behind Martha Weinberg, a woman he has never met before today although she also knew him, by name and reputation, and was cool with him, but impressed. She'll be asking me for an article before the day is out, he thinks. He is happy to have slept with Helen, and to have been left by Yvonne, happy that Stefania is already flying from wherever she has been towards him, ready to allow him what she's called a seventh chance. Already the idea that he and Helen might be able, after all these years, to live together as a couple strikes him as foolish; he can barely remember having thought of it. How fickle the heart is, he says to himself, the pressure of the girl's hand warm and vital on his arm. Life, he says to himself, is endless with possibilities.

"You're enjoying this, aren't you?" Helen's face is flushed, she seems to be as cheerful as he is and, thank God, she's caught some sun. She looks like a girl in her neat little cotton dress, like a schoolgirl, he thinks. She's always had that quality of innocence about her. People used to think she was cold; Giacomo was convinced that this was what had made her so appealing to Federico. She seemed unavailable, that was her strength. That must have been what appealed to Federico, he thinks now. Federico always wanted his own space, as people say these days. My space. Your space. His or her space. What was that Leibniz term? That's the one: windowless monads. All at once he recalls that parable – Buddhist, is it? He should ask Don Giusini – about the difference between heaven and hell. In both places people sit round a table with chopsticks that are longer than their arms and bowls of food. In hell they try to feed themselves, and fail. In heaven they feed one another. He's always liked this kind of thing. Parables. Stories that make up the world. And now there is this story Helen has made up, about her mother-in-law. Which might be true, he'll give her that, but to what end? She surely doesn't want the woman arrested for the murder of her own son? What good would that do?

"Yes," he says, before she can ask him what he's thinking about. "I'd forgotten what fun it was to be lost in a crowd."

"How many of us are there, would you say? I'm hopeless at guessing."

He looks around him, at the loose knots of people, young and old, families with pushchairs and dogs, red flags and rainbow flags and kaffiyahs wrapped around the most unlikely heads. They must be somewhere in the middle of the march, he supposes. They're moving slowly, unhurriedly, down Via Cavour, on their way to Piazza Venezia. Far in front, already on Via dei Fori Imperiali, what looks from here like a solid mass of protestors, placards bobbing above their heads, is turning right. Behind them, the crowd is equally dense. Dance music comes from a decorated float a hundred yards to their back, fifty yards ahead of them a line of men plays pipes. The roads that lead to Monti and the Colosseum are cordoned off by police, two rows deep, blue armoured vans behind them, but the mood is festive, an air of picnic, thinks Giacomo, smiling at a group of children with painted faces, a Labrador with a rainbow-coloured scarf knotted like a cape to its collar. The march around *Futuri Prossimi* is loose and informal, they might have been tourists. If the shops weren't boarded up he'd buy a souvenir.

"Hundreds of thousands," says Giacomo.

"Multiply the number the ministry says by a factor of three," says the girl on his left. "That usually gives you a rough idea."

"A factor of ten," barks Martha. A man at the side of the road has put down a rucksack and is taking photographs of them with his mobile. "Fuck off," she shouts, "*Vaffanculo*," then turns to the rest of them as the man slips the mobile back into his pocket and walks away. "Did you see that? Who does that jerk think he is?"

"CIA," says Giacomo. "Bound to be. You can tell from the baseball cap worn backwards."

"You're like everyone else. You think being anti-American is funny," says Martha. "What about your own shit? Can't you smell that?" What a humourless bitch she is, thinks Giacomo, and smiles.

"I wish Martin could be here with us," says Martha.

"I don't think that would have happened," Helen says. "Demonstrations aren't his style. I'd be happy to know he was at home."

Giacomo glances at Helen, who looks thoughtful, almost sad. She's thinking about Federico, he supposes, and is himself stirred by sadness. I loved him as much as I've loved anyone, he thinks, and that wasn't enough to save either of us. He's better off dead. What a mess we've made of everything though. Perhaps I should do what he wanted to do, whatever that was, something pure and significant, unambiguous. Some necessary death.

They are turning onto Via dei Fori Imperiali when a thin woman with too much white-blonde hair, a woman he vaguely recognises, breaks through the cordon of police to approach them, holding a microphone to her chest as if to conceal it. She is followed by a man in a T-shirt and cargo shorts and a floppy white hat, with a camera on his shoulder. Giacomo is the first to notice and steps forward, undecided whether to fend her off or play his usual role, mediate, explicate, be both available and aloof, dance along the knife edge of his charm. He is starting to smile when he realises that the woman isn't interested in him, though he knows her now as someone who's worked in Paris for Italian television. No, no. She doesn't want him at all. She wants to speak to Helen. He turns towards her, his initial instinct to protect her. But Helen doesn't seem to need to be protected. After glancing at Don Giusini, who nods, she meets the woman halfway. Giacomo moves in close, in case he is needed. Behind the cameraman, three *carabinieri* detach themselves from the line of armed men along the pavement and cross to the group. The woman is holding the microphone to Helen's face. Judging from her expression, she expects to be rebuffed, but Helen is smiling. "*Ciao, bella,*" she says, as if she's bumped into an old friend at a party. Startled, the woman asks her if she'd mind answering a few questions. "Certainly," says Helen. "Why not?" The woman turns to the cameraman, nods, begins to speak.

"Signora Di Stasi. This is your first public appearance since the tragic death of your husband four days ago. Why have you chosen to interrupt your silence on this particular occasion, a political demonstration against the government and its closest ally, especially in view of the president's visit?"

Helen moves closer to the camera. "Because my husband would himself have been on this demonstration, which is not merely political but humanitarian, which is not against the government and its allies, but against an illegal war. He was firmly opposed to the military occupation of Iraq. He would have taken part in this demonstration as a citizen, not as a representative of the government." She stares into the lens. Her voice is clear and cold. "The least I can do, to honour his memory, his life and his work, is be here to represent him," she says. She was ready for this, thinks Giacomo, with admiration. The girl beside him whispers in his ear, "She's wonderful," and all he can do is acquiesce. Martha Weinberg is clapping her hands behind Helen, thumping the air, whooping with joy. She breaks into a little dance, like a child pretending to be Tonto. She's got more than she expected, far more than she hoped for.

"After the brutal, politically motivated murder of your husband, there has been talk of a state funeral."

"I don't know where that talk came from. I've said nothing about a state funeral. And I wasn't aware that the motivation behind the murder had been established. I spoke to the magistrate only this morning, and he made it clear that all possibilities remained open. No one knows who killed my husband. No one knows why. Only the murderer." The woman is glancing anxiously around, uncertain whether to encourage Helen to expand on this, then speaks again, her tone tinged with panic. You can see she's torn, thinks Giacomo. She'd like to hector Helen, who is nothing, a nobody, a *widow*, and foreign to boot, bully her into toeing whatever party line has been established; but she doesn't dare, because Federico counted. At the same time, she's terrified what Helen might say next.

"Your husband was a senior public servant. He died in the service of the state. Why do you feel it inappropriate of the state to recognise his assassination, officially? Surely he deserves a state funeral?"

Helen is about to speak when Giacomo sees two men elbow to the front of the small crowd that has formed around the interview, pushing the squealing journalist back towards the cameraman, who stumbles under the weight of his equipment and almost falls. As the *carabinieri* step in, whether to protect or restrain Helen isn't clear, the two men move off. Helen turns to Giacomo, hisses *Do something, for God's sake. Don't let them get away*. Giacomo walks, slowly at first and then in an odd half-run, in the direction the men must have chosen. The small crowd that has gathered around the thrill of the microphone and the camera now breaks up to let Giacomo through. He feels both excited and absurd as he dodges among these people, who don't seem to know what he's doing, nor why, who don't appear to have recognised him. He is running now against the flow of the march, breathless but with a sense of purpose he hasn't experienced in years. He sees a flash of T-shirt and tattooed bicep, and pushes on, elbowing his way through knots of demonstrators, until he is blocked by a line of police. They are moving to surround him, closing in. He tries to push them out of the way. They hold him by the shoulders, by the arms, but he twists round, his shirt coming out of his trousers, stumbling over his feet, and begins to shout. "Witness this police brutality. This is how fascist regimes begin. Remember Guantanamo!" He is dragged away, screaming "Collusion!", and pushed into a van. He grins at the others already seated along the sides of the van's interior, tucking his shirt back into his waistband. Some of the buttons have been ripped off. Excellent. He'll sue. He's never felt better. If only he had Federico with him now, he thinks, everything would be possible. He wants to punch the air, and would do if he weren't so breathless and didn't have a fleeting memory of Martha doing precisely that five minutes earlier. "I know who you are," says a teenage girl with orange dreadlocks sitting opposite him. "You were on the news last night. You're that dead man's friend." She sighs. "It's your generation's fault we're in this fucking mess."

Giacomo wants to hug her. "You couldn't be more right!" he says.

7

Martin watches Alina whenever she turns her eyes away from him, watches her walk across to the window and adjust the blind, watches her as she folds the top sheet back to smooth out any creases that might have formed beneath his legs. He is oddly unembarrassed when she checks his catheter, oddly because he doesn't see her as a nurse, or not primarily. He'd say that he saw her as an angel if he believed in angels and could say this without sounding mawkish. He doesn't know how, but he sensed her touching his legs as he lay, unconscious, on the pavement. He remembers her cool hands on his skin. He sees her as a woman.

He's asked her questions about herself, less out of curiosity than to begin to know her voice by heart, although he's been curious too, how could he not be? He just doesn't want to hear about any indignities she may have suffered, he wants to protect himself from that. He isn't being a coward; he's convinced that by protecting himself he will protect her too. I've fallen in love, he says to himself, how unexpected. How unexpected the behaviour of the heart. At first he was worried that whoever had tried to kill him might come back to finish the job they botched. But he doesn't think that now. He's seen, and spoken to, Helen, who'll have spoken to Mura by now and who knows who else. If he thought there was any risk, he'd send Alina home.

He's asked her to turn on the television and to raise his head a little so that he can watch the demonstration. It's being filmed from a helicopter, one of the many helicopters Martin can hear from his bed. The number of marchers, as ever, is a matter of opinion, although half a million wouldn't be far off, thinks Martin, doing the usual sums from the figures provided. She's sitting beside him, her slim hand on the bed.

They have cameras on the ground as well. Watching them move across the faces of the demonstrators, he sees a man he recognises but can't place for a moment. Bald, heavily built, tattoos visible on his arm. It takes him a couple of seconds to realise it's Picotti's son, the one who led him out to Ostia. Now that's a surprise, he thinks, he's not the anti-war type. But, of course, he needn't be in agreement to be there; there are other reasons. Picotti's son. Keeping it in the family, that's what his father said. The camera moves on, in search of news.

As the screen goes back to aerial shots, he wonders if he'd have gone on the march himself. He's tempted to think he would, but doesn't know with whom. At a pinch, he supposes he'd have gone with Federico, assuming Federico would have taken part. What do you think of this bloody war? he asked Alina when she turned the set on and the first few images passed across the screen. She shrugged. There is always war, she said. Not always, he said, not everywhere. She smiled at that and said, "Take me some place there is no war, Martin Frame. We can make ourselves comfortable and wait for it to arrive." It was the way she first used his surname that made him understand what he felt for her, he doesn't know how else to explain it. As though he's been taken on whole, without reservations. He lies here, his neck beginning to ache a little from the effort of holding this awkward position, and repeats it to himself, in his head, his own name made fresh. Martin Frame. He asked her where she came from and she named a town in Ukraine he'd visited once, in another lifetime, on what he'd thought of then as official business. He was about to say, Yes, I know the place, but didn't. She'd have asked to know what he was doing there and he didn't want to have to lie to her.

When Helen appears on the screen, his eyes are half-closed; he might have missed her if Alina hadn't called out. *Your friend! From this morning!* But no, he'd have heard her voice and recognised that. How angry she looks, he thinks, and how determined, as though she's been waiting for this moment. Perhaps she has. They are all there. Would you credit it? Giacomo, that priest chappy, Don Giusini. He even knows the woman interviewing her, a dreadful creature without an ounce of talent, the ex-mistress of some under-secretary, a compromise choice to appease the right. Someone who's never been slow to run to the aid of the victor, as the saying goes. Helen is listening to what she says with a look of disdain. She shakes her head. She answers. Martin smiles, then pulls a face of surprised approval. She's giving as good as she gets. Better. He's about to ask Alina to put another pillow under his head when Helen's face changes, she looks as though she's been slapped by a hard invisible hand. Just as abruptly, it disappears and the screen shows a sweep of heads and banners and then sky and the programme is interrupted for a handful of seconds, but not before Martin hears Helen cry, in English. *Do something, for God's sake.* And then they are watching the march from the helicopter again, the camera drifting from group to group. It all looks so thin from above, people scattered into small informal groups, it might as well be a garden party. The commentator doesn't mention Helen, nor Federico; the interview might as well not have taken place. What on earth could have happened? he wonders.

"I don't suppose you've got a mobile, have you?" he asks.

She is sitting beside the bed on the rigid hospital chair, like a creature from his childhood. "Of course," she says. "Would you like to use it?"

"But I don't have the number in my head," he says. "Perhaps you could see if someone's got mine. It was in my pocket." She smiles and passes him his mobile from the table.

"You found it yourself," he says.

"How do you think I called your friend this morning?" she says. "You'd be surprised at how resourceful I can be."

I must never stop being grateful, he thinks. For as long as this lasts.

It must be an hour later, or more, when he wakes from a half-sleep. Alina puts down her magazine and points to the TV. There is a photograph of Giacomo Mura.

"Wasn't he standing next to your friend earlier?"

"Yes," says Martin.

"Well," she says, "he's been arrested."

8

Helen is standing where the taxi left her, outside the building in which Giulia and Fausto have lived since their retirement. She looks up at the tended balconies that are never used, the grilles and security devices. She's always hated this area; neither she nor Federico understood their choice. She's lost her courage, at the last moment, and if the taxi hadn't gone, she'd have used it to be taken home. But she's missed her chance, and besides, there is so much that needs to be said. She can't put it off any longer. Her talk with Eduardo's son this morning has given her strength. The more she thinks about him, the more she sees his father. How could she not have noticed the similarities that first time? she asks herself; he has his father's eyes and a thoughtful, exploratory way of holding her gaze. But she had so much else on her mind, she thinks now, although all she can recall from that meeting is numbness and an underlying fear of being found out. If she could, she would talk to Federico about this, this closing of a circle she'd thought already closed, and how it might not be closed at all. She'd ask him what he remembered about her then, about the girl Eduardo must have seen. He'd been jealous, she remembers that, jealous and curious all at once. Had he wondered if she might have been attracted? She could talk to Giacomo about him, of course, but she won't do that. She has never talked to Giacomo about Eduardo after that first conversation, when he'd called her sentimental; she won't start now.

She feels as though she has Eduardo with her, taking her hand in an odd sort of way, grounding her as she lets herself into the building with the key she used before, and takes the lift to their floor. She doesn't want to give them any warning.

Standing outside their flat as the lift doors close behind her, she hears faint scuffling sounds from the neighbouring flats and knows she's being watched by their neighbours, old couples, like her in-laws, who behave as if under siege from the world. One of the other two doors on the landing opens a hair's breadth, then closes before she has a chance to explain who she is, see what they know. Neighbours are always the first to know.

But nothing has prepared her for this hunched unshaven figure in a vest and pyjama trousers who opens the door at the third ring, after she has knocked and called out their names, and then her own. This old man, tremulous, foreign to her, smelling of sour milk, hurries her in.

"I don't know what to do," he says, his voice raucous, over-loud, as though he hasn't spoken for days and has lost all sense of volume. "She won't come out. She'll starve to death."

Helen hugs him. To see him reduced to this is more than she can bear.

"Won't come out of where?"

Fausto points hopelessly down the corridor. "Her study." He sighs, gestures with his clasped hands, shaking them up and down. "She hasn't eaten since Thursday. She'll die. She hasn't taken her medicines."

"Haven't you got a key?"

"It won't go in. She's left the key in on her side."

Impatient, more angry than anxious, Helen goes to Giulia's door and raps at it sharply, hurting her knuckles.

"It's Helen," she says. "Let me in. I have to speak to you." She doesn't expect to be answered, but immediately she hears footsteps and the turning of a key. Fausto tries to push her out of the way but she won't budge from where she is, not now, not until the old woman shows herself.

Giulia is dressed to go out. Her hair is drawn up tight into its perfect bun, her necklace and earrings are matching beads of jet. She is wearing a black suit, a different one from the day before, and holding a single short silk glove in her gloved right hand. Startled, uncertain, Helen waits to see if she's going to be allowed in or expected to step to one side to allow her mother-in-law out. Fausto, behind her, is weeping with what might be rage or relief, she can't be sure. Acknowledging neither of them, Giulia walks into the corridor.

"Where are you going?" says Helen.

Giulia stops, turns slowly to look at her, a haughty, determined smile on her lips. "I'm going to pay my respects to my son."

"We did that yesterday," says Fausto, desperate, glancing at Helen, as if to say, You see? You see the state she's in? "Giulia, my dear, we did that yesterday. Yesterday morning. Don't you remember? We went with Helen. They sent the car for us."

"You don't know what you're saying," she tells him. But she doesn't seem to know where to go any longer. She stands in the hall, her eyes misting over with tears. Helen, unexpectedly touched by pity, takes her elbow.

"Come and sit down, Giulia."

"I don't want to sit down," says Giulia.

"I've never seen her in such a state," says Fausto, fretful and accusing, as though all this is Helen's fault.

"I tell you I'm perfectly all right," says Giulia, and now, confusingly for Helen, she sounds it.

"Come and sit down, in the living room," Fausto says. "We can talk there."

This time, Giulia nods and allows herself to be led by Fausto, along the corridor and into the living room, walking as though she were blind.

As soon as they are seated, Giulia and Fausto side by side on the sofa, Helen in an armchair in front of them, Helen opens her bag.

"You know what this is, don't you?"

Giulia glances at the sheets of paper that Helen has thrown onto the coffee table between them, then raises an eyebrow.

"I knew it. You're nothing but a common thief," she says, with great hauteur. "And don't imagine for a moment that I didn't know who had them." She raises her chin as high as it will go. There is something sad, and ludicrous, about her. Helen begins to laugh, then gathers the sheets of paper up.

"Those documents were given to me by Federico," Giulia says. "He asked me to look after them."

"I know what you've done," says Helen, ignoring this.

"Don't talk nonsense," says Giulia. "You know nothing about me. Nothing." Fausto is holding his head in his hands.

"I know what you've done and I think I know why," says Helen.

Giulia looks exasperated, as if to say, Do I really need to discuss this? With you?

"What I still don't understand – and, to be honest, I don't think I want to – is how you arranged it all, the squalor of it. How much you must have dirtied your hands," says Helen. "The people you must have dealt with."

Now it is Giulia's turn to laugh. "If it hadn't been for me, for my work and Fausto's, you'd all have died in jail for what you did. You. Federico. Giacomo Mura. Those friends of yours. You thought we didn't know what you were up to, didn't you? All your little secrets, your little subterfuges. Your silly revolutionary games." Her mouth curls with disgust. "You have no idea what we went through to make this country a place fit to live in. You were all too busy spitting in the plate that fed you."

"You have no right to criticise me," says Helen. "I haven't killed anyone I loved."

"Which makes what you did all right?" says Giulia. "The fact that the people who died because of your foolishness didn't have your love? What an odd way to see the world. You may as well live in caves."

"You killed Federico," says Helen. "Your own son."

"What do you know about mothers and sons? You have no children. Oh no, nothing so compromising. You were both too busy, too self-centred, for children. You dare to talk to me about being a mother. You have no idea what it means to have a son."

"A son you killed."

"Federico was as good as dead," says Giulia, dismissively. When Fausto utters a little cry of shock, although surely this can't be news to him, thinks Helen, Giulia turns her head, throws him an angry glance. "You know as well as I do our son was mad. There's no point in denying it."

"He was ill," says Fausto.

To Helen's surprise, Giulia looks away from Fausto to give her a little conspiratorial smile, shaking her head. This is women's business, she seems to be saying, we understand each other.

"And what about Massimo? Was he as good as dead?"

"Massimo?"

"Federico's driver."

"Oh," says Giulia, after a moment. "The driver."

"I suppose he doesn't matter," says Helen. What was it Giacomo had said, all those years ago, about Aldo Moro? An empty signifier. A box you can change the label on to suit your needs.

For a moment Giulia looks distressed. "His mother won't suffer, I've seen to that. I've arranged for his brother to be taken on as a driver."

"And you think you'll get away with it." You almost killed Martin as well, she thinks, but doesn't say. She wonders how much Giulia is aware of what she's done.

Giulia smiles. "Oh yes, I think so." She looks at Helen, hard, challenging – *unforgivingly*, thinks Helen. "Of course, that also depends on you."

"Are you trying to threaten me?" says Helen. "You're in no position to do that. Not now." All at once, she is tired of this supercilious, unwavering old woman. She can't even bring herself to hate her. There is nothing human left to hate, she thinks. Fausto is rocking slowly backwards and forwards in his chair, his head still held between his hands. You'll have to live with this, she thinks, and is glad. You'll have to live with her. And that will be your punishment.

"I'm not threatening you," Giulia says. "I wouldn't demean myself."

"There won't be any state funeral, you know," says Helen. "I've arranged something else. For Monday afternoon. It's what Federico would have wanted, I think." She lifts her shoulders, as if a burden has been lifted. "More to the point, it's what I want."

"I expected you to behave like this," Giulia says. "No thought for anyone other than yourself. Selfish to the last. You haven't disappointed me, I'll give you that. I assume I'll be invited." She glances at Fausto, who is crying, and corrects herself. "*We'll* be invited."

"Oh yes," says Helen. "I'll want you both to be there."

9

Twenty minutes later, Helen is breathing deeply, holding the filthy sun-warmed air in her lungs, letting it out through her clenched teeth. She'd like to run – not to get away, for the sheer pleasure of it – but doesn't want to draw attention to herself. She's decided not to call for a taxi because the idea of being cooped up in a box is more than she can bear. Now she is a mile from her in-laws' flat and she still hasn't shaken them off, the vicious dried husk of the woman in her outfit of black cloth and beads, the devastated old man who has let it happen. They are still on her skin, like the scent of death. She'd throw herself in the river beneath her, to wash the scent off, if it wasn't so deep and dark and dirty. How many dead this river has seen, she thinks, what a city I've let my life be spent in. Centuries, millennia of statecraft and slaughter, faith and the lies and bloodletting that keep it alive. The blood-dark Tiber, winding its way through the city, appearing where you least expect it, curling and almost doubling back on itself. Sluggish, then fast, swollen, retreating, all the detritus drying on its mud banks. What a city I've chosen to make my home. Giacomo was right to leave.

She is walking as fast as she can, she hasn't felt this strong for ages. She could walk all night and find herself at the coast, although she knows this is impossible, that between her and the coast there are barricades of low-cost housing and car-jammed roads, an airport, military installations. All of it worth protecting, for Giulia, worth protecting so much she would let her own son die for it. There's a precedent for that, thinks Helen, and bursts into humourless laughter as she walks. She's taken the side of the river that runs by the stadium, its impotent marble youths gigantic against the red-streaked sky. Motorbikes, cars go by, but nobody else is walking, people in this part of Rome don't walk when they can drive. Only their servants use their feet. She is alone, and revelling in it. She lets herself think about Federico, about the way he used to walk, long strides, his head held up. He would stroll for hours, along beaches and mountain paths, through woods and gorges. She let herself be led and now she is glad of it, now that he is dead and she is sauntering at her own pace, she is glad that for all these years she's walked at his. She sees him almost, tempted to close her eyes, the way she saw him at the moment of his death, but the smile is less hesitant, less perplexed. She has a sense of rightness about him finally. How awful it would have been, she thinks, if he'd died not knowing who he was, in some hospital ward, in pain. How awful if he'd died some other way, the way he'd wanted, and thought, at the last moment, when nothing could be done, that he'd been wrong after all. That every choice he'd made had been wrong. She has Giulia, at least, to thank for that.

Her mobile rings. It is Giacomo. She's forgotten all about him. She's moved beyond Giacomo, it occurs to her, as though all that has died with Federico, and she's only just realised. She will have to be gentle with him.

"I'm calling from the police station," he says. He sounds annoyed. "In Piazza Venezia."

"What are you doing there?" she says.

"I was about my lady's business," he says. "You may not remember."

"I'm sorry," she says, with a smile, recalling Giacomo's face as he turned and ran into the crowd, and all the other faces she's seen of Giacomo over the past thirty years. So many Giacomos. "I don't know what I expected you to do. I hope you aren't in too much trouble."

"Can you come and get me out of here?" he says. He is speaking English, they must be listening to him. "They're being difficult."

"I'm miles from Piazza Venezia," she says. The last thing she wants to do is argue with the police. But, before he can answer, she has changed her mind. She can't desert him now. "I'll be there as soon as I can. I just need to go home first." When he doesn't speak, she says, "It's like old times," and is relieved to hear him laugh.

"Tell that to Stefania," he says.

"Stefania?"

"Yes. She's on her way."

"I'm glad."

"Are you?"

"Yes." She pauses. "Stefania is what you need."

When her mobile rings again, Helen sees that the caller is unknown. It might be Don Giusini, she thinks, about the arrangements for Monday. She's about to answer, but something stops her, some sense of herself and of the world. She already has enough to think about, she decides, but that's only partly true. She sees a sort of web stretching out from the small bright object in her hand, a tensile web of invisible trembling filaments, infinitely fine, infinitely strong, that binds them together and makes them complicit, each to each, filaments that carry not only words from mouth to ear, from mouth to ear, but everything that lives beneath and beyond those words, that lives within them as both parasite and force, everything people feel and struggle to say and sometimes succeed in saying, attraction and fear, intimidation and love and the offering of comfort. *Bind* is one of those words Federico was talking about, she thinks, that mean not only themselves but also their opposite. Antagonyms. To obligate and to secure. As bondage and swaddling. A vast compelling unifying web that issues from, and gathers to its point in this gleaming metal toy, in the flashing lights and the awful noise it makes. I'm sorry, unknown, she says. You'll have to wait.

She sees him sitting on the step the minute she turns the corner into the square beneath her flat. He is reading a newspaper, his sunglasses pushed up onto his forehead because the side of the building that looks over the square is in shadow by this time of day.

"Hello," she says.

He looks up and smiles. "I called you earlier."

"I didn't know it was you. I'm sorry. I'd have answered if I'd known."

"Well, you're here now." He stands up, shaking his trousers loose in a way that reminds her of Federico, and reaches behind him.

"I've been taken off the case. Too many personal ties, apparently. So it took a little while for me to lay my hands on it," he says, as he holds out Federico's briefcase.

EPILOGUE

Abruzzo, Monday, 7 June 2004

The first car to arrive is Helen's. She's chosen to drive because she likes the concentration it involves, and the distraction it offers. She left the motorway an hour ago, the last part of the journey is uphill, the roads getting narrower and more winding, and now she is parked in front of a small church. It isn't as pretty as she expected, she'd hoped for bare stone and roses, but the over-elaborate façade of this one, with its pink stucco columns and crumbling beige plaster, is the worst sort of rustic baroque. Maybe it's better this way, more appropriate. The last thing she needs to remember Federico is the easy sentiment of beauty. The service doesn't start for over an hour but Helen wanted to get here early, she needs to talk to Don Giusini. She walks into the church.

He is standing near the altar, adjusting a strip of cloth, some flowers in a small pewter vase. She hasn't seen him in his robes before.

"You're early," he says, with a smile, his hand held out. "I'm glad you found us."

"I want you to use this," she says, and gives him a sheet of paper. He glances at it, then reads it more carefully, frowning.

"Where does this come from?"

"As far as I know, it's the last thing he wrote."

"Are you sure?"

She nods. "I'm sure."

After the coffin has been carried from the hearse and placed in the aisle, the church fills up rapidly. The people she knows well are in the first few rows and behind them all the others she has met maybe once or twice, colleagues, friends of Federico's from school who must have been told about the service by one another, their families, a loosely-knit web of affection and sorrow that comforts and saddens her more than she has imagined possible. They spoke to her briefly outside, her hand in theirs, edging forward in a line that made her think for a moment of injections at school, as though she were there to minister to them. They told her things about Federico she had never known. People cried, and she cried too, an effortless crying that brought her relief. There were no journalists. People had taken her at her word.

After all these years in which they have hardly seen each other, Stefania was the worst. *Oh my darling, how can you bear it? How will you manage?* She was weak with howling, her eyes were bloodshot, her nostrils red. Helen calmed her as well as she could. *You'll be all right*, she said and hadn't realised how strange this was, that she should be comforting Stefania, until she'd spoken. Now she has Stefania sitting in the same row as her, with Giacomo between them, his arm around Stefania's shoulder. The place to her right is empty. When she turns round to see who else might be there and notices Piero Cotugno, standing alone by the door, she is startled and pleased; she beckons to him to sit beside her. After a moment's hesitation, he walks across and takes her hand. "Thank you so much," she says in a low voice, and he lowers his head a little, out of respect. "I'm glad to be here," he says.

"I'm glad you're here," she says. When he looks up, she stares into his eyes. He meets her gaze. "I've been thinking about you," she whispers.

On the other side of the aisle, the pew remains empty until, minutes before the service is due to begin, Giulia and Fausto enter the church, unaccompanied, and take their places. Giulia, impeccable, is dressed in the neat black dress and jet beads she was wearing two days ago. Helen wonders if she has taken any of it off between then and now, if she has eaten or slept or washed, or spoken to Fausto, who has shaved and spruced himself up, but still has the same haunted, absent air. Helen wonders if she has thought about what she's done. She looks across at them to acknowledge their arrival, but Giulia is staring straight ahead, towards the window above the altar, with an air of exaltation on her face, while Fausto barely raises his eyes from the floor.

The last people to arrive, with a clutter and the squeak of rubber on polished stone as the wheelchair is eased up the step, are Martin and Alina. Helen turns to see them, raises her hand. Alina clearly wants to stay by the door, but Helen beckons to them urgently to come closer and Martin says something in Alina's ear as she bends towards him. Martin is wearing a dark silk dressing gown over pyjamas and slippers. "There's room over here," says Helen in a loud whisper, pointing to the opposite pew, where Giulia and Fausto are sitting. Giacomo catches her arm, shaking his head to warn her off, but she is insistent. She wants to see Giulia forced to move, to make room for Martin and Alina. She waves them on until Alina has positioned Martin's wheelchair in the aisle and sat down beside him herself, beside Giulia, who edges away, expressionless. "I'm so glad you've been able to come," she says to Martin, in a voice that is low but loud enough to be heard by others. "I didn't expect you to make it." She wants to see Giulia forced to recognise what she has done.

After the final reading, Don Giusini leaves the pulpit and walks towards them, until he is standing beside the coffin. He pauses.

He seems to be waiting for a sign to start, thinks Helen, alert, wound up, only relaxed by the presence of Piero Cotugno beside her. Don Giusini reminds her suddenly of Giacomo, the way he was when she met him, and she is saddened by this, because that Giacomo is dead. What a mess we've made of things, she thinks, as the priest began to speak.

"Helen wanted friends here, no one but friends, so you all knew – and most of you, no doubt, loved – Federico," the priest says, then pauses and smiles, opening his hands to them. "That makes it easier for me. I don't need to tell you what you already know. You have your memories of Federico, and they're what count, they're what will last. But there may be some things you don't know, things that happened to Federico in the last few months of his life and that changed him. Important things." He pauses again, but this time he doesn't smile. He glances at Helen, who nods for him to continue.

"Federico Di Stasi was dying. He had a tumour pressing on his brain, an inoperable tumour that may have affected his thoughts and his emotions. If he hadn't been murdered he would have lived for no more than a few weeks, in a state of great pain and confusion. His death was a sort of release from that. It isn't for us to know whether this was part of a greater plan, this release, or whether it was part of something belonging to this world, the material world in which Federico lived and served and wielded power. Because Federico was an important, powerful man, his actions were designed to change this world, to change it for the better. When he discovered that he was about to die, after the shock and the grief for self that anyone would feel at such a time, he saw his destiny as a source of power. He had an idea that would take his importance to new heights. He thought that with a single act he would be able to change the world, our world. It was a dreadful idea. But that didn't matter. He had only weeks, maybe days, to live. He thought he could ride roughshod over the laws of the world, like a juggernaut, a god. He was beyond human punishment."

He pauses again and looks at the people in the church, as if to ask each of them what they would do if they were about to die. He looks at Helen, whose lips are trembling, who is living with the force of what she has set in motion. He looks at Giacomo, who turns away and comforts Stefania, stroking her hair as she weeps into his shoulder, whispering into her ear. He looks at Fausto, who lowers his head and sighs, and wrings a damp, crumpled handkerchief between his hands. He looks at Giulia, who returns his gaze, unflinching, untouchable.

"It doesn't matter now what that idea was. The night before he died, although of course he didn't know that then, he didn't know that he would die so soon, he wrote these words:

```
The worst thing that can happen to a just man is
to realise, the moment before he dies, how much
he's hated by those for whom he has given his
life. Is this what will happen to me, to realise
this? Will I realise, when it's too late, that I
am hated? That what I have done, convinced that I
am right, is wrong? Am I a just man? And if I'm
not?
   I know now that I can't go through with what
I've planned. I want no more blood on my hands,
or on my conscience. How can I die as a just man
if by my dying more hatred is created?
```

"These are the last words we have from him. They sound like words of renunciation – they are anything but that. In these few words, Federico takes on his full humanity, the power and the glory of it. Federico, in his way, preferred to die not as an important man, as a saviour or lord protector of the world, as a martyr inflamed and reduced to blindness by his belief, but as an ordinary man, a just man, going about his business. He was shot down on his way to work by a common murderer. He will be remembered by us for what he was. A good man cruelly taken from us."

The silence in the church is broken by a guttural suppressed cry. All eyes turn to Giulia as she struggles to her feet, stumbling over Alina's legs in her attempt to leave the pew. If Martin weren't there, in his wheelchair, she'd have fallen to the floor of the aisle. But she lands across him, her breath forced out of her by his knees in her chest. Alina cries out and jumps from her seat as Martin bellows with pain. Helen has expected to find pleasure in this, her mother-in-law's discomfort at this last and most futile understanding of her own son's death. Yet what she feels isn't, after all, pleasure, but an overwhelming sadness, even guilt, as the old woman fights to stand, her hair unwinding in a thin white coil. Alina holds Martin's head to her chest. "You'll be all right," she murmurs as Helen stands, half-turned, hesitant, one hand across her mouth, the other on Piero's shoulder. We've suffered enough, she thinks, the damage is done. I should have spared her this, if only for Federico. She stares towards the back of the church, taking the hand from her mouth to gesture towards the door. But no one notices her. Everyone's eyes are on Giulia, who trips a second time, stumbles, regains her balance, then stumbles again, her stuttering, broken journey through the silent church towards the light seemingly without end. A tall girl Helen doesn't recognise, who was casting shy glances at Giacomo before the service and is sitting in one of the pews beside the door, tries hopelessly to stifle her laughter as Giulia leaves the church.

ACKNOWLEDGMENTS

Among the people who have helped me during the writing of this novel, I'd particularly like to thank my friend and agent, Isobel Dixon, for her unflagging efforts on my behalf, and my group of constant readers, Clarissa Botsford, Peter Douglas, Wayne Harper, Jane Lambert, Joanna Leyland, Sally MacLaren, Jane Stevenson and Phyllida White, for their patience, wisdom and generosity. I'd also like to thank Renata Crea, Sam Humphreys and Rob Redman for their valuable advice at different stages in the book's development, and Emlyn Rees, my editor, for his enthusiasm and good sense. Finally, as always, Giuseppe Mallia was a resilient sounding board for ideas at every stage. I don't know what I'd do without him.

ABOUT THE AUTHOR

Charles Lambert was born in England and educated at Cambridge, but has lived in Italy for more than thirty years. Currently a university teacher, academic translator and freelance editor, he lives in Fondi, exactly halfway between Rome and Naples. His first novel, *Little Monsters,* was published in 2008, the same year as his collection of prize-winning stories, *The Scent of Cinnamon and Other Stories,* won an O. Henry prize. His next crime novel, *Any Human Face*, was described in *The Telegraph* by Jake Kerridge as 'a slow-burning, beautifully written crime story that brings to life the Rome that tourists don't see – luckily for them.' *The View From the Tower* and Charles's next novel, *The Folding World*, will continue this suspenseful exploration of Rome's dark side. Also in 2014, Charles is publishing *With a Zero at Its Heart*, an autobiographical novel in 241 paragraphs, each paragraph composed of 120 words.

charleslambert.wordpress.com
twitter.com/charles_lambert

WITH A ZERO AT ITS HEART

We've teamed up with HarperCollins' dynamic imprint, The FridayProject, to bring you an exclusive excerpt of *With a Zero at Its Heart* by Charles Lambert - to be published in May 2014.

OBJECTS *or* GHOST BALLOONS

1

He has never seen a ship inside a bottle but the day he discovers their existence he knows that he wants one more than anything in the world. He is seven years old. He imagines men no bigger than his fingertip working at the building of the ship, singing as they nail long boards to the hull, and sew the rigid sailcloth panels for the mast, tall and straight as a tree, and coat the ship with burning tar to make sure it never sinks. He watches them gather on the deck. There is a bird above their heads. He imagines he is on a ship and there is glass all around him, as far as the eye can see.

2

He comes across the pendant in his great-aunt's drawer. It is heavy, warm in his hand, the size of a just-fledged bird. At the heart of the pendant is the skeletal form of some insect, some winged insect, more than an inch long, longer than any insect he has ever seen, its flesh eaten out and engulfed by the same warm yellow that surrounds it. It is hollowed and sustained, its wings barely furled, it floats in a substance for which he has no name, which could be plastic but isn't. There is a loop for a chain at the pendant's top, but he will never wear it. It is amber. The insect has been trapped for a million years.

3

His father buys him a bicycle, but it is the wrong sort. The bicycle he wants has sweeping racing handlebars and no mudguards and is green and white. This one has small wheels and can fold into two. It is the colour of bottled damsons. He pushes his new bicycle into the road and rides away as hard and fast as he can, but it is not fast enough; it will never be fast enough to escape the shame of the thing that bears him. His eyes are blinded by tears. When he skids and scrapes the skin from his arms he is glad. He shows his father the blood. This is your blood, he thinks but dare not say.

4

He finds an owl pellet in the barn beside his house. It is round, the weight of a dove's egg, and roughly made, as though pressed from earth or some other substance he can't identify. He does what he's read in his book, soaking and prising it apart. Some of it crumbles and is thrown away, but he's left in the end with a tangle of tiny bones, as fine as rain, and puzzling, like a jigsaw without its box. One by one, he lays the bones out on his table until he finds at their heart a hollow skull, a jewel. That night he sees an owl swoop from the bare eye of the barn towards his bedroom window.

5

His favourite aunt gives him a typewriter. The first thing he writes is a story about people who gather in a room above a shop to invoke the devil. When they hear the clatter of cloven hooves on the stairs the story ends, but the typewriter continues to tap out words, and then paragraphs, and then pages, until the floor is covered. He picks them up and places them in a box as fast as they come, and then a second box, and then a third. There is no end to it. I am nothing more than a channel, he whispers to himself, and the typewriter pauses for a moment and then, on a new sheet, types the word 'possession'.

6

He's looking for Christmas presents in an antique shop behind the station when he sees a small, black lacquered box with a hinged lid. On the lid is a row of Chinamen. Their robes are exquisitely traced in gold, their wise heads tiny ovals of ivory, inset, like split peas bleached to bone. They seem to be waiting to be received – supplicants before an invisible benefactor, some mandarin perhaps. Many years later, the box survives a fire, but the shine of its lacquer is destroyed and the fine gold lines that delineate the robes of the men are seared away. All that's left is the row of heads, like ghost balloons, tethered down by invisible cords to the general darkness.

7

He reads his work at an international poetry festival. The local paper calls him a small, bearded man with one earring, which is two parts false and two parts true. At the party that evening, horribly drunk, coked-up, he pretends to adore the work of a Scottish poet whose shallow musings he despises, and ignores the two poets he most admires out of shyness and misplaced pride. These poets both die soon after, the first beneath a passing car, the second alone, choked by her own vomit. He feels accountable for their deaths. He takes the reading fee he has been given and uses it to buy a Bullworker – a contraption of wires and steel that will make him invincible.

8

Before leaving the country he buys himself a single-lens reflex camera. It is more than he can afford, but how else will they believe him? Without the lens his eye is drawn by what moves, by skin and sinew and eyes and mouths, by the shifting of an arm against a table or the way one shoulder lifts without the other, but he's too inhibited to photograph what he sees. He's scared it might answer him back. Through his lens what he sees

322

is the perfect empty symmetry of doors and windows, and the way light catches the concrete of a bollard a boy has been sitting on moments before, the light still there, the warmth refusing to be held.

9

They live in a rented house with a billiards room, a spiral staircase and a ghost. The local laundrette is filled with drunken Irish poets. It is cold, and getting colder daily. When they're forced to move, traipsing knee-deep in snow through the back streets of London, they take a single trophy with them, a Chinese duck with a pewter body, and brass wings and beak. The duck splits into two across the middle; they use it to keep dope, papers, all they need to hold the misery of their failure at bay. It is their stash duck and they love it. Everything else from that time has gone, everything except the ghost. The ghost is alive inside the duck.

10

His father keeps his ties in a flat wooden box. Each tie is tightly rolled, with the wide end at its heart. There are ties of all widths, all styles. His father throws nothing away and will never leave the house without a tie. The ties are held in place by a wooden grille, placed over them before the lid is closed. His father dies and he finds himself with the box of ties, many of them gifts he has bought at airports or hurriedly in shops he would normally avoid. He opens the box and rolls the ties open across his bed, their silk and wool a reproach to him as they wait to be taken up and worn.

CLOTHES *or* UNRIPE STRAWBERRIES

1

His first pair of long trousers are rust-coloured jeans his mother
buys him from a catalogue. He's ten years old, his legs are sweaty.
He rolls the jeans up at the bottom, cowboy-style, and wears them
with a brand-new green pullover from the same catalogue, then
goes to play with his friend next door. He's tense, excited. He feels
that he has finally grown up. His friend's mother opens the door to
him, before calling up the stairs to tell her daughter he's here. I hope
you aren't planning on doing anything dirty, she shouts, flicking
ash into her free hand. Your little friend looks ready to muck out
stables. He blushes. He hates the woman with all his heart.

2

He wants a velvet frock coat like the ones worn by The Kinks.
He's seen them in a shop down the road from Beatties called
Loo Bloom's. He hadn't noticed it before, but now he stands
outside the window and stares at the mannequins for hours at a
time. His favourite coat is burgundy crushed velvet, with metal
buttons that go from the collar to the waist. He has no trousers he
could wear it with, but that doesn't matter, not yet. It will soon
be Christmas. His mother hasn't said no, which gives him hope.
Christmas morning he unwraps a double-breasted jacket in dark
green corduroy, which he hangs in his wardrobe that evening and
will never wear again.

3

His friend next door has a room at the top of her house with chests full of clothes her family has collected. They spend whole days there dressing up – as pirates, duchesses, washerwomen, spies. Sometimes, alone in the house, they wander from room to room, inventing stories about themselves, inventing selves. One afternoon, they leave the house. His friend chooses a cocktail dress that belonged to her mother, baggy at the chest, red stiletto heels. He wears a long gypsy skirt and a sort of bonnet that covers much of his face. If anyone stops them, they'll say he's her long-lost American aunt, but no one does. That evening, his father forbids him to see her and won't say why.

4

It is July, but he still won't take his blazer off. The playground is used by the first three forms at school; there are ninety boys in all. He is one of the youngest. They all have the same school uniform: grey trousers, white shirt, brown blazer with the brown-and-yellow badge, and yellow-and-brown striped tie. Even the socks have a brown-and-yellow stripe around the top. At morning break they are allowed to remove their blazers and tuck their ties into their shirts, but he stands and watches the other boys in their white shirts and grey trousers, the younger ones like him still in shorts, and he won't take his blazer off. He feels safer with it on. He's sweating.

5

He roots through his mother's clothes until he finds one of her tops, a fine wool crew-neck pullover, salmon pink, identical to one Keith Richards is wearing in the November number of his Rolling Stones fan club magazine. He holds it against himself in front of his mother's dressing-table mirror, then takes it into the bathroom to try it on. It's cold, there's no heating in the house. He shivers as he takes off his shirt and pulls his vest over his head. He puts on the top. His nipples poke out like disgusting unripe strawberries. He rips the top off and screws it into a ball, throws it behind the toilet. He'll be in trouble but he doesn't care.

6

He gets a Saturday morning job at Skinner's hardware store, selling garden implements, screws and nails, buckets and brooms, household objects of various kinds. When he's saved enough he buys a pair of genuine Levi 501s, a size too large because they're supposed to shrink to fit. He gets them home and locks himself in the bathroom, fills the bathtub with water as hot as he can bear, strips to his skin, then puts on the jeans. They're hard and stiff, and so is he. He eases himself into the water, wincing at the heat. When he's lying in a cold bath, he gets out. The lower half of his body is stained indigo. The 501s hang from his hips.

7

At university he opens an account in a bookshop and another one at Austin Reed's gentlemen's outfitters. The first things he buys with his cards are a book about the Cultural Revolution and a long green cashmere scarf. He twists the scarf twice round his neck, the fringed ends trailing like dangling vines. His hair is long and catches in the scarf; at night he picks out teasels of bright-green cashmere from the curls at the back of his neck, like decadent angel down. He's sitting in the college bar and saying how much he would prefer to live in China. You don't see people dressed like you in China, someone says. Really? he answers, put down but also flattered.

8

Each Saturday afternoon they leave their cold water flat by the Arco della Pace. They cross the park, walking past De Chirico's stranded figures in the drained pool, they leave the Castle with the room they call the knotted room behind them and cross the square until the Duomo is to their right and they are walking into Rinascente, and Fiorucci, and the smaller shops of the Galleria, and along Via Montenapoleone. It is summer and people are dressed in the colours of sorbet and ice cream cups from the small provincial cinemas of his childhood. Pistachio. Lilac. They shop for T-shirts, jeans, belts and sweaters. It is hot, and so are they, and they have no idea how hot.

9

The night he meets his true love he's wearing a jacket he bought in a second-hand shop in Via del Governo Vecchio. It's blue check, unlined cotton, and has a retro American feel about it that makes him feel sexy and ironic. He's wearing it with a baby-blue Lacoste and a pair of chinos the same beige as the beige in the jacket check, and Timberland boat shoes, without socks. It's a warm evening, and he's pulled up his jacket sleeves to show off his tan. It's late April. Decades later, his only memory of what his lover is wearing is a cap, the kind people wear in Greece, and a smile, and the cap will be a false memory.

10

He visits the second-hand clothes market every Sunday morning, returning home with bargains he never wears, but discovers months later behind the sofa or under the bed, still stuffed into pastel-coloured plastic bags. A woman from Naples has a stall of suits, and he goes through a period of imagining himself as the type of man who wears nothing else, filling a section of his wardrobe with suits that are too small, too large, too formal, too spiv-like, too dull to wear. One day he finds a suit made by Valentino, a grey so dark it's black, a wool so light it floats from the hand, the pockets still sewn shut. Weeks later, he wears it to his father's funeral.

SEX *or* HONEY AND WOOD

1

He sits in the middle of the living-room carpet, piling up wooden blocks that have letters pasted on their sides while his mother watches *Emergency Ward Ten* on the black-and-white set. He's spelling out his name when one of the nurses says something about sex rearing its ugly head. He doesn't know what this means, but he can tell from the odd way his mother shifts in her armchair and glances down at him that it's something bad. He waits for a moment, and then asks her why sex has an ugly head and what rearing means. She tells him he's too young to understand. When he spells the word SEKS with his blocks she takes them away from him.

2

Visiting his aunt's house, he plays with the daughter of the family two houses down. She drags him out of the house and into the outdoor lavatory, then lifts up her skirt and pulls down her knickers. They're supposed to be where someone can see them, he says, but she reaches for his shorts and quickly, as though she's done this before, unzips them and pushes them round his knees, then makes him sit on the lavatory. She squats on his lap, her shoulders against his jumper, and wriggles. He can't see over her head. His face is pressed into the cotton of her dress as she leans back into him. Do you like it? she asks. No, he says.

3

They're in the greenhouse. It's tomato season and they're surrounded by tomatoes when his best friend suggests they play nudist camps. They take their clothes off and then stand there not sure what to do next. They don't touch. It's hot and the smell of the tomatoes is almost overpoweringly strong. After a while, she suggests they play charades. He watches her growl, her chest as flat as his, then mount the handle of a spade the gardener has left in the corner and run with it pressed between her thighs. She puts the spade down and mimes the opening of a door. I'm a book, she says, but he can't guess which one. He feels faint. Everything looks red.

4

Some weeks later they're in her playroom, at the top of the house. This time they both take off their clothes and get into bed. It's a single bed, beneath the window. They lie there, shivery at first, and then hot. She pushes his head down under the sheets until his mouth is on her tummy, then further down. There's a sprinkling of hair he doesn't expect, which tickles him and makes him want to laugh, but he's scared as well. Kiss me, she says, and he does. Harder, she says, but he doesn't know what she means. He struggles back up until he can see his watch. It's time for *Five O'clock Club*, he says. I have to go.

5

They stand in the tent his father bought for him, a tall square tent like the kind you see in films about knights in armour. They all have their jeans around their ankles. The tent is made of some orange material. One of them has a handful of pigeon feathers. The boys push the hard end of the feathers into the ends of their dicks until they stick. The girls put the hard ends into their slits. They wriggle their hips to make the feathers move from side to side. He's told them it's what Red Indians did, to show they belonged to the tribe. Their skins are bathed in orange. They're sweating. One of the girls starts to cry.

6

It's a sleepover with one of his friends from school. They've been put in the same bed, a double bed, with a bolster and a quilted eiderdown. They start off in their pyjamas, but his friend waits until the house is quiet, then asks him if he's still asleep. No, he says. Neither am I, his friend says. They lie together, listening to each other breathe. It's hot, his friend says, and takes off his pyjama jacket. He sits up to do it, his slim bare chest turned silver by the moonlight. That's better, he says. He gets out of bed and slips his pyjama trousers off, then gets back in. Aren't you hot? he asks. His hand is hard.

7

It's the afternoon of the boat race. His father wants them to watch it together, but he goes upstairs and lies on his bed. After a while, he opens his fly and reaches in, stroking himself until he's hard. He carries on stroking and something strange happens, like soft white feathers pushing to come out. For a moment, he thinks he's going to pee, to burst with pee, and will flood the bed, but then he's moaning and he has some white stuff on his belly. He's so excited he runs downstairs. He wants to tell his mother, but his father catches him in the hall, and he has time to reconsider. You missed a grand race, his father says.

8

He's in the common room, between classes. One of the boys is being picked on by a group of other boys for being cocky. He keeps his head down, he doesn't want to get involved. He's had his eye on the boy for some time. Short blondish hair, solidly built. He's never spoken to him, but he has had a dream in which the boy's dick looked like honey and a piece of polished wood all at once, and he was stroking it. When they wrestle him to the ground, his shirt comes out of the waistband and his torso arches back, bare-bellied, taut. The whole world and his heart are blinded by the light of the boy's white skin.

9

He buys *Health & Efficiency* from a newsagent's where he isn't known. He cuts out his favourite images of men and sticks them into last year's Stoke Arts Festival programme, alongside the underwear pages from out-of-date catalogues, a photograph of Kevin Keegan, shirtless, running across an empty field, a smaller photograph, scissored from the paper, of the dark one from *Starsky & Hutch* dressed up as Houdini, wearing chains around his neck and wrists, and not much else. He's hiding a new copy of *H&E* in his satchel the day his mother tells him about a piece of pig's liver in some friend's fridge, so riddled with cancer it wrapped itself around the milk. For the protein, she says darkly.

10

He's sitting in the back of the car reading *Brideshead Revisited* when he hears the thwack of a leather ball against a bat. He glances up. His father is driving through a village and he sees a game of cricket being played. He hates cricket, but he has a vision of waiting beneath a tree, an ash tree perhaps, with a hamper of sandwiches and champagne, and his friend is walking towards him, his bat under his arm, his cheeks flushed. He flops onto the picnic rug, and his hair falls into his eyes as he reaches across, his hand barely brushing the knee of his friend, his lips slightly parted, his words the merest whisper. And so they come.

Charles Lambert's haunting and highly original With a Zero at Its Heart is a sequence of short texts, each of exactly 120 words. Arranged by theme, including objects, clothes, sex, danger, travel, work, theft, animals, money and language, these form striking glimpses – comic, tender, shocking, enigmatic – of one man's life.

ISBN: 9780007545513

It's time to finish
what he started.

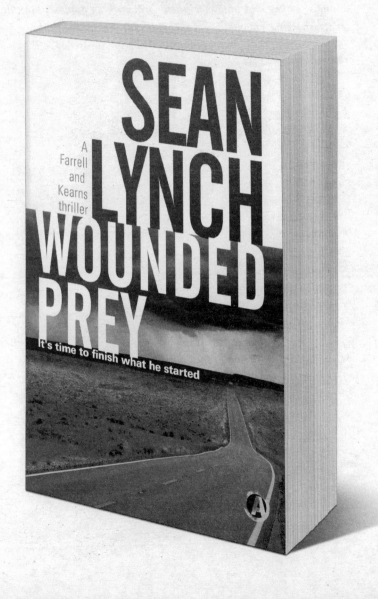

SEAN
LYNCH

A
Farrell
and
Kearns
thriller

WOUNDED
PREY

It's time to finish what he started

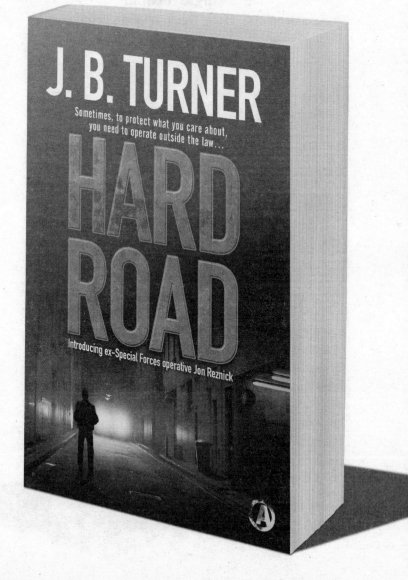

"Sometimes, to protect what you love, you need to operate outside the law..."

J. B. TURNER

Sometimes, to protect what you care about, you need to operate outside the law...

HARD ROAD

Introducing ex-Special Forces operative Jon Reznick

A taut, timely thriller ripped from today's headlines. Blisteringly paced, authentically told, here is a novel that demands to be read in a single sitting."

James Rollins, New York Times *bestselling author of* The Eye of God

No child should ever stay missing...

"A taut thriller, blisteringly paced."
James Rollins, bestselling author of *The Eye of God*

KAREN SANDLER

CLEAN BURN

INTRODUCING DETECTIVE JANELLE WATKINS

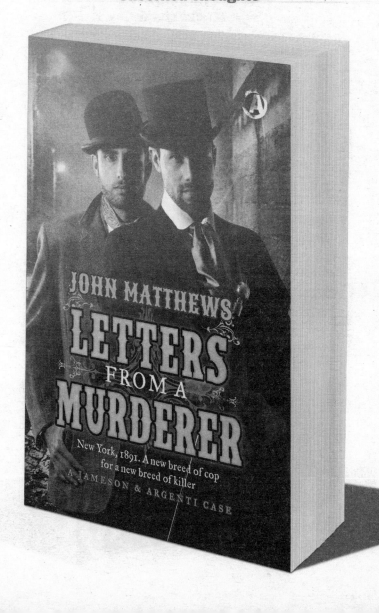

JOHN MATTHEWS

LETTERS
FROM A
MURDERER

New York, 1891. A new breed of cop
for a new breed of killer

A JAMESON & ARGENTI CASE

**In 1976, four boys walked into the jungle.
Only three came out alive.**